**Jackie Ashenden** writes dark, emotional stories, with ⸮⸮ha heroes who've just got the world to their liking ⸮ y to have it blown wide apart by their kick-ass ⸮ines. She lives in Auckland, New Zealand, with her ⸮and, the inimitable Dr Jax, two kids and two rats. ⸮en she's not torturing alpha males and their gutsy ⸮ines she can be found drinking chocolate martinis, ⸮ ⸮ing anything she can lay her hands on, wasting time ⸮ social media or being forced to go mountain biking ⸮ her husband. To keep up to date with Jackie's new ⸮ases and other news sign up to her newsletter at ⸮kieashenden.com.

⸮en **Kali Anthony** read her first romance novel ⸮ ⸮urteen she realised two truths: that there can ⸮ r be too many happy endings, and that one day she ⸮uld write them herself. After marrying her own tall, ⸮rk and handsome hero, in a perfect friends-to-lovers ⸮ance, Kali took the plunge and penned her first story. ⸮iting has been a love affair ever since. If she isn't ⸮ing her cat for access to the keyboard, you can find ⸮ playing dress-up in vintage clothes, gardening, or ⸮walking with her husband and three children in the ⸮ forests of South-East Queensland.

# THE ITALIAN'S FINAL REDEMPTION

JACKIE ASHENDEN

# BOUND AS HIS BUSINESS-DEAL BRIDE

KALI ANTHONY

MILLS & BOON

First Published in Great Britain 2020
by Mills & Boon, an imprint of HarperCollins*Publishers*
1 London Bridge Street, London, SE1 9GF

The Italian's Final Redemption © 2020 Jackie Ashenden

Bound as His Business-Deal Bride © 2020 Kali Anthony

ISBN: 978-0-263-27842-2

This book is produced from independently certified FSC™ paper
to ensure responsible forest management.
For more information visit www.harpercollins.co.uk/green.

Printed and bound in Spain
by CPI, Barcelona

# THE ITALIAN'S FINAL REDEMPTION

## JACKIE ASHENDEN

To JA. For true leadership.

# CHAPTER ONE

LUCY ARMSTRONG HAD planned her own kidnapping meticulously.

Something simple, that wouldn't cause a fuss, and that would ultimately allow her to get away from her controlling father once and for all.

It wouldn't be easy. She was a valuable commodity to Michael Armstrong, and not for being his daughter, no, that was the very least of it. A tutor her father had hired for her had discovered she was a genius with numbers and had understood money from an early age, and had passed that discovery on to her father. He'd soon found a use for her, making sure she laundered all that ill-gotten money, and he would definitely not let her go without a fight. He guarded her assiduously and jealously, the same way he'd guarded her mother.

However, Lucy only needed an hour's physical freedom, long enough for her to implement stage two of her three-stage plan.

Stage two being to throw herself on the mercy of her father's enemy.

Stage three to request that he kidnap her and hide her for the short amount of time it would take to ensure that she disappeared without a trace so Michael would never find her again.

It wasn't the best plan she could come up with—she didn't like relying on other people—but her mother's death could not be in vain. Lucy had made a promise to her mother before she'd died, that she wouldn't let herself be kept a prisoner the way her mother had been. That she would get away from Michael, no matter what the cost. And of the few other scenarios she'd run, this one was most likely to keep her out of her father's clutches for ever.

Or so she hoped. She'd allowed for all kinds of variables, and could predict most things with surety, but she couldn't account for everything.

The main variable being him.

Vincenzo de Santi. Her father's enemy number one.

She'd done her research. The de Santis were an old and infamous Italian crime family for whom her father had once worked—at least until the matriarch had been imprisoned and her son, Vincenzo, took over. Then his crusade against the big crime families of Europe began.

One by one Vincenzo had taken them down and turned them in, including his own mother, it was reputed. The de Santi business empire—once a hotbed of white-collar crime—had been cleaned out, all sources of corruption and illegal activity removed. Now it was the very model of a business that excelled. Legally.

Vincenzo de Santi had been ruthless in his quest to drag his family back over to the right side of the law, and with other families in his sights he'd made a lot of enemies. Including her father, who hated him and had sworn to take him down.

Which made him both the perfect target and the perfect refuge.

Lucy peered up at the old, graceful ivy-covered building opposite the bus stop she was currently sitting in.

She'd managed to get hold of de Santi's schedule, and his visit to London to check on several of his family's businesses was timely, not to mention useful—for her plan to work she had to talk to him directly and not be dismissed by flunkeys. Right now he was checking on one of his family's auction houses and she'd decided this was the perfect place to throw herself on his mercy. Far less security than the big skyscraper near the river and it was in a quieter area of the city.

Still, she didn't have a lot of time. The security detail that followed her wherever she went had no doubt already figured out that she hadn't gone to powder her nose after all and were tearing up the cafe she'd insisted they stop at trying to find her.

And find her they would, she had no illusions about that.

Which meant she needed to get to stage two of her plan, and quickly.

Keeping her head down, Lucy hurried across the road to the de Santi auction house and pushed through the ornate double doors.

It was cool inside, her footsteps echoing on the marble floor as she walked towards the reception desk. A nearby waiting area was furnished with richly upholstered couches, but there was no one currently waiting. There were pictures on the walls, sculptures on the tables and various other precious items displayed in cases. Silence permeated the place. The kind of silence that only the astonishingly rich and important could buy.

Lucy ignored the art the way she ignored most things, keeping her attention on what was in front of her, since what was in front of her was always the most important thing, and approached the large and obviously antique reception desk.

A beautifully dressed young man sat behind it, looking intently at a paper-thin computer screen, and he glanced up as she approached, his expression pleasant and professional. 'Can I help you, miss?'

Lucy gripped the strap of her handbag tightly, her heart beating very fast. 'I need to speak to Mr de Santi immediately, please.'

The man's pleasant expression didn't change. 'Do you have an appointment?'

This part of her plan was always going to be difficult.

All she had was her name, and even though most people didn't know it, they surely knew of her existence. Or at least, Vincenzo de Santi would know of her existence.

'No,' Lucy said. 'But he'll want to see me. I'm Lucy Armstrong.'

That clearly meant nothing to the receptionist. His smile changed to one of polite refusal. 'I'm sorry, Miss Armstrong, but if you don't have an appointment I'm afraid you can't see Mr de Santi. He's a very busy man.'

She'd have only twenty minutes now. Twenty minutes and then they'd find her. They'd track her down and then she'd be dragged back to Cornwall. She wouldn't be allowed back to London again, and then her mother would have died for nothing.

Ice collected inside her, small tendrils of frost working their way through her veins. She'd become adept at ignoring her emotions, at not seeing anything but the task in front of her, which was generally numbers on a screen, the financial markets she lived and breathed. And for years that had worked very well.

But with freedom so close and the loss of it approaching fast, the fear she'd been trying to suppress was battering at the box she'd locked it in, trying to get out. It had taken her years to muster the courage to put this plan into motion. It *had* to work. She wasn't going to get another chance.

'It's Armstrong,' Lucy said, hoping her voice was firm and not shaking. 'Lucy Armstrong. I'm Michael Armstrong's daughter.'

The man's expression still didn't change. Her father's name meant nothing to him.

She swallowed, the chill inside her deepening. She'd expected de Santi's gatekeepers to at least know of her father, but it was obvious that wasn't the case.

The fear was reaching higher, cold floodwaters threatening to drown her.

Her mother lying on the floor, blood pooling on the carpet where she'd fallen as she'd grabbed Lucy's hand.

*'Promise me,'* she'd gasped out. *'Promise me you'll survive long enough to get away from him. Escape, have a life, be free. I want you to be happy, darling. I don't want you to end up like me...'*

She'd promised and her mother had died right there in front of her.

*Think.*

Right. She couldn't freeze, couldn't let the fear get the better of her. Concentrate on the immediate problem and figure out a solution.

Although there didn't seem to be any security around, she wasn't fooled. De Santi's security team were legendary, which was part of why she'd chosen him to start with. If she made herself a threat in some way, she'd be instantly grabbed and hustled away somewhere secure.

Maybe that would be the way to go.

She was just sorting through that option, when a door behind the reception desk opened and an expensively dressed older man strode out. 'And I'll see you in hell, de Santi,' he flung over his shoulder before storming over to the exit.

The receptionist was halfway out of his chair, no doubt to soothe the other man's ruffled feathers, and Lucy saw her chance.

She was good at remaining unnoticed and, since the door to de Santi's office stood open, she moved quickly, heading straight to it.

No one stopped her.

She went in, her heart beating far too fast for comfort, turning and shutting the door quickly, and locking it for good measure. Then she turned around.

The atmosphere of luxury and astonishing amounts of money was here in this office too. No marble on the floor this time, but a thick, deep carpet in midnight blue. Dark wood panelled the walls, the lighting of various paintings on it discreet and subtle. Bookcases and display cases, a couch, a low coffee table and a huge oak desk.

There was a man behind the desk. And he was looking at her.

He said nothing.

Lucy's heart thundered in her ears. The minutes were ticking away and yet somehow she'd lost her voice. As if the man behind the desk had struck her dumb.

He wore a dark suit that had clearly been made for him, but it wasn't the suit that Lucy noticed first. It was his height and the broad width of his shoulders, and the hard plane of a very muscular chest. He was strength incarnate, the epitome of power. Although he lounged in the big leather chair as if waiting for a boring meeting to finish, one ankle resting on the opposite knee, he radiated that power like a king, all determination and purpose and casual arrogance.

She blinked, a feeling of safety filtering through her.

Yes, she'd been right to come here. If there was any-one on earth who could protect her from her father, it was this man.

He still didn't say anything, watching her with eyes so dark they verged on black.

He wasn't handsome, though he possessed a power-ful and undeniable charisma. It was there in his deeply set eyes, in the hard cast of his jaw, high cheekbones and straight nose. An aristocrat turned crusader. The air of ruthlessness around him made him utterly compelling.

*Are you sure you were right to come here?*

But Lucy shoved the thought away. She couldn't start second-guessing now.

This was Vincenzo de Santi himself and it was time to implement the next stage of her plan.

She forced herself to walk forward to the desk, stop-ping in front of it just as someone rattled the handle of the office door.

'Mr de Santi!' a voice called from outside.

She swallowed and said very quickly, before Secu-rity came bursting through that door, 'Mr de Santi, my name is Lucy Armstrong and I'm here because I need your protection.'

De Santi ignored the shouting and simply watched her with no more than minor curiosity. And said nothing.

'Mr de Santi!' The door rattled again. 'I'm calling Se-curity right now!'

He stirred, as if only mildly bothered. 'No need, Raoul,' he called back, his English lightly accented, his voice deep and cold. 'Security are already aware.' He sounded bored.

Except the black gaze that speared her was not.

*He is dangerous.*

Fear moved through her again and she had to force

it down hard. That was the problem with strong men. Strength meant safety but it could also mean danger, as she knew all too well. Especially for her.

He was a fanatic, the rumours said. He couldn't be swayed and he couldn't be bought. He was incorruptible and merciless against his enemies.

*You are his enemy.*

She was. But she had no other choice. She couldn't go to the authorities, not when she was a criminal herself, and that limited her options. Vincenzo de Santi was the only one who could keep her safe, she had no doubt. Anyway, though he was dangerous, he couldn't be more dangerous than her father, surely?

'Mr de Santi,' Lucy said, preparing her speech again, in case he hadn't heard her the first time, 'my name is—'

'I know who you are,' he interrupted in the same bored, calm way.

'Oh.' She was a little nonplussed. If he knew who she was already, then shouldn't he be more…interested? Wouldn't the daughter of his enemy simply walking into his office make him pleased? Certainly he should have been asking her questions. Except he wasn't. He was simply sitting there, at his leisure, in that big black leather chair. Staring at her.

It was unnerving.

Lucy shifted on her feet. She wasn't used to being stared at the way he was staring at her. As if those dark eyes were X-rays and they could see right through her clothes to her skin and deeper, right through her flesh, down to her bones.

*You're freezing again. Don't get distracted, keep your attention on the goal.*

That's right, she had to concentrate. The minutes were ticking away and she didn't know what would happen when her father's men burst in here. They might drag her away and she didn't want that, at least not before she'd put her proposition to him.

Steeling herself, Lucy pushed her glasses up her nose and stared right back. 'If you know who I am then you'll also know who my father is. I need your protection, Mr de Santi, and I'm willing to pay handsomely for it.'

'I see.' He didn't look at all surprised at this, nor one whit less bored. 'Please explain why I should give you anything at all.'

But Lucy didn't have the time to answer questions. She knew what she was bringing to his door in coming here: a war. No more and no less, and he needed to know immediately.

'I'll explain when you've agreed. You probably have ten minutes before my father's men track me down and come pouring through your door ready to drag me home.'

Vincenzo de Santi didn't react. He remained in his chair, his hands loosely clasped in his lap. Her father favoured big gold rings, but this man wore no jewellery. He was austere as a monk. Except monks generally did not have eyes that glittered like polished onyx; he reminded her of a great black panther about to pounce.

Time was going faster and faster, and the fear was harder and harder to contain. She gripped on to the strap of her handbag for dear life, her nails digging into her palm, the slight pain holding panic at bay.

This was obviously deliberate, this silence he was giving her. Hoping to rattle her possibly. Well, she wouldn't be rattled and she wouldn't panic. She'd got this far and she couldn't allow herself to fail.

Failure was her mother dying in a pool of blood after

trying to protect her from her father's wrath, and she couldn't let that death be in vain. She wouldn't.

'Please,' she said. 'I am throwing myself on your mercy.'

The young woman—it was difficult to tell her age, given the quantity of dark hair covering most of her face, but he thought she was a woman rather than a girl—was plainly terrified, yet trying very hard not to show it. The knuckles of her right hand where it clutched the strap of a ratty brown leather handbag were white, and her skin was very pale. Her eyes behind her glasses were very large and an indeterminate colour between brown and green, and she wore a shapeless dress of the same muddy colour.

Vincenzo eyed her. Silence was a useful interrogation tactic and so he used it often. People didn't like it. It made them uncomfortable. It made them want to fill the dreadful quiet any way they could, letting slip all kinds of interesting information.

Not that Miss Lucy Armstrong was someone he was interrogating.

At least, not yet.

'Mercy,' he said, tasting the word, because it was strange to hear it used in conjunction with himself. 'I'm afraid if it's mercy you're wanting, Miss Armstrong, you've come to the wrong place.'

Her gaze, for all that it was trapped behind two pieces of thick glass, was startlingly direct. In fact, he couldn't recall a woman—or, indeed, anyone—staring at him the way she was staring at him. People were generally too afraid to look him in the eye, and with good reason.

She should be afraid too. Especially being Michael Armstrong's daughter.

He'd tried to take down that particular piece of scum

for years now, but the man had evaded all Vincenzo's attempts to bring him to justice. And Vincenzo had tried *very* hard to bring him to justice. A couple of centuries ago, when crime families warred against each other, the war was carried out physically and brutally, and the authorities left well alone if they knew what was good for them. It had a certain...efficiency about it.

These days though, the battles were conducted on twenty-first-century battlefields; online, in the financial markets, in numbers and money. In shell companies and tax havens.

Vincenzo had tried many times to shut down the lucrative money-laundering business Armstrong had going on, since money and all the ways to hide it was a relatively easy way to take down someone's illegal empire. Yet every time Vincenzo thought he had Armstrong, the man managed to get away. It was puzzling.

Armstrong wasn't a subtle man and Vincenzo was almost positive he didn't have the kind of understanding required to evade Vincenzo's team of financial forensic specialists, yet somehow he did. One would almost suspect that Armstrong himself was far more sneaky than anyone thought, but Vincenzo didn't think he was. What Armstrong had was help. And Vincenzo thought he knew who that help might be.

The woman standing in front of his desk right now.

There had been many rumours throughout the European underground about Armstrong's daughter. That he guarded her closely, jealously, because she was the secret of the success of his empire. She knew numbers and money, was a genius with computers, could hide anyone's digital tracks with ease...

A dangerous woman. Yet she didn't look very dangerous. She looked very small, her body hidden away behind that awful, shapeless dress and thick, dark, frizzy hair hanging over her face. Her features were mostly hidden too, behind those thick glasses, but he thought he could see a scattering of freckles over her nose.

Not dangerous, perhaps. Just very, very unremarkable.

Interesting, though, that she should come here. That she should blunder through his doors seeking him. His security had informed him of her presence the moment she'd set foot in his family's auction house and despite his inclination to have her instantly taken and imprisoned, since her arrival was the kind of windfall he couldn't pass up, he'd decided to let whatever she was here for play out.

Raoul needed the practice in dealing with difficulties anyway.

Lucy Armstrong took another step forward, still holding his gaze. There was a certain ferocity to her, a determination that on another day he might have admired.

But he wasn't going to admire her. She was Armstrong's partner in crime, fully complicit in his evil empire, and so he would use her instead. Get her to reveal all her father's secrets, and once Armstrong was in prison, where he belonged, she would join him.

'Mr de Santi—' she began yet again, her voice low and slightly husky.

'Don't worry, Miss Armstrong,' he interrupted. 'Your father's men won't even get through the front door. My security is excellent.' And it was, because it needed to be.

When you were conducting a crusade against the most powerful crime families in Europe, having people try to kill you was an everyday occurrence.

It didn't bother him. If people were trying to kill him it meant he was doing something right.

'You don't understand,' she said. 'He will—'

'No.' Vincenzo didn't raise his voice, didn't put any

emphasis on it. Just let it cut across her, cold as an icicle. 'He will not.'

Her mouth opened then closed. It was, Vincenzo couldn't help noticing, a rather full and soft-looking mouth.

'Now,' he went on, dismissing the observation and nodding at the chair near his desk. 'Sit.'

She frowned, a deep crease between two straight dark brows, and he thought she might be working herself up to argue with him. But, clearly thinking better of it, she did as she was told, holding her worn handbag protectively in her lap.

He tilted his head, studying her. She was still very afraid. He could almost smell it on her. He was a connoisseur of fear. He knew how it worked and what it did to people, and how it could be used to manipulate them. He himself didn't use it that way, since that was an approach he loathed above all others. But he wasn't averse to people letting themselves be manipulated by their own emotions. And he was constantly amazed by the fact that they did.

Another reason, if he needed one, that it wasn't a gun that would kill you, it was fear. Or hate. Or anger. Or love. Emotions were far more dangerous than any weapon.

'Explain,' he said, finally breaking the silence that had fallen. 'Why are you here, Miss Armstrong? Apart from throwing yourself on my non-existent mercy?'

She was sitting in the chair completely rigid, almost vibrating with tension. 'But my father's men will be here any minute.'

Fear, again. And she was right to be scared. Coming to him directly would be a betrayal her father would not forgive.

He glanced at his computer screen and, sure enough,

she wasn't wrong. Some of Armstrong's thugs were already at the doors of the auction house.

Vincenzo touched a button on his keyboard and swivelled the screen around so it was in front of her. 'Top right-hand corner is a camera feed of the front of the building. As you can see, your father's men are already here. But they are being dealt with.'

It was clear he'd get nothing out of her until she was satisfied that she was safe from her father, so he might as well let her watch the proceedings. It would also serve as a good reminder to her that he was no less dangerous.

She watched the camera feed avidly, her eyes unblinking from behind her glasses. She didn't move, clutching her handbag and looking like nothing so much as a small brown owl.

Fanciful of him. And he wasn't given to fancies. Nor was he given to mercy for small, unremarkable women, who also happened to be accessories to the crimes committed by their father.

Really, he didn't know why he was letting her sit there watching a feed of his security team dealing with her father's men. Especially when what he should be doing was to call his head of Security and get Alessio to hand her over to the British police immediately. After all, if his crusade against the crime families of Europe had taught him anything it was that immediate action was the best kind of action.

Then again, she could be useful to him in all kinds of ways, especially if he wanted to eventually bring Armstrong down. Perhaps he wouldn't be calling Alessio quite yet.

'Seen enough?' he asked, watching her.

She glanced at him, frowning ferociously. 'How do you know that your security dealt with it? You didn't look once.'

'I don't need to. My team is the best there is.' He swivelled the screen back. 'Your explanation, if you please.'

She took a little breath. 'Okay. So, as I said, I'm here because I need your protection against my father. I managed to get away from him, but he'll never let me go free. He'll come for me whether I want to go back or not, and the only way to stay safe from him is to have someone to protect me. Which is where you come in.'

'Lucky me,' he said dryly. 'Presumably you know who I am, Miss Armstrong? I mean, you didn't wander into my office at random looking for a place to hide?'

The look she gave him was almost offended. 'Of course I know who you are. I planned my escape meticulously, including coming to you. You're my father's enemy number one. You're powerful and strong, and you have a great many resources. You don't owe my father anything and apparently you can't be bought.' She pushed her glasses up her nose again in what was obviously a nervous gesture. 'You're incorruptible, which makes you perfect.'

She had done her homework, hadn't she?

'I'm not as perfect as I'm sure you'd like me to be,' he said flatly. 'What's to stop me from taking you direct to the authorities right now, for example? You're an accessory to a great many crimes, Miss Armstrong, and, as you're no doubt aware, it is my stated aim to make sure people like you and your father are brought to justice swiftly.'

Her frown turned into a scowl. 'I am *not* like my father.'

'And yet you're complicit in a number of illegal activities if my sources are correct, and they usually are.'

She went even whiter than she was already, making

the dusting of freckles across her nose stand out, and highlighting the shadows beneath her eyes.

Now the little owl wasn't just afraid, she was terrified.

Vincenzo had a reputation for ruthlessness, and some would have called him cruel. He supposed they could be correct about that. His world was a very black and white one, and it needed to be, since his personal mission in life didn't allow time to debate moral quandaries or sort out grey areas. He turned everyone over to the authorities and let them sort the innocent from the guilty, which could be interpreted as cruelty by some people.

It didn't bother him. He didn't care how other people interpreted his actions.

And he wasn't sure what the strange tightness was that whispered through him when he looked at the terrified young woman sitting across his desk. But it was there all the same. It was almost like…pity.

Her chin came up then, her narrow shoulders squaring slightly, as if she were facing down a firing squad.

'Yes,' she said. 'You're right, I am complicit. But prisoners don't get choices, especially when they're being threatened, and I didn't have the luxury of refusing. Believe me or don't, it's up to you. Just promise me that you will keep me safe from my father.'

She was wrong. Everyone had a choice, even if you didn't like the choice you were given.

'And why would I promise you a single thing?' he enquired, keeping the question casual.

Her gaze turned ever more determined. 'Because I can give you everything you need to take my father down.'

# CHAPTER TWO

LUCY HAD KNOWN nothing but fear for most of her life and was used to it. But the fear that gripped her as she sat opposite Vincenzo de Santi was unlike any she'd ever known.

And she couldn't work out why.

Her father's men had been dealt with efficiently—she'd seen just how efficiently on that camera feed—and so there shouldn't have been any reason for her to remain scared. Yet she was, and now it had less to do with her father than it did with the man sitting opposite her.

He was still lounging there in that casual pose, to all intents and purposes bored. But his eyes glittered like black jewels and they did not move from her face, not even once. He was all coiled menace and a ruthlessness that she could almost feel like ice against her skin.

She hadn't expected to be confronted about her own crimes, not so soon, though in retrospect she should have. But she didn't like having to think about the things her father had made her do and, since she was very good at not thinking about certain things, she'd simply pushed it out of her head to be dealt with later.

Except later had now come. And Vincenzo de Santi calmly stating that she was complicit in her father's crimes wasn't something she could deny.

But she'd told de Santi the truth. She hadn't been given a choice. It was either she did what her father asked, or there were consequences. Survive, that was what her mother had told her and so that was what she'd done, any way she could.

Maybe one day there would be time to address her crimes, but she would see her father taken down first if it was the last thing she did.

Yet it wasn't her guilt or otherwise which scared her. It was something else. Something about Vincenzo de Santi himself that she couldn't put her finger on.

She wasn't used to men. Her father kept her secluded in Cornwall, her every move watched by the guards he employed twenty-four-seven. She had a few online friends, but she made sure any identities she used online were heavily cloaked. She didn't really see anyone but the guards in real life, and she kept away from them, because they made her uncomfortable. It would have been a lonely existence if she'd let herself think about it, but she didn't ever let herself think about it. Never let herself see the bars of the cage she was locked in. Never contemplated the tightrope she walked between being useful enough for her father so he'd keep her alive, and refusing to do certain things that would anger him and make him deal out the same punishment he'd given her mother.

Her attention must always be on what was directly in front of her, never looking right or left, or anywhere else. Otherwise she would lose her balance and fall to her death.

She stared hard at Vincenzo de Santi, not letting her focus waver, not paying any attention to the new fear that lived inside her, just under her skin. An electric, prickling kind of fear that made her heart beat fast.

'Of course, you will give me everything you have on

your father,' de Santi said easily, as if that had always been a foregone conclusion. 'Immediately, if you please.'

Lucy eyed him warily. 'And you will then hand me over to the police?'

He lifted one powerful shoulder and she found herself watching the way the fabric of his suit jacket pulled in response to the movement. She didn't know why. She already knew he was strong; she didn't need to watch him in order to confirm that.

'Naturally.' He put one hand on the arm of his chair, one long finger tapping out a soundless, slow, meditative rhythm. 'I should imagine the police would be very happy to get their hands on you.'

They probably would. But she didn't want to go. She hadn't survived for years waiting for her chance to escape, only to be put back in yet another cage. That wasn't what her mother had wanted for her.

*But you have committed crimes. You deserve prison.*

It was true. And to a certain extent she'd protected herself from the knowledge of what she'd done by not enquiring too deeply about where all her father's money had come from. Because she knew, if she did, she'd discover things that would make her life even more untenable than it was already. So she hadn't enquired. She'd only done what she was told. She'd made some money disappear into offshore accounts, pouring the rest into other investments, making her father's bank balances grow.

It had been survival, pure and simple.

But did survival really deserve a jail cell?

Because Vincenzo de Santi would hand her over to the police, that was obvious. She could see it in his mesmerising, compelling face. He was her judge, jury and executioner, and she couldn't look away.

Her hands tightened on her handbag and the laptop

hidden in it. The laptop that contained all the information he required. But not the passwords he would need. Those were all in her head.

'When you say you will hand me over to the police, when will that happen?' It was very difficult, but she held his gaze. Because she had to know. His handing her over to the authorities had always been a possibility, but she'd held out a tiny sliver of hope that perhaps he wouldn't. That he'd help her disappear into obscurity somewhere in the US, far away from her father. Where she could make sure her mother's death hadn't been in vain.

He tilted his head and she had the impression that he could see every single part of her. From her guilty conscience to the fear she lived with every day. Every aspect of her small, narrow, confined existence.

'You give me the information I want,' he said in that easy, casual voice, 'and then I will notify the authorities. This afternoon probably. The quicker you do it, the quicker I can take your father off the streets for good.'

Perhaps he'd meant that to be encouraging, or maybe an incentive for her. But it wasn't.

And her expression must have given her away, which was a shock in itself, since no one ever noticed her emotions, because he said, 'This does not please you?' His mouth curved slightly and she found herself watching that too, as if she was compelled. 'But Miss Armstrong, if you'd done your research you would know that I do not care for criminals. And, as I've already told you, if it's mercy you're looking for, you'll find I have none.'

She'd underestimated him. She'd thought that perhaps she would be unimportant to him. That her father would be his ultimate goal and he'd let her slip away to pursue her own redemption far away from the constant fear.

But she'd been so fixated on her immediate plan she'd miscalculated.

*That's always been your greatest failing.*

Yes, that was true.

She shifted her hold on her laptop, her fingers nervously gathering up the fabric of her dress and pleating it.

*Okay,* she told herself, *so don't think about what he was going to do, don't think about police cells and having to survive for years in a prison with fear your only companion yet again. Don't think about your mother dying in a pool of blood, begging you not to end up like she did.*

Only think about how to change his mind.

She steeled herself, met his black gaze head-on. 'It'll take some time to give you this information, since I don't have all the data yet. Probably, say, a week.' Was a week long enough to change his mind? She didn't think she could push for more. And the reality was that she'd have to work with whatever he gave her.

If he even gave her anything at all.

One black brow rose. 'A week?' he echoed, as if it was the most preposterous thing he'd ever heard. 'Forgive me, Miss Armstrong, but I've heard all the rumours about you. I know what you're capable of. You could get me that information in ten seconds if you wanted to.'

'But I don't want to,' she said flatly, before she could stop herself. 'A week, Mr de Santi. A week and I'll give you all you need to not only take my father down, but his entire empire along with him.'

De Santi's eyes narrowed, an obsidian blade getting sharper. So sharp it might cut. 'Why would I wait a week? In ten minutes I can make you tell me anything I want to know.'

The icy flood of fear inside her rose higher. His ruthlessness was legendary, as was his single-minded determination. He'd betrayed his own parents to the authorities, it was rumoured, which meant he would have no qualms about torturing her into giving him whatever he wanted.

Lucy gripped on to her courage, held it tight, and didn't look away. 'You can torture me all you like, Mr de Santi, but I'm not going to give you a thing.'

If being accused of potential torture bothered him, he didn't show it. 'And what makes you think you can hold out against torture, Miss Armstrong?'

Well, that was the problem. She didn't think she could. Then again, she'd doubted she'd ever be able to escape her father and yet she had, so anything was possible.

'I have a very high pain threshold,' she said, because that was true. Certainly her father wouldn't let her have painkillers, so she'd had to deal with severe period pain and migraines by herself. 'You can put glass under my nails or break my fingers, but I won't tell you a single thing.'

De Santi blinked once. 'Glass,' he murmured. 'Break your fingers… Hmm. Both good options that yield results, certainly. But I could just take that laptop you're clutching on to and save myself the drama.'

'You could,' she allowed. 'But it wouldn't do you any good. All the information on this laptop is encrypted, and the passwords are all in my head.'

The edge of his stare was pressing against her skin, cutting her.

She gritted her teeth, refusing to give in and look away. She might not know much about men, but she did know that strong men liked to test that strength on others. She'd seen her father do it with his associates and his enemies, and he enjoyed it. When he was in the mood, he even appreciated strength in others, too.

Perhaps de Santi was the same. In which case maybe letting him test his strength against her determination might buy her the time she wanted. Maybe it would even go towards him changing his mind about handing her over to the authorities.

Whatever, it was clear that remaining unnoticed and slipping beneath the radar the way she normally did wouldn't work with him. In which case, if he was going to notice her, then she couldn't allow him to see her fear, her weakness. And, since she wasn't particularly strong, she'd just have to be determined instead, and if there was one thing she was it was determined.

'Looking at me ferociously won't make me any more likely to tell you,' she said, clutching tighter to her laptop. 'I can hold out against you.'

He tilted his head, his eyes gleaming from beneath surprisingly long, dark lashes. 'I'm sure you can. But I've broken hardened criminals, and I'm sure one small, soft one would be no bother at all.'

Was he mocking her? She couldn't tell. The expression on his brutal, aristocratic face was utterly unreadable, his gaze absolutely opaque.

He frightened her. And yet she realised that, even though she was frightened, the prickling feeling she got between her shoulder blades whenever she thought about her father had gone.

De Santi had dealt with him for now. For now, at least, she was safe.

That thought steadied her.

'You can try,' she said, glaring at him. 'I'm not afraid of you.'

'Yes, you are.' His voice was very deep and very cold, his gaze as merciless as the man himself. 'You're terrified of me.'

* * *

It was obvious she didn't like him pointing that out to her. Anger glittered in her eyes, her delicate jaw getting a stubborn cast. She opened her mouth, no doubt to deny it, but he forestalled her.

'Don't lie to me, Miss Armstrong. I can smell a lie a mile off. And I have a feeling you're not very good at it anyway.'

She bit her full bottom lip, small white teeth worrying at it. He found his gaze had fixated on that soft mouth for absolutely no reason that he could see. He liked a woman's mouth, but unless it was doing something interesting to him he wouldn't tend to notice it in the general scheme of things. Certainly not when the owner of said mouth was a criminal he was hoping to bring to justice.

He took his pleasures with women only when it suited him and did not allow himself to be subject to the whims of his body. It was true that he'd been too busy for female company the past month, mopping up the last of the St Etienne family and their drug empire, but that didn't concern him. His body might protest but he rather enjoyed such exercises in self-control. It kept him sharp.

Regardless, even if he'd been desperate he wouldn't have let his interest fall on the woman opposite. He preferred his lovers less…unkempt. And definitely not criminals.

Especially criminals who had the gall to accuse him of using torture. Which he didn't. He would never stoop to using the same tactics his own family had once employed, even if only in centuries past. He didn't need to now, anyway. When it came to information gathering, the team he'd assembled to assist him was the best in the world, and most of the time he didn't even need his quarry to be physically present. He collected the information, handed it to the police, and let them do the rest.

Miss Lucy Armstrong continued to glare at him, while at the same time her knuckles were white as she simultaneously clutched her laptop with one hand, the other gathering and releasing the fabric of her shapeless dress. 'Well?' she demanded in her sweetly husky voice, ignoring what he'd said about her fear. 'Will you give me a week or not?'

'Why should I? I can take your laptop and turn it over to my forensic specialists right now. They can crack any encryption within—'

'No, they can't,' she interrupted flatly. 'Not the encryption I put on the information on the laptop. No one can crack it except me.'

An unaccustomed irritation rippled through him. Being interrupted was not what he was used to and especially not being interrupted by people he was going to turn in.

Most especially when those people were small women who were afraid of him and yet couldn't quite stop themselves from challenging him.

It…intrigued him that she couldn't and spoke of a certain courage. Unless she was stupider than he'd initially suspected. But no, he didn't think she was stupid. A woman who'd escaped a violent crime lord like Michael Armstrong would never be stupid.

'Then you won't mind handing it over and letting my specialists take a look,' he said mildly, deciding to let the interruption go.

'Any attempts to access the data without the passwords will result in all the data being deleted automatically.' She glared owlishly at him from behind her glasses. 'So I guess if you want to risk losing it all, then that's up to you.'

No, definitely not stupid at all.

Vincenzo's irritation deepened, along with the curiosity he'd been trying not to pay any attention to. It stretched out inside him, lazy and subtle, making him think of questions. Such as, how had she managed to escape her father? And why had she come to him now? What made her think he would protect her? If she'd done her research, she must have known he'd simply hand her over to the authorities, surely?

*You could give her a week. What would it matter in the long run? You'll turn her in eventually. And in the meantime you can get everything you need to know from her about Armstrong.*

It was true, he could. And there were other things he could get from her too. If she was indeed the reason Armstrong had evaded all his traps, perhaps he could use her to entrap others. Because, after all, he had a long list. And hadn't he made the decision to employ hackers in his IT section to make sure their own online security was watertight? Use a criminal to hunt down other criminals... Why not?

He was a patient man. A week was nothing.

Vincenzo studied her carefully, taking his time. He kept his finger tapping on the arm of his chair and saw her attention zero in on it. A useful distraction technique.

She was still hunched in her chair, narrow shoulders collapsing in on themselves like the wings of a bird trying to hide itself beneath its own feathers.

It didn't surprise him. Armstrong was a man much given to casual cruelty and there had been many rumours about his first wife and her death years ago. Rumours that only made Vincenzo even more determined to bring the man down.

He didn't have any particular sentimentality towards women—he knew that they could be just as ruthless and cruel as men, and he'd had personal experience of this—but he despised physical cruelty. It was the weapon of the weak, in his opinion, and he had no doubt that Michael Armstrong was one of those weak men who needed to use it in order to enforce his power over people.

Had Armstrong used it on his daughter? Was that why she was hunched in her chair trying to make herself small? Was that why she was so afraid of himself?

*Why are you thinking about her like this? She's his daughter and a criminal, and now she is a tool you can use.*

All very good points.

He moved, sliding his ankle off his knee and leaning forward, elbows on the desk. He watched her reaction as he did so, observing how her eyes went wide and how she held herself very still in her chair, her knuckles whitening even further on her handbag.

Yes, this little brown bird was very afraid. And of him.

Yet, for all that, she watched him very intently, as if he was a large cat stalking her. And, yes, there was fear, but it was clear to him that she also had a stubborn, determined spirit that wouldn't let her give in. An interesting combination.

*Why? Since when are you intrigued by the people you bring to justice?*

Vincenzo ignored that thought, since he didn't have an answer to it. Instead, he held her fixed hazel gaze with his and said, 'You are enterprising, Miss Armstrong. I'm impressed. Your encryption might hold out against my experts or it might not. But perhaps I'm not in the mood to wait for them to break it. Perhaps I'm in the mood to make a bargain with you instead.'

Her gaze was ferocious. 'What kind of bargain?'

'Your skills are obviously valuable and I could use them, and not only to take your father down. There are plenty of other men and women just like him around. Those who need to be behind bars, and I think you could prove very useful in helping me bring them to justice.'

Those small white teeth worried at her bottom lip. It was very red now and very full, and it had the sweetest curve. A vulnerable, soft mouth. Would it taste as sweet if he took a bite out of it himself?

*Why are you thinking about her mouth, fool?*

The thought was sharp and bright and shocking. He had no idea why he was thinking about her mouth. None. He shouldn't have even noticed it.

'Why would I want to do that?' she asked bluntly, not noticing his sudden stillness. 'I'll help you with my father and that's all.'

Irritation rippled through him once again, his temper not helped by his own wandering thoughts. 'I'm afraid you do not have a choice.' He kept his voice flat and cold. 'If you want a week before I hand you to the authorities it will be in my custody and you will do anything I ask. That is the price. If you don't want to pay it then I will get my security team to hand you over to the police immediately.'

She bit at her lip, the expression on her face—what he could see of it behind all that hair and those big glasses—turning angry. 'But you won't be able to take down my father if I don't help you.'

'Of course I can take down your father without you.' He made a negligible gesture. 'It would only take longer. Your help would expedite the process, but it's not necessary.'

'Then why bargain with me at all?'

Another good point. She was astute, he'd give her that. Because he really didn't need to bargain with her. He could make her do whatever he wanted, since he was the one with all the power here. But doing so would make him no better than those he brought to justice, and he would never use those kinds of tactics.

'Because, although you are not necessary, you could prove to be useful,' he said, just as blunt as she was. 'And a tool is only useful if it is not broken. I have no wish to break you, Miss Armstrong, believe me.'

'But you want to use me.' There was no anger in her tone, only a kind of…resignation. As if the situation she now found herself in wasn't unfamiliar.

And it wouldn't be. She was as much a tool for him as she was for her father and he was very aware of that fact. Not that it bothered him. Not given what was at stake.

The old crime families of Europe were like a disease, rotting the body from the inside. Corrupting everything. That corruption was inside himself too and he knew it. Knew his own family's history and the stain they'd left behind them over the centuries.

He wasn't exempt from that corruption, but at least he wasn't here to hasten its spread. No, he was a surgeon and he would cut it out completely.

'No, *civetta*,' he said, because a surgeon needed a sharp scalpel, 'I do not want to use you. I *will* use you. If you want your week of freedom, then you must pay for it and that is my price.'

She continued to stare at him, frowning, as if he was a problem she wanted to solve. 'When you say "freedom", what exactly do you mean?' she asked. 'Because you won't be letting me go, I assume.'

'No, I'm afraid not.'

She only nodded, as if that was the answer she'd expected. 'Well, I suppose if I were truly free that would leave me unprotected, which would undermine the whole point of me coming to you in the first place.' The line between her brows seemed etched there, marring her pale skin, and he found himself idly wondering if that skin was as soft as it looked. Whether it would be as soft as her mouth. 'I wouldn't like to be in a cell,' she went on. 'My father kept me in his house in Cornwall with a lot of guards. I could walk in the garden but that was it. It was by the ocean, but the house had no view so I couldn't see it. I could hear it though.' A thread of some emotion he couldn't place crept into her voice. 'I'd like to be able to see the waves.' Her gaze had turned distant, looking through him as if he wasn't there. 'In fact, I don't think I've ever seen the ocean. How ridiculous is that? When we live on an island?'

Slowly, Vincenzo leaned back in his chair, studying her. A strange criminal indeed to escape her father, throwing herself on his non-existent mercy then demanding his protection despite her obvious terror, only to talk with wistfulness about an ocean she'd never seen.

Perhaps it was an act. One could never tell. People of her ilk were liars and used all kinds of emotional tricks to get what they wanted. Already he was thinking odd thoughts about her mouth and about her skin... Thoughts he'd never normally have about a woman like this one. He'd encountered women who'd used seduction as a way to get close to him, either to murder him or manipulate him for other reasons. Women who weren't aware that their techniques wouldn't work on him. He was impossible to manipulate, especially when it came to emotions, because he didn't have any.

A lesson he'd learned the hard way. From his mother. A lesson this woman, this little brown owl, would soon learn too. Also the hard way.

*So what are you going to do with her, then?*

A good question. She was either exactly what she seemed and relatively harmless apart from the information she carried in her head, or she was far more dangerous than she appeared. Either way he would need to watch her closely.

'Prisoners do not get to determine what cell they prefer,' he said after a moment. 'That is what being a prisoner means.'

The line between her brows was deep, a carved furrow of worry or of concentration. Or maybe both. 'I know what being a prisoner means, believe me. I guess it's too much to ask for a week of a normal life.'

Vincenzo frowned. 'A normal life? Is that what you were expecting when you came to me? That I would simply let you go?'

Her gaze behind her glasses wavered, colour staining her cheeks, softening the drawn look on her face. 'Yes. I was hoping that you would help me…disappear, if I gave you the information you want.'

'Disappear?

'You give me a new identity, help me get to the States or somewhere else, away from Dad. And then I could vanish where no one would ever find me.'

For a second all Vincenzo could do was stare at her, conscious of a certain shock echoing through him. Did she really think he would help her? That she, a known criminal, would put herself in terrible danger simply on the expectation that he would do exactly what she asked?

She was either very stupid or very arrogant, or maybe a combination of both.

Then again, as he'd already thought, she wasn't stupid. And the woman huddled in her chair in an ugly dress with her hair in her eyes definitely didn't seem arrogant either.

*Perhaps she's telling the truth. Perhaps she genuinely thought you would save her.*

A foolish belief. He wasn't in the business of saving people. He was in the business of delivering them to justice. And if she thought she would be different, then she was wrong. Mercy was a luxury he couldn't afford.

'Then I'm afraid you're destined for disappointment,' he said, keeping his voice hard. 'You should have been more thorough with your research, Miss Armstrong. I keep telling you that I am not a merciful man. You should have listened.' He pushed himself out of his chair and strolled around the desk towards the door.

Her eyes had gone very wide and she didn't move, obviously frozen in place by fear. A gentler man might have felt sorry for her, but he had no gentleness left in him.

He crushed the ghost of that strange emotion he'd suspected was pity. Crushed it flat completely. Then he unlocked his office door and opened it. 'Get Security, Raoul,' he ordered casually, not raising his voice. 'This prisoner needs a cell.'

# CHAPTER THREE

LUCY SHIVERED. A cell.

There had been a few times when she hadn't wanted to do what her father had told her, when she'd pushed against the bars imprisoning her, and his response had always been the same. Since she was too valuable for him to kill or maim, he would drag her down to the basement in that house in Cornwall—or get one of his guards to do it—and lock her in one of the tiny rooms there. The room had no windows and when the door closed the darkness was absolute. A crushing weight that stole her breath. She never knew how long he would leave her there, but it always felt like aeons.

She hated the darkness. Hated that room. And without fail, whenever he dragged her out of it, she would always do what he asked. Until eventually she learned to always do what he asked every time.

She'd thought that when she'd escaped her father she'd leave that room behind her for ever. It seemed she was wrong.

Vincenzo de Santi had always been the variable she couldn't predict and yet she should have been able to. She'd ascribed to him a morality that it was clear he didn't have, and in retrospect she didn't even know why she'd thought he would help her in the first place.

He was everything the rumours had said about him. Cold, incorruptible, ruthless. Without a shred of mercy. He stood there staring at her, so tall, so powerful, a certain cold, brutal beauty to him that her stupid brain couldn't help appreciating even as everything inside her felt as if it was collapsing in terror.

*You're not brave, not like your mother.*

No, that was true. She wasn't. She was made of fear instead and that fear in turn had made her stupid. She'd thought that the knowledge in her head would be worth more to him than her physical presence. More than the weight of her own crimes.

She was wrong.

'Please.' The word was a scraped thread of sound, which was all she could muster up. 'Not a cell.'

*Begging now?*

Her mother hadn't begged. Her mother had been fearless, stepping between her and her enraged father, taking the blow that had been meant for her.

She could only dream of being that brave, that strong.

The sound of footsteps came and two security guards dressed in black appeared in the doorway. She knew how skilled they were. She'd watched them in the camera feed de Santi had shown her. There was no escape for her. There never had been.

Always, in every way, she was trapped.

Fear had locked all her muscles, her breathing getting faster. They would drag her away, wouldn't they? Drag her into a hole, into the darkness, and she would be trapped there. It was like dying, that darkness. A weight that would crush all the life and the breath out of her…

The guards came towards her and her vision wavered, turning black around the edges. The darkness was coming for her. It would swallow her whole.

She opened her mouth to scream but there was no air in her lungs, no air anywhere, and she was falling, falling into that blackness, and there was no end to it…

'Breathe, *civetta,*' a deep, cold voice ordered in her ear. 'Breathe.'

It was to be obeyed, that voice. It brooked no argument. So she tried, sucking in air, pushing back against the crushing weight on her chest and the darkness pressing in.

A wave of dizziness caught her, making her tremble. She was so cold. She couldn't feel her fingers or her toes.

'Breathe,' the voice ordered again, and so she did.

More dizziness and she was trembling even harder. But something was around her, something strong. Something hot. Holding her. The heat made her feel less cold and she was held very tightly, which seemed to ease the shaking.

A warm scent surrounded her, cedar and sandalwood, oddly comforting, and she could have sworn she could hear the beating of someone's heart. It was strong and steady and slow, and she found herself trying to breathe to match that rhythm. In fact, if she concentrated, it steadied the frantic race of her own heartbeat too.

Gradually the tight pull of her muscles relaxed and the cold feeling in her hands and feet began to ease, the weight on her chest lifting. Everything was still dark, but as her consciousness returned she gradually realised that it was because her eyes were closed.

And then she realised something else: that the thing holding her was a person and the strong bands around her were arms. That the warmth was someone's body. She was lying against someone and it was their heart she could hear beating.

Shock rippled through her.

'Breathe,' the voice reminded, a deep rumble in her ear.

So she breathed and kept on breathing as she became conscious of more, that she was being held by someone very strong and very hot, and that the warmth of their body was helping her to relax, making the panic—and it had definitely been panic—recede.

Strange how the fact of being held made her feel safe, because she definitely did feel safe. And that was an unfamiliar feeling in itself, since it had been a long time since she'd felt safe anywhere. So she held on to it, kept it tight in her grasp, not wanting to move, not even wanting to breathe in case the feeling disappeared.

But she had to breathe and she kept on breathing, and she became aware of where she was. Of what had happened. Of whose arms surrounded her and who it must be holding her so tightly.

Vincenzo de Santi. Who was going to put her in a cell.

Lucy opened her eyes.

She was sitting on a sofa in the same expensive, luxurious office she remembered, in the lap of the same man who'd stared at her so intensely from across that big desk. A man with black eyes and the face of a warrior angel.

His powerful arms were around her and she was leaning against his chest as if it were her favourite pillow. Her glasses were gone and everything was blurry, but she remembered those eyes and that face. They would haunt her dreams.

She must have had a panic attack. How humiliating.

And then she realised that two other men were standing in front of the sofa, dressed in black uniforms. Tall, powerful men... The guards, come to take her away.

Instantly cold fear poured through her veins, her hands clutching on to de Santi's shirt, and she was pressing herself against him, as if he could keep her safe.

*You idiot. He's the one who wants to imprison you.*

Her fingers were going cold again and she could hear the frantic rush of someone's frightened breathing. Hers.

'Out,' de Santi ordered flatly, then said something else, deep and low in fluid Italian.

The guards instantly turned and left the office, closing the door behind them.

'Keep breathing,' he murmured. 'Relax your muscles.'

Helpless to do anything else, Lucy did what he said, leaning against his very hard chest and cushioned by the expensive wool of his suit. His body was so warm and the beat of his heart was in her ear, a steady, relentless sound. She concentrated on that, since it had worked so well before, and her breathing slowed, her muscles losing their rigidity.

It was strange to be held like this. She couldn't remember the last time anyone had held her. Not since her mother had died, certainly. She'd been around seven then, so...a long time. And definitely not by a man. Were all men this hot? This hard?

*You're an idiot. He wants to put you in a cell.*

The thought made her stiffen again, his arms tightening in response.

'No,' he said casually and without emphasis. 'Be still.'

And, since those arms gave her no other choice, she did so. Yet, though the panic lost its bite, the fear wouldn't go away. Not now she was fully aware of who held her and where she was. And what he was going to do.

'What happened?' she asked, her voice rusty-sounding. 'Did I faint?'

'Very briefly.'

The low rumble of his voice was oddly comforting, though she had no idea why. 'Why are you holding me?'

'Because you were shaking and you'd gone very cold.'

He shifted slightly, the movement of his powerful body beneath her sending a bolt of some strange sensation through her. 'I removed your glasses for safety's sake.'

She blinked, remembering something. 'And my computer?'

'It's on the sofa beside me, along with your handbag.'

A brief silence fell.

Lucy closed her eyes again, suddenly exhausted. She'd been operating on nothing but adrenaline since she'd woken up this morning with her plan in place, and now, the panic attack having burned through all the rest of her reserves, she had nothing left.

She was literally in the arms of her enemy, the prospect of a cell in front of her, and all she wanted to do was sleep.

*Pathetic. Do you really want your mother to die for nothing? Pull yourself together.*

Lucy gritted her teeth and forced herself to ignore her own weariness.

'Do you have panic attacks often, Miss Armstrong?' he asked after a moment.

'Not usually.' She hadn't had one for weeks, not since she'd stopped resisting her father. But did the nightmares count? Maybe they didn't.

'What is it about a cell that frightens you?'

She hadn't wanted him to know the depth of her fear, but that ship had long since sailed. And perhaps, if he knew, it might make him more sympathetic towards her. Useful, given the fact that she was still hoping to change his mind and have him not hand her over to the police.

'There's a room in the basement of our house in Cornwall. My father locks me in there sometimes when I won't do what I'm told. It's dark. There are no windows.' A shiver coursed through her, making de Santi's arms tighten once more.

'I see,' he said, his tone very neutral. 'And do you not do what you're told often?'

As a child, she'd been fearless and curious, always getting into things she wasn't supposed to, which had made her father angry. Her mother had shielded her from the worst of his rages—until she hadn't been able to shield her any more and Lucy found out just how much her mother had protected her.

'I used to,' she said, because there was no need to get into that. 'Not so much any more.'

'Except for escaping from him.'

'Yes, except for that.' She had relaxed against him fully now, the warmth of his body stealing through her. How could such a cold man be so warm? It didn't make any sense. 'Why are you so hot?' she asked, opening her eyes again. 'Are you sick?'

His face was blurry and she couldn't read it, but she could feel his muscles tighten beneath her as if in surprise. 'No, I'm not sick.' There was a thread of something in his tone, marring the casual sound of it, but she couldn't tell what it was. 'Are you dizzy? Still a little faint?'

'No. I'm okay now, I think.'

Instantly he moved, gathering her gently without a word and shifting her off his lap and onto the sofa. The whole of her left side where she'd been resting against him felt hot, the withdrawal of his arms like a loss, which was very strange and she didn't understand it, not one bit. A wave of sudden vulnerability flooded through her, and she fussed with her dress, hoping he hadn't noticed.

It seemed he hadn't though, because he moved over

to the desk, picking something up off it and holding it out to her. Her glasses.

'Thank you,' she murmured awkwardly, taking them and putting them back on.

De Santi was leaning against his desk, his arms folded, his dark gaze fixed on her with unnerving intensity.

Lucy wanted to stand up, not have him loom so threateningly over her, but she wasn't sure if her legs would even support her, so she stayed where she was and lifted her chin instead. 'I suppose you're now going to put me in a cell?'

'I haven't decided,' he said.

An echo of fear shivered through her once again, but she borrowed some of her mother's courage and steeled herself against it, meeting his gaze head-on. 'If it's to be a cell, then you'll have to either drug me or knock me unconscious, because I won't go in there willingly.'

'Clearly.' He continued to stare at her for a couple of moments longer, then he muttered to himself in Italian again, and abruptly reached into the pocket of his suit trousers and brought out a slim, complicated-looking phone. Pushing a button, he raised it to his ear, then began to speak in rapid Italian, his gaze still resting on her.

The feeling of unease widened. What was he going to do with her now? Would he really drug her or knock her unconscious and put her in a cell?

Then again, he'd obviously had every intention of doing just that before and he hadn't. She'd had her panic attack and, instead of simply picking her up and dumping her in whatever holding facility he'd intended to put her in, he'd held her in his lap instead. Calming her down, soothing her.

*Perhaps he isn't as merciless as he told you he was?*

Certainly a merciless man wouldn't have held her like

that and eased her fear. A merciless man—and she knew all about merciless men—would have dumped her in that cell and left her there, panic attack or not.

Something hard inside her, a knot that had pulled so tight it felt as if she'd never get it undone, relaxed slightly. Perhaps there was hope, then. Perhaps she might change his mind after all. Perhaps she might be able to make good on the promise she'd made to her mother after all.

She swallowed, and smoothed her dress again, keeping her gaze on the green fabric while listening to the fluid lilt of his voice.

Eventually, he stopped speaking and she looked up at him. He slipped his phone back into his pocket, his dark gaze impenetrable. 'You can relax. There will be no cell for you.'

Relief swept through her and it was a good thing she was sitting down, otherwise she would have fallen. 'Oh?' she managed thickly. 'Then where will you keep me?'

'I have a house here in London. You will be going there.' His gaze was as hard and sharp as obsidian. 'It's not a cell, Miss Armstrong, but believe me, it is still a prison.'

She didn't doubt that, not for a second. Yet somehow the knot inside her had become a little less tight. It wasn't freedom, no, but at least it wasn't some dark hole where she would be left for hours on end.

'I didn't think you had any mercy left,' she said, which in retrospect probably wasn't the wisest of things to say to him.

He only looked at her, his expression as neutral as his tone. 'As I said, I don't like my tools broken. And you're no use to me if you're catatonic with fear.'

Lucy swallowed again. Perhaps she was wrong after

all. Perhaps the way he'd held her and soothed her had purely been from self-interest.

*Why do you care what his reasons are? You're safe. That's the only thing that matters.*

It was true. And she didn't care about his reasons. She only wanted to know so she had hope that she might be able to change his mind about handing her over to the police. That hope was still there, especially if he thought of her as useful.

In which case, she would make herself as useful as she possibly could for as long as she possibly could.

'Thank you,' she said.

'Don't thank me yet.' His gaze was very intent. 'You're not going alone.'

Vincenzo took a dim view of people's emotional…difficulties. He'd encountered them many times in his little crusade for justice and they always left him cold. Some people pleaded with him, weeping and going to pieces, while others got angry, throwing punches and shouting curses. Some even did what Miss Lucy Armstrong did, collapsing in fear as their lives unravelled before their eyes.

He was always impervious. He didn't let any of those emotional storms touch him, refusing to be manipulated by tears or curses, or white-faced panic. Much of the time it was all for show anyway, people thinking they could get him to change his mind with a few moving emotional scenes. They were always wrong.

His mother had been the queen of emotional manipulation and he could see through such fakery very easily.

So he wasn't sure what had made him gather Michael Armstrong's daughter up in his arms as her eyes had rolled back into her head and she'd nearly fallen off her chair. It was just the kind of thing that some people tried to get his sympathy or his pity, and so he should have let her fall onto the ground. Or let his security drag her off to the small office bathroom he'd planned on locking her in.

Yet he hadn't. No, he'd darted forward as her glasses had fallen off her nose and she'd started to list to the side, pulling her into his arms and going to sit on the sofa with her in his lap. Holding her tight as she'd shivered and trembled. She'd been so pale, and without her glasses guarding her face he was able to see clearly the scattering of freckles across her small, straight nose. A delicate, vulnerable face, with a decidedly stubborn, pointed chin and that luscious, full mouth. Not beautiful and yet not without charm. Her lashes were long and thick and dark, the same as the untidy mass of hair flowing over his arm. And he'd been surprised by the feel of decidedly feminine curves against him. He could have sworn she'd be very slight and skinny, but she definitely wasn't. No, she was warm and soft. And then when she'd come to and had seen his guards, and had clutched at his shirt, trying to press herself closer against him, as if he could protect her...

His chest had gone oddly tight and he'd sent his security away before he'd even had a chance to think straight.

Why had he done that? Why had he held her so tightly? What on earth was the feeling that had coiled inside him, because he could have sworn he was immune to both pity and sympathy? He should have ignored her and had her dragged away, treating her panic like the award-winning performance it no doubt was...

Yet he didn't think it was a performance. Her panic had been real.

He watched her as the unmarked, nondescript car

he'd used to transport them both to his house in one of the quieter parts of Kensington drew up to the kerb. Since assassination attempts were a daily part of his life and since Armstrong would now no doubt be aware of where his daughter was, Vincenzo had sent a decoy limo heading in the direction of the city, while he'd bundled Lucy and himself into another car out the back of the auction house.

There had been no incidents in the short trip and nothing out of the ordinary now as his bodyguards checked the quiet square where his house was situated. He had a few in London and he changed where he stayed with each visit.

So far no one had worked out that this place was his and so it was relatively safe. He still hadn't decided what he was going to do with her though. He had to fly back to Naples in the next couple of days to deal with a few issues with one of the de Santi business subsidiaries, and hadn't expected to be dealing with Michael Armstrong's notorious daughter. Hadn't expected to be giving her a week's reprieve from justice, either.

It interfered with his plans and he didn't like it.

The bodyguards pulled open the door and Lucy got out. He followed, striding past her and up the stairs to the front door. It opened immediately, one of his housekeepers having been alerted to his presence on the drive over.

Lucy was hustled inside and directed to the lavishly appointed sitting room at the front of the house, with the opaque windows that made looking inside very difficult.

His housekeeper had put some refreshments on a small tray—tea and some expensive chocolate chip biscuits—on a table next to one of the armchairs and Vincenzo guided Lucy over to the chair and made her sit down.

She glared crossly at him from underneath her curtain of hair, her hazel eyes looking very green behind the lenses of her glasses.

A strange woman. Almost catatonic with fear one moment then angry the next. Was this another performance for his benefit? Or had her fear been the performance? But no, it couldn't have been. He'd already decided it wasn't, hadn't he?

'Drink the tea,' he ordered. 'And have a biscuit. You could probably do with the sugar.'

'I don't want a biscuit. Or the tea.' She continued to glare at him for no reason that he could see. 'What are you going to do with me?'

He turned away, pacing over to the fireplace and stopping, laying a hand on the marble mantelpiece.

It was a good question. What *was* he going to do with her? He could leave her alone in this house for the next week, which would be the most logical thing, and have his security team get the answers he required from her. And yet...he was strangely reluctant to do so.

He'd told her that he hadn't wanted a broken tool and he hadn't lied. It had been the most likely explanation for his catching her before she'd fallen off the chair and holding her. It certainly wasn't because he felt sorry for her. No, if she was frozen with fear then he wouldn't be able to get any information out of her at all, so he'd had to do something. She was to be the scalpel with which he cut out the corruption that was Michael Armstrong, but one couldn't cut with a broken blade. That blade had to be sharp and whole.

His thoughts scattered then rearranged themselves with their usual orderly precision. If he wanted the information she held in her head, he would need to be careful with her. He would need to be subtle and delicate. His usual methods would break her, which meant he would have to try a different approach.

Leaving her to his security team ran the risk of breaking her and, since that couldn't happen, the most logical thing was to deal with her himself.

Something coiled inside him, a certain sense of…anticipation. He ignored it the way he ignored most of his emotions, since there was absolutely no reason for it. No, handling her personally would be the best option all round and, though he couldn't really afford the time it would take for a more delicate interrogation, he'd make time.

The information she held was valuable. Michael Armstrong was powerful in England and did a lot of work for several Russian families, as well as some for French and Italian families that he was also in the process of dealing with. Taking Armstrong down would be a blow and would effectively end their influence in England.

It would be worth it.

*Are you sure that's the only reason you want to deal with her personally?*

A sudden memory filled him, of the softness of her in his lap, her hair over his arm, her fingers clutching his shirt. She'd smelled sweetly of apples ripening in the sun, reminding him of summertime in the valley at his family's *palazzo*. Playing as a boy with Gabriella, before his mother had used him and changed everything.

'Mr de Santi,' Lucy said from behind him. 'What are—?'

'Drink your tea,' he interrupted, staring down at the empty fireplace, going over plans in his head. 'I will not have you fainting on me again.'

There was an annoyed silence behind him, then came the clink of a cup on a saucer.

He straightened and turned around.

She was holding the cup in her hand, sipping very pointedly on the tea, still looking highly irritated. A less perceptive man might have thought her fear had vanished, but he could see that it hadn't. Her knuckles had remained quite white and there was a certain darkness to her eyes.

Her father had locked her in a room in a basement with no windows when she wouldn't do what he told her...

Vincenzo felt something inside him shift and tighten. He'd asked her how often she refused to do her father's bidding and she'd said not very often. He could understand why if that panic attack was anything to go by. There were many ways to break a person's spirit, and leaving them alone locked up in the dark would certainly do it.

Except she wasn't quite broken, was she? There were glimmers of defiance and stubbornness in her hazel eyes, and certainly a broken woman would never have got up the gumption to escape her father in the first place.

Brave. He'd give her that at least.

'I'm drinking, see?' She lifted her cup again.

'Good.' He gave her a critical look, noting the colour in her cheeks. Probably she wouldn't faint again, and certainly not if he didn't threaten her with a cell. 'Are you going to give me the information I want?'

'About my father?'

*'Si.'*

Her gaze turned wary. 'I'm not sure. You might hand me over to the authorities if I do.'

A strange restlessness took hold of him and he wasn't sure if it was irritation or something else. 'I told you I would give you a week and I meant it.'

'A week of what?' She peered up at him from beneath

her lowered brows, her wealth of dark hair curtaining her face again. 'A week of being in a cell?'

'There will be no cell, I've said so already.'

'But you didn't say what else there will be. I operate best with clear parameters, Mr de Santi.'

It was definitely irritation, he decided. 'Are you trying to bargain with me, *civetta*? Because I should tell you now that you are in no position to do so. You are only out of a cell at my pleasure and I can put you in one at any time.'

She continued to glare at him, but her hand was shaking a little, the tea in her cup rippling in response. And he had the oddest urge to put his own hand around hers to steady her. Or perhaps gather her into his arms again and hold her until she'd stopped shaking. Ridiculous. Where on earth were these urges coming from? He'd thought he'd put his protective instincts behind him a long time ago, especially when it came to women. Women were treacherous—more so than men, as he had good reason to know. His father had been ineffectual and weak, while it had been his mother who was the dangerous one. Small and exquisite and utterly merciless when it came to putting the de Santi name and its poisonous history before everything.

Even before her own son.

'But if you do that, I won't tell you anything,' Lucy pointed out. 'And you want me to tell you things, don't you?'

He gritted his teeth. 'I do not make bargains with prisoners.'

Lucy put her tea down, the saucer clattering on the table as she did so, tea spilling on her hand. She gave a little hiss of pain and he found himself instantly moving over to the table and reaching for one of the napkins on

the tray, taking her small hand in his and dabbing the
tea away gently.

She tried to pull her fingers from his, but he held on.
He shouldn't give in to these urges and he knew it, but
the hot liquid had burned her.

*Because you are scaring her.*

But he scared a lot of people. Why should scaring her
feel so different?

'Let me go,' she murmured. 'It's just a little burn.'

He ignored her. Beside the tea and the plate of biscuits
was a glass of water with ice in it, so he took one of the
ice cubes out of the glass, wrapped the napkin around it
and then pressed it gently against the burn on her hand.

'What do you want?' he heard himself ask, even
though he'd told himself he wouldn't. That he definitely
would enter into no negotiations with her.

Her hand trembled lightly in his grip and then, slowly,
steadied.

'What do you mean?' she asked, her voice husky.

'You wanted a week of a normal life, you said. Is that
the kind of thing you're talking about?' Her fingers were
slender, her skin pale. Her hand looked very small in his.
He couldn't think why he was tending to a tiny burn in
this way. What was it about her that was making him do
this? She wasn't beautiful and she wasn't charming. She
didn't flutter her eyelashes and seduce him the way some
women did. She didn't weep and she didn't scream. She
was only scared. And wary. And guarded. Trying to stay
in control even when he had all the power.

'You can't give me a normal life,' she said. 'You're
going to hand me over to the authorities.'

He glanced up from her hand. 'You don't think you
deserve to face justice for your crimes?'

Colour tinged her cheekbones and her gaze wavered.

But he could read her very easily. She was ashamed and he thought that was genuine. Which meant she also thought she was guilty.

*Your mother never thought she was guilty.*

That was true, she hadn't. Not once. Not even when the police had dragged her away. It was a war, she'd kept telling him. And sometimes in a war there were casualties.

But it wasn't a war. Because if it had been, he'd have felt like a solider and not a murderer.

'No,' Lucy said, a little less certain now. 'I don't think that. I mean, I—'

'You have broken the law, Miss Armstrong. Numerous times.' Her hand in his pulled against his hold, but he didn't let her go, and he didn't look away. 'Do you think you should not have to answer for that?'

He could see her pulse beating very fast at the base of her throat, and as he watched she swallowed. She was radiating fear again and that angered him, though he didn't understand why. Because she had to fear him. She was supposed to.

*As if she hasn't spent most her life being scared.*

He didn't know if that was the case or why he should care even if it was. She wasn't any different from any other criminal. Her father might have forced her compliance by locking her in a dark basement, but that didn't change the fact that she had committed a crime.

*Your mother used the same tactics on you, or had you forgotten?*

No, that had been different. This little brown bird had only been locked in a room, fear keeping her in line, while his mother had used a far sharper tool. His mother had used his own love for her against him.

*But Lucy didn't do what you did...*

'I know I broke the law,' she said quietly. 'I know

that. I hid his money for him and I helped him make more, and no I didn't do it legally. And I…' She stopped and pain flickered through her gaze. 'I know what he did with that money. But I was forced into it. I didn't *want* to do it, not any of it.' All the breath went out of her then and her shoulders slumped. 'I guess if that doesn't make a difference to you, then it doesn't. All I wanted was…a taste of what it would be like to be free.' Her voice had got soft, her fingers lax in his. She was staring down at her lap, all the defiance and mulishness leached out of her.

She looked defeated.

It should have satisfied him that he'd managed to break her, should have counted it as a win, and yet he didn't feel satisfied. And this didn't feel like winning.

This felt as if he'd destroyed something fragile and precious, and he didn't understand why. In fact, none of this made any sense. She was a criminal, regardless of whether she'd been forced into it or not, and as far as he was concerned she was guilty. He should have no feeling about her whatsoever. So why he should feel something tight in his chest and an anger in his soul he had no idea.

Perhaps it was only that he was annoyed with himself at his own clumsiness with her. He wasn't supposed to break her after all. He was supposed to be subtle. It wasn't his usual way—he preferred the direct approach, always—but he was going to have to try it at least, that much was clear. He didn't want her so terrified that she was useless to him, and if he carried on the way he was going that was exactly what she would be.

It was time for what the English called the 'softly, softly' approach.

'Give me your other hand,' he said quietly, and when

she did so without protest he laid it over the top of the hand he was holding, keeping the napkin pressed to her skin.

Then he released her and straightened, looking down into her pale face. 'I can give you a week. No, it will not be complete freedom, but I can give you a small taste of it none the less. The price, though, remains the same. All the information you have on your father and your expertise to take down anyone associated with him.' He hesitated then said, 'If you do this, I will put in a good word with the authorities. Perhaps it will help make your sentence lighter.'

Her forehead creased, her gaze still wary. But he could see something glowing in it, something that looked a little like hope.

Poor *civetta*. She shouldn't hope. Hope was merely a drug to ease the pain and it only made everything worse when it ran out.

'Okay,' she said slowly. 'How do I know that you'll keep your word, though? That you won't put me in a cell or hand me over to the authorities the moment I give you anything?'

'You won't know.' He was not in the habit of sugar-coating anything and he didn't now. 'My word shall have to suffice.'

# CHAPTER FOUR

LUCY TRIED NOT to be excited, but she couldn't help it as the small private jet touched down in Naples. She'd never left England before, had barely even left Cornwall, and now here she was in an entirely different country. It was almost overwhelming.

De Santi had dealt with customs technicalities with astonishing ease. He'd somehow produced a passport for her, even though she'd never had one, and she'd barely had a chance to look around after disembarking the aircraft before she found herself bundled into a helicopter. Then they were in the air again, flying over the sprawling city of Naples and then over the deep blue water of the ocean.

She couldn't drag her gaze from the sight of it. She didn't know where they were going—de Santi hadn't told her—and she didn't care. All that mattered was the wide blue of the water below her.

Finally, the sea. She'd listened to the waves at night in her bedroom in her Cornwall prison, but the house had no views and so she'd never seen the source of the sounds. Never seen such an expanse of blue.

She didn't know why it hypnotised her but it did.

*Liar. You know exactly why you're letting it hypnotise you.*

Okay, so, yes, she did. Staring at the sea was infinitely better than being conscious of the man sitting so closely beside her. Tall and powerful and utterly silent. He hadn't said a word the whole trip, at least not to her. He'd spent most of it on the phone talking to other people or looking intently at his laptop. A busy man, was Vincenzo de Santi, with a vast family business to run—since both his parents were now in prison and he had no other siblings, he had to run it alone—and a personal mission to take down as many of the European crime syndicates as he could.

Except somehow he'd found the time to whisk her away from London almost as soon as she'd agreed to pay his price for a week of freedom, and into Italy.

Once he put his mind to it, things certainly got done, she'd give him that, and if this was part of the taste of freedom he was offering her, then she was going to take it.

She wasn't sure what had changed his mind back in England, because it had seemed as if he was hell-bent on handing her to the authorities immediately. And she'd just about given up. She hadn't wanted to mention her mother—that was a private pain she wouldn't reveal to anyone—and so she'd waited for his judgment, feeling her defeat sweep through her.

And then he'd said that he would give her one week. It hadn't been exactly what she'd hoped for, but it was better than nothing. And it might be enough time for her to get him to change his mind about handing her over to the police. Because if he'd changed his mind once, then maybe he could change it again. If she was…persuasive enough.

*You will have to be.*

The thought was a warning and it made her afraid, so she ignored it. She was very good at ignoring the things that scared her, at seeing only what was right in front of her, and, since the sea was right in front of her now, that was where she looked.

Except she couldn't quite ignore the presence of the man beside her, no matter how hard she tried. His warmth was distracting, as was his intriguing scent. She'd never even thought a man could smell intriguing, but he did. It was disconcerting, too, that she could still feel how he'd held her hand when she'd burned herself on the tea, the heat of his skin on hers and then the cold press of the ice.

She'd been afraid of him then and she still was, yet she was drawn to him as well and she didn't understand how that could be. His strength and his power were both attractive and terrifying, as was the merciless way he looked at her, the cold ruthlessness of him, and yet how tightly he'd held her when she'd panicked.

No, she didn't understand how she could find him so fascinating and yet be so terrified of him at the same time. He was a panther, sunning himself on a rock, and she couldn't help wandering closer, wondering what it would be like to run her hands over his fur…

*You're thinking of touching him now?*

Lucy stared hard at the ocean. No, she definitely was *not* thinking of touching him. He was her enemy. He didn't care that she hadn't wanted to do any of the things her father had forced her into doing. In his eyes she was guilty and he would hand her over to the police once this week was done.

A creeping sense of cold threatened, only to vanish as the helicopter eventually soared over a big jewel of an island, all green with soaring cliffs and lots of expensive and very grand-looking mansions.

Ten minutes later they were coming in to land on a rolling flat green lawn that seemed to stretch to the edge of the ocean itself, an old, sprawling building constructed out of white stone sitting in the middle of it. There were lots of terraces and balconies, beautifully laid-out formal gardens and winding paths, the sun glittering off the sea beyond.

De Santi got out of the helicopter, ducking his head beneath the lazily turning rotors as he held the door open for her. She slipped out into the cool, salty air, the hot sun providing a delightful contrast. She wanted to just stand there and look around, but de Santi's fingers gripped her elbow and she was being guided along one of the paths and up some stone steps towards the big house.

A few people in uniform met them on a beautiful terrace that overlooked the sea, guards and probably housekeepers, all greeting de Santi in rapid Italian. He issued a few of what sounded like orders and then ushered her through some open double doors and into a large white room with big, deep sofas upholstered in a thick, textured white fabric. The floor was parquet and worn, as if centuries of feet had walked over it, the walls were white, with a few pieces of artwork here and there, decoratively displayed. A few antique pieces of furniture—shelves and a sideboard—also displayed various other artworks as well as being stuffed full of books and other knick-knacks.

The place was cool and quiet, and she could hear the sound of the sea. It might have bothered her, that sound, reminding her of things she didn't want to think about, but it felt different here. The air smelled different, was hotter, drier, and she could see the sea right there in front of her.

'Where are we?' she asked, as de Santi finished speaking with one of the uniformed women.

'Capri,' he said shortly. 'This is Villa de Santi, my family's holiday villa.'

She blinked, staring around the room. 'A holiday villa? This is…pretty amazing.'

'It's built on the remains of a historic Roman palace and has been in my family for generations. My family's actual estate is inland, near Naples, but I thought you would prefer to be near the sea.' He gestured towards the doors. 'You may wander at your leisure around the grounds, and don't worry, you'll be completely safe. My security is excellent.'

As if she'd needed any extra confirmation of his power… He had another house—no, estate—somewhere else on the mainland. But then, her research had confirmed that his resources were vast. An auction house in London was only the tip of the iceberg.

*You will never escape him.*

It was a strange thing to think when escaping him wasn't what she actually wanted, or at least not right now. She only wanted to change his mind about handing her over to the authorities.

*Even though you deserve it?*

No, she didn't. That was her fear talking. She ignored the thought. 'But only around the grounds,' she asked, to clarify. 'Not anywhere else?'

His eyes were dark as midnight and just as impenetrable. 'Of course not anywhere else. Your freedom is of a specific kind, *civetta*, and entirely at my pleasure.'

Not that she expected a different kind of answer. And this was already better than the house in Cornwall. Yes, she was still a prisoner, but at least she could see the sea. She could maybe even swim if she was lucky.

'Why do you call me that?' She frowned at him, distracted from swimming for a second. 'What does it mean? Is it "filthy prisoner" in Italian?'

An odd expression flickered over his face. 'No. It's nothing.'

'If it's nothing, then why say it?'

'It means "little owl".' He turned abruptly away. 'We will have a late dinner out on the terrace there. Martina will show you to your room and collect you when it's time to eat.' He was already moving towards the door. 'My staff do not speak English, so do not attempt to use them for any escape plans.'

She wasn't thinking of escape plans. 'Little owl?' she echoed blankly.

But he'd already vanished through the doorway.

How strange. Why would he call her that? Was she particularly owl-like? Perhaps it was an Italian term of disdain?

She had no more time to think of it, however, as one of the uniformed women bustled in, letting out a stream of musical Italian and gesturing at her.

Lucy followed her as the woman led her through the echoing halls of the house. It was a wonderful place, the ancient walls whitewashed, giving it a light and airy feel. Sometimes the flooring was smooth tiles, sometimes it was parquet, but there were always beautiful artworks on those whitewashed walls and richly coloured rugs on those floors. It was an intoxicating combination of simplicity and richness, the scent of the sea everywhere and the sound of the waves permeating the house. And she felt the hard knot inside her loosening a little further.

Martina showed her to a big room on the next floor, with that warm wood on the floor and those lovely white walls. Gauzy curtains hung over big windows that looked out over the intense blue of the sea, and there was a big, dark oak bedstead covered in white pillows and a white quilt against one wall. Through one door was a blue-tiled bathroom, and through another what looked like a dressing room.

Martina, still talking, disappeared then came back with a length of lustrous red fabric thrown over one arm. She laid it across the bed, gesturing emphatically at Lucy's dress. Lucy frowned then looked down at what she was wearing. 'What? I don't understand.'

Five minutes later it was apparent what Martina wanted, her firm hands briskly divesting Lucy of her handbag and then her dress. Shocked, Lucy could only stand there as Martina draped the red fabric around her shoulders, then tied it around her waist with a long red sash. The housekeeper stepped back, gave Lucy a satisfied look, then, holding Lucy's dress between one thumb and forefinger, as if it were something nasty she'd picked up after her dog, she went through the door and closed it behind her.

Well, that was interesting.

Lucy took a breath, looking down at herself again. It appeared that she was wrapped in the most gorgeous Chinese robe made out of thick, brilliant red silk and embroidered all over with gold dragons.

Clothes hadn't ever interested her, mainly because she had no one to dress for. She'd never cared about her appearance, didn't even think about it. But there was something…cool and delicious about the feeling of the silk against her skin.

Not sure what else to do, she poked around the room, picking various things up and examining them before putting them back down. And when she'd examined everything thoroughly, she went into the bathroom and examined that too.

The shower was vast and, since the journey had been a long one, she decided a shower was in order. Half an hour later, feeling better than she had in the past twenty-four hours, or even longer than that, she towelled herself dry and then considered her dirty underwear. She didn't really want to put it back on, so she didn't, wrapping herself up in the red silk dressing gown again and wandering out into the bedroom.

De Santi had mentioned something about a late dinner, which meant she had a bit of time beforehand, judging from the light outside the window. She stared at the door for a moment, then crossed over to it and gingerly tried the handle, expecting it to be locked.

It turned easily.

A wave of some emotion she couldn't identify washed through her. So she wasn't locked in, the way she was at home. He'd genuinely meant what he said when he'd told her she was free to wander.

Lucy stepped back from the door, the knot inside her almost coming undone. Then she turned and went over to the bed, got onto it and lay back, curling up on the white quilt. She felt tired, and now she knew the door wasn't locked the urge to get out and explore had left her for the moment. She closed her eyes instead, only for a second.

At least, it should have been a second.

When she opened her eyes again the light had changed, long streaks of twilight painting the white walls in vivid pinks and reds and oranges. She lay there a second, getting her bearings, remembering where she was and what was happening. Then she slipped off the bed.

She felt hungry now and ready to eat, so she went into the bathroom to get her underwear, looking around to see if Martina had brought her dress back. But not only had the dress not been returned, her underwear had gone too.

Lucy frowned, wrapping the silk robe more tightly

around her. Annoying. She felt underdressed wearing only a dressing gown with nothing underneath it. There was nothing to be done about it, however, and, left with little choice, she eventually had to venture out of the bedroom wearing only the robe belted tightly at her waist.

The house was quiet and she encountered no one as she retraced the route Martina had led her on earlier, back into the big white lounge and out to the stone terrace again. It was beautiful in the twilight, the white stone glowing, the view framed by ancient olive trees, the table set for dinner.

Lucy stared at the table for a second, her chest feeling a little tight. There were candles and a white tablecloth and pretty wine glasses. It looked special. Not like a table set for a criminal and a prisoner.

Was this his doing? Or his staff? Did they know who she was? Perhaps they thought she was his girlfriend or his lover...

The tightness inside her twisted, making her feel hot. Disturbed, she turned away from the table and went to the edge of the terrace bounded by a low stone parapet. She sat down on it and looked out over the sea, taking in the amazing view.

There were so many boats, yachts with white sails and launches creating wakes, big super-yachts—floating palaces for the rich and famous—and smaller fishing boats. She imagined being on one and heading out to sea towards the setting sun, leaving everything behind to disappear over the edge of the horizon...

Maybe that would be her one day, finally escaping.

*You think you really deserve to escape? Your mother didn't, so why should you?*

Despite the view and the peace of the twilight, a chill whispered over her skin, curling through her soul.

Then a footstep sounded on the rough stone behind her, and she turned, thankful for the distraction, even though she knew who it was already.

It was him. De Santi. He'd obviously come through the French windows from the lounge area, and now he stopped as he approached the table, his dense black gaze flicking over her.

He'd removed his suit jacket, his white business shirt open at the neck, his sleeves rolled up. His skin was a smooth, dark olive, the muscles beneath it lean and sinewy. He should have looked casual and relaxed, but he didn't. Somehow the open shirt and rolled-up sleeves only served to make him appear even more ruthless, even more intimidating. The warrior angel ready to do battle.

He said nothing as he pulled a chair out and sat down, his movements loose and fluid. The setting sun bathed the almost medieval lines of his aristocratic face in gold, which should have softened him. Again, though, it was as if his presence rejected any attempts to mitigate it and instead the light simply illuminated even more strongly his dark ruthlessness.

He frightened her. Mesmerised her. Compelled her. She didn't know why. Yet again, she couldn't understand how a man could scare her and yet make her want to keep looking at him, as if she'd miss something if she glanced away.

Kathy, her mother, had been afraid of Lucy's father, she knew that much. It hadn't always been that way, Kathy had told her once. He had used to be a good man. But the years had turned him darker and he'd fallen in with bad people, and she had become afraid. Lucy had asked why they couldn't go away and live somewhere else. Her mother had only looked sadly at her and said, 'I love him.' As if that was explanation enough.

Lucy had never understood that. All it told her was if love was staying with someone who hurt you, then that was something very much to be avoided.

Not that love had any place here, with this man.

'Don't be like me,' her mother had said and yet here she was, inexplicably drawn to a dangerous man, and that scared her too.

He leaned back in his chair, his gaze still roving over her in a way that suggested he was hungry and she looked like something good to eat. It brought colour to her cheeks, made a strange, buzzing tension collect in the space between them and then go crackling over her skin like sparks.

Her cheeks were hot, her breathing oddly short, and the sound of her heartbeat echoed in her head. What was happening to her?

*You know. You are more like your mother than you thought.*

Lucy dragged her gaze away, back to the boats, an unfamiliar fluttering sensation in the pit of her stomach. No, that wasn't true. She didn't know enough about men to have any opinion on whether she was like her mother in that regard. Why would she? The only contact she'd had with them had been to be threatened by them. None of them had ever made her feel like…this.

'Sit at the table,' de Santi ordered coolly. 'Now, if you please.'

He didn't know what was wrong with him. Miss Lucy Armstrong was sitting on the stone parapet, the long twilight falling over her like gold dust, setting fire to the scarlet silk of the dressing gown and making the dragons embroidered on it dance. The colour made her skin look like porcelain and she must have done something to her hair because instead of the mat of dark brown, there was a wealth of glossy chestnut curls falling down her back. The gold in the embroidery of the robe picked up glints of gold in the depths of her hazel eyes and somehow, within the space of a few hours, this small, dull *civetta* had turned into something of a siren.

He couldn't take his eyes off her.

She slipped off the parapet she was sitting on, fumbling with the silk of the dressing gown as a bit caught on the rough stone. One side slipped a little off one shoulder, revealing a quantity of pale skin, and it was clear she wasn't aware of it because she didn't put the material back in place. Instead, she tied the belt tighter and came over to the table, pulling out the chair opposite him and sitting down. The movement made the fabric that should have covered her shoulder slip further down her arm, making it very apparent she was not wearing a bra.

Perhaps that was understandable. She had no clothing except the ghastly dress she'd been wearing when she'd appeared in his office, and there had been no time for her to get any more. At least some of the afternoon he'd spent in his office had involved ordering her various items via one of his assistants. The villa didn't contain much in the way of female clothing or anything else, since he never brought any lovers here, or, indeed, anyone.

He was still puzzled as to why he'd brought her here. He'd told himself that it was because, although the de Santi *palazzo*, deep in the Campania countryside, was a much better place for a prisoner, being, as it was, built along the lines of a medieval *castello* rather than a palace and thus very secure, it was also a place that she might find frightening with its ancient walls and dark rooms. This villa was brighter, airier, and being on the sea with cliffs on one side made it easily defensible, not to mention the fact that Capri was an island and therefore it was less likely that she would escape.

All very good reasons and justifications for bringing her here, where he never brought anyone. And yet all he could think about was her voice telling him that she could hear the waves from her house in Cornwall and yet had never seen the sea.

*You are getting soft, perhaps? Tired of the crusade?*

No, of course not. And he would never tire. He needed her unafraid of him and willing to share the information in her head, that was all. And all of this was in aid of lulling those fears, making her relax, and who knew? Perhaps he could even get her to trust him?

She was staring down at her plate, her hands fussing with the silk of her robe as if she didn't know what to do with either them or herself. He made her uncomfortable, that much was clear. She'd blushed before, when he'd looked at her, and had glanced away, as if she'd felt the sudden tension between them too.

*There is tension now?*

Vincenzo gritted his teeth, trying to force the thought from his head as Martina and a couple of other staff members bustled over bearing quantities of food. Olives and bread and cheeses. Plates of fresh pasta with the excellent oil that she made from the olives in the gardens, and a tomato sauce to go with it. And a bottle of a very good red wine from the de Santi vineyards themselves.

The consummate professional, Martina arranged the food, poured the wine, then left, taking her staff with her.

Silence fell and he still couldn't take his gaze from her pale, uncovered shoulder.

Lucy reached for a piece of the fresh bread, but his patience was thinning, and when the robe slipped even more it ran out completely. He shoved back his chair and rose to his feet.

She looked up at him, her eyes wide and startled behind her glasses, and he knew he shouldn't do this, but he couldn't stop himself. He moved unhurriedly around the table to where she sat and paused beside her chair. Then gently he lifted the slipping fabric of the robe up and over her shoulder, covering her. A better man wouldn't have touched her, but he'd always known, deep down, that he wasn't a better man, so he allowed the backs of his fingers to brush over her bare skin. It was warm and even softer than the silk that covered it.

Her eyes went even wider, that vulnerable mouth of hers opening slightly as her breath caught. Colour flooded her cheeks, making her freckles turn pink, though he was more interested in the row of goosebumps that rose as he touched her.

It would be so easy to push that silk away instead of lifting it up, to uncover instead of conceal. Examine the curves he'd felt when she'd rested in his arms in his office, caress them, see if they were as satiny as the curve of her shoulder.

She was staring at him as if she'd never seen anything like him before in all her life, and though there was fear in her eyes there was also something else. Something that he'd seen in the eyes of other women who'd stared at him just like this one.

She was attracted to him, it was clear.

*Perhaps you could use that to your advantage?*

The thought streaked through his brain, bright and clear as a comet at midnight, but he dismissed it almost as soon as it had occurred to him. Those were his mother's tactics and he would never stoop to using those. Just as he would never indulge himself with her. Seduction was not and would never be one of his weapons. He was better than that. He had to be.

He turned away, ignoring the tight feeling in his body as he headed back to his chair. She was still staring at him, a bewildered look on her face.

It occurred to him, as he sat, that the slipping of her robe might have been purposeful, but one look at her expression told him it hadn't. She seemed to have no guile at all, which was definitely a rarity in a criminal.

'Why did you do that?' she asked, her voice slightly husky.

He ignored her. 'I have ordered clothing for you. It should arrive tomorrow. In the meantime you can continue to wear that robe.'

She frowned and he thought she might push, since he hadn't answered her question, but she didn't. Instead, she reached for the bread she'd been going to have before he'd interrupted her.

So, she was uncertain about this…chemistry between them, was she? It certainly seemed that way. She'd had no trouble speaking about other subjects, but she didn't want to push him on this. Interesting. Perhaps she was inexperienced. He wouldn't be surprised, given how her father had kept her prisoner.

'Why are you doing this?' she asked after a moment, small fingers tearing apart the piece of bread. 'With the candles and the food. This beautiful house.'

'What do you mean?' He reached for his wine and picked up the glass, swirling the liquid around inside it.

That deep crease between her brows was back. 'I'm a prisoner. A criminal. Yet there are candles on the table.'

'I did tell you that you wouldn't have a cell.' He leaned back in his chair, sipping his wine, letting the flavour warm him, since nothing else did much these days; justice was a cold mistress. 'The candles were Martina's idea.' They were not. They were his. He'd been concerned about the incipient darkness and wanted her to have some light, because he didn't want a repeat of her panic attack, that was all. But he didn't want to tell her that. It felt like giving away an advantage. 'You don't like them?'

'Oh, no, they're lovely. I just…' She stopped. Then lifted a shoulder as if the subject was one she'd lost interest in, and began layering some of the dip onto her bread with a knife. 'This smells very good,' she offered after a moment. 'I'm quite hungry.'

'That is obvious,' he observed dryly as she ate the piece of bread with small, precise bites then proceeded to get herself another. 'Are you ready to give me some information yet?'

She ate the other piece of bread then picked up her wine glass and took a sip. 'Is that why there are candles and nice food? You're hoping to bribe me into giving you what you want early?'

Irritation gathered inside him. It was true. He had promised a week. 'No,' he said shortly, even though he had a suspicion that was a lie as well. 'The candles and food are an added bonus. I do not bribe anyone, nor do I manipulate. You will give me what I want because I ask for it. Because we have made a bargain.'

She sipped again at her wine, frowning at him from behind the thick lenses of her glasses. 'Why is taking down my father so important to you? Did he do something to someone you know?'

'He's a criminal who has hurt others. He's a murderer, *civetta,* in case you didn't know. That's all the reason I need.'

An expression he couldn't read flickered over her face. 'Oh, I know what he is, believe me. But is it him in particular? Or merely the fact that he's a criminal?' She regarded him curiously. 'Why don't you let the police deal with it?'

Was she really expecting him to tell her his reasons? To justify himself to someone like her? She'd be waiting a long time in that case, because he did not have to explain himself to anyone. Rumours followed him, naturally enough, but he didn't concern himself with them. The facts were his own and he gave them to no one.

No one else, for example, needed to know how his mother had seduced his father into the de Santi family 'business'. Or how she'd manipulated Vincenzo himself into doing the same thing, using his love for her against him.

He'd been her creature through and through. Her perfect boy, her heir. Her tool. There was a war, she'd told him, and their family had enemies that they had to defend themselves against. All lies. Lies he'd been too busy basking in her attention to see. Too busy being the chosen de Santi prince to care.

*You knew. Deep down, somewhere inside, you always knew.*

Some nights he lay awake in the dark, going over and over the things she'd told him to do, searching for signs he'd somehow missed. Signs he perhaps should have noticed—a cruel glint in her eye or a betraying curl to her lip. Something that would have told him that what she'd said about wars and soldiers and fighting were lies.

But there had been nothing. His mother had spent years perfecting her lies and he'd been sucked in completely. It was an evil he could never be free of and so all he could do was mitigate the damage by pursuing justice relentlessly.

No, he couldn't tell her that.

'I do let the police deal with it.' He kept his voice level and without emphasis. 'I give them the evidence they need, and they do the rest.'

'But isn't gathering the evidence their job?'

Annoyance gripped him. He didn't want her questioning him. 'They miss things. And they do not have the resources or the knowledge that I do. In some instances the police are corrupted by the very people they're trying to bring to justice.'

'You don't trust them, then?'

'No one can be trusted.'

'No one except you?'

Vincenzo realised he was holding his glass far too tightly and that if he held it any tighter the slender stem would snap. With a conscious effort he relaxed his fingers, staring across the table at the woman opposite.

There was nothing sly or knowing in her gaze, only curiosity. She wasn't goading him, it seemed; she genuinely wanted to know and obviously hadn't picked up on his irritation.

'You're not very polite, are you?' he observed casually, turning the conversation back on her.

Her eyes widened as if the statement had surprised her. 'Aren't I? Is asking questions wrong?'

'You are my prisoner, *civetta*. And a prisoner does not interrogate her captor.'

Colour tinged her cheekbones, giving her face a rosy flush. She really was quite pretty, now he thought about it. Which was not at all helpful.

'No, I suppose not.' She took another piece of bread. 'I just don't get to talk to people very often.'

'Why not?' he asked, since what was clearly sauce for the gander could also be sauce for the goose.

She looked down at the piece of bread in her hands,

tearing it once again into tiny pieces. And stayed silent. Her shoulders had hunched, her glossy hair a curtain over her face. The chestnut colour gleamed almost auburn in the fading twilight.

He was trespassing on painful subjects, it was clear, and no wonder. If her father had locked her in a dark basement, then what else had he done? But then, Vincenzo knew already. There were rumours about her, as there were about him; her father kept her well-guarded, deep in the English countryside. No, not just well-guarded. Her father had kept her prisoner.

The strange sensation in his chest that he'd felt earlier when he'd held her trembling body in his arms shifted again. A constriction.

He didn't like it and he knew he should let the subject alone, move on, even get up from the table and leave her here to finish her meal alone. Yet he didn't. Something compelled him to remain in his chair and to look at her all wrapped up in red silk, with her dark hair everywhere. Small and vulnerable and very, very alone.

'He kept you prisoner,' Vincenzo said, voicing his thoughts aloud to see her reaction. 'Didn't he?'

Her fingers shredded the bread to crumbs. 'I was too valuable to be let out, or at least that was what he told me. It was for my own protection. There were a lot of people who wanted to use me or kill me, and so I was safer in the house with the guards.'

The sensation shifted again, getting tighter.

'So you had no one at all you talked to? No friends? No family?'

'No. I had some online friends he didn't know about, but no one in real life. The only people I could speak with were him and my guards. But I didn't like speaking to the guards because they were...' She stopped.

But he could fill in the blanks. 'They frightened you?'

She lifted a shoulder, clearly not wanting to admit it.

'How long have you been a prisoner?' he asked, even though he shouldn't want to know, that it didn't matter. That being a prisoner was no less than what she deserved.

'Since I was seven.' Her hands rested beside her plate, still and tense.

'And how old are you now?'

'Twenty-two.'

Fifteen years she'd been her father's prisoner. Fifteen years.

He was aware that another sensation had joined the tightness in his chest, something hot that felt like anger, though it couldn't have been. Because she was a criminal and needed to face justice, and it seemed that she'd served fifteen years of equivalent jail time already. A just sentence. Especially when she would have been committing even more crimes in that time.

*She has been alone all her life. Like you have been alone.*

No, it was not the same. And he wasn't alone. He had his staff and business colleagues, and anyway, he didn't need anyone. The path he'd chosen for himself was one he could only walk himself. No one else could walk beside him and he'd known that when he'd chosen it.

*You are serving a sentence just like her.*

He ignored that thought. His own guilt had nothing to do with this and he didn't need that contributing to the already tangled knot of emotions inside him. Emotions that he would have told himself even a day ago he no longer felt.

He was a fool. He shouldn't be sitting here talking to her about her life. He had better things to be doing with his time.

Vincenzo put his glass down on the table with a click. 'None of that matters, of course. You are guilty, Miss Armstrong. And at the end of the week you will pay for your crimes.'

# CHAPTER FIVE

LUCY COULD HEAR the certainty in his deep, cool voice and it sent yet more chills through her. Clearly he'd finished making conversation. And he had been making conversation, that was obvious.

She shouldn't have asked him all those questions. She'd only been…curious about him and why this justice crusade he was on was so important, and she shouldn't have been. Curiosity had always got her into trouble and she shouldn't indulge it.

Sadly, he hadn't given her reasons for his crusade, though that was understandable. As he'd said, a prisoner didn't interrogate her captor.

*And he's right that you should pay. You are guilty.*

A shiver chased over her skin. If she was guilty of anything, it was of not standing up to her father. Of cowardice. Except cowardice didn't deserve a jail term.

However, he certainly seemed to think it did. She had to change his mind somehow, convince him to let her go.

Incorruptible, they said of him, but, as her father liked to remind her, every man had his price.

What was Vincenzo de Santi's?

Slowly she raised her head and looked at him, her heart thudding strangely in her chest as she met his inky gaze.

He was leaning back in his chair, the casual arrogance

he carried around with him everywhere he went even more palpable. The menace that gathered like a cloak at his back even stronger. He was dark and he was dangerous and yes, she was frightened.

But she was always frightened. Of everything. She'd been frightened since she'd been seven years old and her mother had died right in front of her eyes.

Yet Kathy hadn't let fear of her husband stop her from protecting her daughter. She'd been brave; why couldn't Lucy follow her example?

*You have other weapons at your disposal, remember?*

She frowned, trying to puzzle the thought out, because what other weapon could there be?

*He is a man and you are a woman…*

A flash of heat seared her skin, passing over her so fast she barely had time to draw a breath before she could feel burning in her cheeks. Burning everywhere.

Because he *was* a man and the way he'd looked at her earlier, unable to tear his gaze from her bare shoulder, had been very much the way a man a looked at a woman. He'd been…hungry…

The heat deepened. She'd never thought of having a lover, had never liked the idea of getting that close to a man, not after what her father had done to her mother.

She had never regretted her decision. She didn't think of the future beyond her mother's promise. Have a life, Kathy had told her, but Lucy didn't let herself think about what that life would contain, because it was only the escape that mattered.

But if she *had* thought about it, a man wouldn't have featured anywhere. Yet a part of her now wondered if this would have been easier if she'd managed to find herself a lover.

Not that her father had given her any opportunity to

find one, but still. Maybe if she had she might know what to do, how to use de Santi's definite hunger to her advantage.

Because she could, couldn't she? This could be a way for her to take control, to get some power for herself. She could offer herself in return for her freedom. Some women did that, didn't they?

Of course, he could just take what he wanted from her whether she let him or not, but it was unlikely that he'd force himself on her physically the way some men did. Surely a man who'd held her in his arms while she'd been paralyzed with fear, who'd tended to her burn, wouldn't be physically violent, not the way her father had been. De Santi was a much more controlled man.

Her heartbeat had speeded up, her breathing becoming unsteady. He watched her as if he could read every thought in her head and knew exactly what she was planning, his eyes gleaming obsidian black in the night.

Was she really contemplating using her sexuality to get what she wanted? Hoping that she could earn her freedom that way? Because what did she know of seduction? Nothing. She was a virgin in every way there was, while he was a man of no doubt infinite experience. Plus, she was a terrible liar and an even worse actress. She wouldn't be able to pretend something she didn't feel.

*Are you sure you don't feel it?*

Her heart beat harder, fear like a fist slowly closing inside her. Yet…not only fear. Or maybe it was a different kind of fear, because this type didn't feel bad. No, it felt…like a fine electrical current, sparking over her skin, sizzling wherever it touched.

She wasn't a seductress. She didn't know how to do this with any subtlety or grace. Direct was the only approach she knew. So she took another sip of wine—it was more of a gulp really—and put down her glass. Then she made herself hold his dark gaze and put one hand on the knot of her sash. 'Are you sure I can't get you to change your mind? Perhaps there's something I can give you that might help.'

Then she pulled the sash and let her robe fall open.

The last rays of the sun had gone, leaving only a deepening purple darkness that crept over everything. The candles flickered and danced, catching the gleam of his ink-black eyes as he stared at her. A breeze moved over her skin, making goosebumps rise on the thin strip of flesh she'd bared. Though that could have been the heat of his gaze.

She didn't look away, conscious that it wasn't only fear inside her now, but something more complicated than that. Like a delicate fabric shot through with threads of silver and gold, her fear had other things woven through it, emotions she'd barely felt before. A breathless excitement. The tight coil of anticipation. A nagging ache right down low inside her, between her thighs.

'What are you doing, *civetta?*' The question sounded idle, as if she'd done something mildly curious that he was puzzled about. But there was nothing idle about the tension that gathered around his powerful form. He was very still, the panther about to pounce.

Her pulse was loud in her ears and she wasn't sure if this was a good idea, but she'd taken this step and there was nothing to do but go on with it.

'Isn't it obvious? I undid my robe.'

'I can see that. Are you hot, perhaps?'

Had he misunderstood her? Were her seduction skills that bad? Or was he deliberately misreading the situation? Probably deliberately misreading it, surely?

'I'm not hot. I would very much like not to be handed

over to the police at the end of the week and I thought that perhaps I could…change your mind.'

She wanted to cover herself, conscious of how the flickering candlelight was illuminating the bare curve of one breast. It wasn't the same as being wholly naked, but she'd never even been partially naked in front of anyone, let alone a man she was afraid of. A man she'd only known a matter of hours. A stranger.

It made her feel very vulnerable. But she was tired of feeling alone and powerless. Tired of feeling afraid all the time and so she didn't look away. He might be frightening, yet she refused to give in to her fear.

His face remained unreadable, his eyes glittering. 'Are you trying to manipulate me with sex, Miss Armstrong? Because I should warn you now, I don't respond well to it.'

She shivered slightly at the chill in the words. Clearly she was on dangerous ground. 'I…didn't intend it that way, no.'

'Then what did you intend? Do you think I'm a man who would be swayed by such things?'

The urge to cover herself returned, stronger this time as his gaze slid slowly down her body, dipping to where her robe opened. But she didn't move. She had the distinct impression that he was not…unaffected.

'I don't know,' she said, her voice hoarse. 'Are you?'

He lifted his gaze to hers again, unhurried. 'No. I am not. Especially when the woman concerned is afraid of me and doesn't want me.'

A little shock went through her. Did she want him? She'd never wanted anyone before, so how would she know? Was it possible to want someone you were afraid of?

*But it's not just fear that you feel for him.*

The shock deepened as she stared at him in the darkness, the light from the candles flickering over his strong features, touching on the harsh planes and angles of his face, shadowing the deeper darkness of his eyes and the hollow of his throat...

She wanted to tell him that she didn't think it was only fear that she felt for him, but her hesitation must have given her away, because he moved abruptly, shoving back his chair with some force. He didn't say anything, merely gave her one last, fierce look that she couldn't interpret, then turned and left her sitting there in the dark, with her robe open and the shock getting deeper and wider inside her.

Vincenzo didn't know what to do. He was furious, both with himself for wanting what he shouldn't, and with Miss Lucy Armstrong for offering something he couldn't help wanting and in such a way as to ensure he could never take it.

Not only was she a criminal whose crimes had hurt people, but she'd also used her body as a bargaining chip. She'd said that she hadn't meant it that way, yet he felt manipulated all the same.

*'Ask Gabriella out, Vincenzo,'* his mother had told him all those years ago. *'Go to the cinema and have some dessert afterwards. Get her to tell you what her father's movements are, especially whether he's planning on returning home after the play on Friday night or whether he's going out. And if he's going out, we need to know where.'*

He'd been older then, eighteen, and starting to suspect that his beloved mother's casual requests were never as casual as they seemed, and so of course he asked why this was necessary. Why he couldn't just enjoy a date with his childhood friend and whom he was beginning to have feelings for.

*'Oh, it's just some family business, my handsome boy. Nothing to be concerned about. I like to keep tabs on people. You know that.'*

And she'd given him the most radiant smile, and he'd forgotten his doubts and suspicions. All he'd wanted was to make his mother happy.

Of course it was just business. Of course it was nothing to be concerned about.

So he'd taken Gabriella out and casually asked her about her father, then later relayed the information to his mother. And two days later, Gabriella's father had died in a hit. No one knew which family had been responsible, but Vincenzo had known. And so had Gabriella.

She'd realised Vincenzo had betrayed her. That he was the one who'd got her beloved father killed and that he'd made her complicit in it too. That the downfall of her own family was her fault, and all because a childhood friend had asked her a few seemingly simple questions.

He'd never forgotten the sound of Gabriella's devastated voice ringing in his ears as she'd called him the next day, confronting him with what he'd done, full of fury and grief. Nothing he could say would have made it better, because he knew what he'd done just as she had.

Afterwards, he'd gone to his mother as the shock of the assassination of a major player echoed through the crime families of Europe. She'd merely shrugged her shoulders.

*'As I told you, Vincenzo. It's just business. So I would get used to it if I were you.'*

She'd given him another of those radiant smiles.

*'If you want to remain part of this family, that is, which I'm sure you do. You've already done so much for us as it is...'*

But he knew he would never get used to it, just as he knew what his mother had issued with that lovely smile was a threat. She'd never done that before, but he understood what it was all the same. A reminder of his own actions, that he wasn't innocent and never would be, and that what she gave she could also take away.

It was in that moment that he'd realised what he was to her: not a son but a tool to build her empire. She'd never loved him. He'd never been her handsome boy. He'd been spoiled and pampered and paid attention to, but only so she could turn him into her creature. The way his father had always been her creature.

So that night he'd pretended to be her loving son, her yes-man, just as he always had. Then he'd gathered what information he could about her activities and sent it to the police.

Two days later she and his father had been arrested, justice served.

But he would never again let himself be used the way his mother had used him. Never let his own feelings blind him to the truth. He would always listen to his conscience and never let his emotions sway him.

He would always do what was right, and sleeping with the little *civetta* because she offered, and because he wanted her, was wrong.

And he did want her. And he was furious about it.

He kept away from her the following day, to give her some distance and to give his recalcitrant body some time to rethink its choices. There were matters that needed his attention anyway. Her father was trying to contact him, no doubt to offer terms for her return, and Vincenzo was almost tempted to see what the man would say, but then, he knew anyway. Armstrong only used either bribery or threats, neither of which would work on Vincenzo. He couldn't take his daughter by force, either, since he didn't have the resources to touch her on Capri, not without getting allies at least, and that would take time.

Regardless, Vincenzo could afford to wait. He'd let Armstrong suffer for the next week, or for however long it took Lucy to give him the information he wanted.

So he closeted himself in his office in the villa, dealing with the thousand and one things he had to deal with, while his brain kept replaying the memory of her sitting in the dusk with her robe half-open, the shadowed curves of her body a temptation he hadn't envisaged. The rounded shape of one breast—fuller than he'd expected, given how small she was—and the graceful arc of one hip. Her skin had been such a pretty pink, highlighted by the red silk she wore, and his desire had risen, thick and hot. Shocking in its intensity.

He wouldn't have taken her even if she had wanted him, but he knew that she didn't. Her eyes behind the shelter of her glasses had been very wary, the fear glittering greenly in their depths.

It had angered him, that fear. His desire angered him. Her offer had angered him.

Everything had angered him and so he'd pushed himself to his feet and left before he did something he regretted, such as reaching for her and dragging her across the table and burying that anger between her thighs.

Yet even immersing himself in business didn't help. He felt restless and unable to concentrate, her presence an itch he couldn't scratch, and he was further annoyed that he had to wait until the week had ended before he'd get the information he needed to take down her father.

He would have gone back to the de Santi estate himself and left her here if he could have. But he couldn't. Even though his security was impregnable, he didn't want to leave anything to chance. He had to be here to keep an eye on her.

She might try to manipulate him again, of course, but if she was hoping that he'd change his mind about her she was mistaken. He would not be changing his mind. She needed to answer for her crimes so justice would be served.

The thought hardened his resolve, though it did nothing for the restlessness that coiled through him as the day progressed into night. He stayed in his office till midnight, and only then did he leave, stalking back to his bedroom in search of sleep.

He didn't find it, however, and after several hours of lying there, staring at the ceiling, he admitted defeat and slid out of bed, pulling on some jeans and prowling downstairs to the salon that led out onto the big terrace.

It felt hot and airless, so he went to the double doors and pushed them open, allowing the salt-soaked night air and moonlight to pour in. He stood in the doorway a minute and took a deep breath, trying to find his usual clarity of purpose, the bone-deep knowledge that what he was doing was right and necessary.

He couldn't allow himself to be distracted from it by an inconvenient attraction to the worst possible woman. He wouldn't. He must keep on with his crusade, right the wrongs his family had perpetrated over the centuries, that his mother had carried into this century too. It would end with him, that was certain.

Behind him came the sound of a soft footstep and a whisper of an indrawn breath, and he was turning, instantly on his guard. He normally had a weapon with him, but since the villa was well-protected he hadn't bothered with one tonight.

Not that he needed one.

A small figure stood in the darkness near the door to the hall. There was enough moonlight for him to see golden dragons gleaming on red silk and the gloss of dark curls, of light reflected off the round discs of her glasses. The sweet scent of apples reached him and he felt himself go still, his entire body tightening in anticipation.

*You're getting ahead of yourself. She didn't want you, remember?*

He remembered. She'd been made of fear, not desire.

'I'm sorry,' she murmured in her husky voice. 'I didn't know you were here. I'll go if you—'

'What are you doing up, *civetta*?' He shouldn't ask. He should leave her the way he'd left her the night before. Yet he didn't move.

'I...couldn't sleep.'

'Why not?'

'I don't know.' She shifted on her feet, silk rustling, sounding uncertain and nervous. 'I was just...restless.'

As he was restless.

*Perhaps it's for the same reason?*

Perhaps. But again, last night, he hadn't seen desire in her when she'd opened her robe. Only uneasiness and nerves.

*You could be wrong.*

A thread of heat wound its way through him and he found himself wanting to see her face, see what expression was in her hazel eyes.

'Come here.' He had to put some effort into not making it sound like an order, but he managed it. Part of him wanted to know if she would come if it wasn't a command. If she would come because she wanted to.

She hesitated, but only for a moment, and then she came slowly towards him, the moonlight moving over glorious red silk, dark curls, and pale skin.

He could see her face now as she stopped a few feet from him, laid bare in the light coming from behind his back. The moon had bleached all the colour from her cheeks, turning her eyes very dark. With the lenses of her glasses reflecting the light, she looked even more owlish than she normally did.

The night before when he'd told her that she didn't want him she hadn't denied it. She'd simply looked at him as if wanting him hadn't entered her head, even though she'd been fully prepared to offer him sex. And he couldn't lie to himself. The fact that she hadn't wanted him had angered him too.

'Yes?' The word was tentative, her gaze full of familiar wariness.

'Perhaps you can't sleep for the same reason I can't,' he said.

'I...' She stopped, and her hands moved nervously to the sash of her robe, touching it before falling away again. 'What reason would that be?'

He might have thought she was deliberately misunderstanding him if he hadn't known already that she had no guile whatsoever. But, as he was learning, she wasn't like his mother; her response had the ring of truth to it. She genuinely didn't know. Which meant that she had no sexual thoughts about him at all, or she was so desperately inexperienced she didn't recognise them.

*Does it matter? You're not going to take her anyway.*

It didn't matter. And of course he wasn't.

'Were you thinking of me?' he asked, not moving, not taking his gaze from hers.

Even in the moonlight he saw the flush rise in her cheeks.

'Yes,' she admitted hesitantly.

The confession hit him like a jolt of electricity, unexpected and raw as a lightning strike, making his hands curl into fists at his sides.

'Why?' This time he couldn't make it sound like anything less than a demand.

'I don't know. I can't work it out. I'm…afraid of you. And yet I can't stop thinking about you.' The blush in her cheeks got even deeper. 'That was too honest, wasn't it?'

But that was what she was, wasn't it? Too honest. And in ways he was only now beginning to understand. Honesty had been so rare in his life, he barely recognised it. Yet there was more to her than simple honesty. She was also wary and guarded, as if she didn't know what parts of herself she should be protecting.

He wasn't sure why that was, but one thing he did know. He didn't want her to be afraid of him. Thinking of him, yes. Scared, no.

He held her gaze. 'Honesty is rare these days and it is precious. Never apologise for it.'

She blinked, then her gaze dropped from his, down to his chest, which was bare, since he hadn't bothered with a shirt. And stayed there a second before she looked away, nervously fiddling with the knot of her sash.

She wasn't a seductress, he knew that already, and he knew, too, with sudden insight, that she would never have offered him what she had if she hadn't on some level been attracted to him. It simply wouldn't have occurred to her.

But she was attracted to him. Her problem was that she didn't know what it was, because she had no experience. She had no experience of anything at all.

'And are you afraid now?' He searched her vulnerable face. 'Afraid of me?'

Her fingers pulled at her sash. 'Yes.' She said the word tentatively, as if she wasn't sure whether she should reveal it to him or not.

That wasn't what he wanted, not here, not now. She'd been afraid for a long time and right now he didn't want her to be. Just as he didn't want to be only one more man who scared her.

Vincenzo didn't stop to question himself. He merely reached out and took one of her nervous hands in his and slowly drew it towards him. She tensed, looking up at him, her eyes widening. But she didn't pull away, allowing him to place that small hand palm down on his bare chest. Then he put his own over the top of it, holding it there.

The hiss of her indrawn breath echoed in the still darkness, her touch on his skin as warm as sunshine resting on him. Her eyes were wide, that soft, vulnerable mouth open.

'And are you afraid now?' he asked quietly.

# CHAPTER SIX

LUCY WANTED TO tell him that she wasn't afraid. But she was. She was terrified.

Of the smooth, oiled silk of his skin. Of the heat of his body. Of all the hard muscle she could see clearly etched in sharp, carved lines all over his torso. Of the strength and power that hummed through him like electricity through a high-tension wire.

His eyes were the night itself beyond the terrace and his face was all brutal beauty and ferocity, a combination that mesmerised her.

She'd told the truth. She'd come downstairs, restless and unable to sleep, because she'd been thinking of him. She'd been thinking of him all day and she didn't know how to stop.

The words he'd said to her the night before kept revolving in her head, taking up space. Making her angry that he would dare to tell her what her own emotions were and yet also making her examine those emotions. Examine the fear that lived inside her and had done so ever since her mother had died.

Yes, she was afraid of him, but it was such a complex fear. And she'd never wanted anyone before, had never thought about physical hunger that wasn't for food. Had never felt drawn to anyone at the same time as she was afraid of them. It made her think of her mother and how afraid she'd been of Lucy's father. Yet she'd stayed with him all the same.

Love, that had been the issue, though, Lucy was sure. And she didn't love Vincenzo.

The whole day she'd done her best to do her usual thing, which was to pay attention only to the moment as she'd explored the villa, to never think about anything else. Yet it gradually became clear to her as the day went on that she wasn't just exploring the villa. She was also looking for him. Wanting to see him, talk to him. Ask him how he knew that she didn't want him, because she wasn't sure that was the case.

She didn't think it was the case now as he held her hand to his powerful chest, the inky black of his gaze holding hers. She wanted… She didn't know what she wanted. Not love, that was for sure. In fact, she'd never want that, but sex? Maybe.

Sex wasn't a mystery to anyone with an internet connection and she'd looked up various things. It had all looked faintly ridiculous and like nothing she'd ever want to participate in, but what she'd seen on her computer screen had nothing to do with the reality of Vincenzo de Santi, half-naked, in the middle of the night in a villa on Capri, watching her with heat in those black eyes.

There was nothing ridiculous about him. Nothing ridiculous about the heat inside her either.

*Why isn't he simply taking you?*

A good question. Powerful men took what they wanted, as she knew all too well, but he wasn't taking her. He hadn't the night before either, even though she'd offered herself to him. In fact, he'd got up and left rather than reach for her, and that only added a layer to the complex puzzle he was turning out to be.

An incorruptible man, yet not a man without hungers. A man with a strong moral code who stuck by that morality regardless of what he might want for himself.

*He is not your father. You don't have to be afraid of him.*

Lucy swallowed, her mouth dry. It was true. He *wasn't* anything like her dad. And she wasn't anything like her mum. Once she'd been fearless like her. Brave and inquisitive and curious, too. But that had been before those things had led to her mother's death, so these days she locked them away. Fear kept her safe, after all.

Yet last night she'd realised that she was tired of being afraid, and now she realised something else. She was tired of being afraid of Vincenzo. The frightened little girl she'd spent so many years being wanted to pull her hand away and run to the safety of her bedroom. But the woman who'd spent a day near the sea, who'd smelled the salt and watched the boats, who'd opened her robe and offered herself to a dangerous man, didn't want to leave. Right now there was a fascinating and beautiful panther in front of her. And she was ruffling his fur and nothing bad was happening. He wasn't being violent. He wasn't hurting her. He was only holding her hand to his chest. And she was so very curious about what would happen if she stroked him…

*You're not afraid of him. You're afraid of yourself, of what you want…*

She took a breath, feeling something shift and turn inside her, a hunger of her own that she'd ignored. A hunger that there was no way of satisfying, held prisoner as she was in her father's house. So she'd ignored it, shoved it away. Forced it down.

But it was still there. And it was strong. And yes, it scared her.

'Yes,' she whispered and she felt him tense, the expression in his eyes changing, as if that wasn't the answer he wanted. 'Does it matter?'

A muscle in his jaw leapt. 'Of course it matters.'

'Why? Isn't my being afraid what you want?'

His hold remained gentle on her hand, but his gaze was not gentle in the slightest. 'No. You've been afraid for too long, *civetta*, and I don't want that for you. Not now. Not here. Not with me.'

She wanted to ask him what made now different. But that was a rabbit hole she didn't want to go down, not with her hand on his warm chest and the hunger inside that kept on getting wider, getting deeper. That she was afraid of, because it felt bottomless. It felt as if it would swallow her whole.

'I don't think it's you,' she said. 'I think... I'm afraid of myself.'

'Oh?' His thumb moved on the back of her hand, a gentle caress that sent sparks glittering all over her skin.

'I'm afraid of what I want.' A shake was beginning in the pit of her stomach, a tremor like a small earthquake. 'I think I'm more afraid of that than I am of you.'

Tension was gathering in him, but his hold on her hand remained gentle. She could pull away at any moment. 'And what is it that you want, *civetta*?'

He knew, she could see it in his eyes. But he wanted her to say it.

*You can't be so afraid all the time. You only have a week. You only have now. Tell him and let him give it to you. This chance won't come again.*

And he would give it to her. He wanted to.

Lucy took a slow, silent breath and made herself hold his gaze. 'You were wrong last night.' Her voice was little more than a hoarse whisper in the night. 'I do want you.

And I spent all today exploring the villa, but I think… I wasn't exploring. I was searching.' She tried to moisten her dry mouth. 'I was searching for you and I couldn't find you.'

The moon was behind him, glossing his black hair and throwing his face into shadow. But that shadow couldn't hide the flare of heat that leapt in his eyes. 'Well,' he murmured, and this time his voice wasn't cold or casual, 'you have found me.'

The tremble became deeper, wider, the tremor turning into an earthquake. 'Yes,' she said, unable to think of anything else to say.

His thumb moved on the back of her hand again. 'And now you have found me, what are you going to do with me?'

'I don't know.' Her pulse was getting louder and louder in her ears. 'I don't know anything. I've never… I haven't…' The hunger inside her felt too big to contain and she knew if it got any bigger it would shatter her. But she had no experience of this, had no idea what she should be doing. She could hide millions of dollars in offshore tax havens, make them disappear completely, but she had no idea how to touch a man. 'Please…' That one word was a request, a plea, an order. Encompassing everything she didn't know how to say.

An expression she couldn't read rippled over his face, then it was gone, and he was looking at her, the blackness of his eyes becoming the entire world. He raised her hand from his chest and brought her palm to his mouth, pressing a kiss to it.

She gasped, the feeling of his lips against her skin like a hot coal being held there.

Then, keeping her hand in his, he reached out with the other and slowly threaded his fingers in her hair, cradling the back of her head, drawing her closer. She was shivering now, but she didn't pull away; she didn't think she could even move.

And when he lowered his head and that burning mouth covered hers all thoughts of moving vanished entirely. Every thought vanished entirely.

His kiss had taken them all, including her fear.

Something opened inside her like a flower opening for the sun, a knowledge that had been sitting in her soul all this time. That she'd been waiting for this moment her entire life. Waiting for him. She was Sleeping Beauty and he was the prince waking her from sleep, and now he was here there was nothing to be afraid of. Nothing at all.

The trembling took over as he kissed her and so did her need, and her mouth was opening beneath his as if she knew what to do already, letting in his taste and his heat. It felt as if the kiss was a match, igniting her, and now she was burning so hot it felt as though the flame would never go out.

She hadn't meant to deepen the kiss, because he'd started off so gentle, but now his tongue was exploring the inside of her mouth, tasting her with more demand, and she didn't know how to hold back. She followed his lead, tasting him in return, taking in the rich, spicy flavour of him and letting it settle down into her bones. Into her heart.

One of her hands was still held in his, pressed hard to his chest, but she wanted more than that. More than his beautiful mouth talking to her in a language made of teasing kisses, gentle nips, and coaxing licks. She wanted the heat of that powerful body against hers, wanted to press herself to his velvet skin, explore what he felt like, because she didn't know and the lack of that knowledge was an ache inside her.

She moved closer, put her other hand on his chest, glorying in the heat of his body and the feeling of strength. It didn't frighten her, not any more. She knew to the depths of her soul that he would never use that strength to harm her, not the way her father did, and now all she wanted was to explore that strength. Touch that power. Have it turned on her to bring pleasure, not pain.

He released her hand and his arms were around her, pulling her close so she was where she wanted to be, pressed up against him. His mouth had turned hot on hers, the kiss more demanding, and yet even now expertly controlled. More and yet not more than she could handle.

She wanted to handle it though. Because, now she wasn't afraid, all that was left inside her was strength.

His hands slid from her hair down her back and suddenly she was lifted in his arms, held tight to his chest as he crossed the room to one of the long, low sofas. He put her on the cushions, sitting her upright, then came down on his knees in front of her.

She reached for him but he only took her hands in his, turning them palm up and pressing a kiss on each one. Then he put them on the couch and held them there, his gaze fierce on hers. 'Keep them there,' he ordered, his voice full of dark heat. 'Let me give you this, *civetta*. Let me show you how good I can make you feel.'

Lucy took an unsteady breath, shivering all over, held fast by the fierce, hungry look in his eyes. She nodded.

He took his hands away from hers then put them on her knees, easing them apart so he could kneel between them. She took another trembling breath as he came closer, his lean hips between her thighs, his bare chest inches away. He was so tall that, even sitting, she was barely at eye level with him, the breadth of his shoulders blocking out the night behind him.

Calmly he took her chin in one hand, holding her still as he leaned down and kissed her again, his lips hot, the kiss so achingly sweet that she moaned. He deepened it, his tongue dipping inside her mouth, and as he did so she felt his fingers slide beneath the silk of her robe.

Clothes had arrived for her that afternoon, but she hadn't gone through them all, and she hadn't been bothered to find any nightgowns or pyjamas. She'd gone to bed naked and now he knew that too, his fingers burning like a brand on the sensitive skin of her shoulder as he stroked her.

It felt so good that she trembled harder, shivering all over as his grip on her chin loosened and his fingers spread out along the side of her jaw, cupping it, his thumb stroking along her skin as he kissed her deeper. With his other hand he eased the silk of her robe aside, the tips of his fingers brushing down her side and lightly following the curve of her bare breast.

Lucy shuddered, the tips of her nipples abruptly achingly sensitive. She wanted him to touch them, but he didn't. He only caressed her side and then traced circles over her skin, teasing her, maddening her. His mouth left hers and trailed down the side of her neck, leaving kisses like fallen stars and nips like hot sparks. Making her shake, her fingers curling into the material of the sofa cushions, holding on tight.

She wanted more, so much more, but he was going so slowly and being so careful, and he didn't need to. She wasn't afraid, not of him. Not any more.

'Please, Vincenzo.' She'd never called him that to his face before, but it felt right on her tongue. It felt perfect. 'Please... I w-want—'

'Patience,' he murmured against her skin, kissing down between her breasts as his hands caressed her hips and thighs. 'I know what you want and I'll give it to you, I promise. But anticipation will make it sweeter. And besides, I want to savour you.'

He did? Was she worth savouring? Her mother had died protecting her and sometimes, in her lowest moments, she wondered if her mother's sacrifice had really been worth it. Because after Kathy had died her only value lay in what she did for her father, her analytical brain and her facility with numbers. And it was a value predicated on hurting others…

So no, sometimes she didn't think she'd been worth saving. But now here was Vincenzo, telling her that he wanted to savour her, making her feel almost as if she had been worth it after all…

Inexplicable tears collected behind her lids, but she blinked them back fiercely. She wasn't going to cry, not while he was doing this to her. And she wasn't going to protest, either. Not while he was making her feel so good. She didn't want to be sad with him, she only wanted this feeling, this pleasure to never end. Because she'd never had it before. There were so many things she'd never had before and all because of him.

He kissed down her stomach, his hands stroking, making the sweet ache between her thighs become more acute, more demanding, sending delicious chills everywhere. Then he was pushing her thighs wider, his mouth moving lower, and she found herself arching back, ready for anything he might give her. It would only be good, surely.

His fingers stroked her inner thighs, his mouth finding the hot, wet centre of her. Exploring gently, tasting lightly, and she was shaking so hard she thought she might come apart, her breathing loud, her heartbeat louder.

An ocean of pleasure rose up around her, hot and liquid like honey, drowning her, but she didn't care. She wanted to drown. She never wanted to come up for air again.

His hands slid beneath her thighs, drawing her close to the edge of the sofa, and she leaned back, gasping as he lifted her leg and draped it over one powerful shoulder, allowing him greater access, and then his mouth was back on her, tasting her deep inside as his hands caressed her.

There were lights behind her eyes, falling stars and supernovas, galaxies glittering, the end of the world approaching. And she had a front-row seat.

Until even that was lost as the pleasure took everything from her, leaving her with nothing, not even her name. But it wasn't frightening. She threw herself into it, happy to leave it all behind, the only anchor point Vincenzo's hands on her, holding her still, and his tongue working his magic.

And when the end of the world finally came she called his name as the galaxies exploded and she was exploding too, a star blazing in the night, her soul flaming before dissolving into bliss.

Her hands were on him, stroking his shoulders absently as she lay back on the sofa, her face flushed, her mouth curving in a smile as old as time—that of a woman well satisfied.

He couldn't look away from her. He had her flavour in his mouth, a salty sweetness that had to be the most delicious thing he'd ever tasted, and he was desperate for more. Strange, when he'd never been desperate for a woman before. Needing sex, yes, but not a particular woman. Not like this.

Everything in him was urging him to pick her up and

take her upstairs to his bed, because he had protection up there and he wanted to be inside her more than he wanted his next breath. Yet he didn't move, because he hadn't seen her smile, hadn't seen her face when she wasn't scared, and the sight of that smile made his chest get even tighter than it already was.

He'd done that to her. He'd been the one to give her that smile. And he couldn't remember the last time he'd made anyone feel good, made anyone feel happy. All he ever did was cause pain.

*They deserve it though.*

Yes, there was no question that they did. But…looking at Lucy's smile, he found he liked that he'd been the one to give her that. And he liked that he'd given her pleasure, made her call his name. Wiped the fear from her lovely hazel eyes…

*This is not what you should be doing.*

No, but he was going to do it anyway. He'd crossed the line of his own control, and anyway, to leave her now would be cruel and he couldn't do it. This would all be so new to her and he wanted to show her what more there was, what more that lovely body of hers was capable of.

*Don't pretend you're not selfish. You want her for yourself too.*

Oh, he wasn't pretending. He did want her for himself. And even though allowing himself to want a woman like her, a criminal, went against his own moral code, he wasn't going to let that stop him. He'd denied himself many things in pursuit of the justice he craved, but she wouldn't be one of them.

Her robe had fallen open, the red silk in perfect contrast to her pale skin, and her hair was spread everywhere, lush, dark lashes lying still on her cheeks. She was naked and everything he'd imagined. Full, perfect breasts with hard, berry-like nipples. Rounded hips and thighs, soft and graceful, with the pretty little nest of dark curls between.

He was hard now, so hard, and he couldn't wait any longer.

Vincenzo leaned forward and gathered her into his arms. Her eyelashes fluttered, her eyes opening as he straightened, holding her close.

'Where are we going?' Her head rested against his shoulder, her body utterly relaxed. She didn't sound concerned and her gaze was only curious.

'To my bedroom,' he said, unable to keep the roughness from his voice. 'We could go to yours, but there is no protection in your room.'

'Protection?' Her forehead creased. 'Oh… Oh, of course.' A shy little smile turned her vulnerable mouth. 'I was hoping that we might… That you would… I mean, I would like you to be my first.'

That soft confession shouldn't have affected him. It shouldn't have made his chest ache or cause bitterness to gather inside him, and yet it did both. An ache for the gesture of trust that it was, and bitterness because, God knew, he didn't deserve that trust.

He was going to hand her over to the police at the end of this week and nothing would change his mind. He would be giving her to people who would put her in a cell and there would be no one to hold her if she panicked. No one to soothe her fear.

That thought shouldn't have been so bleak, shouldn't have made him feel so hollow inside. Shouldn't have made him so angry. But it was and it did. And he didn't understand it. If he'd had any sense at all, he would have put her down and walked away.

He wasn't going to, though. He was going to make love

to her, because he wanted her. And he wasn't going to mention anything about the police or a cell or her guilt, because he wasn't going to scare her.

Tonight he didn't want her to be afraid of anything and, even though he had no idea why that would be important to him, he was going to accept it.

'There are better men for your first,' he said shortly.

'There might be,' she agreed. 'But I don't want them. I want you.'

Her honesty…it killed him. Made the knot of feelings inside him tighten unbearably, drawing attention as it did to his own failings and the gaps in his morality.

*You're a hypocrite and you always have been.*

Perhaps he was. After all, only a hypocrite would set himself on a course of justice, all the while knowing that he was a criminal himself. That the only reason he'd escaped paying for his own crimes was that he'd handed over his parents instead.

'You look so serious.' She leaned against him, looking up at him. 'What are you thinking about?'

But he wasn't going to talk about the past. That had no place here.

'You,' he said, and it wasn't far from the truth. 'Naked and in my bed.'

'Why? What is it about me that you want?'

He should tell her lies. Tell her that he had no idea why he wanted her, that she must have drugged him or bewitched him to make him so hard for her.

Yet he couldn't do that. He might be a liar and a hypocrite at heart, but he couldn't lie to her. Not about this. Not when she was small and soft in his arms, and the scent of apples and musk wove around him, making his groin ache. Making him want to put her down on the stairs right here, right now, and have her.

'You're beautiful,' he said, and again this was the truth. Her beauty was a secret thing, slowly revealing itself like a photo being developed, a gorgeous picture gradually coming into perfect focus. 'And you're very brave. And you're honest.'

'Beautiful? No, I don't think so. And I'm certainly not brave. I don't know if I—'

'Those things are all true,' he interrupted and not without gentleness, because she wasn't to argue with him on this. 'Whether you believe them or not.'

The look on her face softened and she reached up, her fingertips brushing his cheekbone in a touch that felt like fire against his skin. 'You're really very kind, aren't you?'

Kind. She thought he was kind.

He was nothing of the sort, but that was something else that he wasn't going to tell her. So he stayed silent instead as he came to his bedroom, kicking the door shut behind him as he went through the doorway. Then he carried her over to the big white bed and laid her down on it, before stepping back and stripping off his clothes.

She watched him, her glittering hazel eyes alive with curiosity and fascination and hunger, and when he was naked she reached for him in instinctive welcome.

That stole his breath, made his heart feel heavy in his chest. There was an affectionate, caring, and generous spirit beneath her wariness, and he was uncovering it, bit by bit.

*You don't deserve it. You don't deserve her trust. You'll betray her like you betray everyone.*

Vincenzo shoved that thought from his head as he reached for the protection in the bedside drawer. And locked it away as he prepared himself. Then he moved onto the bed with her, easing her onto her back and settling between her thighs. She made a small, throaty, satisfied sound as he did so, her body arching beneath his, pressing herself harder against him. Her hands were on his shoulders, stroking, as if she couldn't get enough of touching him.

'You're beautiful, too,' she murmured as he eased himself against the soft, damp heat between her thighs.

But he didn't want words now, not with her silky skin against his and the light, feminine musk of her scent intoxicating his senses, making the need hammer in his head so loudly that he could barely hear a thing. So he bent his head and took her lovely mouth, tasting the sweet fire that he was beginning to suspect lay at the heart of her. And she didn't protest, kissing him back, all shy inexperience and untutored hunger.

That sweetness felt unbearable to him all of a sudden, as did her inexperience. He didn't want any reminder of how vulnerable she was, or how alone and unprotected she'd been all her life. How she'd only ever been in the power of a man who'd hurt her. Scared her.

It made him feel things he didn't want to feel, emotions that he had no place for in his heart. He didn't want to protect her, care for her, keep her safe. All he wanted was to be inside her and this hunger for her sated.

He kissed her harder, with more demand, stroking down her body to the wetness that lay between her legs, his fingers circling the sensitive little bud. She gasped, trembling, her nails scraping over his skin. And that was better. That was much better than softness and vulnerability, better than the tightness in his chest and the ache in his heart.

So he kissed her harder still, deeper, nipping at her, biting at her until she moaned and her nails scratched him as she quivered and shifted restlessly beneath him. He was relentless, making her come against his hand, her breathing wild and ragged, and only then did he finally allow himself his own pleasure.

He wanted to thrust hard, show her that, though she might think him beautiful, he had no mercy to give her. That if she persisted in being soft with him, there would be nothing but pain in store for her. But he couldn't bring himself to do it. The thought of her pain in amongst this pleasure anathema to him.

So he pushed inside her slowly, carefully, watching her pretty face, searching for any signs of discomfort in the wide, dark eyes that looked up into his. She groaned, her gaze going even wider as he pushed deeper, but he saw no pain in it. Only a kind of wonder. As if he was a secret she'd always wanted to know, a secret that in the discovering was even better than she'd thought.

She was so hot. Slick. Perfect.

His brain blanked and for a moment he couldn't think of anything but her. Anything but the heat of her and the pleasure that was unfolding inside him, many-faceted and complex. Fascinating. Demanding.

He pushed his hands beneath her hips, tilting her, enabling him to go deeper, and she cried out, her hold on his shoulders almost painful. But she wasn't hurting, he could see that. She was as much in the grip of this pleasure as he was.

'Oh, Vincenzo,' she gasped, shuddering. 'Please, oh, please…'

And he moved, harder, deeper, his hands gripping her hips, losing himself in the tide of pleasure that washed over him, sweeping away the tightness in his chest and the poison in the centre of his soul. The corruption he could never escape, since it was part of him and would always be.

Sweeping away everything but the feel of her around

him, the tight grip of her sex as she stiffened and arched beneath him, calling his name.

Everything but the pleasure that raced up his spine and exploded in his head, an excoriating fire that gave him finally what he hadn't realised he'd been searching his whole life for: a single moment of purity.

It wouldn't last, though, and deep down he knew it. Which was why this could never happen again.

# CHAPTER SEVEN

LUCY WOKE THE next morning knowing exactly where she was: Vincenzo's bedroom.

Sunshine came through a gap in the heavy white curtains, leaving a trail across the crisp white sheets, making it abundantly clear that she was alone.

A thread of disappointment wound through the pleasant, lazy, sated feeling inside her. She wanted him next to her so she could explore that powerful, masculine body in the daylight, discover what made his breath catch and turned his black eyes to flame.

She shivered deliciously as memories of the night before flooded through her. Of the feeling of him sliding inside her, pushing in deep, and how strange it had felt and how wonderful too. There hadn't been any pain, only a momentary discomfort that had gone almost as soon as she'd felt it. And then there had only been the most incredible feeling of connection, of being so close to another person. She'd never experienced anything like it.

His face had been stripped of everything but hunger, a fierce need that had echoed in her own soul. And for a brief, crystal-clear moment before the pleasure had washed it all away she'd seen something vulnerable in him. Something lost.

But the moment had been so brief that now, in the

sunshine of the morning, she wondered if she'd seen it at all. Because what would make a man as strong and powerful as Vincenzo de Santi vulnerable? What would make him lost?

Curiosity tugged at her, that fatal flaw, but this time she indulged it. Staring at the ceiling, she remembered the research she'd conducted into him as she'd planned where to run to. The de Santi family was an old one, going back to medieval times when they'd been spies for a now lost Italian duchy, before an ancestor had found that there were more riches to be had in illegal activities.

In modern times they'd managed to stay one step ahead of the law, concerning themselves only with the jostling for precedence and constant need to earn respect among the crime families of Europe, fighting petty private wars and constantly stoking ancient feuds, and they probably would have continued in that vein if not for Vincenzo.

He'd betrayed his ancient heritage, his lineage, and reported his parents to the police in exchange for immunity.

Then he'd turned himself into the scourge of Europe, feared and loathed by the all the families who'd once considered the de Santis allies.

Lucy frowned at the ornate plastered ceiling.

What had made him turn his back on his family? Loyalty was the lifeblood of the old families, it was ingrained deep in their bones, but something had happened to Vincenzo. Something had shattered that loyalty. Or perhaps he'd never had it at all.

But no, that couldn't be. A man who held to such a difficult purpose as the one he'd chosen for himself wouldn't be a man with no loyalties or beliefs. If anything it was the opposite. But then, where did those loyalties lie? And to what? To justice? To making up for the sins of his family? Or was it something else?

*What does it matter? In a week you'll be in custody and then you'll never see him again.*

That thought hurt and so she ignored it in favour of slipping out of bed and heading for the shower in the en-suite bathroom. She washed herself, enjoying the cool water falling on various aching parts of her body, and when she was done she wrapped the familiar red robe around herself—which was the only item of clothing to hand—and went back to her own room.

The clothes he'd bought for her that had arrived the day before had been put away by Martina, and so she had to pull open the drawers on the big oak dresser and hunt through them. They were all very expensive, in beautiful fabrics, and all her size, and she, who'd never been much of a clothes person, found herself smiling as she pulled out a light, gauzy dress made out of pale green silk.

It was pretty, and when she put it on she could see how the colour brought out the green in her eyes. Immediately, her first thought was about what Vincenzo would think if he saw her in it and whether he would like it.

*Your mother would have liked it too.*

Oh, she would. She'd loved dressing Lucy up and Lucy had loved it too, but after Kathy had died she'd lost all interest in her appearance. Faint glimmers of interest were returning, though.

Perhaps it was silly to want to look nice for a man, especially a man who was still her enemy in many ways, but she decided she didn't care if it was silly or not and kept the dress on. She attempted to do something with her mass of hair, but, since she wasn't sure what, having never paid much attention to styling it before, she left it loose. Besides, she was hungry and wanted some breakfast.

She went downstairs to the terrace, where all the main meals of the day were served, hoping to find Vincenzo already there. But he wasn't. The table was set and food was on it, but the place was empty.

The disappointment she'd felt on waking returned and she turned around to go back inside and search for him, only to stop.

Why was she going to find him? What did she think she'd say? They'd spent the night together, that was all. No promises had been made, nothing had been said.

He'd given her pleasure and it had been the most incredible experience of her life, but he was still who he was. That hadn't changed. Nothing had changed.

*But perhaps you have.*

A strange feeling pulsed through her, part certainty, part strength. As if last night he'd given her some of his, along with the pleasure.

Yes, she had changed. She felt…different. More sure. Less afraid. And maybe if she had the urge to find him, to tell him that she wanted him again, then she should do it. He'd told her to be honest, that it was precious, so why shouldn't she be honest with him?

Avoiding things and hiding was what she'd done in the past and that had kept her safe. But safety was beginning to look overrated to her now. He'd given her a night without fear, a night of pleasure and warmth, and she wanted more.

She only had a few days left of it, after all—if she couldn't change his mind, that was.

First, though, she would eat.

Fifteen minutes later, full of coffee, bacon and some delicious pastries, Lucy went to find Martina to ask where Vincenzo was. Through some emphatic gestures, she understood that he was in his office and wasn't to be disturbed.

That gave her a moment's pause. Did that apply to just her or did that mean he didn't want to be disturbed by anyone? She only needed five minutes. That was allowable, wasn't it? Deciding that it was, she made her way to his office.

It was at the other end of the villa and the door was closed, so Lucy gave it a discreet knock. When there was no reply she stood there a second, debating, but then, nothing ventured, nothing gained, so she opened it quietly and went in.

The room was large, with fabulous views out over another terrace, a formal garden below that led all the way to the edge of the cliff and then the sea. A big desk stood near a set of high, arched windows and behind it stood the tall, powerful figure of Vincenzo.

He faced the windows with his back to the door, talking on the phone in his beautiful Italian, his voice calm and casual-sounding. His usual tone.

He wasn't in a suit today, wearing a pair of well-worn jeans that sat low on his hips and a faded blue T-shirt. As casual as his voice. A man doing a bit of light work on the weekend.

Except there was nothing casual about the tension that gathered in his broad shoulders and back, and even standing where she was by the door she could sense it. Was something bad happening? Did it have to do with her father?

She slipped into the room and closed the door behind her, moving over to the desk and pausing in front of it. Obviously hearing her footstep, he swung around, his obsidian gaze catching hers, the ferocity in it driving all the air from her lungs.

Had that fierceness always been there? Had she simply not seen it? Or was this new?

No, it had always been there, the driving force of his will allied with the flame of purpose. A man who would stop at nothing to get what he wanted or to do what was right. Who wouldn't let anything get in his way, not mercy, not sympathy, not tenderness. No soft feeling at all.

Yet…last night he'd been nothing but gentle with her—at least initially. Until she'd shown him that she didn't need gentleness.

He kept talking, the tone of his voice not changing one iota, holding her gaze with his. She couldn't breathe, couldn't move. The seething tension that gathered around him held her fast.

Something was wrong. He was angry. No, more than that. He was furious.

Male anger was always something to be wary of. Her father's rages had been terrifying and she'd seen the consequences of that rage first-hand. After her mother had died, being in his vicinity had always made her go icy with fear and she tried to avoid him at all costs when he was like that.

Yet, even though Vincenzo seemed no less angry, she wasn't scared. His was a coldly controlled anger and the threat of violence that hovered around him wasn't directed at her. He told her he would never hurt her and she'd believed him then; she believed him now too.

She didn't back away and leave the room the way she might have done even a week earlier. Instead she lifted her chin and stood there, waiting for him to finish. She'd been going to ask him why he'd left her that morning, but now she wanted to know why he was so angry. Was it her father? Business? What?

Quite suddenly he disconnected the call and flung the phone back down on the desk with a clatter. 'What do you want?' There was an edge to his cool voice. 'I told Martina I wasn't to be disturbed.'

Lucy took a breath, studying the hard cast of his features and the black glitter of his eyes. 'Why are you angry?'

'Why do you think? I gave orders that I wasn't to be interrupted and yet here you are.'

'That's not why.' Something more was going on here, she was sure of it. The hot breath of his fury was too intense to be about a mere interruption. 'Is it my father?'

He muttered something vicious under his breath and looked away, the tension pouring off him.

The urge to go around the desk and put her hands on those hard, muscled shoulders to ease him was almost overwhelming. But they'd only had one night together and she couldn't presume anything. He probably wouldn't welcome it anyway.

She clasped her hands in front of her instead. 'Vincenzo?'

'You should leave.' The words were bitten out. 'I'm not in the mood for conversation.'

'Why? What's happened?'

He lifted his head, his gaze clashing with hers again. The darkness in it made it hard to breathe. 'You happened, *civetta.*'

Shock slid down her spine. She stared at him, not understanding. 'What do you mean, I happened?'

He straightened, a muscle in his jaw leaping. 'Last night you compromised my moral code and it cannot happen again.' The anger threading through his voice was like hot metal piercing a block of ice, making his accent more pronounced. 'I do not sleep with my prisoners.'

Oh. So that was the issue. *She* was the issue. And he regretted it.

A heavy disappointment settled in her stomach, though she knew she had no right to be disappointed. There had been no promises made, no indication that it would happen again. She'd just assumed, because it had been so good…

*For you. But perhaps not for him.*

Her mouth dried, the disappointment turning inward, growing sharp edges. 'I…see,' she said huskily. 'I didn't mean—'

'You didn't mean to sleep with me? Is that what you're trying to say? You didn't mean to compromise me? Or cause me to forget everything I stand for?' He gave a harsh laugh. 'You overestimate your charms, Miss Armstrong. It wasn't you and your lovely body, believe me. It was my own weakness.'

The edges were razor-sharp, cutting her, pain seeping through her. She wanted to turn away and leave the room, run away and hide. She'd thought that what had happened between them had been special, had been precious, and now he was looking at her as if it had meant nothing. As if she'd meant nothing.

He'd told her that she was worth savouring, but…had he not meant it?

*Are you worth it, though? After what your mother sacrificed for you? You were where you shouldn't have been and that's all your fault.*

The thought ran like acid through her. No, she wasn't going to think about that. Yet she couldn't pretend to herself that his opinion didn't matter to her, either. Pretending wouldn't change the emotion sitting in her heart. It did matter, because the night with him *had* been special and it *had* meant something. And maybe she was assuming that because it had been that way for her, it had been that way for him, too. But clearly she was wrong. While she'd felt changed on some fundamental level, he simply felt angry.

That hurt, she couldn't deny it. She didn't expect anything from him—an emotional attachment was the last thing she wanted—but she wasn't going to act as if it meant nothing either.

He'd told her to be honest and so she would, both with herself and with him, and if he didn't like that then too bad.

'Yet it's me you're apparently angry with.' She pushed her glasses up her nose. 'Shouldn't you be yelling at yourself in that case?'

He gave a short laugh that held no amusement. 'I should, yes.'

'You might regret what happened last night, Vincenzo, but I don't.' She lifted her chin, holding his ferocious gaze. 'I don't regret any second of it. In fact, that's why I came to find you. I wanted to know why you left and whether you wanted to—'

'No,' he cut her off harshly. 'I will not sleep with you again.'

But she didn't let his tone get to her. 'I wasn't going to ask if you would, only if you wanted to.'

The tension gathered tighter around him, like a fist closing, and all of a sudden it was clear to her what that tension was and where his anger was coming from: he *did* want to. He wanted to badly, because she knew that fierce look in his eyes. She'd seen it the night before as he'd moved inside her. It was hunger, fierce desire, and denial.

He was at war with himself and what he wanted.

The raw feeling inside her eased; she'd been hoping he might feel the same way she had about the night before, but she hadn't been sure. Now it seemed clear that, despite himself, it had been good for him. And that he wanted more.

Except she didn't know what to do, whether to let him put her at a distance or to close it.

'I do not want to,' he bit out, his whole posture rigid with tension.

'You told me honesty was precious,' she said quietly. 'And yet you're lying.'

There were black flames in his eyes, his temper a cold fire. 'Don't presume to know me, *civetta*. You have no idea—'

'You want me, Vincenzo. I can see it in your eyes.'

The muscle in the side of his jaw leapt again. 'It won't happen, Lucy. I've already told you that.'

'Then why are you still so angry?' She came closer, the width of his desk all that separated them. 'If it's not going to happen again, then why should what's already happened matter?'

He said nothing, staring at her, the panther starving for his prey.

She swallowed, the sound of her heartbeat getting louder in her head.

Perhaps she should leave after all. Perhaps it was selfish of her to force this issue with him. He was a man of strict principles and she was essentially asking him to go against everything he believed in. Then again, he was also a man of strong passions, passions that he hadn't given in to and yet clearly needed release from.

Would it be wrong to encourage him to release them with her? He'd already done so the night before after all, and a second time couldn't hurt. And anyway, when was the last time anyone had made him feel good? Did he even have anyone?

Lucy put her fingertips on the desk, steadying herself. 'Do you want to know why I'm here, Vincenzo?'

'No.'

She ignored him. 'I came to tell you that last night was special to me. That you made me feel…so very good. And so very safe. I've been afraid for so long, but I wasn't last night. I wasn't afraid at all, not for one second. And I… want that again.'

The flames in his eyes burned like cold wildfire. 'You are my prisoner.'

'So you keep saying. And I know you care about that, but I don't.'

'You should care. I'm going to hand you over to the police and they're going to put you in a cell, and there will be no one to ease your fear then, *civetta*. No one to hold you or calm you.'

Something vulnerable inside her shivered, but she ignored it.

*You won't be able to change his mind. He'll never release you.*

She ignored that too.

'I know that,' she said and didn't look away.

'You will get no gentleness from me. No mercy.'

Lucy arched a brow, her own temper stirring. 'Did I ask for any?'

He muttered something low and vicious in Italian, then continued in English, 'You don't know what you're asking for.'

She lifted her chin even higher. 'Then show me.'

There was only the desk between them. Only a paltry length of wood that he could have reached across and dragged her over the top of at any time. It was all he could do to stop himself from doing just that.

She looked so beautiful this morning in a green silk dress that made her skin look creamy and deepened the chestnut of her hair, making her eyes seem greener too. The fabric was sheer and he could see the curvaceous shape of her through it, and it made him so hard he could barely think.

Then again, he'd been trying to think all morning and been unable to, his mind full of her. He'd thought going to his study and burying himself in work would be the answer, but it wasn't. Even the news he'd just received, about how Armstrong wanted to do a deal for her return, hadn't distracted him.

The whole night had been a mistake and he knew it. That moment of clarity, of purity, when pleasure had annihilated all thought and he'd lost himself in the darkness of her eyes, had been the turning point. If it had only been sex between them, if she'd been just another in the long line of women he'd had before, then it wouldn't have mattered. He'd have taken his pleasure as often as he could with her and the rest of the world be damned.

But she wasn't just another woman and it wasn't only sex. He'd known it wouldn't be the moment she'd told him that she wanted him to be her first. And it certainly hadn't felt like only sex when he'd touched her, when he'd buried himself inside her.

There was something in the way she looked at him, the way she touched him, as if he was her white knight, a man who would save her, not lock her in a cell. A man who would protect her, keep her safe. A man she trusted…

But he could never be those things for her. Not if he didn't want to compromise his entire life up to this point.

Justice had always been his driving force and he didn't allow himself to be swayed or manipulated. Wouldn't allow his emotions to be twisted or turned the way his mother had twisted and turned them. Yet somehow Lucy had done both.

Correction. She hadn't done it; he'd allowed it to happen. The problem was him, not her. He'd been weak. He should be burning with the holy fire of justice, not the sensual flame of desire.

Yet that flame wouldn't go out and now she was here, so close, offering him more of what his body so desperately wanted, and the need inside him wouldn't be leashed.

She was a criminal, though. She'd broken the law. She was his prisoner. She was everything he'd been fighting against and he couldn't allow himself to have her.

*But why not? She wants you. And no one need know. You've told her that you won't be kind and you won't show mercy, and that you're still going to hand her over to the law, so she will have no expectations. After all, you've already crossed the line once…*

His hands clenched tight, all the reasons for holding back suddenly seeming spurious. Maybe he was turning this into a bigger issue than it needed to be. Yes, he'd thought the night before had been about more than sex, but it didn't need to continue like that. She wasn't a virgin any more. And besides, it would only be for another few days and then the time limit he'd imposed would be up. He would give her over to the police and hopefully by then this madness—because it couldn't be anything other than madness—would have left him.

The look in her eyes from across the desk now was all challenge, an emerald glow glittering in the depths. A familiar emerald glow. It had burned bright as she'd climaxed beneath him, his name torn from her all husky and raw.

*Show me,* she'd said, and so maybe he would. Maybe she needed to see what kind of man he was at heart.

He unclenched his hands and moved around the side of his desk, approaching her slowly. She didn't move, watching him come closer, her gaze steady. There was nothing wary or guarded about it now—she was an open book, her desire for him easily readable in her pretty face.

The urge to take that face between his palms and kiss her, give her more gentleness, was strong, but he resisted it. He'd told her he had no mercy and so he would give her none. And if she wanted to know what that was like, then he *would* show her.

'On your knees,' he ordered coldly.

She blinked, but after a moment's hesitation she knelt on the silk rug in front of him, her head tilting back as she looked up at him. Pink tinged her cheekbones, her eyes a deep, fascinating green behind the lenses of her glasses.

His breath caught, the ache in his groin almost overwhelming now. He reached down and took her glasses off, laying them carefully on the desk beside them.

'What do you want me to do?' she asked breathlessly.

There was no fear either in her voice or her expression, only a sensual curiosity that made his pulse accelerate. There were so many things he could teach her, that they would both enjoy, and why not? Why not take the entire day? If he was going to do this, he might as well commit himself whole-heartedly.

'I'll tell you.' He dropped his hands to the fastenings of his jeans and undid the button, drawing down the zip. Her gaze followed his movements, the pink in her cheeks deepening into red.

'Give me your hand,' he murmured.

She did so without hesitation and he took it in his, guiding her fingers to him, showing her how to draw him out of his boxers and jeans, then how to hold him in her fist. Her touch was searing and it was all he could do to make himself go slowly. Because even though he had no mercy, she was still new to this and he still couldn't bring himself to frighten her.

'Now,' he went on, his voice husky as the pressure of her fist around him sent pure electricity to every nerve-ending he had. 'Take me in your mouth.'

She obeyed, taking him in as if she'd been waiting her whole life to taste him, and the second the heat of her mouth encircled him he had to grit his teeth against the urge to thrust deep.

Instead, he dropped both hands to her hair and threaded his fingers through it, guiding her mouth on him gently and showing her what to do. Encouraging her with whispered commands to use her teeth and her tongue, when to suck and when to release, teaching her the rhythm he preferred.

She was eager and didn't balk at anything he asked of her, the softness of her lips and her inexperienced enthusiasm somehow making it ten thousand times more erotic than what he'd had from other women.

He watched her face, pleasure sweeping through him, making his heart race and the blood pump hard in his veins. The feeling of that vulnerable mouth on him was exquisite, something he'd never forget, and when she closed her eyes as if he was the most delicious thing she'd ever tasted, and made a soft, husky sound in the back of her throat, he knew he wasn't going to last.

His fingers tightened in her hair, pulling her head away from him, and as he did so her eyes opened. 'Oh,' she breathed. 'Did I do something wrong?'

But he was beyond speech.

He pulled her to her feet lifted her onto the desk and set her on top of it. Then he pulled up the hem of her dress, gathering all the green silk up to her waist, before pushing her thighs apart. He spent a breathless minute finding some protection in his wallet, ripping open the packet and rolling down the latex. Then he pulled her to the edge of the desktop and dipped a hand between her legs.

Her eyes were very wide, the hazel gone smoky and dark with desire. And as his fingers touched her slick flesh she shuddered, gasping softly.

She was soft and hot, and very wet, and when he positioned himself, pushing slowly inside her, she welcomed him with a sigh of satisfaction. 'Yes,' she murmured. 'Oh, Vincenzo...yes...'

And he felt that peace again. That stillness. As if he'd been in a room full of unwelcome noise and someone had shut the door, leaving him with blissful quiet.

Nothing but heat. Nothing but pleasure. Nothing but peace.

Her thighs closed around his waist, holding him tight inside her, and then her hands were in his hair, pulling his mouth down on hers, kissing him so sweetly, making him feel as if all of this was new to him too, new and wondrous.

The war inside him ceased and he let himself have this moment of ease, beginning to move, allowing the pleasure to set its own pace, slow and languorous.

She sighed and arched against him, and he paused once to pull her dress off over her head and get rid of her bra, getting rid of his T-shirt too, so that there was nothing between them, nothing but her silky, damp skin against his. And then he kept moving, the thrust of his hips driving them both closer and closer to the edge.

Her kisses became hungry and he gave her back the same hunger, gripping her hips so he could move harder and deeper, the easy pace becoming something more desperate. She tore her mouth from his, kissing his neck and his shoulders, her tongue tasting the hollow of his throat as if she couldn't get enough of him, frantic, feverish words spilling out of her.

He'd forgotten he was supposed to have no mercy and that he wasn't going to give her gentleness. Stroking her back and soothing her were automatic and instinctive, as was the need to ease her desperation. He took her hand and guided it down where they were joined, putting his fingers over hers and showing her what to do to increase her pleasure. She writhed as he did so, her body desperate for release, giving harsh little pants and moaning against his neck, so he pressed her finger hard against the bundle of nerves where she was most sensitive, allowing her to tumble over the edge.

And only when she convulsed around him, did he allow himself to thrust hard and deep and fast, letting himself fall over that edge too, tumbling end over end, and down into peace with her.

# CHAPTER EIGHT

LUCY TRIED TO crawl out from under the blanket thrown over one of the sofas in the salon downstairs, only for a powerful male arm to hook around her waist and draw her back in again.

'No, you don't,' Vincenzo growled, pulling her up against his very hot and very naked body. 'I haven't finished with you yet.'

She gave a long-suffering sigh, running a hand down the warm, velvety skin of his back, loving the feel of all that hard muscle beneath her palm, despite the fact that she'd spent most of the day running her hands all over his body. 'But I'm hungry. Lunch was hours ago.'

He moved, settling himself over her, his weight a delicious pressure pinning her down. 'You're always hungry.'

'So are you.' She shivered as he pressed his mouth to her throat.

'It's true.' He moved lower, nuzzling against her breast. 'Luckily I have all the food I need right here.'

'Yes, but I don't.' The word ended on a gasp as he took her nipple in his mouth, the hot pressure making everything inside her go tight.

She couldn't want him again, surely? They'd done nothing else all day.

After the encounter in his office that morning, he'd

been insatiable, taking her upstairs almost immediately and laying her out across the bed, setting about exploring every inch of her body. He'd been slow and relentless and she was pretty sure she'd screamed. More than once.

He'd sent Martina away for the rest of the day after that and forbidden his security to come into the house. Then he'd made her lunch himself, feeding it to her as she lay in bed wrapped only in a sheet. Once lunch had finished, he'd taken her yet again, and she'd fallen asleep in his arms. She'd woken to find herself downstairs on the sofa in the salon, the doors open, and a naked Vincenzo sitting on the floor leaning back against the sofa, doing something on his laptop. He'd known she was awake instantly and had put aside the computer, joining her on the cushions. They'd lost another hour like that and now she was feeling well rested, physically sated, and ravenous.

In other words, she'd never felt better in her entire life. Apart from being hungry, of course.

She pushed at his muscular shoulders. 'Vincenzo. Food.'

Finally, he lifted his head and gave her a measuring look. 'Very well. But you let me organise it, yes?'

'Okay.' She had no problems with that. If he wanted to feed her the way he'd fed her lunch, she was more than happy.

But Vincenzo clearly had a bigger plan than a simple meal in mind, because he made her stay where she was for at least half an hour, before finally coming to get her and leading her down a couple of hallways and out to a small private terrace shielded from view by trees and potted bushes.

A big outdoor bath sat on the stone floor of the terrace and steam rose from the water. Candlelight leapt and flickered from holders placed on various surfaces, casting a gentle glow over everything.

Her chest constricted as he urged her towards the bath, his hand gentle at her back.

'This is beautiful, Vincenzo,' she said huskily. 'Is it for me?'

'Yes.' He eased the robe he'd put around her off her shoulders. 'There's no beach here and it's too late to swim from the rocks. We have a pool built into the cliff but it's a bit cool at night. I thought you'd enjoy being outside and in some warm water in case you're sore.'

She was slightly…achy. And parts of her that were a little chafed would like some warm water to ease them. She definitely would enjoy that.

Then again, she already was enjoying everything he'd already given her, just as she was very determinedly only thinking about what was happening now and not what would happen in a few days, when he handed her over. It wasn't relevant to this moment and, since this moment was all she had, she'd enjoy every single second of it.

She slipped naked into the bath, the water delightfully scented and warm.

'I'll be back,' Vincenzo murmured and disappeared into the house.

Sighing, Lucy leaned her head back on the bath, loving the soothing effect of the water and the sound of the waves at the base of the cliffs below the house. The stars studded the black sky, the candlelight flickering, and yet another moment presented itself. A moment of peace and tranquillity and utter safety.

Her father couldn't reach her here. No one could. She was protected by Vincenzo and he'd let nothing touch her.

*He will give you up, you know this…*

But that thought wasn't part of the moment and so she

ignored it, counting the stars above her head and letting herself drift in the water.

She must have drifted to sleep too, because she opened her eyes maybe only seconds later, to find Vincenzo had returned and had set a tray of food plus a bottle of white wine and wine glasses down on a stone table near the bath. He'd pulled on a pair of jeans, but wore nothing else, and so she lay there for a few moments, watching the play of muscles moving beneath his tanned skin as he opened the wine and poured it.

And she didn't need to see clearly to know he was beautiful. Stunningly masculine and so physically powerful. Also so fierce and passionate, and not at all the cold, judgmental angel he'd appeared to be when she'd first met him.

He'd told her that he had no mercy and yet with her he'd been nothing but kind. Demanding, true, yet also gentle. And his ruthlessness hid a protective nature that she found almost unbearably attractive.

*You feel something for him...*

Lucy forced her gaze away, the water around her suddenly not quite as warm as it had been. She was only admiring him. It didn't mean anything emotionally.

Her skin prickled and she looked up again to find that he'd turned from the table and was now watching her, a familiar expression of hunger on his blunt, aristocratic features. 'I was going to ask if you wanted some dinner now, but maybe we could wait five minutes. I suddenly have a very strong urge to have a bath.'

She flushed at the heat in his eyes. 'Dinner first,' she said firmly. 'It would be very unfortunate if I starved to death at a vital moment.'

He stared at her a second and then, much to her delight, his hard mouth curved into one of the most glorious smiles she'd ever seen. It softened the stern lines of his face, making him seem much more approachable and incredibly sexy. 'That would, indeed, be unfortunate. Perhaps I'll wait, then.' He picked up a large white towel he'd draped over a nearby stone bench. 'Come, *civetta*. Get out of the bath and let me dry you.'

She could have done it herself, but she didn't want to, getting out of the bath and letting him dry her off and wrap her in the lovely red silk robe. It made her feel cared for, and it had been a long time since she'd felt cared for, so she would let herself enjoy it while it lasted.

*Not that you deserve it. Not when your mother died because of you.*

Lucy ignored the thought.

A few minutes later she was seated on one of the stone benches, cushioned by mounds of pillows, a plate full of cold meats, salad, cheeses and delicious fresh-baked bread in her lap. A glass of wine sat on the back of the bench at her elbow, while Vincenzo lounged in a chair opposite, ostensibly making sure her plate was full. To 'build up her strength' since it was apparent he had plans for the rest of the evening. Plans that obviously featured her.

'This is wonderful,' she said, picking up an olive. 'Thank you.'

He inclined his head in wordless acknowledgement, sipping on his wine as she slowly chewed the olive, relishing the sharp, salty taste.

'This whole place is wonderful,' she went on, gesturing around them at the villa and its grounds. 'Did you come here a lot as a child?'

'Not often. I do spend a lot of time here now, however.'

'Oh? Why is that?'

'The *palazzo* is…medieval and dark. I prefer this villa. It's much lighter, and being near the sea is pleasant.'

There was something in his voice she couldn't place. An edge. She wanted to ask him what it meant, but the mood between them was relaxed and easy and she didn't want to upset it.

'I think that was the worst thing about the house in Cornwall,' she said instead. 'It was near the sea, but it had no view. I could hear the waves but I could never see them.'

'You weren't allowed to go out at all?' This time there was no edge in his voice, the question utterly neutral. 'Not even for a drive?'

'No.' She didn't see the harm in telling him. It was only the truth, after all. 'Perhaps I could have argued for a trip to the beach, but I couldn't see the point. It would only make me want what I couldn't have.' The story of her life, really. 'Easier to take a virtual trip via my computer.'

Vincenzo frowned. 'So you never left the house?'

'Dad would sometimes take me to London.' She reached for her wine and took a sip herself, enjoying the cool bite of it. 'But not often. I didn't like going anyway. It meant meetings with some of his contacts and friends and they scared me.'

Vincenzo's frown became fierce, the glitter of his eyes sharper. 'Why? Did they hurt you?'

She could hear the promise of retribution in his voice and it set up a small, warm glow inside her, even though she knew it shouldn't. 'No. Dad wouldn't have been pleased with them if they had and they were afraid of him.'

'You were afraid of him too.'

'I was,' she agreed. 'I am.'

'And yet you escaped him.' Vincenzo tilted his head, his black gaze focusing on her as if he'd never seen anything so interesting in his life. 'What made you run, *civetta*? Was it opportunity or had you been planning it?'

They hadn't talked of anything personal the whole day and she'd been more than happy with that. But now tension crawled through her. Talking about this would involve explaining about the promise she'd made to her mother, and how her mother had died, and the reason for it...

*Then he'll know exactly how guilty you really are.*

A kernel of ice settled in the pit of her stomach. She didn't want to tell him. She wanted him to keep thinking of her as someone worth savouring, someone worth taking care of. She didn't want this warmth between them to end. There was still a chance she could convince him to change his mind about handing her over to the police, but if she told him the real reason for her mother's death, that chance would be gone.

She looked down at her plate, picking up a red cherry tomato and eating that to give herself a moment or two to think, even though her appetite had vanished.

No, she couldn't lie to him. He valued her honesty, which meant she'd have to tell him the truth, face his judgment. Accept her own guilt, because she couldn't hide from it any longer.

Lucy gathered her courage and met his gaze head-on. 'I ran because of a promise I made to my mother. She wanted me to survive, get free any way I could, but it took me a long time to be brave enough to do it. I killed her, you see. The story was that she tripped and fell against a window, sliced her arm, and bled to death. But that's not what happened.' Her jaw ached, but she forced herself to go on. 'Dad had a lot of secret meetings and I was curious about them. I'd always try and eavesdrop, pretend I was a spy, stupid things like that. I knew I wasn't supposed to. Mum warned me not to, that Dad would get very angry if he caught me, and there would be consequences. But… I couldn't help myself.'

She took a breath, her hands now in her lap, her fingers twisting. 'He did catch me that day. And Mum was right, he was furious. He was going to hit me, but she put herself between him and me, and caught the blow instead. It knocked her into a window, which broke, cutting a major artery.' She felt very cold all of a sudden, as if she'd been plunged head first into a pool of snow melt. 'Dad did nothing. He just walked out, leaving me to try and help her. There was so much blood…and I couldn't.' Lucy's throat closed up. 'She made me promise to escape, to have a life away from him. To be happy. And then…she died.'

There was no expression at all on Vincenzo's face, but a fierce light burned in his midnight eyes. 'Lucy,' he said softly.

'And you're right,' she went on, because she had to say it now. 'I am a criminal. I'm guilty of all those crimes I committed for my dad. But mainly I'm guilty of being the reason for her death. If I'd only listened to her, if I hadn't been so curious, so s-stupid, if I'd just done what I was told, Dad wouldn't have found me. He wouldn't have got so angry. And he wouldn't have tried to hit me, and then Mum wouldn't have died. I killed her, Vincenzo. It was my fault.'

*Of course it is. And you deserve everything that's coming to you.*

Fear came bubbling up at the insidious voice inside her head, a black wave of it, and she had to turn away, unable to face Vincenzo's dark gaze and the judgment that would no doubt be there, sticking like a splinter in her heart.

She didn't know when his opinion of her had begun to matter so much, but it did, and she couldn't bear it. She didn't want the way he looked at her or treated her, with so much gentleness and kindness, to change, yet it would, and she couldn't avoid that.

She deserved his condemnation, not soft candles, and delicious food, and a warm bath.

*Face it like your mother faced her death, coward.*

Lucy swallowed and lifted her head, determined now, forcing herself to look into his eyes. Because her mother hadn't hesitated to put herself in physical danger to protect her, and so she couldn't hesitate now.

'I appreciate everything you've done for me, Vincenzo,' she said, her voice hoarse. 'But I don't deserve it. Not any of it.'

She'd prepared herself to meet his judgment—that much was clear from the look on her face. And, given how pale she'd gone, it was obvious that she was expecting that judgment not to be in her favour.

He hadn't meant to have this discussion with her, not here, not now. But that was his own fault. He'd been the one to ask her why she'd escaped when she had. And, of course, she'd answered him with her customary honesty.

And he wasn't sure what horrified him more: that she blamed herself for her mother's death or that she expected him to blame her as well.

*You told her she was guilty, that she was a criminal.*

That was true, he had. But how could he think she was either? After that?

Her little chin was lifted, her eyes shadowed behind the lenses of her glasses, the green lost in the darkness.

She was brave to tell him what she had. And it had cost her. He could see the cost in the gleam of tears she was trying not to let fall, that fogged her glasses, and in the tension that surrounded her.

She'd sat up so straight on the stone bench, telling him in a steady voice about her mother's death. About how her mother had defended her, protected her, and in the end bled to death right in front of her. And for that, Lucy blamed herself.

*'I don't deserve it. Not any of it...'*

She was a criminal and she was guilty. The crimes she'd committed for her father couldn't be erased. But what she wasn't guilty of was her mother's death.

'How old were you when that happened?' he asked carefully.

'Seven.'

Dear God. She'd watched her mother die at seven...

His heart contracted painfully tight. He wanted to put his wine down, cross the space between them, gather her into his arms, take the pain he saw in her eyes away with his touch. But he had to make this clear to her first.

The law was a logical thing and emotion had no part in justice. And he wanted her to know, unequivocally, that, from a legal standpoint at least, she was blameless.

'And did you stab your mother with that piece of glass?' he asked.

She blinked. 'No. She fell against the window because Dad hit her.'

'She died of blood loss, yes?'

Lucy nodded and he could see her swallow. This was so very painful for her. Her jaw and shoulders were so tight. She looked very fragile, so very vulnerable.

His heart contracted even tighter, but he ignored it.

'You could not have killed your mother, Lucy,' he said

in a neutral voice. 'If you had picked up a piece of glass and stabbed her with it, then that would be a different story. But you didn't.'

She shook her head. 'I didn't listen. I should have—'

'You were seven,' he cut across her gently. 'You were a child. What seven-year-old listens to everything their parents tell them?'

The look on her face was bleak. 'She was afraid and yet she still protected me. She stepped in front of Dad and took the blow meant for me. And if she hadn't she wouldn't have fallen against the glass and—' Her voice cracked.

Vincenzo put his glass down then and rose from his chair, giving in to his own instinct, because the sight of those barely suppressed tears… He couldn't sit there, letting her cry, and not offer any comfort. He couldn't.

Crossing to the bench she was on, he sat down and pulled her into his arms before she could protest, holding her the way he had days ago in his office in London.

Immediately she turned her head, burying her face against his chest, her shoulders shaking in a silent sob, and it made him ache that her instinct was to turn to him for comfort. It made him want to hold her tight, protect her, be deserving of the trust she'd put in him.

He disentangled her momentarily to take her glasses off so they didn't hurt her, laying them down on the arm of the bench next to him, then he gathered her in his arms once more and held her close, stroking her thick, glossy curls.

'She was only doing what any mother would,' he said. 'She was protecting her child.' His own mother, for all her faults, would have done the same. But not out of any maternal instinct. She would have done it for her own ends, not his.

'Sometimes I don't understand why.' Lucy's voice was muffled. 'Sometimes all I can think is why? Why did she protect me? What was it about me that was worth dying for? And if she hadn't protected me, then she wouldn't have died and maybe other people might not have got hurt. My father might not have used me—'

'You cannot think like that, *civetta*,' he interrupted quietly. 'The past is something you can't change, so there is no point in going over all the what-ifs and might-have-beens. You did not kill your mother. She made a choice to protect you and she made that choice because she loved you. If you are going to assign blame to anyone, assign it to your father. He is the villain here, not you.'

'A villain I worked for. I did everything he told me to and if I hadn't been so afraid...'

Vincenzo tightened his fingers in her hair, drawing her head back. Her face was wet with tears, her eyes red-rimmed and her nose pink. She looked so sad and yet so unutterably lovely. How had he ever thought her plain?

'You cannot blame yourself for that, Lucy.' He put force into the words. 'You escaped him. You were afraid, but you made a promise to your mother and so you didn't let that stop you. In the end, you were brave and you escaped, and that's the only thing that matters.'

But pain lingered in her eyes. 'If I had truly been brave, I would have stood up to him. My mother did. She knew he would hurt her and yet she stood up to him anyway. I should have done that. Should have refused to do all those things, gone to the police.' A tear ran down her cheek. 'And I didn't. I...allowed him to keep me prisoner because I was just terrified.'

He cupped her cheek in his palm, his thumb brushing away the tear. 'You had reason to be terrified, *civetta*. He is ruthless and violent and he would have hurt you very badly if you'd done any of those things.'

Even the thought of what Armstrong could have done to her made Vincenzo's blood run cold and a red haze of rage descend over his vision.

*Does she really matter that much to you?*

But he ignored that thought entirely.

Lucy shook her head. 'Mum was afraid of him, but she didn't let it stop her. She was so brave, while I just sat in my room cowering for years. She would have been so ashamed.'

'No,' he said flatly and with absolute conviction, tightening his fingers in her hair for emphasis. 'To see you now, she would have been proud. And she would have thought her death worthwhile if it kept you from harm.'

Lucy's lovely face was tearstained, and she looked at him, as if she was searching for something that only he could give her. 'How do you know that?'

He didn't, of course. He didn't know anything about loving mothers who protected their children. But he did know this little *civetta* and what she'd done for him. Because she had changed him. With her honesty and her trust, with the heat of her passion and the cold grip of her fear. With the heart she wore on her sleeve...

'Because you are worth saving, Lucy Armstrong,' he said quietly.

Lucy flushed and the pain in her eyes eased, and he found himself going on, for what reason he didn't know. Maybe because he didn't want her to feel alone.

'And because I have done things I regret too, things I cannot change no matter how I wish I could.'

She blinked, tears glittering on the ends of her lashes. 'What things?'

He shouldn't tell her. No one knew. And he hadn't

thought he'd want anyone to know either. But somehow it felt wrong to hold this back, to let her know that she wasn't as alone in the world as she might think. That he understood in a way few other people would.

*You weren't supposed to let your emotions become a part of this.*

No, but it was too late for that now and he knew it. His emotions were engaged already. All he could do now was to make sure he didn't allow them to get in the way of what needed to be done.

'I never knew what my family was.' He kept his voice quiet, his thumb moving on her cheek. 'My mother maintained a fiction of the proud de Santi legacy, an aristocratic family of warriors fighting to protect what was theirs. I believed her. A proud de Santi prince, she called me, and that's what I believed myself to be. I was arrogant and spoiled. So sure of myself and my place in the world. I didn't see what was wrong with that place until it was too late. Until people died because of what I'd become.'

Lucy's eyes were very wide. 'What did you become?'

'I became complicit.' He couldn't stop the bitterness that coloured his tone. 'Though I was always complicit, I just chose not to see it.'

A deep crease lay etched between her brows. 'What did you choose not to see?'

Even now he didn't like to think about it. But he couldn't not tell her, not when she'd shared what had happened to her.

'My mother was beautiful and very loving, but she was also a de Santi through and through. I wasn't a son so much as her tool. She used me from a young age, mostly as a spy or a distraction, since children could be useful for manipulating adults and since they were so easy to manipulate themselves. She told me I was her brave soldier and that if I wanted to be a general, I had to prove my worth and follow orders.'

He could feel the creeping dread of the night he never thought about. The inexplicable dread that he always tried to hold at bay, because nothing had ever really happened. Or, at least, that was what he'd told himself. What he'd been telling himself for years...

'We were at the opera one night in Naples, and at the end of the production my mother pointed to a woman in the theatre foyer and told me to bring her to the alley-way a couple of doors down from the theatre. She said that if I pretended to be lost, and cry a few tears, no one would question it. I was seven and I loved my mother with all my heart. I only wanted to make her happy, and so I did what she asked.' Years ago now, and yet that dread still wrapped around him and squeezed him tight. 'The woman was so kind. She hugged me when she found me crying, and gave me a sweet, and she followed me when I told her to come with me to the place I'd last seen my family. She held my hand and told me a funny story...' He stopped, took a breath, and then went on, 'There was a van in the alleyway. And when we approached, the door opened and some men got out. They grabbed her and pushed her into the van and drove off. She didn't even have a chance to scream.'

Lucy's gaze darkened. 'Oh, Vincenzo.'

He could hear the sympathy in her voice, but he knew he didn't deserve any of it. 'My mother was so pleased with me. And I felt proud that I'd done what she wanted me to do. And yet... I couldn't stop seeing that woman's face as they grabbed her. The look of fear on it. Even then I knew that something had happened to her, but I didn't let myself remember it or think about it. But that memory was always there, and then Gabriella happened.'

Lucy placed a hand on his chest, her palm a small ember of heat. 'Gabriella?'

He didn't want to talk about this either, but it was too late for silence.

'When I was twelve, Mama encouraged me to be friends with the daughter of a rival family. She was my age and wasn't afraid of me like the other kids were. I liked that very much. I didn't question why my mother wanted me to be Gabriella's friend, I just let her encourage it because it suited me too.'

'Other kids were afraid of you?'

'Because of my family. The de Santis were very much feared, though I didn't understand why at the time.' He paused, the bitterness sinking deeper into his heart. 'I liked that though. I liked being the de Santi prince that everyone was afraid of. And I was very loyal to my mother, wouldn't hear a bad word said about her. I ignored the rumours and doubts that I picked up as I grew older. That the de Santis were a family of murderers and traitors, and that my mother was the most feared of all, because of her reputation for brutality. I didn't believe them. Mama was small and beautiful and adored me. I couldn't even conceive of her being brutal.' Tension wound through him, though he tried not to let it. 'Then when I was eighteen Mama mentioned that we needed to know the location of Gabriella's father on a particular night, and could I perhaps find out? I knew, deep down. After that night in Naples, I suspected. There was a reason why she wanted that information and that the reason wasn't going to be good. But I was so completely her creature that I ignored my doubts. I took Gabriella out and I got the information I needed from her. I knew she had feelings for me, and I used them the way my mother used mine for her.'

His heart clenched tight at the memory. Of Gabriella's pretty face and the way she'd looked at him, as if the sun rose and set in his eyes. 'It was easy. She told me everything, because she trusted me. And I betrayed her. I passed the information on to my mother.' He'd been so oblivious. So stupid. So blinded. 'Two days later Gabriella's father was killed in a hit carried out by unknown assailants.'

Lucy's eyes widened and he could see the shock in them. Now it was his turn to face judgment, and it would happen. She would soon see his own special brand of hypocrisy.

'Gabriella knew what had happened. She knew that I'd betrayed her. But she didn't blame me. She blamed herself instead.'

Lucy's hand pressed hard against his chest, as if she could sense his self-loathing and wanted to ease the burn of it. But nothing would. Nothing would ever make that get any better. Only the fire of justice ever came close.

'I was complicit in her father's death,' he said flatly, so there could be no mistake. 'I'd ignored the doubts I'd had for years about my mother, too blinded by my love for her to think that everything she'd told me about our family, about myself, could be a lie. But after Gabriella's father died I couldn't ignore it any longer.' He remembered the weight of his own realisation. The crushing burden of understanding that had nearly annihilated him. 'I confronted my mother about it and she laughed. Told me it was just business. That if I wanted to remain part of the family I should get used to it. That I'd already done so much to help, after all…'

He gritted his teeth, remembering his mother's warm, familiar smile. And the cold, cold look in her eyes. 'It was a threat and we both knew it. A reminder that I was as guilty as she and that she had the power to do something about it if I became a problem.' His mouth moved in a smile, though there was no humour at all in it. 'It was common knowledge that there was only one way out of the de Santi family and that was in a box.'

Lucy's gaze was dark and liquid, but she didn't say anything.

'So I made a decision.' He could still feel the flame of that decision, burning hot and strong. It never went out. He couldn't afford to let it. 'I gathered all the pieces of information I could find on my mother's activities and I forwarded them to the police. I made sure I was at her trial to give evidence and I made sure she went to prison. She didn't look at me at all as they led her away. I was dead to her already.'

There were so many things that had scarred him in that moment. The knowledge that he'd negotiated his own immunity from prosecution by betraying his mother. An immunity he'd wanted so he could dedicate his life to pursuing his own justice.

The way she'd ignored him so completely. He didn't blame her in the end, but it had hurt all the same. Confirmation, as if he'd needed it, that he'd never been her son to love.

There was silence afterwards, but he couldn't hear anything above the pounding of his own heartbeat.

'If I can't blame myself for what happened with my mother, then you can't blame yourself for what happened with yours, Vincenzo,' Lucy said quietly. 'You weren't complicit. You were used.'

# CHAPTER NINE

VINCENZO'S DARK EYES were full of fire. 'You think I don't know that?'

'I do think you know that.' The anger in his face told her that clearly. 'But you don't feel it, do you?' She'd phrased it as a question, but it wasn't meant to be one. Not when she knew the truth so intimately herself. 'You feel responsible.'

'Of course I feel responsible. I lured that woman to that van. And I used my friendship with Gabriella to betray her father. My actions caused his death, and I knew all along that something wasn't right about it. I knew all along that there was doubt. But I didn't listen to that doubt. I didn't listen to my instinct. And if I had—'

'If you had, what would have changed?' She didn't know why she was arguing with him. It was only that there was pain in his heart the way there was in hers, and that he blamed himself just as she blamed herself. They were so alike. Both children of monsters. It made her feel his agony as if it were her own. 'You might have saved him, but someone else might have got hurt instead. And if the past doesn't matter for me, then it can't matter for you. We can't be complicit when both our parents used us, and we can't change what happened.'

His expression had become hard, like stone, but his eyes glittered, sharp as volcanic glass. 'No, I can't. Which is why the only thing of importance is what I do now. And that is taking down the people like my mother. Those families who have caused so much harm to so many people. Justice is the only way forward.'

And he was burning with it, that was clear.

Foreboding fluttered deep inside her, but she ignored it. She understood all too well where he was coming from and she could see how heavily guilt weighed on him. Gabriella hadn't blamed him, but he blamed himself, and that surely had to be an impossible burden.

*You know about those too.*

Oh, yes, she did. She'd carried the weight of her mother's death for a long time, after all. But this life he'd set out for himself, this crusade, had to be a lonely one. She knew better than anyone how difficult it must be, to be constantly on your guard, to never feel safe. Never to be able to trust anyone.

Her heart ached for him and there was nothing she could do. No words to make the burden he bore for the deaths of those people lighter, no way to ease it. All she could do was offer him understanding, because she carried those same burdens.

He'd told her that she wasn't to blame and that she was worth saving, but the feeling in her heart was still the same, the doubt and the fear.

He felt those things too.

Maybe, though, there was some help she could offer him…

She shifted in his lap. 'Wait here. I'll be a couple of minutes.' Before he could stop her or ask what she was doing, she'd slipped off him, going quickly into the house and to her bedroom. Her laptop was still sitting in her bag on the armchair near the bed, so she got it out and went back to the terrace.

Vincenzo had risen to his feet, that dark menace gathering around him again, staring at her fiercely. But she ignored him. She opened up the laptop and typed in her password, then opened up the files she'd encrypted only a week ago.

Then she held out the laptop to him. 'Here. All the information you need about my father is in this file. It's yours, Vincenzo.'

He didn't look at it or make any move to take it. 'You were going to give me that at the end of the week. That was the deal.'

'I know. But justice is important to you, and I don't want to cower in fear any more. I want to do something. I want to help.'

'But why now? Why not before?'

'Because I understand better now why you're doing it and where you're coming from. And I don't want to keep that information from you. More people could get hurt the longer I hold on to it, and I don't want that either.' She lifted her chin, held that fierce stare. 'Take what's on that laptop. Use it to put him behind bars for the rest of his life, because that's what he deserves. At the very least for my mother's sake. And at the end of this weekend I won't protest. I'll go quietly to the authorities.'

Still he didn't take the laptop.

'If I have the information now, what's to stop me from handing you over immediately?'

He wouldn't, though. She knew in her bones that he wouldn't.

'You won't.' She dared him to contradict her. 'You gave me your word and I think that's important to you too.'

Once again he said nothing, that look on his face like

a judge debating a sentence. 'You're really prepared to give yourself up? Just like that?'

That he didn't deny it caused her heart to miss a beat, just once. But she ignored it, because what else could she do? After all the things he'd told her about himself and his motivations? His reasons for what he was doing? He was taking responsibility for his actions and trying to make amends, and she couldn't fault that. She couldn't pretend that she didn't have amends to make either because, although logically she knew she wasn't responsible for her mother's death, the guilt remained. And maybe answering for the crimes she'd committed afterwards would help ease it.

'You've devoted your life to justice, Vincenzo. You took responsibility for yourself and the wrongs your mother did, and you're making up for that harm by preventing harm to others. By stopping those responsible. Yet what have I done? I broke the law and my actions would have caused people pain.' That guilt was so heavy, weighing her down. 'I need to pay for that. I don't want to go to jail, but not wanting to doesn't put me above the law. And besides... I don't want to manipulate you into helping me escape. That would be forcing you to compromise your principles and I can't ask that of you.'

He had set her an example and all she could do was follow it. She couldn't claim a freedom that she didn't deserve, and she couldn't ask him to ignore everything he believed in just for her sake.

Slowly, Vincenzo reached for the laptop and took it from her. But even then he didn't look at it. He put it down on the stone bench and reached for her, drawing her close. He was so tall she had to tilt her head back to look up at him. Her glasses were still on the arm of the bench, but she didn't need them to see those burning, dark eyes, and the expression on his face, like stone.

What he was thinking, she had no idea.

She didn't know whether she still wanted him to change his mind, or whether she'd be happier in a jail cell. Either way it seemed she'd have to endure pain, so perhaps it was better that she didn't know what he was thinking. Perhaps it was better to just be in the moment with him, where there was only his warmth and strength. The way he looked at her and the way he touched her. Where there was no past and no future.

Only them. Together.

He lifted his hands and cupped her face between them, staring at her as if she was a book in a language he didn't know but had always wanted to learn.

'*Civetta,*' he said softly, 'why should my principles matter to you?'

Honesty was precious, he'd told her, and so honesty she'd give him, even though perhaps telling him this wasn't wise. Even though she was still sorting through the implications of it for herself.

'It's not your principles.' Her voice was scraped and raw. 'It's you, Vincenzo. You matter to me.'

She wasn't sure when it had happened, when he'd suddenly become important to her, but he had. And perhaps she'd only come to the realisation in the last ten minutes or maybe she'd known subconsciously for days. Whatever, the when didn't matter. She only knew that she felt it now, like a fire burning hot and strong inside her. A fire that in the space of the last half-hour, as they'd shared their secrets, had only strengthened.

*You cannot feel anything for him, remember?*

Oh, she remembered. But this was merely a feeling of...kinship. Nothing more than that.

Shock flickered in his gaze and something else, an instinctive heat that made her breath catch. His palms were warm against her skin, resting there lightly, holding her gently. Yet there was nothing gentle or light about the way he looked at her. Angry, almost. As if he hadn't liked her answer one bit.

'Don't.' An underlying thread of ferocity wound through his cool voice. An order that he wanted her to obey. 'You can't let me matter, Lucy. You can't feel anything for me, understand? I negotiated immunity from my crimes so I could dedicate myself to bringing people to justice, and that's my sentence. And it's for life. I cannot be distracted from it, not by you. Not by anyone.'

It was a warning, but she didn't need it. She knew what was at stake already. Not that there was any kind of future for them even if she'd wanted there to be. He wouldn't compromise his principles and she would never ask him to.

Yet they could have this moment and perhaps a night. Perhaps even the next couple of days, too. Surely that wouldn't be too much to ask?

Her mother had wanted her to be happy, and she'd never been happier in her life than when was in his arms.

'I know,' she said. 'Believe me, I know. But I think we could have the next couple of days, couldn't we?'

An expression she couldn't name rippled over his face. 'Oh, *civetta,* I don't—'

'Please, Vincenzo.' She stared up into the inky darkness of his eyes. 'I've never been happy before, but you've given me a taste of it. And I wouldn't mind a little more to take with me when I go.'

He muttered something harsh under his breath, the glitter in his eyes full of anger and desire, heat and regret, and too many other things she didn't understand.

But she understood the demand of his kiss as he bent his head and took her mouth, hard and deep and hot. Knew, too, the taste of his desperation, because she felt the same. She put her arms around his neck, rose up on her toes, kissing him back just as desperately as he was kissing her. And everything suddenly became feverish and raw.

He swept her up into his arms, carrying her from the terrace and through the villa till they reached his bedroom, where he tore the robe from her body and laid her on the bed. He got rid of his clothes, found the protection they needed, then eased apart her thighs and settled himself between them.

He didn't wait and she didn't need him to. There was a yawning emptiness inside her, an echoing hollow space that only he could fill. And he did, thrusting deep and hard inside her. And this time he didn't treat her as if she was made of glass. He didn't go softly or gently, treating her as if she was vulnerable.

He gripped her thighs, hauling them up and around his waist, tilting her hips back so he could slide more completely inside her, and then he was moving in an almost savage rhythm, forceful and hard and demanding.

It felt so good. Exactly what she wanted. Because she wasn't the scared little girl he'd brought to Capri days ago. She was different now. She was changed. She wasn't afraid any more, not of herself and not of him, and not of what she wanted.

And she wanted everything. She wanted it all and now, because she didn't have long to enjoy it. Only a few days. But she would take those days and throw herself into them. Take as much happiness as he could give her and then come back for more. She wouldn't hold back and she'd deny him nothing.

She might not deserve it, but he did. Everything he'd given her she'd give back to him, because, whether he knew it or not, he needed it too.

So she put her arms around him and tightened her thighs around his hips, holding him to her, moving with him. And she kissed him, nipped him, licked him. Let him know how much she liked what he was doing to her, how much she wanted all the pleasure he gave her.

And when she'd reached the point of desperation, when her soul had been drawn so tight with pleasure she almost couldn't stand it, she stared up into his intense face, and felt everything inside her still.

It was as if he held her in the palm of his hand, her whole being gathered up tight in his fist. Then he opened his fingers and her soul flew free, caught in a spiralling ecstasy. Only to fall into the hot darkness of his eyes.

And drown there.


For the first time in his life, Vincenzo had no idea what to do. Always, his path had been clear to him. Always, he knew in which direction to turn and which route to take.

Justice was what he was after. Justice for the woman he'd lured into that dark alleyway. Justice for Gabriella and her father. And perhaps some justice for himself, too. For the way he'd been used and manipulated.

There had never been any conflict within him. He always knew that what he was doing was the right thing, and even when there had been protests and denials from the people he'd put away, he'd never doubted that they deserved what they got.

But now he was made of doubt and the path that had always been so clear was shrouded in fog.

Lucy had accepted that she was guilty of the crimes she'd committed for her father and that Vincenzo would turn her over to the police. And not just accepted it. She felt she deserved it.

Days earlier, there had been none of this conflict. Yes, she was guilty. Yes, she deserved it. But now…things were different.

He sat on a sun lounger under the shade of a big white linen umbrella, gazing at the woman who lay face down on the lounger next to him, her head buried in the crook of one arm, her mass of dark hair in drifts over her pale shoulders. Beyond was the cool blue of the pool built right on the edge of the cliff, and beyond that the deeper blue of the sea dotted with white sails.

The past couple of days they'd done nothing but make love, eat, talk, swim, before starting back at the beginning again. He'd wanted to take her for a tour of the island, but the safety concerns were significant and he didn't want her to feel hemmed in by his security staff, so he'd organised to take her out on his small yacht, which at least gave her the illusion of freedom and meant they could be by themselves, even if his staff followed along behind them in another launch at a discreet distance.

She'd loved that, sitting out on the deck in the sun with the wind in her hair. Then he'd got her to take the wheel while he stood behind her, his hands guiding hers as she steered the little yacht. She'd laughed with delight, leaning back against him as they guided the yacht through the waves. The wind had been up and they'd moved fast, which had thrilled her.

Afterwards, after they'd talked more, sharing pieces of their childhoods that weren't too fraught as they'd eaten the lunch Martina had given them, he'd anchored in a sheltered, private bay and they'd gone swimming off the boat. Then, still wet and salty from the water, he'd taken her down onto the deck and made love to her under the sails as the boat rocked gently.

*'I've never been happy before,'* she'd told him the night she'd handed him her laptop, *'but you've given me a taste of it...'*

He'd given her a taste of that happiness. He, who'd only ever delivered justice, had made someone happy. And she'd wanted more of it, so she'd have something good to take with her when she went to jail...

The thought of that was unbearably painful for reasons he couldn't describe even to himself. Because why should he care whether she was happy or not? And why did he want to be the one who gave her that happiness?

Why did he even think she deserved it? She'd hidden her father's money and had enabled him to make more, helping him build the crime empire he now commanded whether she'd been aware of it or not. She'd helped him evade the law and she'd known that was wrong.

Yes, she did deserve a prison cell.

But she'd also watched her mother bleed to death. A death she held herself responsible for. And she'd lived in fear for years afterwards, threatened and terrorised, deprived of companionship and love and happiness, everything that made life worth living.

She'd been forced into doing things that went against her loving, loyal and honest nature, things that might have broken another person. But Lucy hadn't broken. She'd made a promise to the mother who'd died to protect her and had survived any way she could. He couldn't fault her for that. But it had left scars on her. The weight of a guilt she couldn't escape, just as he couldn't.

Lucy sighed and stretched on the sun lounger. She'd been wearing a swimsuit, but after their last swim, when he'd stripped it off her and had her up against the wall of the pool, she hadn't bothered to put it on again, and so was lying there naked, her pale skin flushed in the sunlight.

His beautiful *civetta...*

*She doesn't deserve that cell and you know it.*

His chest felt tight, as if his heart was pressing hard against his ribcage, a strong, steady ache. He felt as if he was looking through a window that had once been crystal clear, but had fogged up, rendering the view indistinct and out of focus. He couldn't even work out what he was looking at now. A badly hurt innocent or a criminal who deserved prison?

She was both, and that was the issue. That was why he didn't know what to do.

*She is you, you realise that, don't you?*

Vincenzo abruptly shut the laptop he'd been working on, the constriction in his chest getting tighter. No, surely not. She wasn't him.

She didn't have a history of corruption of her own family and she hadn't actually led people to their deaths as he had.

*You think she should pay for her crimes while you escape having to pay for yours?*

He *was* paying for his crimes. What he'd told her that night was the truth. He was serving a life sentence, using his contacts and his knowledge to help the police. Dedicating his life to the pursuit of justice.

He'd put a lot of people behind bars, more than if he'd been rotting in a cell himself. And it wasn't as if the life he had now had anything to do with freedom. Yes, he had money and a life of ease, but he lived in a cage all the same. A gilded one. Hemmed in by security, since not a day went by when someone didn't make an attempt on his life. Isolated, since he could trust nothing and no

JACKIE ASHENDEN                                157

one. Curtailed in everything he did because, as far as he was concerned, everything had one point and one point only: justice.

He had paid and he was still paying. He'd be paying for the rest of his life.

*Fine, but do you really think she should? Hasn't she paid already?*

Putting the laptop down on the table beside him, he got off the lounger and paced over the green lawn towards the stone parapet that stood between him and the cliff face.

Her life had been a misery, spent in fear and loneliness, and so really she *had* paid. She'd been forced into committing offences and, regardless of what he'd told himself about choices, Lucy hadn't had one. Was she really guilty? And did she really deserve to be handed over to the authorities?

But then, what would he do with her if he didn't? She'd asked him to help her escape, find a new life for herself in the States...

*Or you could keep her.*

A fist closed around his heart, squeezing him tight, making it so he could hardly breathe.

He could keep her. She could live here in the villa. With him.

Slowly, Vincenzo turned around, his gaze settling on her where she lay on the sun lounger, a primitive sense of possession filling him. Perhaps he wouldn't give her up. Perhaps he would keep her. She would be there whenever he wanted her, warm and silky and sweet. Giving him her honesty and her passion. Her loyalty and her trust. He wouldn't have to be alone any more. He would have her.

And why not? He was paying for his crimes, but why couldn't he have something for himself? And it wouldn't be only for himself. It would be for her too, because she'd told him that he was important to her, and surely staying with him was more important to her than being imprisoned in a cell?

*Is that really what she needs, though? And isn't being trapped on this island with you really just another cell?*

A chill washed over him, burning away the burst of possessiveness. It was true, he could keep her here with him. And he could make her happy, he was sure. In fact, perhaps he even should, since with her help he'd be able to take down even more people than he would on his own.

But what kind of life would that be for her? She'd be in constant danger from those looking to use her to get to him, unable to go anywhere without security. It would be a curtailed, narrow sort of life.

It was the life she'd escaped when she'd run from her father. The life her mother had told her to get free of.

*You can't do that to her.*

Over on the sun lounger, Lucy sighed and turned her head, her hair trailing down her back. He could see her face, naked without her glasses, and for the first time he didn't see vulnerability and fear there. Her eyes were closed and her mouth was curved slightly in a satisfied way, and she looked at peace. She looked...happy.

He could give her more of that here, but not for ever. She was curious and intelligent and he could imagine her living a life without fear, where she was free to explore everything that interested her. Where she could put those impressive financial skills to better use in a way that would fulfil her, not cause her guilt and pain.

But that life wasn't with him. He'd chosen his path and it was a solitary one; he couldn't make her walk it with him. And if he couldn't trap her in a cage here with him, he couldn't trap her in any other cage either.

The knowledge filtered through him, not fast like a lightning strike but slowly, like the sun rising.

He couldn't give her to the authorities. He couldn't let her go to prison.

Yes, she'd broken the law but there were extenuating circumstances. She'd lost so much and there was so much good she could do out in the world. So much good she *would* do, because of the kind of person she was.

What things could she do if she was allowed to follow her own passions? What kinds of things could she create if she weren't hemmed in by fear?

What kind of person could she become?

Ah, but he knew already. She would be amazing.

He couldn't keep that from her. He wouldn't.

It went against everything he'd thought justice was, but maybe there were more forms of justice in this world than he'd previously thought. And besides, it would be a greater injustice to put her back in a cage than it would be to take her out of it.

Determination sat inside him, a new sense of purpose.

He'd never wanted anything more from this life than to bring down the people who hurt others and he would keep on with doing that. She'd brought him a little space of peace and he would remember that for ever.

But she wasn't his and she never would be. And the greatest gift he could give to the world would be to let her go.

Lucy sighed again and rolled over, glancing to where he'd been sitting. She frowned when she didn't see him, sitting up and looking around.

Then her gaze found his and her face lit up, and she smiled.

No, *that* was the sun rising. That was the lightning

strike. Her and her smile, and the way she looked at him. As if he was a sight that made her happy and gave her joy.

Then she held out her arms to him and he felt something inside him crumble and fall away, like a narrow cliff path collapsing under his feet. There was nothing to stop him, nothing to hold on to. One moment the path was firm and solid, the next he was in the air and he was falling.

It was dizzying, terrifying, a rush of intense happiness and hope, along with a despair that he hadn't felt since he'd betrayed Gabriella.

He didn't know how he was ever going to give his *civetta* up.

But he was going to have to.

# CHAPTER TEN

LUCY PAUSED BESIDE the bed and briefly debated whether to grab the book she'd been reading to bring down to the pool, or the financial magazine Vincenzo had given her. The book was some nice escapism, but the magazine had some interesting articles, and she wasn't sure what she was in the mood for. Both, perhaps?

She picked them up and turned to the door just as Vincenzo strode in.

A delicious shiver worked its way down her spine the way it always did whenever he was near, her heart beating faster, tension and flutters of heat collecting in the pit of her stomach. Along with a desperate, tight feeling she couldn't shake.

He was in a perfectly tailored midnight-blue suit today, with a black shirt that only emphasised his compelling, dark magnetism. With his inky hair and obsidian eyes, the harsh planes and angles of his face, he was the most beautiful man she'd ever seen in her life.

*Don't feel anything for him. You can't.*

No, of course she didn't. She was just…admiring him. And she liked being near him and touching him and having him look at her. She was happy whenever she was in his presence, so happy…

But it was nothing more than that. And it certainly wasn't love.

She smiled and took a step towards him, but he didn't smile back. And he didn't reach for her the way he normally did. The expression on his face was carved from stone, his black eyes cold. He looked the way he had when she'd first seen him in his office nearly a week ago. Unyielding. Ruthless...

A chill crept through her.

'Is there something wrong?' She tried a smile, hoping he would smile back, let her know that everything was fine. 'I was just going down to the pool and—'

'It's time to pack, Lucy.' His voice was cool. 'You'll be leaving in an hour.'

She was aware of a rushing sound in her ears, her vision tunnelling, darkness creeping in around the edges. 'What do you mean, leaving? You gave me your word that—' She stopped dead as he thrust out his hand.

He held something small, square and blue.

A passport. A United States passport.

The rushing in her ears grew louder, her vision wavering, her breath coming short and hard. She didn't understand. Why was he giving her a passport?

*You know why.*

She had an inkling. It was what she'd asked for when she'd initially come to him: an escape. To disappear to a new life in the States. With a new name and identity so no one would ever find her. Where she would be safe at last, just as her mother had wanted.

But that was before she'd realised he would never let her go the way she'd hoped. Before she'd accepted the weight of her own guilt and her need to make amends for the crimes she'd committed for her father. She'd accepted that her future was a cell and, if she wasn't exactly happy about it, she wouldn't balk at it either.

Except this was…not a cell. This was the escape she'd come to him to help her find.

'I don't understand.' Her voice sounded hoarse. She glanced at the passport in his hand and then at him. 'What does this mean?'

'What do you think it means?' There was only granite in the words, the hard edge of stone. 'I'm not handing you over to the authorities, Lucy. I've organised a passport for you with a new identity, visas, social security numbers, everything you'll need to start a new life in the States. Your father will never find you, I'll make sure of it.'

She began to shake, the tremors starting in her stomach and moving outwards, to her hands and knees. This surely couldn't be happening. He couldn't be giving her freedom. Not after everything he'd told her about justice and making amends. About guilt and the law and taking responsibility.

'But…' She tried to make sense of what was happening. 'I was going to be handed over to the authorities. That's what you were going to do and I—'

'I changed my mind.' His voice was like a blade, cutting her off. 'I'm not going to hand you over to the police.'

'Why not?' She searched his face to find some signs of his reasoning, but there was nothing. His features were stone. 'You were very clear that's what you were going to do. I don't understand why you're changing your mind.'

'You were forced into doing those things for your father, Lucy. You had no choice. And even if you had, you've paid many times over for those crimes.'

'But I haven't,' she said hoarsely.

'Haven't you?' His gaze cut like a knife. 'Weren't the years you spent as your father's prisoner a jail term?

Wasn't that house he kept you in a cell? He took your mother from you, *civetta*. And that is a life sentence.'

She felt as if the ground had shifted under her feet. As if she were walking in quicksand that would suck her down at any moment. She'd never thought he'd change his mind. Never thought he'd present her with the freedom she wanted, enabling her to keep the promise she'd made to her mother long ago. A freedom she didn't deserve...

*Is that really true, though?*

Something hot swept through her. He'd told her she wasn't responsible, that she couldn't blame herself, that she was worth saving, and then, over the course of the past couple of days, he'd shown her. He'd taken care of her, made her feel valued, made her feel precious, and more—he made her feel worth the sacrifice her mother had made for her.

*'You are worth saving, Lucy Armstrong...'* he'd told her, and he'd believed it. This beautiful, passionate, strong man who'd changed her, healed her...

She stared at him and the ground kept shifting, the landscape kept changing, that hot, bright emotion continuing to sweep through her, crushing everything in its path. It was raw and intense and it filled her with strength, made her feel ten feet tall and bulletproof.

And she knew what it was. She knew the truth deep in her heart, in her soul.

The feeling was love.

Was this what her mother had felt when she'd protected her? This sweep of power? Blinding and sure and so utterly certain. A burst of purity, filling her with a confidence she'd never dreamed she'd have.

She'd been so afraid of this feeling all this time. Afraid of its power. The kind of power that made someone stay with someone who hurt them. That made them give up their lives for someone else. But she understood now, she got it.

Love wasn't something to fear, it was something to embrace. Because love was strength and it was courage, and that was what her mother had drawn on to take that blow to protect her. Her love for her daughter.

Lucy's eyes filled with sudden tears. She couldn't let that sacrifice be in vain. Her mother hadn't just wanted a life for her, she'd wanted her to be happy. And that was the best monument, wasn't it? Happiness? Not just for her, but for him too, because they'd both been through terrible things and they deserved it.

They deserved to have a future. And it would be love that would give them that future.

She met Vincenzo's hard, midnight gaze. 'No,' she said.

He ignored her. 'Pack your things. You'll be leaving in an hour.'

'No,' she repeated.

Vincenzo's expression became even harder than it already was. 'No? What do you mean, no?'

Lucy looked him in the eye. 'I mean no. I'm not leaving. I want to stay.'

The expression on his face darkened. 'This was what you wanted, Lucy. A new life. That's what you promised your mother.'

'Well, that's not what I want now.' And she didn't hesitate. She gave him the truth, because that was always what she gave him. 'What I want is you.'

A muscle flicked in his jaw, tension gathering around him like a storm gathering electricity. *'Civetta...'*

'I want the moments I'd planned. I want another day. I want more than that. I want a future, Vincenzo. I want a future with you.'

The tension around him became even more electric, a subtle vibration in the air. 'No.' The word left no room for argument. 'You will go and you will go now.'

'Why not?' She took a step towards him, holding his black gaze. 'Don't you want a future too?'

*'No.'* Something broke in him, the stillness shattering. He threw the passport onto the bed suddenly, then he closed the distance between them in an explosive movement, reaching for her, his fingers closing around her upper arms and holding her in a grip that bordered on painful. It might have frightened her once, but there was nothing about him that frightened her now, and certainly not with the emotion blazing in his dark eyes, a black fire that nearly swallowed her whole.

'Yes,' he said roughly. 'Yes, I want that. I want a future. I want for ever with you, *civetta*. But if I take even one day I will *never* let you go. Do you understand now?'

Her heart was full, emotion flooding out of her, and she didn't hide it. She let him see what was in her soul.

'Then don't.' She leaned into his strong grip and his heat. Leaning into him. 'Don't let me go.'

For a second the fire in his eyes blazed so hot it nearly burned her to the ground, the grip he had on her searing her. But that was okay. She wanted to burn. She wanted to burn with him.

But then, as abruptly as he'd grabbed her, he let her go and stepped away, leaving her swaying, leaning into a warmth that was no longer there. The fire in his eyes had gone, the blaze doused. He was cold again, expressionless. Emotionless.

'You say that,' he said, casual. 'But you don't understand what your life would be like with me. People want to kill me every day. I'm a target and so you'll be a target too. You won't be able to go anywhere without a security detail or without planning your every movement. Your life will be curtailed. The only place you'll ever have any freedom is here in the villa, with me.'

'So?' She smiled, wanting him to understand. 'None of that matters, Vincenzo. Don't you see?'

His eyes were black stars, glittering cold and sharp. 'No, I don't see. And you may not think it matters, but it matters to me. I don't want you to be a prisoner with me on this island. I don't want you to have a life limited by safety concerns and security. You should be free to explore the things that interest you, that excite you. And, more than anything, you should be safe. And I can't give you that. I can never give you that.'

A crack ran slowly through her heart, sharp and jagged. Because it was obvious that he didn't understand. And why would he? He'd been betrayed by someone who loved him, the person who'd mattered most. No one had protected him the way her mother had protected her. She might have lost her mum, but she'd known that Kathy had loved her. Had he had anyone who'd cared about him?

He was so hard, so cold. So shut down. All the passion she knew lived in him locked away... No, he hadn't.

'Vincenzo—'

'I don't want to hear it. That is my decision, whether you like it or not.'

She studied him, sensing the battle in him. He'd been at war with himself the whole time she'd been here, torn between his principles and his passions. But he didn't have to choose, couldn't he see that? Didn't he know? He could have both. Love was big enough.

*He's afraid.*

The insight came almost forcibly and she saw it, because she knew fear, knew it intimately. It was there in his eyes, in the lies he was telling himself and her. And they were lies. He was afraid of what was between them and he didn't know what to do.

'If you really wanted me, you could have me,' she said quietly. 'It doesn't have to be a choice, Vincenzo. It's not one or the other. It's not black and white. And all this stuff about keeping me safe sounds good, but it's just a convenient excuse, isn't it?'

He said nothing, the tension around him almost humming.

The crack in her heart became deeper, wider, and her eyes prickled with tears. Because he was desperate, she could feel it. He was fighting so hard, her poor Vincenzo, and she didn't know what to say to reach him. To show him that he had nothing to fear.

She took a step closer, but he didn't move, towering over her, his gaze utterly forbidding. Intimidating. Yet she knew better now what that aura of menace actually was. It was his armour, his protection. His heart had been broken into pieces once before and now he was desperately shielding it.

'It's okay,' she said softly, trying to calm him the way he'd calmed her days ago. 'It's all right. You don't have to be afraid.'

His eyes glittered, cold as the depths of space. 'I'm not afraid. You deserve freedom, Lucy. And what I deserve is freedom from you. You're a distraction. You're getting in the way and taking up my time. I have more important things to do than sleep with you.'

It might have hurt her badly if she'd been the same Lucy that had come to Capri days before. But she wasn't the same Lucy. She was changed, and he'd changed her. He'd shown her where her true strength lay, and it wasn't running and hiding, it was in embracing what was in her heart. And she knew he was lying. That what he was doing was protecting himself. He was a city under siege and he would do anything he could to keep the invaders out.

And she could storm those walls with anger and pain, but she knew that wouldn't work. It would only make him call for reinforcements. No, if she wanted to crack his defences she was going to have to drop her own.

Lucy reached out and gently touched his cheek, the faintest brush of her fingers. 'I've fallen in love with you, did you know that?' The words were soft, yet the power of the feeling inside her vibrated in every syllable. 'You make me so happy.'

And just for a second the walls around his city looked as if they might shatter as shock flickered through his black eyes. The defenders putting down their swords, the battle inside him pausing.

But only for a moment.

'I don't care,' he said in a voice made of ice.

The crack through her heart became a chasm. He couldn't see, he couldn't understand. Because he didn't want to.

Vincenzo de Santi was a man with an iron will and he'd made a decision and nothing was going to sway him, still less the woman who loved him with everything she was.

He was happy in his cage. He didn't want to see that she was handing him a key.

Anger and pain would accomplish nothing. Only love could scale those walls. Only love would help him overcome his fear. But it was something he would have to come to in his own time. He would have to open the gates of his heart himself—she couldn't force him.

It hurt. It hurt so much. But her pain wasn't for herself, it was for him. This beautiful, powerful, passionate panther, stuck in a cage of his own making. Too afraid of the open door standing before him to take a step through it.

All she could do was give him what she always gave him: the truth. And hope that somehow it would stay with him. It would be her last gift to him.

'If that's what you choose to believe, then fine,' she said quietly. 'But know this. All the justice in the world won't change the feeling inside you. It won't do anything for the guilt or the grief. But you can allow yourself to have something good. You can let yourself be happy. You deserve it, Vincenzo. And so do I.'

He said nothing, cold radiating from him so fiercely he might as well have been made of ice, but she went on anyway.

'I think you do care. I think you love me as much as I love you. But you're afraid and I think I understand why. You were betrayed by the one person who shouldn't have betrayed you and now you're protecting yourself.' She wanted to touch him again, but she couldn't bring herself to do it, not when she knew it wouldn't help. 'But I need you to know right now that you can trust me. I won't betray you. I love you and you don't have to be worthy of that love. You don't have to be pure. You don't have to be just. You don't have to prove yourself, not to me. The only thing you have to be is you.'

The silence that fell was deafening.

Vincenzo's gaze had turned flat and black and depthless. 'Are you done?'

'Yes,' she said and her voice didn't shake, even though her heart had cracked into pieces in her chest.

This time he said nothing.

He simply turned on his heel and left.

* * *

He didn't want to see her pack up her meagre belongings. Didn't want to see her tears or hear her husky, sweet voice telling him things he didn't want to hear. Telling him that he was afraid. That she loved him.

So he left her standing there, going down to his office and slamming the door.

Rage burned in his heart. At himself for what he couldn't let himself have and at her for all those things she'd said. Because he wasn't afraid. And he really didn't care. And as for worthiness...

Vincenzo strode to his desk and sat down, preparing to focus on some work, trying to shove all those thoughts from his head.

But it was impossible.

*'You don't have to be worthy,'* she'd said, as if he'd been trying to make himself worthy all this time. Which wasn't true. He *knew* he wasn't worthy. What he was doing was trying to atone. For himself and for his family. Pursuing justice was the only way he could make up for what he'd done, for the weight of guilt that crushed him.

*'All the justice in the world won't change the feeling inside you...'*

Ah, but she was wrong about that too. He'd wait until she'd vanished to the States and was safely ensconced in the new life he'd made for her, letting her father believe she was still with him on Capri. And only once she was settled would he make his move.

And that *would* make him feel better. Delivering justice to the man who'd hurt her.

*You, you mean?*

Vincenzo gritted his teeth. Yes, sending her away had hurt her, but he'd had to do it. And it wasn't because of fear. He'd told her the truth; he couldn't allow her to distract him from his true purpose, because what else would he be without it?

A liar. A murderer. A traitor. A tool to be used, not a son to be loved.

*'You were betrayed by the one person who was supposed to love you...'*

His *civetta*. She knew exactly what to say to appeal to his traitorous emotions. And they were traitorous. He couldn't trust them.

*But she loves you. She won't betray you.*

A spear of ice caught him in the chest, the pain so sharp he could hardly breathe, along with a raw, desperate feeling that made him want to run from his office and find her. Hold on to her. Cup her white face between his palms and kiss away the tears on her cheeks and the pain in her eyes. Give her those moments she wanted, give her the happiness she deserved.

But he'd told her he didn't care that she loved him, and he'd told himself. And he believed it. He *had* to believe it.

So he stayed where he was, his hands clenched in fists on his desk.

In the gardens outside, he could hear the sound of the helicopter's rotors. His security staff would be leading her to the helicopter that would take her to Naples. From there, she'd take the jet to New York. Everything had been organised for her. He wasn't going to leave her in the middle of a foreign city with nothing.

There was a heavy, aching sensation in the centre of his chest. It hurt. He'd never been shot in all the years he'd spent destroying organised crime, but perhaps it felt something a little like this, a bright, pure agony reaching every part of him.

He ignored it. Because she was wrong. Justice *would*

cure this pain. He just had to be more focused, concentrate solely on his mission. He had to work harder.

There could not be any more distractions.

He could hear the rotors spinning faster now, faster and faster, and his whole body tightened with the urge to go to the windows and watch the helicopter take off, watch her fly away from him. But he didn't move. Because he didn't care. He wanted her, yes. Needed her, maybe. Love her? No.

She'd told him she loved him as if love was a truth, but she was wrong.

Love was the greatest lie of all.

Love had controlled and manipulated him. Love had blinded him. Duped him. Love had betrayed him.

He would never allow love to have that kind of dominion over him again.

The noise of the helicopter became deafening now as he heard it lift off from the garden, heading into the sky.

Vincenzo closed his eyes as the sound became more and more distant, listening until, at last, it faded away. And there was nothing but silence in his house.

Silence in his heart.

She was gone.

# CHAPTER ELEVEN

HE ENDED UP waiting a month. Just until the people he had keeping an eye on Lucy told him she was settled. Her father, naturally, thought she was still with him and had contacted him a number of times, offering all kinds of things for her return.

Vincenzo had ignored all of them.

Once he had confirmation she was safe, he contacted Scotland Yard and gave them everything they needed to bring in Armstrong. And put him away for life.

The news of Armstrong's arrest came swiftly after that, and afterwards Vincenzo sat on the terrace, staring out over the sea, a glass of wine in his hand and the peace of the evening closing in.

It should have been satisfying, but it wasn't.

All he could think about was how empty his villa was. How quiet.

How he wanted to look across this table and meet a direct hazel gaze, large and dark behind the lenses of her glasses. How he wanted a pair of warm arms to welcome him, and a curvy, silky little body to press itself against him.

How he wanted her smile. Her honesty. Her understanding. Her bluntness and her direct manner.

He wanted her and she wasn't here.

*'All the justice in the world won't change the feeling inside you...'*

His fingers tightened on his wine glass, the memory of her voice playing in his head.

Over the past month he'd thrown himself into his work, spending hours holed up in his office, sifting through information, looking for his next target.

It should have made him feel better. It should have cleaned the memory of her right out of his head. But it didn't matter how hard he worked, the ache inside him wouldn't go away.

If only that ache was guilt, because that was easier to deal with. But it wasn't. It was her and her absence, the silence around him not one of peace, but of loss.

*You made her happy and you sent her away.*

Pain deepened in his chest. Happiness. What was that anyway? He didn't need it himself. He didn't want it. He had a vocation, a calling, and that fulfilled him. It brought him all the satisfaction he required.

*'You can let yourself be happy...'*

No, he couldn't. Happiness and peace weren't for men like him and she was a fool if she thought they were.

He raised his glass and took a sip, wanting to savour it, but it tasted of nothing. Even the food he ate these days had lost its flavour, just as the world had lost its colour. The sun its warmth…

She'd taken even those small pleasures left to him.

Anger began to burn in his gut, unexpected and fierce, an anger that he'd thought he'd put behind him. And the more he tried to force it away, the more it grew.

She'd done this to him. She'd taken all the little things that had made his life bearable. She'd shown him what peace felt like, what it was to be free of guilt, what it meant to be able to smile at something amusing. She'd shown him how to take a moment and enjoy every second of it.

*You made her happy, but she also showed you happiness and now you can never forget it.*

The anger burned hotter, flaming high and wild, incinerating everything in its path.

She'd been right, hadn't she? She'd been right all along. Justice would never be enough for him, not now she'd shown him what else he could have, and because he could never have it she'd doomed him.

Vincenzo shoved his chair back so hard it fell over. He rose to his feet, the rage inside him a column of fire, burning him alive. The wine glass was still in his hand, and before he'd even realised what he was doing he'd flung it to the stone floor, crystal exploding in glittering shards.

It was her fault. She'd made him feel like this. And now he'd be Tantalus for ever, desperately thirsty and unable to drink. Starving and unable to eat.

*Or you could just accept that what she said was true, that you can let yourself be happy.*

Rage coursed through him. How could he accept that? How could he be happy? When he'd hurt people? When he was as guilty as his mother? She was in jail at least, but he wasn't.

*You thought Lucy had served her sentence and deserved freedom. Haven't you served yours?*

He was shaking, staring unseeing at the remains of the wine glass, glittering in the last rays of twilight. Years he'd spent pursuing his crusade. Years. And still he felt the crushing burden of guilt. That hadn't eased one bit, no matter how many people he had put away. She hadn't lied about that, had she?

No, there had only been one thing that eased him and

that was her. Being deep inside her, looking into her eyes. Feeling her arms around him, holding him. Making him feel as if he was more than his mother's broken tool. More than a ruthless, merciless crusader, fighting to fill the gaping void inside him.

The void his mother had left when she walked away from him without a backward glance. The void left by betrayal. Left by love.

He sucked in a breath and then another as the knowledge filtered slowly through him, another truth that Lucy had given him that he'd thought was a lie.

*'You're afraid...'*

Was he? He hadn't thought he was, but... What if that was true? What if he just hadn't wanted to believe it? And if that *was* true, then just what the hell was he afraid of?

*You know...*

Vincenzo closed his eyes. If he didn't have justice, if he didn't have guilt, if he didn't have atonement, then what did he have? Who was he?

Just his mother's tool, her weapon. The puppet she pulled the strings with. An empty void. Unworthy of even her tainted, conditional love.

Fear curled through him, so sharp and bright he shuddered. He didn't want to face it. He wanted to turn and go to his office, lose himself in doing something, anything so this fear didn't choke him. The fear that he was nothing and no one. That he was unworthy, undeserving.

*She loves you. She believes you deserve happiness.*

What if...she was right? What if his *civetta* had told him the truth? Ah, but then, of course it was the truth. She'd always given him that. So maybe the question wasn't what if she was right? Maybe the question was more what if he believed her?

Something shifted inside him, the urge to run back to

his office and bury himself in his crusade. But he knew, with a sudden flash of insight, that if he did that, he'd be doing exactly what he'd been doing for years. Escaping.

Escaping pain. Escaping betrayal. Protecting himself...

Ah, *Dio*, that was what he'd been doing all this time, wasn't it? Running from his fear, running like a coward for decades. Using his justice as his shield and righteousness as his sword.

But he wasn't just or righteous. He was a man cowering in fear. Afraid of his own emotions. Afraid of pain and betrayal. Afraid of the most powerful emotion of all: love.

*'I think you love me as much as I love you.'*

Vincenzo took a ragged breath, his heart raw, chewed up and spat out, scarred and full of holes, beating hard in his chest as the greatest truth of all settled down inside him. His skin was sensitised, as if the slightest breath of air would cut him to shreds.

Yes, he loved her. He'd loved her for days, for weeks. The entirety of his life had been spent waiting for her and the rest of it would be spent aching for her. She was his fate and his destiny. She was his truth.

And he'd been afraid of her. Afraid of her honesty. Afraid of her strength. Afraid of her courage, because she had more courage and strength in her little finger than he had in his entire body.

And when he'd sent her away he'd been afraid of her love. Afraid of the power of it, of the acceptance and understanding in it. The absolution he could sense it would give him and the happiness and peace it promised him.

He didn't deserve any of those things, but she thought he did. She thought he deserved happiness. She thought he deserved peace. And really, in the end it was a simple choice. He either trusted in her belief, or he didn't.

Ah, but was that even a decision to make? He knew the answer. It lay in his heart, in his soul.

Of course he trusted her. He loved her.

This time, Vincenzo didn't run. He faced his fear. And he accepted her love. Felt it flow through him like a purpose, like a vocation, a calling. Yet so much stronger, so much deeper. So much more complex.

And it wasn't a flame, burning through dry paper, only to crumble to ash when there was nothing to feed it. It was a glow, steady and bright and unending, self-sustaining. True strength in its purest form.

It would never flicker and it would never die. It would be with him always.

Peace came over him, easing the anger, dissipating the last remains of the blaze, cool and soft like Lucy's touch on his skin, a balm to his wounded soul. Bringing with it an absolute certainty.

He would find her. He would lay his heart at her feet. He would give her everything she ever wanted and if what she wanted was to never see him again, he would leave and count it a privilege to have even known her.

It would hurt and he might not survive it, but then, he wouldn't survive without her anyway.

She was more important than justice and she was certainly more important than fear. She was the most important thing in his life and he couldn't let another day pass with her thinking that she wasn't.

Vincenzo reached into his pocket and grabbed his phone, punching in a number, his hands now steady, the path before him clear and true.

'Get the helicopter now. I'm going to New York.'

Lucy had eventually found herself a little house by the sea in Cape Cod. It wasn't Capri, of course, or the Mediterranean, but the wild Atlantic wasn't far from her door, and there was a beach. And she could walk along that beach, have sand under her toes.

It was a lovely place and she had a job with a small finance firm that enabled her to work from home. It wasn't the most challenging of positions, but she was able to earn a living, which was all she required. She was starting to think longer term, now she had a future ahead of her, and had been toying with the idea of a financial crime consultancy business, but that was still to be decided.

She might even have been happy if it wasn't for the fact that she was missing one thing.

Vincenzo.

She had everything she'd promised her mother she would have. A life away from her father, a life of safety, of freedom.

But she didn't have him. And because she didn't have him, she could never be truly happy. Her heart remained broken and always would.

It was late in the day, the sun going down, and Lucy walked along the beach as she did most late afternoons, her feet sinking into the sand.

She shouldn't give in to these long, solitary walks, because they gave her too much time to think. Too much time to remember how she'd let him turn his back and walk away a month earlier. How she'd collected her things and followed his security staff out to the helicopter, not even watching as it lifted off and flew away because she'd been blinded by tears.

She couldn't force him to see what he didn't want to, and, though love had given her strength, it didn't shield her from the pain of her heart breaking.

Pain for him and what he couldn't allow himself to have.

\* \* \*

She remembered the flight to the States and the tears she'd cried for him, weeping herself into sleep at last. Then arriving in New York with an aching throat and gritty eyes.

A kind woman had met her after she'd got off the jet, giving her all the information she needed and showing her to some accommodation in the Village where she could spend a couple of days acclimatising.

She didn't remember that either.

All she remembered was the hollow feeling inside her. Which made sense in a lot of ways, since she'd left her heart in Capri, in Vincenzo de Santi's strong and capable hands.

*You just let him have it. You gave it to him and then you walked away.*

Lucy bent and picked up a shell, brushing the sand off it.

Of course she had. He'd wanted her to leave and even telling him that she loved him hadn't changed his mind. And not because he didn't want her, but for all those lies he was telling himself. About keeping her safe. About being distracted. About justice.

It was fear and she knew all about fear, how it could get inside you, trap you. And she'd confronted him with his own. But he'd refused to see it. And if he refused to see it, what more could she do? There was nothing.

She stared at the shell, her chest aching. Her throat tight with grief for the lonely path he'd chosen and the life he'd trapped himself in. He was a prisoner just as much as she'd once been, but his cell was one of his own choosing.

It made her ache.

She lifted her wet face to the sky, letting the tears

dry on her cheeks in the wind. And then her gaze narrowed as she saw the tall figure of a man coming down the beach towards her.

It looked like… But no. It couldn't be him. It couldn't be Vincenzo.

She should walk on. The sun would be going down soon and she needed to get home. Yet she didn't move, watching the man walk towards her instead.

Her heart began to speed up, beating wildly in her chest, because it knew who he was, even as her mind balked. And her body tightened, because it knew too. The easy, powerful way he walked. The darkness of his hair. The hard, carved angles of his face…

Lucy stilled. Afraid to move in case he disappeared. Because surely he couldn't be real. Surely he couldn't be here on a beach in Cape Cod. With her.

But he came closer and closer and soon it was apparent that it was him, and he *was* here, and her heart raged behind her breastbone and she couldn't breathe.

All she could do was stand there as he came to her and, without saying a single word, swept her into his arms.

She stiffened, pushing hard against his solid chest. This couldn't be real. She was dreaming. She'd offered him her heart and he'd refused it.

'Vincenzo? What are you doing here?' And then anger in a cleansing fire hit her and she struggled. 'Let me go.'

He shuddered, as if in pain, and then abruptly his arms opened and she was free. His face was taut with some vast, passionate emotion burning just beneath the surface of his skin, his black eyes blazing with it.

'I need to say something, Lucy,' he said, his voice raw and rough. 'Will you let me?'

She was trembling now, half of her desperate to throw

herself back into his arms while the other half was desperate to send him away.

'Say what?' she demanded, shaken and unable to hide it. 'Didn't you say everything you needed to back on Capri?'

'No.' The word was hoarse. 'I didn't. What I said to you then were lies.'

Shock washed through her, the trembling getting worse. 'What lies?'

Vincenzo's gaze was full of something hot and vital, burning steady as the fire at the centre of the earth. 'That you were a distraction. That I didn't care. That I wanted you to leave... You were right, *civetta*. Right about so many things. And it took me a while to see them, to accept what you were trying to tell me, but I know now.' His hands were in fists at his sides, his whole body radiating a familiar tension. 'You told me I was afraid, and you were right. I was. And if you want to know why, it's because of this.' He paused, his great, powerful chest heaving as he sucked in a breath. 'My mother betrayed me. She manipulated me. She took my trust in her, my love for her, and she broke it. She broke me. I was the tool she used to make herself powerful. Not her heir and not her son. Nothing. No one.'

Her heart quivered at the desolation in those words, her eyes filling with tears. 'Oh, Vincenzo. That's not true.'

'I was afraid it was, though, so afraid. I filled my life up with justice, with a crusade, and used it as an escape, a way to hide. So I didn't have to face the truth that she didn't love me. She never loved me. And perhaps there was nothing in me to love.'

A tear rolled down her cheek, the cracks in her heart aching. 'That's not true,' she said hoarsely. 'There so much in you to love.'

'I didn't believe you back on Capri. I used so many excuses to run from what you were trying to show me. But... I'm tired of running. I'm tired of not believing, of not trusting. I'm tired of filling my life up with something that changes nothing. I want something else, I want something better.' He paused, his eyes dark and full of heat. 'I want you, Lucy Armstrong. You were brave. You facing your fears helped me face mine. And if there's one person in this world I know I can trust, it's you.'

Her throat closed up at the certainty in his face and voice; she couldn't speak.

'You and your honesty and your strength, my *civetta*. You helped me find peace, you gave me a taste of happiness, and I... I want that more than I have wanted anything in my entire life.' The desperate, burning look in his eyes had dissipated, and there was something else there: a steady, bright glow. Calm and sure and certain. 'I'm afraid of being nothing more than what my mother made me, of being no one, and I thought justice would somehow make that feeling go away. But it didn't. It was you who made it go away, Lucy. It was you all this time.' The glow in his eyes became brighter, hotter. 'I love you, my *civetta*. I love you so much. And I know it took me a long time to understand and you will never know how sorry I am that I hurt you, but I can't bear another day of you not being in my life.' Slowly, he raised his arms and held them out, his soul laid bare in his eyes. 'Will you come to me, Lucy? I would very much like you to be mine. And I very much want to be yours.'

There was no thought, only certainty. Only the truth of the feeling that had burned in her heart so long it was part of her.

Lucy closed the distance without hesitation, giving him her answer.

And when his mouth found hers, she knew she'd found everything she'd ever wanted, right there in his arms.

The perfect moment to find her for ever.

The for ever they both deserved and the happiness they'd finally found.

Together.

# EPILOGUE

THEY HAD SO many plans. Lucy had informed him of her idea to use her financial skills to help institutions combat fraud and other financial crimes, and so he'd helped her set up a consultancy. As for himself, he'd decided to step away from his crusade. He was going to devote more of himself to his family's auction house and the other various businesses he had. It should keep him busy until they started a family, which they would. After all, someone had to be around to look after the children, and he fully intended to be that someone.

And if he passed on a few titbits that he'd heard through the grapevine to various law enforcement agencies on occasion, then it was only what a fine, upstanding citizen would do.

But the most important plan of all was the wedding Vincenzo had insisted on the moment they returned to Capri.

And that was where he married her, at their villa, the place where they'd both discovered what happiness was. And they discovered it anew as they said their vows to each other in front of the priest.

Lucy wore the most beautiful wedding gown of ivory silk that hugged her curvaceous form, a veil tumbling over her glossy dark curls. They'd been left loose down her spine, but some combs held it back from her lovely face.

No, she was more than lovely. She was beautiful.

She'd given up her glasses today for contact lenses, and not for vanity but because her glasses fogged whenever she cried and she was apparently going to cry a lot—or so she told him.

But she wasn't crying now as he held her small hand and pushed his ring onto her finger. Only looking at him with so much love he could hardly meet her gaze.

Yet meet it he did as he made her his and he became hers.

And he wasn't unworthy or undeserving. He wasn't nothing and he wasn't no one.

He was her husband and he had a new purpose: to love her for the rest of his life.

So he did.

\* \* \* \* \*

# BOUND AS HIS BUSINESS-DEAL BRIDE

## KALI ANTHONY

To Philip.
My own romance hero and happily-ever-after.

# PROLOGUE

*Then*

'ARE YOU HURT?'

Eve shivered as Gage pulled his coat close around her, covering the wet clothes clinging to her body. A cold trickle of rainwater drizzled down her spine from the hair plastered to her head. She reached her hand to her temple, probing the area where a dull throb ached. 'Only a bump, but I'm okay.'

'Where?' Gage's voice sounded urgent. A torch flicked on. She winced as the brightness of it cut through the dark.

'Here.' She touched her head again and his gentle fingers brushed her own out of the way, tracing over her skin where it hurt the most. She shivered again, but not from the cold. This one was something warmer and suffused with pleasure.

'I'm sorry,' he said. His soft lips touched the middle of her forehead. He bent down and placed the torch on the floor, the small halo of light like a cocoon around them. 'Anywhere else?'

She shook her head. 'What about you?' He'd been driving when they'd slid off the road in the deluge. They'd been in a rush, trying to get away quickly because she was sure her sister, Veronique, had seen her sneak out of the house to meet Gage and run.

'I'm fine,' he said. 'Don't worry about me.'

She searched his face, shadowed as it was by the grim darkness that surrounded them in the abandoned building they'd found after grabbing their packs and fleeing the wrecked car. He looked okay, but he'd never tell if he wasn't. Gage always tried to protect her from every hurt. She wished he'd let her protect him sometimes.

'Did we have to leave the car?'

'It wasn't going anywhere, and we can't drive with that damage. It'll draw attention. At least it's off the road and not a hazard.'

Gage wrapped his arms round her and drew her close. She nestled into his damp chest as rain pattered on the roof above them. In places where the roof wasn't secure water leaked through, pooling on the floor.

'It'll be okay, *cher*. We've got some money.' He squeezed a pocket on the coat she wore. A few thousand dollars wasn't much, but it would get them where they needed to go, she supposed. Gage promised it would, and he always kept his promises. 'We'll hole up here tonight and catch a bus to Montgomery first thing. It's only a few hours away. Then we can get married and no one can stop us. Not your family, not Mom and Dad...'

His voice trailed off as sadness tainted it. Gage loved his parents, but the Caron and the Chevalier families had loathed each other for as long as she and Gage had been alive. His mom and dad had made it clear to him they didn't approve of their relationship, even though he'd tried to convince them that while she was only twenty and he twenty-three, they loved each other and that's all that mattered. It hadn't changed their minds.

As for her family...a knot tightened in her stomach, a

sickening ache that had been present for so long she barely noticed it some days. She couldn't think about what would have happened if they'd known. Eve wrapped her arms tightly round Gage's strong torso.

'You're sure about this?' she asked. They might love each other, but he was still losing something by being with her—the support of his family, who were important to him.

Gage pulled back and looked down at her. The pale yellow torchlight bled the colour from his eyes, making them appear greener than the unearthly blue that filled her waking thoughts and dreams for the future. 'I love you. And we don't need anyone's consent to marry in Alabama, not like home.'

If only she'd been twenty-one, they wouldn't have had to run. But they couldn't wait. She was afraid of the parades of eligible suitors her father had forced on her, and what they might mean. Now, with her enrolment in a French finishing school finalised, there was no escaping the truth. It was a choice between running or not seeing each other for a year, maybe longer. No contact at all. The thought was unbearable. She couldn't. It had made the decision easier for her, at least. For Gage, she knew it had cost something more, even though he didn't say so.

Gage ran his hand through his wet hair, his normal blond darkened by the rain. She couldn't miss the tightness round his eyes, that look of worry present most of the time in recent months. 'You're not having second thoughts, are you?'

'Never.'

He smiled, and it was the most beautiful thing she'd ever seen. The chill dissolved as she was warmed from the inside out. The mere memory of his smile made every day better. Even the ones where even the music turned up too loud at home couldn't drown out her mom and dad's shouting. The days when her mom took to her room, with only her pills and gin-spiked iced tea for company.

Gage cupped her jaw. Dropped his lips to hers. His mouth was so tender and gentle she melted into him, her hands gripping his wet Henley. She needed more than this, kisses in a grimy, falling-down building.

Once they were married they could find a hotel, make love in a proper bed like they had a few weeks before, when they'd sneaked into the guesthouse on his parents' property. It could have been the Waldorf the way he'd treated her like a princess on the crisp, white sheets. A flush of desire flooded through her at the memory of his bare skin slipping over hers. How he'd filled her, body and soul. She'd cried in his arms because he'd made her feel so perfect, at a time where everything had seemed broken.

His tongue touched hers and she threaded her fingers through his hair as they deepened the kiss. She needed him close to her again, craved it in a way she could never explain. He was her everything, the only man she ever wanted. Soon no one could stop them. The thrill of that thought surged through her, the realisation that in a matter of days she'd become Mrs Gage Caron.

He stopped, wrenched away from her and bent down, the loss immediate and shocking. Everything plunged into midnight as the torch was shut off. 'Wha—?'

Gage pressed his finger against her lips. Behind him the ghost of a light flickered, a brief flash in another part of the building. The scrape of something. Shoes on floor? She froze, her heart pounding in her chest like drumsticks, drowning out the sound of anything else. Gage's breath caressed her ear. 'Someone's here.'

His warmth had left her. She didn't know where he was, but he wouldn't leave her alone. Not ever. She flinched at a rustling sound nearby. As her eyes adjusted to the darkness, she saw him hunched close, stuffing things into his pack.

'Hide,' he whispered, his voice like a mere breath over the sound of rain falling on the roof above them.

'It might not be my father.'

'Can't take that chance.'

'What about you?'

She could barely make out the shake of his head. 'You take the money, head to Montgomery and I'll meet you. Call me when you get there. Now up.'

She looked into the black, ominous rafters above her and hesitated.

'You scared?' Gage asked.

*Terrified.* But his words lit a fire in her belly. After they'd first met as children, spying each other through an ivy-covered hole in the wall that separated the Chevalier and Caron family estates, he'd ask that whenever she hesitated. She'd never backed down from his challenges, always pretending they hadn't bothered her a bit, even when they had.

'It's just like climbing the old magnolia. Remember?' Gage's face was hidden by the darkness but brittleness cracked in his voice, telling Eve just how scared he was too. Her mouth dried. She nodded, peering into the rafters again.

'I remember.'

She'd never forget sitting in those branches, looking down at the world as if one day they could bend it to their every whim. Her mom would have had a conniption to know her precious baby girl was up a tree, especially with a *filthy Caron.* But with Gage anything had seemed possible, no matter how bad things had been. Up there, in their world of fantasy, trying to shut out real life and touch the sky, had been the place her childhood crush had turned into full-blown love.

Gage bundled some more belongings into his pack. He stuffed hers through a punched-out hole in the wall into the cavity space, out of sight.

'Now's the time to climb like a tiger's on your tail, *cher*,' he whispered. The sounds of the searchers drifted closer. Men's hushed voices. Sniggers.

*'Come out, come out, wherever you are.'*

Like some sick game. They were hunting and she was the catch of the day. She almost lost her meagre dinner there on the floor, but swallowed down the saliva flooding her mouth. Gage closed the space between them, kissing her again. Not gently this time. His lips were hard and fast against her own, bringing her back to herself. She didn't want to let him go. Not now, not ever.

'I'll get them away from here. Then you run.'

He released her and bent from the waist, clasping his fingers in front of him. She put a foot into his cupped hands, just like when they'd been kids and he'd always helped her into the tree. Gage hoisted her up and she grabbed a rough beam with her bare fingers. Splinters bit into her soft flesh. She clung to the wood, huddled in the darkness as she perched in the old rafters, trying to make herself as small as possible.

She was good at making herself small.

Dim light from the street bled through the dirty, broken windows. Gage gave her a long, last look. Flickers of torchlight came closer. He kissed his fingers and reached them out in her direction.

'Soon.'

He hoisted his pack and crept away quietly till he was almost out of sight. Then he scuffed his trainers on the floor, deliberately making a noise. He was the decoy, like a mother duck leading hunters away from her ducklings. Eve took a deep breath, trying to steady her anxious heartbeat. She had money in her pocket. When Gage and her father's men were gone, she'd swing down somehow and make her way to Montgomery. They'd find each other. Marry like they'd planned. It would be fine.

Shouts.

*'There! He's there!'*

The pounding of booted feet. A commotion, scuffling. A cacophony of sound she couldn't make out.

*'Got him!'*

'Let me go!'

Gage's voice, like she'd never heard it. He'd always made her feel safe. Now he sounded as terrified as she felt. She gripped the beam under her so tight it cut into her fingers and she closed her eyes, trying to make out the voices over the rain falling on the roof. She hoped he was just acting, playing it up for the men who'd caught him.

'Where is she?'

Eve froze, stopped breathing, because that voice she knew. *Her father.* There were a few beats of silence then a thud, a grunt. A swift, sharp crack like a snapping twig. Then Gage's voice, thick and broken.

'She's gone.'

Had they hurt him? Eve's breathing burst in quick pants. Her head spun as she tried to stay calm. If she fainted and dropped from her hiding place, everything would be lost.

'She left you?'

'You'll never, ever find her. I've made sure of it.'

She couldn't hear her father's response, only the murmurs of men that became louder and louder. More torchlight, now below her, flicked into the dark corners of the space. She jumped as one man kicked over some dirty crates in his search. He sneezed loudly and she flinched.

The disturbed dust tickled her own nose and she held her breath. They couldn't look up. Not up. *Please.*

The rain fell heavier now, beating staccato on the roof. Another deluge on the way. She strained to hear over the sound of it, which meant the men below would have to as well.

'Nothing, boss!' one of her father's cronies shouted, before doing a last sweep of the room with his torch. Then they left, drifting out of the space and away.

Eve dropped her head to the strut in front of her. Burning tears threatened behind her eyelids, stinging the back of her nose as she held them in. She wouldn't cry, not now. Gage needed her to stay strong. There would be time to fall apart when they were together again.

'Boy, your grand-daddy was a liar and your daddy's a thief.' Her father again, cold and cruel. The tone all too familiar. 'Now you try to steal my *daughter*? If it's the last thing I do, I'll ruin you and your family. I will destroy everything you love.'

That voice sent icy dread freezing through her veins. She bit her lip to hold back a gasp. The metallic, salty tang of blood flooded her mouth. Hugo Chevalier would do exactly as he'd threatened. What had she done? She shouldn't have run. She should never have risked Gage or his family.

Someone spat, the sound full of disdain. She huddled closer to the beam but couldn't see anything. Her hands stung where the splinters had now worked beneath her skin.

A low laugh. Gage's. She trembled, wanting to scream out a warning. He didn't understand. Her father wasn't a man to taunt.

'You can't destroy everything I love, Chevalier, because you'll never have Eve. She's safe from you.'

A crunch like a fist on flesh turned her stomach to

stone. She couldn't move, even though she was desperate to know Gage was okay. Shouts, noise. Cries of pain as he took a beating because of her. She should jump down, save him like he'd always tried to save her. He claimed she was one of the bravest people he knew, yet tonight she'd made him a liar, hiding like the coward she was.

She buried her face in the arm of Gage's coat, the earthy scent of the man she loved permeating the fabric. Reminding her of everything they were set to lose if things went wrong. There was no going back, not now. Eve sobbed into the damp fabric, the sound drowned out by the rain pounding on the roof above her.

# CHAPTER ONE

*Now*

EVE SAT AT the expansive table in the plush boardroom with its million-dollar view over Seattle. Everything here screamed of a company on the top of its game with sparkling glass, gleaming wood, bright chrome. A company winning at everything, taking no prisoners. The last place on earth she wanted to be, yet a place she couldn't avoid.

She checked her watch. Ten past the hour. He was making them wait. She tapped her finger on the papers in front of her, stomach churning in a tumult of emotion she didn't think she'd ever untangle, no matter how many years she lived.

'I'm not sure this is a wise idea, Ms Chevalier.' She shot a stern glance at her lawyer, the man who'd served her family company for years. He was part of the problem and not the solution for what had gone catastrophically wrong. Yet she'd been forced to bring him, the board having trouble accepting her at the helm in lieu of her father. Trust was in short supply where she was concerned. She doubted she'd get any here either.

'It's our only option.' That was a truth that even the most pious believer in miracles could accept. The family company, Knight Enterprises, sat on the brink. Teetering, ready to plummet over the precipice into oblivion. If it died a swift and public death she'd survive. She'd been through worse than anyone could imagine—this was nothing.

Eve ignored the bright stab of pain that at any other time might threaten to crack her heart in two, the fleeting memory of a tiny white coffin in an empty church on a bright sunny day. There were far worse things than a company failing, but her mother and little sister had no chance if Knight folded. Protected to obsession, *controlled*, they'd fail right along with it. She wouldn't let that happen.

She'd done some things; terrible, hurtful things in her life. Destroying her mother and baby sister would never be one of them. *Never.*

'Your father would say otherwise. Your father—'

Another sharp glance sideways from her and the lawyer stopped talking. She'd become good at silencing people with a glance. Like father, like daughter. The burn of gall rose in her throat. Would Daddy be proud of her right now? She hated that he might be.

'My father is unconscious in hospital. He has no say here.' He'd been cut down in a way his enemies had never been able to accomplish. A mosquito bite, an overwhelming infection. It was hard to contemplate that something as mundane as an insect had felled the man now lying in an ICU bed in Jackson. She searched deep down for a shred of emotion, but all her energy was taken up with hiding the truth of her father's illness for now, while keeping Knight afloat.

Her father had forced them into this mess when he'd reset a ticking time bomb seven years earlier. She either defused it in this room or the whole thing blew up in their faces. Eve was an expert at defusing things. She'd done it her whole life. She'd do it again.

'Caron has been chewing at your father's heels for years.

You do this and it will be the end for Knight. Do you want that on your conscience?'

Caron Investments did more than chase after them. It was a behemoth, mouth agape, waiting to swallow them whole. A hatred between two families and business rivals had led her to this boardroom. She was currently reaping the toxic reward of all that loathing, but in her case that punishment was deserved. She'd fuelled the enmity, throwing petrol on a bonfire. In many ways, she was the reason they were sitting here.

Ultimately, one of the companies was destined to consume the other—she'd just never thought it would be Caron devouring Chevalier in its bloodied maw.

But today, it seemed, Caron would win the battle.

'If someone had told me what was going on, we may not have ended up here,' she hissed. She hadn't seen it coming, having been tucked away safely overseas. Hidden, inured from it all. She raised an eyebrow at the man sitting next to her, who now fidgeted with a pen and his compendium. 'But they didn't. And I still haven't received an explanation as to why I was never informed about the parlous state of things in the US. It's gross negligence on the board's part, which you should know, being the company lawyer.'

She reached for the glass of water in front of her, condensation slipping down the sides and pooling on a coaster protecting the mirror-like wood of the table. Gage was being rude with this lateness. A deliberate message.

*'You're nothing. You have no importance to me. You are here at my bidding. Your fortunes survive or fail on my word alone.'*

She could stand up. Go. Refuse to tolerate the slight and walk from here with her head held high and let everything implode around her. There was a certain wicked satisfaction in imagining that. Her father's one true love, his company, being destroyed at her whim.

But Gage had called *her* and requested the meeting. Well, not Gage himself but an assistant, requesting her attendance at his Seattle headquarters. That was enough to keep her in the chair, because she hadn't seen Gage in the flesh since that night seven years earlier. When he'd looked up at her in that gritty abandoned building, kissed his fingers and run, drawing her father and his men away from her.

The door cracked open and her heart rate spiked, a pounding that punched at her throat. Eve swallowed down the sickening sensation. She wouldn't allow anyone here to know her blood pressure pushed critical. She took a deep, steadying breath. Frosted herself over. Icy was a veneer she'd perfected years ago. No one could touch her, not anymore. She'd no tears left to shed. She'd cried them all as a naïve twenty-year-old. Her well was now truly dry.

Finally, he appeared, filling the doorway. Her breath was crushed in her chest, there was no air in the whole world enough to fill her lungs. All the years of seeing photos, reading about his business exploits on the internet, was not enough to prepare her for seeing Gage in the flesh again.

He strolled into the room, looking down at his phone, no acknowledgement of her presence at all. Not even that could hurt her, though, as she devoured the sight of him. His hair golden and perfect, every part of him the *golden boy* the press claimed him to be. He owned the room in a dark blue suit, crisp white shirt, red and blue tie. Bespoke, tailored to fit his impressive body. He loomed as a presence more than a mere man. Like he owned everything around him—in perfect control.

Eve tried to keep breathing, tried not to show the effect he had on her because, damn, after all these years he still owned her body.

She hated him for it.

Gage grabbed the back of a chair while flicking through something on the phone screen. The leather dented under his grip. He pulled the chair out from the table. Undid the button on his suit jacket with calm precision and sat. Then—only then—did he look at her.

It was like being stabbed by an icicle. A cold thrust, deep into the heart of her, his vivid blue eyes piercing and frigid. Was he remembering the last time they'd spoken, in that terrible phone call her father had given her no option but to make? It was all she could do not to rise from this chair, say *Thank you for your time* and flee.

She'd never expected to have to face him again. She'd hidden out in France after being banished there seven years ago—the deal she'd struck to save Gage, to protect him from secrets he could never know. Secrets that would destroy him, and his family. She'd hold those in her heart for ever. Except she was done running. Running turned things into a disaster, as she and Gage both knew. They'd reaped the poisoned rewards of their own actions years before.

'Ms Chevalier.' His voice was all dark nights and silk sheets and her damned heart tripped over itself in guilty pleasure at the sound. 'Thank you for coming.'

Eve forced herself to look into his beautiful face. It was chiselled in a way it hadn't been in his early twenties. All softness had been hewn away, leaving a specimen of male near-perfection. The only thing marring it was the sliver of a scar under his right eye and the merest bump on the bridge of his nose where it had no doubt broken under the crack of a clenched fist. Her fingers itched to stroke over the flaws, to whisper how sorry she was for the wounds her father had left. But the cold disdain in his gaze told her there were no number of apologies she could offer that would make him forgive her.

'Gage. Thank you for inviting us here.' His eyes widened a fraction. She'd bet anything that everyone called him Mr Caron. Eve refused to play that game. While she might be prepared to beg for his help eventually, she'd start this negotiation as his equal.

'You can thank me at the end of the meeting when you see what I'm offering.'

'Getting straight to business. I like that.'

The corner of Gage's mouth kicked up in the hint of a smile that told her she'd pay, and he'd enjoy extracting the price. 'If you'd liked business a little more, perhaps Knight Enterprises wouldn't be in the desperate state that it is.'

Eve gritted her teeth. She'd tried to grab the reins when she'd sensed things were careening off track, but no one had wanted to listen to her. They'd parked her in France and let her play with the businesses there. The US was her daddy's domain, and he'd taken risks on things he shouldn't have. Too many chances that hadn't paid off. Now the company was fat and bloated and incapable of surviving the coming storm.

'My father and the board were responsible for the US division.'

'And yet you're here instead of him.'

Eve stiffened. She'd locked down news of her father's illness, determined to keep it quiet until she'd been able to assess the full scope of the disaster he'd wrought. The silence had bought her time, and that time had almost run out.

'Right where you want me?'

'I'd say almost the perfect position. Are you going to prostrate yourself? Beg me to help you wade your way out of the mire you've created?

Her solicitor started forward, beginning to rise from his chair. If he stepped in, she'd lose ground here. She wasn't some little girl who needed defending. She'd been fighting for herself and winning for years. Eve held up her hand and her solicitor stopped, sat back down, muttering under his breath. Gage raised an eyebrow but said nothing.

He'd soon learn she was no pushover, not anymore.

'The failings were my father's. His choices are not mine, and I refuse to own them for that reason.'

'I'm pleased to see you owning *your* decisions, Eve. Does that mean you'll take responsibility for what's coming your way?'

She reached for her glass, tried to keep the water inside still and steady as she sipped. The cold liquid hit her knotted stomach, which heaved in protest. She swallowed the sickening sensation down. She was made of stronger stuff now. She'd fought and won against bigger demons from her past than Gage Caron.

'I've never shirked responsibility for my actions, ever.'

He laughed, but there was nothing entertaining about the sound. Gage straightened some papers in front of him. Laid his perfect hands flat on the polished table-top. 'Well, hasn't this been fun. Let me be blunt. Knight's financial state is parlous. You've not grown organically or strategically but instead purchased anything and everything, particularly companies that Caron was considering.'

'If Caron considered them, I'd assume they were sound investments.'

Gage's eyes sparked something of a warning, a vicious kind of pleasure burning behind the polar blue.

'I rejected them as high risk with too little return.'

That's not what her father had said. Hugo Chevalier had taken delight in gloating, especially to her, about how he'd stolen yet another company from Gage, like some brutal, never-ending purgatory. Gage speared her with his frigid gaze again.

'Knight was welcome to them. Each and every one.'

Cold dread trickled through her. It wouldn't have been hard to manipulate her father, his quest for revenge all-encompassing, an unhealthy obsession. She'd only fuelled it by running with Gage, when all they'd hoped had been that the inevitability of a youthful marriage might heal the wounds between their families.

What a naïve, childish dream.

'Aren't you clever,' she said. Gage had planned this. Where once he'd been an avenging angel on her behalf, the sword he carried today would be used against her. He was revelling in their fall and part of her couldn't blame him for that. 'Let me share something with you. So am I.'

'If you're so clever, where are the investors? No one will touch you. The juggling act must be exhausting. Drop one ball and it's the beginning of the end. All it would take is a whisper in the wrong ear...'

The only piece of information held back right now was her father's incapacity. If that came out in an uncontrolled fashion, it was all over. She couldn't let that happen. Her mom and sister would never survive it. They were clueless about what was going on here, and that's how she wanted it to stay for now.

'It seems you know a great deal.' More than she'd expected. He was right, she'd tried everything, and doors kept closing in her face. It was as if someone had been chipping away, determined to make the Chevalier name meaningless. She was staring at the man responsible; she was sure of it.

'I've had seven years of solid study.'

'I like to think I can still surprise people.'

'There's nothing you can tell me about yourself I don't already know. It pays to have the measure of your enemies.'

A shiver ran through her.

*Heaven hath no rage like love to hatred turned.*

She'd bet anything that Gage didn't know everything, and she *knew* that she had some devastating surprises she could spring on him if she wanted revenge of her own. In some respects, she believed her father hoped that one day she would tell Gage all the secrets she held. But no matter how much vitriol he spilled on her, she wouldn't lower herself to joining the battle that had been waged by the two men so far.

'I understand what led us here. That's in the past.'

He picked up his sleek black and gold pen, twirling it nonchalantly in his fingers. 'If you don't learn from your mistakes, you're doomed. The past is instructive on what never to repeat.'

'Thank you for the lesson. Today is for looking forward.'

Gage smiled. Once that smile would have lit her up like a candle. Warm, genuine. Now there was no heat in it. It was a shark's smile, full of teeth and hinting of blood in the water and the bite to come. *That* smile chilled her to the marrow.

'Knight should be allowed to topple and fall. It's not a business. It's your father's vanity project.'

'Yet you called me.'

This wasn't an attempt at investment. It was a ritual humiliation. Revenge at its most acute from a man determined to destroy them all. If that was the ultimate end, Eve wanted to get it over with. She was tired of trying to prop things up when everyone around her seemed intent on cutting them down. If Madame Guillotine was bound to fall, she didn't have the energy to watch Gage sharpen the blade while she waited for it to slice her.

He steepled his fingers. 'There might be *some* aspects of the business that interest me.'

Eve let out a long, slow breath.

*Let the games begin.*

'What are you offering?'

'A lifeline.'

'I can feel the "but". What are the conditions? I'm assuming I won't like them.'

'Medicine isn't supposed to taste pleasant, Eve.'

'And I'm sure you're going to take pleasure in administering my first dose, so let's get started. I'm not big on procrastinating.'

'Your father will be removed as CEO.' Her lawyer spluttered. Funny, she'd forgotten he was even there. No matter. Since her father was currently in a hospital bed and she'd been carrying out the CEO's role in his absence, that was no problem. 'There will be a restructure. My word is *final* on what Knight keeps and discards. It needs to discard a great deal.'

'And will Knight retain its name and integrity as a company?'

'Caron will own eighty per cent.'

That was no answer at all.

Eve suspected there were many things Gage had become, but a liar was not one of them. This wasn't a lifeline, it was a takeover. The members of her family held shares. Her mother and sister weren't interested in the business side of things, other than the money and security that it bought. If Gage took so much, there'd be nothing left and he'd squeeze them out. With their shares' current value, the offer on the table was almost worthless. She could rebuild. She had skills, determination and contacts outside her father's sphere. Her mom and Veronique wouldn't have a chance if she agreed to Gage's terms. She shook her head.

'Knight has a brand. The goodwill of the name is worth millions. You want that for some reason, so we come to this as equals.'

'How entertaining. There's nothing equal about us. You are so far below me in all respects, it should be considered a miracle I'm talking to you.'

She'd thought, "Better the devil you know", hoping that maybe Gage had wanted to see her, that things had mellowed over the years. That thinking had been a terrible mistake. She'd have to try elsewhere to find a saviour. A private equity firm perhaps, someone from overseas who hadn't heard the rumours. They might carve up the company but at least they'd treat her with respect to her face, even if they laughed behind her back.

'I will not sit here and be insulted, which seems to be the only reason you called me to your office. We have nothing more to say.' She stood. Her lawyer stood.

'Liar,' Gage murmured. Eve froze. Was she so easy to see through? Most other people couldn't read her, the frosty veneer she'd perfected years ago renowned. If she couldn't keep secrets from Gage, this would be a huge problem because her life was full of them. Gage leaned back in his chair, a smirk on his face. He turned to her lawyer. 'Mr Stoddart, I'd like to talk to your client alone.'

Eve nodded. She'd travelled halfway round the world to be here. May as well not waste the airfare before judging how this would play out to the end. Her lawyer looked at her with a raised eyebrow.

'I'll be outside the door if you need me. For the record, it has been a monumental error coming here.' He looked back at Gage as he reached the door and hesitated. 'You, sir, are no gentleman.'

'Ouch,' Gage said with a sneer as the boardroom door slammed shut. He motioned towards her chair. '*Please* take a seat.'

'You're using your manners now?'

'I may as well, since I've just worked out how far I can push you before you walk.'

A fierce heat bubbled in her blood. He'd been playing her, and she'd fallen for it. She took a slow breath, trying to restore the equilibrium that seemed to have fled her. Lowered herself into the warm leather of her seat. Smoothed out her slim skirt, and there they sat in silence at either end of the long boardroom table. But no matter how large the room or expansive the wooden surface, the walls closed in on her. She took another sip of water. Tried to steer the conversation back to some level of civility. It was the polite thing to do.

'I admire what you're achieving in Detroit. Repurposing those factories for renewable technologies and retraining staff is admirable.'

'Flattery won't work here.'

'I'm not flattering you, it's the truth.'

He hesitated. Most people wouldn't have noticed. With Gage, she noticed everything.

'You been keeping an eye on me?'

She thought about the contents of a small, battered, yellow suitcase safely stowed in a hotel room in the heart of the city. A suitcase that travelled with her everywhere and held all her memories, physical proof that her eyes were always on Gage. She couldn't look away, even from France. But she'd never let him know it.

'I read the business pages like everyone else.'

'Giving unemployed people jobs and hope is the right thing to do. You believe in doing the right thing, don't you, *cher*?'

The pet name he'd once called her with so much love sounded bitter and poisonous on his tongue now. There were some memories she wouldn't allow to be tainted by all that had happened since, and this was one.

'It's Ms Chevalier, or Eve.'

Gage leaned back in the chair, the corners of his mouth kicking up for the briefest of moments. 'Eve, then. The original temptress.'

If that's what he believed, so be it. She deserved his rage, so she'd let him use it. As long as her mother and Veronique's fortunes were protected, she'd allow him to take his hurt and anger out on her. But Gage always liked a challenge, so she'd give him one.

'People only take the fruits offered them, if it's something they already crave,' she said, with a smile of her own. 'But enough of this. Why do I get the feeling you've asked me here only to mock me?'

'Allow me to indulge myself for a few moments. I enjoy watching you writhe under a good tongue lashing.'

His voice was low, soft. Overtly sexual. Heat roared to her cheeks and she was back on a picnic blanket, hidden under the cascading boughs of an old willow where he'd threaded flowers in her hair and indulged her naked body till she'd wept with pleasure. Gage smirked and the burning in her cheeks flamed hotter.

How dared he? He would not rekindle those memories, not now.

'That's childish and beneath you.'

He shrugged. 'I seem to recall you've levelled that accusation at me before. Or was it that you called me *common*? I'm not sure. Our final conversation seems to have been lost in the annals of my memory somewhere.'

It hadn't been in hers. She'd never forget each second of that last phone call, or the way it had cleaved her heart into a million pieces. With her father sitting next to her and Gage all but begging to see her again, she'd delivered the death blow to any chance they may have had of a reconciliation.

*'It's over. You're being a child. This excess of emotion is common.'*

She'd been cruel to be kind. Her father had promised that if she rejected Gage, he'd never reveal the secret he'd somehow discovered at a critical time for the Caron company: Gage wasn't the true heir to Caron Investments. He wasn't his father's child.

She'd refused to believe her father at first, until he'd produced evidence. A sworn statement from Gage's real father about an affair and the man's photo—it had been shocking to see how closely Gage resembled him. Then there were letters from Gage's mother about the pregnancy. Eve's father had been right when he'd threatened to find a way of destroying Gage's family. The information he had was the perfect bomb. It would have broken Gage to find out as he adored his parents.

She had refused to allow her father to destroy the illusion of his happy family, especially as Eve's own had seemed so bleak. Her father's obsession and quest for revenge. Her mother's illness, a woman always so frail and scared, preferring pills and liquor to her own children. Her sister's whole future hanging by a thread.

Gage's solid family was something he'd held onto like a shield. Promising that if she entered their fold, she'd be protected as well. She'd so wanted that solidity and love to surround her too, like a goose-down comforter. The realisation all those years ago that Caron had been struggling, and that news of Gage's parentage could tip the company and him over the edge, had devastated her. She'd do anything to save him from it. That's what true love was, protecting those you adored, even if it went against your own self-interest.

In her short life she'd become a master of it.

'Now that you've stopped watching me squirm, I propose Knight Enterprises keep its name. I'll take Caron's guidance on the less profitable aspects of the company and I'll support Caron purchasing a forty per cent stake.'

Gage's eyes darkened and then he laughed. Part entertained, part jeering. 'You really think you have anything to bargain with?'

She shrugged. It was more vain hope than an expectation of reality, but she couldn't give up now. Because he'd come to her. Everyone wanted something. She just had to find out what Gage wanted from her.

'I'll give you points for audacity. I'm putting up the money and taking the risk for your poor decisions.'

'It's fixable and you know it. That is what you do, Gage. Break up what's worthless and rebuild the good. If you were speaking the truth and this...' she waved between them '...is just business, then this is a good deal.'

'I'm taking the company. Seventy per cent. Knight is *mine.*'

'Fifty-five. My mother and sister's shares must remain unaffected. There's to be no detriment to their position. And they're to receive a parcel of shares each in Caron Investments.'

'A Chevalier owning shares in Caron?' he asked, his voice quiet and deadly.

She owned some. Privately. An investment through a trust so Gage would never find out she held part of him, for ever. It only seemed fair, since she'd come to realise he owned her, body and soul.

She'd shown her hand now, what she truly cared about. It was a risk, but if Gage understood one thing, it was the love of family. That's why she'd not allowed his own to be destroyed when her father had threatened it. 'You'll never let Caron fail. Their future will be assured.'

'What about yours?' Gage cocked his head, his eyes softened a fraction, and she saw the man she'd thought the boy might become one day, had fate and her father not intervened. He was breath-taking, and her heart ached for what might have been. But she cast the thought aside. No matter how Gage affected her, it would never have worked between them. Even ignoring the enmity between their families, they'd been too young to commit to a life-time together.

'I can look after myself.'

She hadn't been able to once. But she'd grown up fast after being shipped off to France. At least she hadn't been locked up in a finishing school, which had been her father's first intention. Instead, she'd fought for a university education, negotiating with a ferocity she hadn't known she had while promising to make Gage suffer. Her father had agreed. So long as a Caron was hurting, he was happy.

To protect Gage, she'd denied everything other than an infatuation. Denied Gage had touched her. Denied their love. Each one of those denials made her feel like Judas.

'I'm sure your trust fund makes life very comfortable.'

Let him think that was the only reason she'd gone back to her family, the money she'd been set to receive when she'd turned twenty-one. She didn't care. When her dreams of being with Gage had died, she'd used that blood money to fund another, her flower farm in Grasse. Her father had never understood her love of growing things, had refused to allow her to study horticulture, as she'd wanted to. It had been either a society wedding or joining the family business, nothing in between. So she'd chosen the family business and bought her dream for herself.

'It sure doesn't hurt.'

'It was all about the money, wasn't it?' Gage asked, eyes as hard as diamond chips. 'But I own you now.'

'Not yet you don't, since you haven't accepted my counter-offer.'

Gage sprawled back and the leather chair creaked as he did so. He turned to look out over the city that lay beneath them. Seemingly uncaring. A slight smile toyed on his perfect mouth.

'Sixty per cent. Your mother and sister can have their shares.'

Relief broke, washing over her. Not perfect, but she'd known she'd have to cede the majority of Knight to him. So long as her mother and sister's futures were assured, she was happy. She'd banked on him not destroying them too, and it seemed she'd been right. She released a long, slow breath. 'Thank—'

He held up his hand, stopping her. 'I'm not done. If you want this deal, I want something more.' He swivelled his chair round and stared her down. A ferocious businessman, burning with a vengeance. The shark had returned, circling. Even though the expansive boardroom table separated them, she wanted to get as far away as possible from the coming attack. She shivered and pressed back into her seat. He smiled again.

'Congratulations, *cher*. You're my new fiancée.'

# CHAPTER TWO

THE COLOUR BLED from Eve's face till she was as white as the stark walls of his boardroom. It seemed surreal now that he'd had his hands all over that pale flesh once. A body now dutifully hidden under an impeccable, silver-grey suit that fitted her slender frame to a perfection. A fit that might make a lesser man weep with thanks. Not him. Not anymore.

He'd seen more of that skin than she'd probably care to remember, considering the way he'd seemed to disgust her only weeks after they'd parted. He'd stroked her in wonder, marvelling at the privilege of being permitted to touch her, to enter her lithe, luscious body. He couldn't shake that thought now, of stroking her responsive flesh till she moaned with pleasure.

He hated it. Hated that in the months after she'd finally rejected him, he'd tried to get over her. Had attempted to drown his sorrows in spirits and women who'd deserved far better than he had been offering. And still the memory of her had tainted everything. They'd been each other's first and some days it had felt like she was the only woman he'd ever truly enjoy, all others fading like a pale imitation beside the vivid memories of her. Like his body had recognised only one person as its own. Its other half. And without that there'd been a part of him missing.

He shook those thoughts aside. He didn't need them, not today. Not when he knew what she was. Flighty. Duplicitous. A consummate liar. She still hadn't responded to his pronouncement. Her plush pink mouth was opening, closing then opening again. Gaping like a fish caught on a hook and hauled from the water. For he *had* caught her and, by association, her father.

Bitter bile rose in his throat, but he swallowed it down with a grimace. All he'd needed to do was to choose the right lure and reel them in inch by inch. Just like fishing for bass with his dad. Easier, because Hugo Chevalier was nothing if not predictable. Anything he'd thought he could steal from a Caron he had, even if the deal was a dud. So long as Gage pretended to be interested, that was all Eve's father had needed. It had been surprisingly easy. Unlike this.

He hadn't expected Eve to put up so much of a fight. That she had stitched a thread of something like pleasure right through him. Another thing he'd be forced to ignore in time. And he had plenty of that. If she wanted to have some semblance of a company left at the end of all this, she'd do what he demanded. He relaxed back in his chair and waited. Made a show of checking his watch then looking back at her. He'd been waiting seven years so what were a few more minutes?

She seemed to compose herself. Gave a tremulous little laugh. 'You can't be serious.'

His simmering anger began to boil then. He'd done well to keep it under control so far. Playing this little game because he always knew the end point. Eve and her family had tried to smear his family's name since the night her father had hauled him off and given him the hiding of his life for having the *temerity* to steal away his precious daughter.

In the years that had followed, nasty whispers had

abounded. Not enough to cross over into defamation, and nothing too public. Just a quiet word in the right ear whenever a deal was going to be struck or Caron Investments had achieved something great. That Eve hadn't been a willing party to their flight that rainy evening. That Gage was not a man to trust.

He'd be damned if that falsehood continued, especially now. It was time for Eve to pay. He'd make sure of it.

'I'm *deadly* serious.'

'Have you forgotten that in our great-grandparents' time it was frowned on for people who worked at Knight to even date a Caron employee and vice versa? The enmity has only become worse since then. This is insane.'

Yes. It was. But there was only one person who could quell the rumours that dogged him. The cause of them herself. She sat there stiff and straight, almost prim with her generous mouth pulled to a taut line. Not a part of her was anything other than perfect, right down to her sleek, tamed, golden hair. All the wildness smoothed and ironed out of her. He'd been witness to that wildness underneath. It was still there in the way her pale blue eyes flashed at him, making him crave for them to spark for reasons of pleasure, not anger.

He loathed how his body still reacted to her. A siren's song calling for him to dash himself bloody on the rocks of their memories.

'It's the perfect narrative. I can see the headlines. "Fated childhood sweethearts together again, despite their warring families". A Romeo and Juliet story, without all the annoying death at the end. The press will eat it up.'

'We're not barely-out-of-our-teens runaways anymore.' She shook her head. 'No. It's not happening.'

How quickly she'd dismissed their past, but it would happen or she'd lose everything. She had nothing to bargain with here. He'd take Knight, carve it to tiny pieces. What he sought from her was more important than anything. Redemption, in the eyes of the business world and his family.

He would never forget the crunch of fist on bone or the cold cuffs crushing his wrists when he'd refused to tell Hugo Chevalier where Eve was. Then the disappointment on his father's face later that night when he'd come to the police station, bailed Gage out for the trumped-up charge levelled against him that had dissolved as soon as his father's lawyers had got their teeth into it.

All the approbation had been worth it…till Eve had resurfaced in the bosom of her family. The days he'd waited frantically for her call. Planning to go and meet her. Marry her and to hell with everyone. Until he'd realised he'd been fooled. That while she'd professed love, it had really been the thrill-seeking of a bored little princess who in the end had just wanted to dally with someone till she could get her hands on her trust fund. He gritted his teeth.

'I didn't make myself plain. That's the offer.'

'You can have seventy per cent, so long as my mother and sister's investments are protected.'

'No.'

He stood and strolled towards her. She pushed the chair out from behind the table as he neared, her hands gripping the arms.

'Eighty per cent.'

'You're part of the deal or there's no deal at all.' He towered over her now. She tilted her head back, eyes wide and pupils dark, her breathing fast and shallow. He shouldn't have enjoyed it as much as this, but he couldn't help himself. 'How long will it take before the creditors come to your door? Before your precious mother and sister are out on the streets? Till I own everything anyway?'

'If you're going to own everything anyhow, what do you possibly have to gain by this?' Her voice was rough and breathy. The throaty sound of it scored down his spine like he remembered her fingernails had.

He stilled. How dared she pretend? She was complicit in the suspicion that followed him. The women who'd chosen him, only wanting the bad boy. He was all too aware how a carefully placed whisper could bring everything crashing down. Sure, he'd done well. Working with his father, Caron had become a powerhouse, exceeding their wildest expectations. But Gage wanted more. Caron would be truly international. If he could secure the current deal he sought with the Germans—a deal he needed Eve's help to achieve, as much as it galled him—then the world would see what he was capable of. It's what he was owed, and Eve would pay up.

'I gain everything I want.'

'You want to marry me?' She blurted that out and he could tell she hadn't meant to say it. The mottle of red creeping up from her throat, marring her flawless skin, told him so. He laughed.

'Of course not. Don't worry, *cher*. It's only temporary and won't hurt a bit. Not unless you want it to. You know I always give a woman what she wants.'

The column of her slender throat convulsed. The thought of laying his hands on her flawless skin, had his body tight and on high alert. It was as if everything slowed, the air in the room becoming thick with possibilities. If he could touch her again, maybe she would be burned from his system once and for all.

'I don't want any of it.'

'Another lie, *cher*? How disappointing. You still want me. The whole of you tells me that like you're screaming it out loud.'

He could see it in the way her eyes tracked his every move. Surveying him, fixing on his hands, his mouth. Those parts of him he'd used to toy with her mercilessly the rare times they'd been able to sneak away from family and indulge their obsession with each other. And it *had* been an obsession. That's one thing she could never fake. The delicious heat of satisfaction slid through him.

'You'll agree. The engagement will last as long as it needs to, then I'll end it. And all the while you'll fake it with a smile on your face. History tells me you're good at doing that.'

She didn't even balk at the jibe, proving exactly what he'd accused her of being.

'And what if I want it to end?'

'That's not how this works.'

'I need to know.' She licked her lips, leaving them moist and kissable. Would her kiss still have the power to obliterate all rational thought? He craved to swoop down, capture those soft lips with his own. Loathed the fact that she still held some power over him. 'What's in it for you?'

'Apart from crushing your father by forcing him to believe that a Caron's hands are all over his daughter again, and that I've finally won? Let me see…'

He wanted to witness the look on the man's face when he realised he'd lost everything. His company. His beloved daughter. The world coming to know that the falsehoods he'd secretly whispered in the right ears had all been lies.

A look shifted across her face, fleeting, like clouds over the sun. 'There's something you need to know. Is everything that's said in this room absolutely confidential?'

'Don't you trust me, *cher*?' She winced at the endearment but he didn't care. Once she'd meant everything to him, and she'd thrown it in his face by trying to take him down. He'd never forgive her, ever.

'You're an intelligent man. This whole meeting was designed to take revenge against my family and we both know where that leads, to nowhere good. Of course I don't trust you.'

'The only person who has a problem with the truth, is you.'

'And yet here I am trying to tell you a truth and you don't seem interested.'

'I'm all ears.'

'I—I need to know that this deal is safe.'

'If you agree to my whole proposal until *I* say we're done, then yes. It's safe.'

The whole of her slumped a little. Her shoulders dropped. Her eyes shut briefly, dark lashes feathering over her cheeks. Then she opened her eyes, and that hint of vulnerability disappeared. Her eyes lost their soft baby-blue colour. Now they were all hard steel.

'My father's in hospital. The ICU.'

It was as though the earth shifted under his feet. The whole of him a morass of sensations that jumbled together in an uncomfortable soup of feelings he barely understood. There was disappointment that Hugo Chevalier wasn't going to see this, wouldn't feel the full weight of horror at the realisation that Gage had taken it all from him, but there was something else too, something that stuck like a knife under the ribs. A spike that felt a whole lot like sympathy.

He shook his head. He didn't have a sympathetic sentiment left in him. Eve had seen to that.

'How bad is it?'

She must be hurting. She loved her daddy. She had to, considering she'd chosen to go back to Hugo and her trust fund rather than keep running with him. Eve looked up at him, no expression on her face. 'He has an infection.

They're worried about multi-organ failure. It's as bad as can be without being told to call a priest.'

She said it like she was asking him how he wanted his eggs for breakfast.

'I'm sorry.' The words stuck in his throat, but it was the right thing to do, to give his sympathy. He wasn't a complete savage—on most days, at least.

Eve didn't soften but appeared completely unmoved. 'No, you're not. But you needed to know because if it's revenge you're after, all you have is me.'

Her face was still impassive, as if it was merely business they'd been discussing. Hugo Chevalier's name had been the single thing holding that company together. One word about this spoken to the wrong person and Knight was done. He could have his revenge with no effort at all, but that would never satisfy him. He wanted the axe to fall by *his* hand. To know he'd won and taken everything for himself. So he still needed Eve, to achieve public redemption.

He hated it. Hated that he required her for this. Hated that all he'd ever wanted was her. Desire lashed him like a whip-crack as he watched Eve now. Her wide-set blue eyes, petite nose, luscious mouth, sleek hair. That beautiful body all trussed up in a business suit he wanted to snip at and unravel till she fell apart. It had always damned well been her, whether in love or revenge. She shifted in her seat and the gentle scent of jasmine and spring teased his nose, inflamed his blood. Made all of him hot and tight under the suit. He'd shrug off his jacket if he wasn't so damned hard she'd tell in an instant that while his head might loathe her, his body craved her with an unhealthy obsession.

'You'll do,' he said, his voice grinding out all rough and unrecognisable. She blinked fast, like something had been flung at her face.

'Was that meant to sting? Because nothing can hurt

me anymore.' He wondered fleetingly what possible hurt she could have suffered in her privileged, protected life. 'It was such a long time ago, and we both know where revenge leads. It's beneath you.'

Sure, it might be beneath him, but while some memories in life had dimmed, one hadn't. Eve and those last weeks before the end haunted his dreams. Trying her phone in increasingly frantic efforts. Getting nothing then one day having her pick up. The relief that she was okay had flooded him, until she'd cruelly discarded him. From the tinny, hollow sound of the call he'd known he was on speaker and her father had been in the room, listening to it all. Doubtless gloating.

No, he could never forget.

He'd tried to exorcise her from his life. But to his fury every time he'd touched another woman, his body had rebelled. He'd cut a swathe through the female population at college, trying to drown out the memory of her, but he'd never been able to. Any time he'd seen the bright splash of golden hair or a flash of pearly skin his heart rate had spiked, thinking it might be her. But she'd been happily getting on with her life in France as he'd been trying to rebuild the pieces of his broken heart. It had taken years to forget the breathy sounds she made as she came. The smell of her, like the flower gardens she loved so much and wanted to create for herself. Time now to rid her from his life for good.

He sat on the table near her. Her gaze trailed down his shirt, hesitated on his tie, drifted to rest on the buckle of his belt and lower still. A swift shot of adrenaline punched right through him as her gaze lingered there a bit damn long. If she kept looking, she'd know exactly how much his cursed body still wanted her.

What if he kissed her? Would she react? By the flaring of her nostrils and her blown pupils he bet he could lay her out on this table and take her hard and fast till she screamed so loudly the lawyer outside would hear. Show her that, while he might not have been good enough to marry, she still wanted him.

*That* would be beneath him. Not this—an engagement as fake as the woman in front of him. If it could get the European deal over the line, it would be worth *everything*. Revenge was just a tasty morsel on the side. An *amuse-bouche*. Cleansing his palate for better things. It was time to get Eve out of his system once and for all. Because he'd never trust her, not again. She'd cured him of that gentler sentiment.

'That's easy for you to say, isn't it? You haven't suffered any consequences.'

Her brow creased. 'Consequences? I don't—'

'Enough. The innocent act, as compelling as it seems, doesn't suit you.' He stood, stalked to the other end of the table and grabbed a glass of water, taking a long, cold gulp. It didn't help cool the fire of anger burning in his gut. 'But don't worry. All it'll require is for you to pretend for a little while, which should be easy. I'm not trying to rekindle old flames and I don't want to tie myself to you permanently. Just long enough to get a deal over the line and then you're free.'

'A deal? Who is this merry charade for?'

He hesitated. She didn't need to know, there was nothing he had to tell her, and yet…she'd told him about her father. That was a devastating secret being kept from the business world, which he could have used to destroy everything without any effort on his part. She could have kept quiet about it till she had his money. He didn't understand why she had so willingly handed him the perfect means to ruin her.

Maybe it wouldn't hurt to tell her why he needed her. If she worked with him on this, rather than against him, their association could be over sooner. It's what he wanted, wasn't it? A tightness settled low inside him, like that thought was somehow wrong.

'Greta Bonitz.'

Eve's eyes widened. The German industrialist was renowned for her investments in renewable technology. Reclusive, private and family minded, it had taken one hint that Gage may not have had impeccable morals for her to cool and put their discussions on permanent hold.

With Eve as his fiancée, that would change. A partnership with the Bonitz group of companies would give Caron Investments what it should have had years before, premier billing on the world stage. He'd do that for his father, for all the times things had not gone as planned because of what Gage had done as a stupid twenty-three-year-old drunk on lust and a belief in true love.

He'd *finally* be relieved of this burden of guilt he'd carried.

'Why?'

'She needs to believe the lie that you and I are together. Help me get an agreement over the line and Caron will bail out your company and keep your precious mother and sister safe from the wolves already coming down the mountain for them.'

He saw the flare in her eyes, the intelligence ticking in a way that said she thought she might be able to find a way out of this. 'Take care, Eve. You've got more to lose than me. Fail, and I might lose a deal. You'll lose everything.'

'You're the only wolf at the door, Gage. You have been for years, haven't you?'

He smiled. She'd come to realise just how determined

he'd been to bring them to this point, sitting across the table from one another with her future in his grip.

'Seven, to be precise.'

He saw the moment she knew she'd been backed into a corner she couldn't escape. She took a deep breath, straightened her spine and looked him in the face, her lips a tight, tense line. 'When do we start this fantasy?'

'You've got twenty-four hours to get things in order. We leave for Europe in forty-eight. I want to go through Knight's French holdings first. Then we meet with Frau Bonitz.'

'That—that's not long. How do I prepare my family?'

'I assume that's a rhetorical question. If it's not, tell them that after rigorously thrashing out our differences in the boardroom we concluded that we'd never stopped wanting one another. That should do it. Everyone loves a fairy-tale.'

Her cheeks flushed a gorgeous rose. Even though he loathed her, she was a beautiful woman. In her early twenties, he'd thought she was incomparable, but she'd been a pale imitation when compared to the woman who sat before him now. Fleshed out, with grown-up curves. It was all he could do not to reach out and haul her to him.

'We need the business side committed to an agreement.'

Business. Yes. He needed to remember. He opened the folder sitting on the table in front of him, scribbled relevant percentages in the blank spaces his legal team had already left on his instruction, and drafted a short paragraph allowing for the provision of Caron shares. That bit galled him, but it didn't matter. He would win far more than he lost in this deal.

He signed and dated the back page and slid it to Eve with a pen on top.

'Here's a memorandum of understanding. Our lawyers

can sort out more formal details but this will do for now, since I never go back on my word. Unlike some.'

She picked up the papers and his pen slipped with a clatter onto the gleaming wood table-top. Then she read through the document slowly, her jaw clenched tightly. He fancied he could almost hear her teeth grinding. When he'd walked in today, he'd known almost exactly what he was prepared to offer, no more, no less. It was all about filling in a few blanks, which had cost him less than he thought. It told him how desperate she really was.

'Aren't you well prepared?' Eve ignored his pen like it was a snake sunning itself in front of her. Instead she slid an elegant silver fountain pen from her bag and signed in neat, precise script. 'How commendable.'

'I've had a long time to prepare for this day, *cher*.' Nothing took him off guard anymore. He allowed for every contingency. He'd never be surprised ever again. He'd waited long enough for today. He'd left nothing to chance.

'I thought after seven years you wouldn't care.'

He couldn't read what was going on behind her intelligent eyes, but she'd get a warning nonetheless that he wasn't one to be crossed.

'Oh, *cher*. Beware the fury of a patient man.'

Eve nestled into the plush leather seats of a jet sitting on the tarmac of a private airfield. She rubbed at her temple, trying to ease the throbbing that had taken up residence and didn't seem fit to move any time soon. It was as if her body had set out to spite her, ignoring the painkillers she'd downed as soon as she'd boarded. Even though her head pounded, she wasn't sure what hurt the most, that or her heart. It had been a close-run thing since Gage had burst back into her life.

She'd thought it would make things better, knowing

the company and her mother and sister were at least safe from the worst that creditors could throw at them, but it hadn't made any difference, the dread replaced by another fear. Old doubts and regrets had resurfaced. The more she tried to shut them down the worse things became, so she allowed herself to sit with the thoughts for a short while. The 'what-ifs' she'd discarded years before.

They'd been too young. It would never have worked long term. These were the things she *knew*, that she'd told herself every day until the fantasy had died. Even if they'd survived the disclosures about his parentage and the ruination of his family, the seven-year itch would be settling in about now. It would be far worse for things to have ended up in a mess of recriminations at the hands of divorce lawyers than the way they had. A swift, clean break, no matter how painful at the time.

She just had to get through this, however long it took to play out. She could do it; she'd been through worse and while she allowed herself a few reminiscences right now, she wouldn't dwell on some memories. Not those of a tiny white coffin in a lonely church. Not of a baby born too soon.

No good ever came of memories like those.

Eve glanced over at the baggage cupboard where she'd stowed the little yellow case that travelled everywhere with her, which held all her grief and tears. She'd have preferred to keep it at her feet, but the flight attendant had reassured her with a smile that it would be safe. Maybe she could just go and check? She resisted the urge that welled up inside and bit at her heels. There had been days where all she'd done had been to sit and weep over the contents. Now, to simply know it was with her was enough.

Instead of needless worrying, she grabbed a magazine from a low table in front of her and flicked through it.

Beautiful people, salacious gossip, fashion. It all blurred in a whirl of colour till she turned to an advertisement of a flower-filled field with a bottle of perfume overlaying the scene. A picture she recognised, the warmth of pride flowing through her.

That was *her* field. The farm she'd bought in the south of France with the help of her trust fund and a loan from Knight's French arm. A breakout luxury perfume brand had bought *her* flowers to make their new flagship scent, and was keen to contract her exclusively. Especially since she'd hinted about the new rose she and her chief grower had developed. Her only regret was that she couldn't keep the property all to herself. Renting out the house for part of the year to fund her loan was a sad necessity. One day it would all be hers, but not for a while yet.

She smiled at this indulgence on the side her father didn't know about. He'd never understood her love of growing things. That was for gardeners—*staff*—and not his daughter. Getting dirty in the garden was something to be discouraged. Something beneath her. But it's how she'd first spied Gage. She'd been picking jonquils in the lower reaches of the garden and there he'd sat, staring down at her from the dizzying height of a huge old magnolia tree, framed by a sky as blue as his eyes.

That was another memory she shouldn't be wasting her time on. He wasn't that mischievous boy in the tree any longer. She wasn't that hopeful girl. They'd grown up, grown hard and moved on. Her focus was on building her farm. She could almost smell the scents of lavender, rose and jasmine hanging on the warm air and her head-ache eased a fraction. This was her happy place, where her worries seemed to leave her, the place she now felt most at home. She lingered a little longer on the picture as the flight attendant moved through the cabin and to the rear door of the aircraft.

'Mr Caron, it's a pleasure to see you. You're cutting it fine today.'

'Thank you, and my apologies to the captain and flight crew. Has my fiancée arrived?'

The ache inside intensified at the sound of his voice. She snapped her magazine shut and gripped it tightly in her lap.

'Yes, and may I offer my congratulations. Please take your seat and buckle up. If there's anything you need after we reach cruising altitude, just ask.'

Eve turned to see Gage coming on board. There should be a fanfare of trumpets heralding him. He was like some glorious corporate angel. Briefcase in hand, sporting a dark grey suit, pale grey shirt and silver tie, he stalked into the space with an authority that made her silly little heart swoon. He checked his phone before sliding it into his pocket and dropping into the seat opposite her. He was so tall his knees almost brushed hers. It was all she could do not to move away.

'Darling, it's good to see you,' he said, his gaze tracing over her body. She tugged at her shirt and wished she'd done up all the buttons rather than leave a few open, giving the merest hint of cleavage. At least she was dressed for business in a trouser suit. A reminder that for the foreseeable future every moment of her day was work. 'How did your family take the news of our engagement?'

The flight attendant walked back towards the cockpit with a warm smile for them both. Eve tried to return it, but felt sure what she gave in response looked more ill than pleased.

'As well as could be expected.'

Not well at all. She'd told her mom and sister that Gage had agreed to save the company. That they had unfinished

business. Her mother had wailed about liars and cheats, be-
trayals and blood money, before taking to her room where
she'd no doubt still be. Veronique had simply turned her
back with the words 'It's treachery. He's a filthy Caron.'
She'd ignored them both.

'What did your parents say?'

'My parents only want me to be happy,' he said. A tiny
muscle in his jaw clenched, and she wondered about the
truth of what he'd said. There was no warmth or caring in
that voice. She could almost hear the sneer of *My family's
better than yours.*

And as far as he knew, that was true. He was the only
child, and doted on. Which was one of the reasons why
the secret she held must always be kept. He'd idolised his
father. Did Gus Caron even know Gage wasn't his? They'd
always seemed to be such a small, happy family whenever he'd spoken of them. She wasn't sure her parents ever
thought about her happiness. Not really. Her father was
only interested in the dynasty, as if that warmed you on
a cold night. Having two daughters had been a profound
disappointment.

'I thought we could visit for Thanksgiving,' Gage said.

'That's…four months away. Will we still be playing
this game then?'

'Since game-playing is your forte, it doesn't matter how
long this goes on. Sit back, relax and enjoy it.'

She blew out a slow breath and buckled up her seat belt
as the captain announced take-off. 'Fooling people we
don't know is one thing, but carrying on a charade in front
of your family, in person? I can't and I won't.'

'You scared of being caught out as a fraud?' His eyes
were on her, cold and hard like blue steel. He could hate
her all he liked. She'd take his approbation, but he wouldn't
push her around.

'No, but people get excited about weddings and you're their only child.' The lie almost stuck in her throat. 'I'm mindful of hurting the family you love.'

He looked out the window as the world raced by. Her stomach swooped as the wheels left the tarmac and the plane began to climb. She swallowed as her ears popped, and stared out the window too. Anything to ignore the man who sat like a force of nature in front of her. She could feel him, the air almost bristling and shimmering around him with restrained energy. It put her on edge, just when she needed to relax.

When he turned back to her, his face had softened a little. Like the hard edges had been sanded away. 'No Thanksgiving, then.'

The plane levelled out and the captain announced they could release their seat belts, so Gage unbuckled his and strolled to the front of the aircraft into the cockpit. Eve couldn't help watching him go. His strong, broad shoulders, tapering into a narrow waist. The way his suit trousers sat low and firm on his lean hips. A prickly kind of heat rushed over her. She looked away before she ogled his backside because that had always been one of her favourite parts of him. The way she'd gripped him as he'd moved over her…

No. She would not go there. He'd grown up, that was all. Lost his youthful softness, his angles now hard and one hundred per cent adult male in his prime. Any female on the planet would be transfixed by all that golden hair, tanned skin and muscular physique, but obsessing about something she would never have wasn't worth the energy.

Eve sank back into her seat and closed her eyes, the painkillers she'd taken earlier finally taking the edge off her headache. She could work but nothing held her interest right now, everything depressingly bleak for the US operation. She didn't need to read the most recent reports emailed to her to know most of the businesses her father had purchased in the last few years hadn't lived up to the heady expectations of them. Or to know that the board's lack of due diligence was also to blame, believing her father when they should have been questioning the madness of his obsession with beating Caron Investments at all costs.

She might try to snatch a bit of sleep but as she tried to blank her mind and relax, the atmosphere changed again, like everything held its breath. She opened her eyes and looked up to find Gage standing in front of her. He reached into his coat pocket and removed something then sat in the seat opposite.

'This is yours.' He held out a small blue box. The knot in her belly tightened because she knew what it was and didn't want it. This was all a mockery, eating at her like a rat in corn. Still, she reached out to meet him halfway, trying not to touch him, not to let their fingers brush. She needn't have worried. Gage was as keen to avoid her as she him. He pulled back his hand as if any contact between them would singe. She looked at the exquisite, embossed leather ring box. It was still warm from the heat of Gage's body.

'It's unnecessary.' Why did her voice sound so faint? Once she'd been desperate to wear his ring. They'd talked about getting one after they'd crossed the border and married. There was no time beforehand and Gage had been devastated he couldn't do things the right way around— treat her like a princess, or so he'd said at the time. There was no point remembering any of that but, still, the difference between their dreams then and the reality now tore at her heart a little.

'You and I will soon be officially engaged. Of course

it's necessary. Completes the blissful picture of our impending happy union.'

She could do this. It was only a piece of jewellery. It meant nothing.

And that was the whole problem, how meaningless this all was. It dirtied the memories of what they'd had together. Memories that had kept her going through seven years of long, cold, lonely nights. Memories of what love could be and what she might find for herself again one day.

No. There was no going back there. Her father had made it plain what would happen. Gage's family would be destroyed. Their business ruined. Gage would have hated her. Not immediately, but eventually. When the beautiful gloss wore off and everything was tarnished, he would regret the day he'd ever peeked over the back wall separating the two family's estates from his perch high in the magnolia tree, and said hello to a little girl picking flowers. That love of theirs would have morphed to hatred and they'd still be here, yet his life would be in tatters. She could never have done that to him. Love meant sacrifice. They were in the same place they would always have been. She'd done the right thing.

She had.

Eve lifted the lid of the box. Nestled in black velvet sat a huge emerald-cut sapphire, not dark but almost a cornflower-blue. The same colour blue as Gage's eyes. The magnificent stone was surrounded by baguette diamonds and framed in white gold. It glittered under the lights, precious and perfect. She breathed through the burn at the back of her nose. She'd dreamed once of a ring like this when she'd been innocent, and everything had been simpler.

Her hands trembled as she lifted it from the box. Slid it onto her ring finger. 'It fits perfectly.' The gem sat there,

heavy and warm; almost comforting, when there was nothing comforting about this at all. 'How did you manage
that?'

'I knew your ring size once.' Back then she'd never
expected anything like this. While their families were
wealthy, as two runaways they'd had very little. 'I just
sized it up a bit.'

She stilled. Stopped staring at the gorgeous gemstone
on her finger, as if trying to ascribe a meaning to the sapphire it didn't have. Was he saying what she thought he
was trying to say? She looked at him, narrowed her eyes.

'What do you mean by that, Gage?'

In all the time she knew him, she'd only seen him
embarrassed once. The first time had been when they'd
sneaked a kiss at the bottom of the garden on her sev-
enteenth birthday and he'd tried to touch her breast. He
looked a little like that now. Eyes not quite holding her
gaze. A faint stain of colour on his cheekbones. It made
him look young, uncertain. Her heart ached for that simpler time when everything had been perfect and new.

'It means I took into account that you'd be more…' He
cleared his throat. She almost smiled at his discomfort.
'…womanly now.'

He was right. Even though it had happened in her twenties, pregnancy did that to a woman's body. After she'd
overcome the crippling grief of losing her child, losing
every hope for her future, she'd relished the changes in
her body the experience of pregnancy had wrought. The
breasts that had never gone back to their normal size. Her
wider hips. The curves she'd once have starved away in a
quest for perfection, which she now wore like armour, always reminding her of the child who might have been. The
little boy lost to her for ever. She refused to think about
whether he'd have looked like Gage or like her.

She shut her eyes. Controlled the tears that she wouldn't let fall, not here. She coated herself in the icy indifference she'd perfected and opened her eyes again. Hiding from everyone what had happened to her. She looked Gage up and down to make a point but immediately regretted it. Being up close to him only accentuated how much he'd changed from a lean twenty-three-year-old to a vital man of thirty.

'Yes. We've all grown and sized up a bit.'

His nostrils flared. Gage looked down at the ring on her finger. A kind of heat burned in his eyes, which seemed even bluer than before. It slid through her like a jolt of spirits.

'Do you like it?' His voice was softer. He said it like he almost cared what she thought.

'I adore it,' she whispered, and he looked at her with the faintest of smiles teasing at the corner of his mouth. Vulnerability here was a mistake. She'd allowed herself that weakness once but now he'd wield it against her. She hardened her heart and her voice. 'It suits the narrative you're trying to fabricate perfectly.'

That banked heat in his eyes bled away till all that was left was a cold, unfathomable blue. Almost like he couldn't believe they'd had a civil conversation. He stood and she couldn't help but snatch a fleeting glimpse of the tight pull over the fly of his trousers, the unmistakeable bulge there. Heat rose from her throat to her face as he tugged his suit jacket closed and buttoned it, hiding the evidence of his arousal from view. The realisation that she might still affect him thrummed through her, potent and intoxicating. She could have moaned at the thought of it. How he tasted, how he smelled. Those memories didn't fade either, no matter how many times she tried to file them firmly in the annals of her past.

'It's a long flight. There's a bedroom down the back.

You look tired. While it suits my narrative to have the world think I'm exhausting you with hours of lovemaking every night, you might not want the dark rings under your eyes for the inevitable pictures.'

She responded with a tight smile as he gave with one hand and took away with the other. She'd asked for it, and he'd delivered. Did he know how much he still affected her too? Did he care?

'I might just do that.' At least it would get her away from him, from this shimmering attraction that zapped through her. That made her crave things she couldn't have. Because that's what exhausted her every night. The lack of sleep, being woken by dreams of their bodies intertwined. His hands all over her skin. Exploring, probing. Those midnight fantasies were like an endless torment. 'Thank you for your concern.'

'I'm not concerned, *cher*,' he said as he turned and began to walk towards the cockpit again. 'I really don't give a damn about you at all.'

As she sat back in her seat, crushed under the emotional weight of the engagement ring on her finger, she realised they were both liars.

# CHAPTER THREE

HE SHOULD HAVE allowed Eve to travel alone, but he'd wanted to test himself. To show that she didn't affect him anymore. That he didn't care. Yet those hours on the plane with her were a nightmare because his body cared, the clawing desire for her like an addiction that no drug could fix.

Even when she'd taken herself to the bedroom of the airplane it had ridden him hard—the need to open the door, slide onto the bed with her, see where it led. He'd lost control and had almost embarrassed himself after he'd given her that infernal engagement ring. Why the hell was he interested in what she thought of it? And yet the look on her face as her eyes had lit up, as she'd stared at the perfect gem on her finger... One of a kind. It had warmed something inside him.

He'd told her he didn't give a damn, and that was the truth. He didn't care, not even when he'd stood and she'd looked at him like her favourite kind of candy. None of that mattered. She was a means to an end. And then he'd end it. Redeem his family name, take Caron Investments and conquer the damned world. Move on with his life and finally be free of her.

To hell with his unruly hormones.

The car ride ahead of them now they'd landed was

around an hour. But he was an adult and could survive at least that long. Gage grabbed his tablet from his brief-case and scrolled through some emails—tried to read a few financial reports—but his concentration kept wander-ing back to Eve with every elegant move she made, from checking her phone to reapplying her lip gloss or merely crossing her long, slender legs. His heart began racing in a thready, excited kind of rhythm like he'd been for a damned run without the benefits of taking any exercise.

Why hadn't he hired a helicopter to fly them the dis-tance? But that would have been excessive. He understood his position of privilege in the world based on luck of birth and tried not to abuse it. Though right now he wished he wasn't trapped in this ever-shrinking space with her.

After not nearly enough time and yet far too much, she looked out the window and frowned.

'We should be there now. Aren't we going in the wrong direction?'

'And where should we be?'

'Nice.'

'That's where we're meeting Greta for dinner, but that's not where we're staying.'

He went back to work, numbers swimming as her scent filled his head. Something fresh and sweet and floral. Every time he saw damned flowers, smelled flowers, he thought of her. So he wouldn't have them in his offices or any of his homes, no matter how hard his staff tried to en-courage him, because when he'd first spied Eve from his vantage point in the old magnolia tree she'd been clutching a handful of blooms and looking like the mythical fairy at the bottom of the garden.

He'd never forgotten that first glimpse of her, he would probably remember it till his dying day. How innocent life had seemed then…

'Earth to Gage. Some communication would be nice.' He realised he'd zoned out and gritted his teeth. Going mad as a result of this endeavour wasn't his plan, but much more time with Eve and he might totally lose his mind. He looked at her as she worried her lower lip. He wanted to slide his mouth over hers, ease the redness her perfect white teeth had left. Kiss her till they both forgot who they were.

Time to wrest back some control of this situation, let Eve know where she really stood in the hierarchy of things.

'My secretary no doubt advised you of our itinerary. Other than that, I'll inform you of anything I believe is important.'

'I see.' Her eyes narrowed, the watery blue of them darkened to something wilder, like the Gulf in a storm. 'You say jump and I ask how high. Is that how this is supposed to work?'

'You're getting the picture.'

'No, I'm not. You may be on your way to owning Knight, but I'm not some young thing you can push around. It doesn't mean you own *me*.'

The freeze of those words chilled his veins. He hadn't pushed her around when they'd been together. She'd wanted what he did, he was sure of it. But her words echoed every lie told about him. He couldn't let them go unanswered.

'What the hell are you trying to say?' That chill started cracking under the banked heat of his anger, always simmering just below the surface.

'I accept you'll never like me. You can hate me for all I care. But just because this ring is on my finger...' she waved her hand in front of his face '...it doesn't mean I have to accept you being any less than the gentleman your mother raised you to be.'

The desire to be a gentleman, to be a good man by any

measure, had almost been wrung out of him years before. When he'd been beaten by her father and his henchmen, cuffed by the police, thrown in a cell, all for having the *temerity* to love the woman sitting in front of him. Wanting to *protect* her. He'd taken the beating, accepted the scars on his face and his soul for their love. Had kept his mouth shut as a *gentleman* who'd made promises would, and it meant nothing. 'And this assessment of proper conduct comes from who? You? Shouldn't a *lady* keep her promises, Eve?'

'It's a lady's prerogative to change her mind. Let's just say we owe each other nothing but civility. We're trying to pretend to have rekindled a great love. People will notice your barely concealed contempt of me. So let's start over. Gage, I'd like to know where we're going.'

Straight to hell was where he was headed. Right now the colour ran high on her cheeks, making her vibrant, captivating. Incomparable in too many ways he refused to think about. He hated that he noticed this, how being round her made him feel more alive than he'd felt in years. As if he'd been in a torpor and all it took was Eve to awaken him. Because all he could think about now was how passionate she looked when she was angry, and how that flush on her cheeks reminded him of the colour that bloomed when she came.

But there was no room for those thoughts here, no matter how tempting they were, whispering seductively in his ear the things he'd like to do with her. France was all about work. The perfect start to his quest for redemption in the eyes of the world.

'Funny that you should ask, Eve. We're going to Grasse to stay at your flower farm. Since we're talking about rationalising the business, I thought it was good place to start.'

All that beautiful colour drained from her cheeks. He

should have felt a spike of triumph, but instead he felt…
*less*. Like a villain of some sort. But he steeled himself.
It didn't matter. He'd been unjustly cast as some type of
scoundrel for so many years he may as well wear the title
with pride.

Eve didn't say anything. She dragged a tablet from the
odd little yellow suitcase that she resolutely refused to re-
linquish even to his driver and which now sat at her feet. It
looked like it had seen better days or a great deal of travel.
He wondered at her keeping it when she was a woman who
could afford a luxury brand. She was quite secretive about
what it contained, manoeuvring the latch to make sure he
couldn't see inside. In the brief glimpse he had, it looked
like it was filled with old papers.

She tapped away with a kind of fury on the retrieved
device, stabbing at the screen as she worked intently on
something until they pulled into the property. As they
drove through the gate and down the long gravel drive
she looked up, out the window. Something on her face
smoothed out. He hadn't realised that the merest of frowns
had been marring her brow most of the time since he'd seen
her again, until he looked at Eve now. A gentle smile tilted
the corners of her mouth. A look of happiness, a quiet joy.

She used to look at him like that, once. As if he were her
safe place, her…home. Now he'd been replaced by this, a
property, not a person. He didn't know what stung more.

The car pulled up in front of a quaint, two-storey French
farm cottage of rustic stone overlooking fields of flowers.
The pink of what he assumed were roses, the purple of
lavender. He got out of the car and Eve followed, carrying her handbag and clutching the small suitcase tightly
in her right hand. He reached into his pocket for the key
handed to them by their driver at the beginning of the journey, but Eve was ahead of him with her own. She opened

the front door and walked inside. It was a clear reminder to him that she believed this place to be hers.

'I trust this meets your approval,' Eve said, her voice clipped and sharp. She was dressed for business and he couldn't help admire the perfect fit of her deep blue pants as they moulded to her backside with every step. The cut of her jacket's waist that accentuated rather than detracted from her figure.

He followed the tap of her heels on the stone floor through a receiving room to the back of the house where French doors opened onto a patio, overlooking a lap pool and more flowers. Sheer curtains billowed in the gentle breeze. The rooms were full of provincial French furniture, all wood and warmth. Paintings of flowers and landscapes adorned the walls.

The cottage was unlike any of the properties he owned, which were mere places he laid his head. They held about as much attachment to him as a hotel, kitted out by interior designers in cool greys, granite and chrome. This space, as exquisite as the décor was, looked like a home.

'It's beautiful,' he said. That was nothing less than the truth, when there'd been too little truth between them. 'You always wanted somewhere like this.'

Eve turned, put her bags on a table, its warm wood burnished by care and age.

'Don't forget. So did you.'

It was the type of home that they'd talked about owning together when their hopes and dreams had seemed to coalesce. But she hadn't wanted that future with him, and he'd been too blissfully ignorant being yanked around by the chain of his misplaced adoration to see it. It was a reminder. They didn't need each other. Once he'd thought that inconceivable but now he realised everything he'd done had been done in spite of her. He'd reached the pinnacle on his own.

She walked outside and leaned on the balustrade overlooking the sparkling water of the pool below and the beauty of the view beyond. In every direction were flowers, the scent of them lingering sublimely in the air. It all smelled like her—of gardens, of the life he'd expected to have. He stood back a little, not wanting to get too close. The warmth of the French afternoon sank into his skin and bones, unknotting him in ways he didn't want to contemplate. Everything here spoke of opportunities lost and fresh ones waiting to be plucked. He shrugged out of his jacket. Began unravelling in a way all too pleasurable to be safe, especially with her.

'You should have told me we were coming to Grasse,' she said, looking down at the azure water below her. 'I didn't bring anything to swim in.'

'I'm sure that doesn't matter here. It looks secluded enough.'

The words were out of his mouth before he could think. He imagined her in the glorious pool, naked, sliding through the water. Him right there with her, their bodies slipping against each other... Eve shot him a look over her shoulder, her cheeks tinged pink. She pushed herself off the railing and walked towards him, her lips slightly parted. Her pupils were big and dark in the pale blue of her eyes. It wouldn't take much to drop his head. Put his lips against hers. Kiss her like he had all those years ago. The need for it gripped him hard. This was a test as to whether he could finally overcome this craving for her. He hesitated then took a step back, rather than plunging his hands into the thick curls of her hair and dragging her against him.

'As tempting as all that sounds,' she said, stepping close and invading his personal space with a wicked tilt of her lips, 'I might just take a car to Nice and buy myself a bikini.'

She strolled through the doors into the house with her hips swaying in a kind of hypnotic rhythm and the thought of her in any of the boutiques, trying on their skimpy swimwear, filled his head with visions he was sure even a hundred laps in a cold pool wouldn't extinguish.

Eve adjusted the ties at the hips of the yellow and blue-two piece she'd found in Nice. She hadn't meant to purchase something so daring with its vibrant patches of fabric and alluring bows at the side, but she'd spent most of her life trying to stay safe and she was sick of it.

There was a fire in her blood that wouldn't be extinguished, not with Gage in *her* house, invading the space she'd once called her own. Fear gnawed at her stomach and she pressed her hand over the ache there. He'd brought her here for a reason and if revenge was that reason, he couldn't have designed a much better punishment than to take this place away from her. The one thing in her life she'd claimed for herself. She might not own it all, but she'd be damned if she would lose it without a pitched battle.

Eve checked herself in the mirror to make sure her stretch marks were mostly hidden. They'd never worried her before, the pale silvery lines being a reminder of what she could survive. She especially needed that reminder right now because a fight was coming. She couldn't hear Gage around so he was probably working on the press release for the announcement of their engagement, or planning some other kind of ordeal for her. One or the other, they were both the same right now, so to hell with it and with him.

She grabbed a floaty wrap that matched the sun and sea tones of her swimwear and made her way to the pool.

As she stepped out onto the patio she heard a splash. Eve looked over the balcony to see Gage's powerful form striking out in freestyle. Wearing tight black swimming trunks and gleaming bronze in the afternoon, the shimmering water sluiced from his back, his muscles rippling as he powered down the length of the pool, executed a perfect turn and powered back to the other end. Again and again. It was mesmerising, seeing him slice through the water, each stroke as hard and driven as the man himself.

It was all she could do not to sashay down there in her provocative bikini and slip into the pool with him. If this had been a grand affair, she would have. Would have stripped the little scraps of fabric from her body with a deft pull of a few ties and pressed herself into him. He'd probably reject her if she tried that now his level of disdain so strong it almost caused her physical pain to experience it.

No matter how strong the desire that flooded her with need, she wouldn't put herself in harm's way because of misplaced memories of a youthful love that they'd have outgrown had they stayed together. It was only because they'd parted that it had achieved such a mythic status in her own mind.

Anyhow, what did she know about seduction? Gage was her first and her only. She'd tried dating in the years after they'd broken up. Had tried to kiss another man but it had made her skin crawl. She'd resigned herself long ago to there being only one man her body wanted. Unlucky for her he was the wrong man. A man who hated her.

She turned her back on the tantalising view and instead found a spot in the shade on a sun lounge. Throwing on her sunglasses, she breathed in the warm, scented air and stared up at the flawless blue sky. The rhythmic splashing from the pool below lulled her. Whenever the world became too much, this was where she came. She'd never wanted to take over the family business. It had been her father's demand, drilled into her when the reality that he'd never have the son he wanted had hit home.

This, growing things, had always been her dream. To one day own the farm outright, move here and immerse her life in the soil and the scents of what she grew. Now it was possible that Gage had other ideas. That man did everything for a reason, and she wasn't sure of the reason why he'd elected to stay here in *her* home rather than in Nice proper.

As she ran through the possibilities, Gage appeared, towel lashed around his waist. His hair was rough dried and unruly. Drops of water sprinkled across his torso, sparkling in the sunlight like dew on petals in the morning. Dripping down his pectorals. Sliding over the ridges of his abdomen. Balmy heat bled over her, settling low and intoxicating. A delicious ache was building between her thighs. Her nipples tightened and she hoped evidence of her arousal was hidden by her wrap. He stopped when he saw her.

He made such an imposing picture, framed by the blue sky. His eyes a darker colour, boring into her. After the exercise his breathing was heavy, the muscles of his biceps and pectorals firm and defined. Would he look like that if he loomed over her now in bed? Naked, breathing heavily with passion and not exercise. A shiver of pleasure tripped through her and she tightened her wrap a little further, feeling weirdly exposed lying there, as if spread out for his pleasure alone.

And she had to say something, not just sit and stare like the fool she was, brain turned to mush by his hard, perfect body.

'Enjoy your swim?'

He ran his hands through his hair and droplets of water

sprinkled the ground. 'Did some laps. I see you bought a bikini.'

His gaze drifted down her body to her bare legs, paused for a moment before coming back to her face. The heat of it was as sure as the caress of his fingers. A drop of water slid from the side of his nose to his lips. He licked it off. That, and the incendiary burn in his eyes, fired up the devil in her.

'I thought it was better than skinny dipping, since that wouldn't have been very businesslike of me, which is why we're here after all.'

'And yet neither of us is dressed for work right now.' Gage's voice was the rough burr of a sun-dried towel over her skin.

'I'm surprised you're not hard at it, drafting a press release on our engagement. I see the tasty morsel of gossip that you're off the marriage market hasn't hit the press yet.'

He cocked his head. 'Still keeping tabs on me?'

That wasn't far from the truth. For years she'd taunted herself with every alert about him. His success, failures—though there had been very few of those—the women…not as many as she thought she might see, but even one woman on his arm who wasn't her was too many. A constant reminder of what she'd lost, even though she'd convinced herself they wouldn't have lasted the distance.

No. Not lost. Given away because there had been no alternatives. She needed to remember there was a price she'd paid for loving him back then, and that was letting him go.

'It pays to know your enemies. And keep them close.' She crossed her legs and Gage watched the movement, his eyes darkening.

'So, now I'm your enemy, *cher*?' His voice was quiet, a mere whisper in the breeze. Their eyes locked. There was a heat in his, like a flash of sunshine on water.

'You tell me.'

'Perhaps you're not keeping me close enough.'

'Are we talking business or pleasure here?'

Silence between them stretched for a heartbeat. A moment in which hers fluttered in anticipation of his answer.

'Business, of course.'

Her shoulders slumped a fraction. No, she wasn't disappointed. Not at all. It was relief she felt. Blissful relief.

'No rest for the wicked, then,' she said. Except he didn't look wicked, he looked angelic, standing there half-naked, his hair drying in the warm breeze to the glorious blond gossip magazines raved about. Only soaring wings and a blazing halo could complete the picture.

Gage Caron. Golden Boy. Voted USA's most eligible bachelor three years running.

He smirked and she wanted to wipe that look of disdain from his beautiful face.

'No rest for you, at least.'

His words made her feel reckless when faced with all this potent masculinity. And she didn't care that they were enemies or that he loathed her. All she cared about was showing Gage that he might be a little affected by her, too. So she eased out of her reclined position, stood and took a few steps towards him.

'All work and no play makes Gage a dull boy.'

Another step and the pupils in his fathomless eyes blew wide as she let the front of her wrap fall open. His gaze dropped to the slice of body it showed.

'You wanna play, *cher*?'

His voice was like midnight and sin and she desperately wanted to ignore caution and sell her soul to him, if only for the afternoon. Instead, she slid her wrap from her body. Tossed it behind her onto the chair she'd just left. She was close to him now and his eyes burned on her, his nostrils flaring, jaw clenched hard. Part of her was gratified she could still do this to him, that despite everything there wasn't indifference but an incendiary desire that threatened to consume them both.

It was her turn now to look him up and down. Long and slow. The bulge behind his towel was unmistakable. The power of that roared through her, making her feel as wicked as he accused her of being. If that's what he thought, that's what he'd get. She could almost feel herself sprouting horns and a tail.

Eve invaded his space, smiling as his fists clenched hard at his sides. She dropped her voice to as low and sexy as she could make it. For a moment she held his gaze. His lips parted, like he needed extra air too.

'Oh, sugar,' she said, her voice dripping sweetness as she pointedly stared at the impressive evidence of the arousal there was no way he could hide, and drifted her fingers over the knot on his towel. 'I'm going for a swim. Looks like you'll have to play on your own.'

She revelled in the hitch of his breath as she brushed past and sauntered to the pool.

# CHAPTER FOUR

GAGE FOUGHT TO overcome his desire for Eve, but he hadn't figured that being around her in person was *very* different from his distant memories. This morning he'd woken gripping himself hard after a night when his sleep had been plagued with images of her, his dreams and feverish desire bursting to life in full colour.

The feel of her as she'd brushed past him near the pool and his skin had become electric. The trace of her fingers over the knot of his towel that had caused his blood pressure to spike to near coronary levels. Now he was back to seven years ago when his need was fresh and the pain of unrequited adoration unbearable.

She was toying with him and he wouldn't let her get away with it. He'd recognized something when his mind had finally clicked back into gear yesterday. When he'd stopped salivating over her smooth skin on display in that magnificent bikini that had exposed much yet covered more. An item specifically designed to tease and tempt. Yes, once he'd stopped lusting after all that pale skin, elegant curves and her perfect breasts he'd noticed a few things as she'd stood so very close to him. The delicate flush of her cheeks, the way her nipples had pressed like hard knots against the fabric of her bikini top. Irrefutable signs she'd wanted him too.

What if he'd wrapped his arms round her waist, drawn her close? Plundered that pink, pouting mouth of hers. Laid her out on one of the sun lounges and buried himself inside her till she'd screamed his name.

She'd screamed his name long ago. He could get her to do it again.

Gage raked his hands through his hair. Took a long mouthful of hot coffee to try and jolt some sense into himself. Now was not the time or the place. He had to get his head on straight. Today they were talking Knight Enterprises and he'd been picking that company apart piece by rotten piece. There were aspects which were useful to him. As for the rest, it could go. Eve would soon learn that this was no game, and he wasn't to be played.

'Good morning.' Eve strolled into the room, head high, a picture of confidence misplaced. She wandered over to the sideboard where a continental breakfast had been laid out, grabbed a large, white bread roll and poured herself a coffee.

Black. One sugar. He'd never forgotten.

She sat to the side of him. This morning she was dressed in elegant, slim-fitting black trousers and a crisp, white shirt, with her hair pulled back into a messy bun. She looked cool, businesslike, ready to do battle. Nothing like the pampered trust-fund princess he knew her to be. Her engagement ring glittered under the lights each time she moved her hand. Something hot, potent and possessive slid through him at the sight of it there.

*Mine.*

Absurd. Seven years ago he might have been desperate to see his ring on her finger. Not now.

'You don't have to wear it.' He nodded at the bright jewel. 'Not here, in the house.'

It did something to his equilibrium. Better she have it

on only when necessary, which would be almost never, given that it was only for show.

She looked down at the twinkling gemstones. Splayed her fingers a little. Turned her hand so they caught the light. 'It feels safer here. I'd be scared to leave it somewhere, like the bedside drawer.'

Warmth kindled low in his gut. It felt good to watch her admiring it. When he'd seen it on a tray of jewels presented for his selection, it had immediately caught his eye and he'd only thought of her.

*Yes. Mine.*

That damned insistent voice. He ignored it. She wasn't his. She never had been and never would be. He wouldn't be fooled again, by anyone. He wasn't that young man anymore, full of hope for the future, desperately in love and made stupid by it. He'd *never* allow himself to be that man again and wouldn't waste more thought on what might have been.

'How was your swim yesterday?' he asked.

She took a sip of her dark coffee. Closed her eyes for a brief second in pleasure. Her lip gloss left a perfect pink stencil on the white porcelain and he wondered whether, if he kissed her, she'd taste like strawberries.

'Invigorating. How did you sleep last night?'

His blood rushed south as those dark, erotic dreams flickered in the back reaches of his consciousness. Not well at all. He'd ached for her the whole night. Lying naked in bed as he always did. The sheets torture against his overly sensitive skin. He'd never let her know.

'Perfectly. And you?'

'To be honest, I had a little difficulty. Until I…took things in hand. If you're ever having trouble sleeping, you should try it too.'

His mouth dried. Visions of her lying naked. Thinking

of him. Touching herself and… He shut the heated thoughts down. Poured cold water on them. 'Try what?'

His voice sounded too rough and raw. He took another mouthful of coffee.

'Warm milk and honey, with a shot of bourbon.' Her lips turned up in a sneaky smile. 'Always works for me.'

She was playing him like a finely tuned instrument. No more. His desire for her was something he *would* control. He'd done it in the past. Having her here with him was the ultimate test and he'd win, get his deal done and move on. But how would it feel to turn the tables on her for once? Make her crave him like some addiction. Perhaps he could give her a small taste. He'd have her panting and begging and wanting him. He was older now. Wiser. More experienced than he'd been as a callow youth in his twenties. He knew how to push her buttons and push them he would, with immense satisfaction.

But that could come later. Pleasure would wait for now. He didn't want anything she didn't want to give. That was the triumph for him. Her desire. Her capitulation. Her *needing* him. It made the anticipation of what might come all the sweeter.

He finished his coffee, moved his breakfast plate aside. There were more important things at hand, for now at least. He was sure she wouldn't like what he had to say.

'We need to talk.'

'Ooh. Sounds serious.' Eve gave an exaggerated sigh. 'I suppose it's about business again. Remember what I said about you becoming dull.'

He opened his tablet and clicked on a file full of spreadsheets. 'About the French arm of Knight. I can email you—'

'I have all I need here.' She reached down, grabbed a tablet of her own and placed it on the table. 'But for this discussion I need some fortification.'

She buttered a fluffy white roll then slathered it in strawberry jam. Bit into it and slowly ate her mouthful while she swiped her finger over her screen, pulling up some documents as well. 'Go ahead.'

Her dismissiveness niggled at him like a stone in his shoe. He tried to ignore it. She was baiting him, and he wouldn't fall into that trap, not now.

'It's not doing as badly as the US business but there are a few areas of concern.'

Eve glared at him. 'We're doing far better than that and holding our own. Turning a profit.'

'You could do more.' He looked at the financials he had before him. He might have been more aggressive in his approach to some acquisitions, but the decisions that had been made had been sound, if not on the conservative side. 'The vineyard goes.'

She stared at him for a moment and he waited for the argument to come. Instead, she nodded. 'Fine. Next?'

That was too easy, and Gage was deeply suspicious of anything that came too easily to him. He expected more of a fight from her, on all things. 'You don't want to ask me why?'

A smirk played at the corners of her mouth. 'Why, sugar, you're my fiancé. I want to keep you happy. You should be pleased.'

He loathed it when she called him *sugar*. Gage narrowed his eyes. 'Are you treating any of this seriously?'

She narrowed her eyes right back at him. 'Deathly.'

'Then prove it.'

'You hold my life and my business in your hands and can do what you want.' Eve fiddled with the engagement ring on her finger. 'Will anything I say make a difference?'

'It might. I'm not an ogre.'

'I'll hold you to that the next time you behave like one.'

She took another bite of her roll. Chewed deliberately. Washed it down with more coffee. 'The reasons for selling the vineyard are twofold. First is that it was my father's folly. You talked about vanity projects. This was one. Second, I'm betting Greta Bonitz wants a vineyard and that you want to sell Knight's to her.'

Gage sat back in his chair. What she thought about her father surprised him, because that's exactly what the vineyard was. As for the rest… 'Why do you think Greta Bonitz wants a vineyard?'

That little kernel of information shouldn't have been widely known. He had it because he'd been discussing it with Frau Bonitz before she'd turned cold on him.

'When you told me you were keen on doing business with her, I started researching. In an article a year ago she talked about honeymooning with her husband in Provence when they were young. Stomping the grapes at a winery. How it was such a fond memory. It got me thinking.' Eve finished off her breakfast. Drained her coffee.

'About?'

'How, given her husband's recent passing, she might want to hang onto those memories a little harder. Since she can't have him to share them with, maybe a vineyard in Provence might do.' Her voice was quiet and she stared out the French doors of the dining room to the view beyond. Still twisting the engagement ring like it irritated her.

As the silence stretched, he began to feel like there were things unspoken, subtext he couldn't translate. Eve got up from the table, walked to the coffee pot. Her long, lithe legs being encased in conservative black trousers in a strange way made her all the more tempting. A narrow waist he'd once loved to span with his hands. His pulse kicked up a notch. She turned and waggled her cup at him. He'd already had two cups this morning, which was probably the reason his heart rate was being unruly. Not the thoughts of how she felt in his arms, how he might try to get her back there. He shook his head as she poured another for herself.

'So, am I right?' she asked as she came back to the table with a full cup.

'Surprisingly, you are.'

She straightened in her chair, put down her cup and planted her hands flat on the table. 'There's no surprise about it at all. Do you have any idea what it was like, being a woman in her early twenties and given the responsibility of running a company without training?'

'You seem to have forgotten my involvement in Caron after college.'

'You had your father, who no doubt supported you. I had *nothing*. I might have topped my business degree at the Sorbonne, but I'd been thrown the French company as a punishment. Sent to a place I couldn't do much damage with every expectation I'd fail and be put in my place. I've had to work harder and be more prepared than anyone to get the board to listen to me. Even then it was a battle. Every day.'

Her breathing was hard, the colour high on her cheeks. A fight in her eyes, which were as hard and cold as blue diamonds. No society princess anywhere to be seen, and not the soft, sweet girl he'd known either. She was enthralling like this. He wanted to unpick all the complicated knots in her and see her unravel.

'I was *never* going to fail, and I didn't. So, Gage, what else have you got to throw at me? Because I'm ready for it.'

Her voice was as sharp as a prick of guilt. He looked at the long and mundane list on the computer of things that needed to change and back at her.

She ran her finger over a glob of jam on her plate, scooping it up and bringing it to her lips. His mouth dried.

Memories assailed him of years ago. Of Eve on her knees in front of him. The biting pleasure even though neither of them had really known what they were doing. Well, he knew exactly what he was doing now. He'd have her on her knees soon enough. Perhaps he already did. That warm slide of pleasure through his veins was satisfaction. Nothing more.

'Here. The flower farm.'

She'd always loved growing things. Hanging around with the gardener, who'd indulged her. When they'd talked of the houses they'd own, her criteria had always been one surrounded by gardens, where the climate was right so she could grow roses. He'd planned to buy her fields of them when he could afford it. Instead she'd bought her own.

She stiffened. 'No. It's *mine*. Purchased with my own money.'

'Spent your trust fund, *cher*?'

'I could spend it in any way I saw fit and I did. On something just for me for once.'

As if he hadn't been enough, but history had shown him he hadn't been. It galled him that this was the symbol of her treachery. Well, she'd spent her money on what she'd wanted and now she'd have to deal with the consequences.

'It's not quite yours. There's a not so small matter of the loan Knight gave to support the purchase because you didn't have enough yourself. It's a liability the company doesn't need. Debts can be called in and this one should be because, like your father, you have a vanity project.'

'If you cared to ask, the farm is a business that's holding its own. You know it's making repayments to Knight on time, with interest. There's no vanity here. But this has nothing to do with how well it's doing or not.' Her hands clenched into tight fists on the tablecloth. Her lips a thin, taut line. Pale blue eyes burning like a gas flame. There was something enticing about her anger. He wanted to take it and channel it. Let it explode and consume them.

But he wouldn't fall into the trap that was Eve Chevalier.

Instead, he crossed his arms and settled back for the fight to come, the fight he'd been waiting for. 'What's it to do with, then?'

She stood and began pacing the room. Bristling with a tight and furious kind of energy. Her accent broadened then. Nothing like the smooth tones she'd obviously cultivated, those of a stateless world traveller. Hers was now a curious mix of Southern belle and French *ingénue*. The exotic sound of it raked down his spine as surely as her neat fingernails would.

'Revenge. Been there. Done that. Won't do it again. You don't care how well the business is performing, you only care that it's important to me so you can punish me with it, which is petty.' She wheeled round and stopped, her eyes shining brightly as if there were tears there. Was she going to cry over this? Something sharp and painful stabbed in his chest. He rubbed at the spot. 'If there's anyone in this room like my father, it's you.'

'I'm *nothing* like your damned father.' He would not be compared to that man, ever. In response, she gave a sharp, bitter laugh.

'You've decided that because this place is mine, you're going to take it away. So tell me, how aren't you like my father? What is this, if not spite? Because, *sugar*, it sure isn't about business, since you know nothing about mine.'

He gritted his teeth, wanted to stand, face her and shout to the room that he was better than Hugo Chevalier. He'd proved it, in every way. Especially now, by winning. Except... Eve looked upset. The colour was high on her cheeks. Breathing hard. The tightness round her eyes that

still sparkled too brightly. He didn't make a habit of up-
setting women. He'd been taught better by both parents.

But more than that, if he broke through the anger, the
emotion, there were things Eve said that didn't add up. Because she'd been given everything by her family. Money,
security, running the French business. If there had been
the expectation she wouldn't succeed, it had still been an
opportunity some would almost kill for. Even then, she
felt she'd lost…

'What did your daddy take away from you, Eve?'

Something flashed across her face as if she was stricken,
and then melted away so fast he might have been mistaken.
She walked to the French doors overlooking the flower
fields and pulled the gauzy curtains aside as she stared
at the view.

'That's not important anymore. This place is.' She worried at her lower lip with her teeth. 'I want to stop dwelling
on the past and look forward. So, are you going to call in
the debt? If so, I need time to re-finance.'

He heard the message loud and clear. He was the past,
and that's the box she'd locked him into, but today there
was still a niggle of something he couldn't put his finger
on. Something he'd missed. Since Eve, he'd honed his ob-
servational abilities because he wasn't going to be blind-
sided by anything ever again. He'd get to the bottom of
this, sooner rather than later.

'What if I was the bank? How would you sell it to *me*?'
He didn't know why he was asking these things. Maybe
he could indulge her, maybe he was going soft, maybe if
the business stacked up…

'What did you say?'

She turned around slowly, like she didn't believe he
could be reasonable and was waiting for the trick in his

words. He didn't like that at all and didn't know why it mattered to him so much.

'Talk to me about your flowers.'

Even if this was the smallest of chances, she'd take it. She'd spent most of the night working on a proposal that she'd outlined in the car on the way from the airport the minute Gage had told her they were coming here. This was her one shot at saving what she'd fought so hard for. She strode to the table and turned her tablet to him. 'It's in here. Prove to me this is just business.'

He took the device and read. What she'd prepared was rougher than she'd like. There'd been little time to perfect it and too many emotions roiling around for it all to be cold, hard numbers and facts, but it would have to do. And still she had more, a snippet of information that she hoped would show Gage the possibilities. Excite him as much as it excited her.

He worked through what she'd done, scrolling through the document, his expression giving nothing away. She became transfixed by his hands. The way the veins stood out as an elegant cording under his skin. The strength she knew they held, cradling the device like it was something precious. His perfect fingers with their blunt, square nails shifting, moving back, forward. Sliding over her screen in the same gentle way he'd used to stroke her skin. Stopping...

He'd stopped. She swallowed down the knot tightening in her throat and sat at the table as Gage looked up. His eyes narrowed slightly, as if assessing her. The business was sound, the farmhouse rented most of the time, it was paying its way and its bills. These were things she knew a man like Gage would be looking for. Yet she couldn't get a read on his thoughts when he looked at her like he was trying to peer inside her.

'When did you prepare this?'

'Last night. I told you I couldn't sleep.'

Everything stopped at that moment. Even the birds outside seemed to have fallen silent, the breeze dropped. Like the world was holding its breath for her.

'Well done.'

The warmth of that small praise flooded over her, like the first brush of morning sun on her skin. No one had ever thanked her for her efforts or the job she did. Too many wanted to tear her down, whispering about how she'd been handed her position by her daddy, rather than earning it. No one knew the price she'd paid to be here, what she'd lost in the process. How much harder she'd had to work than anyone around her.

'But,' he went on, and she stilled. Her heart rate spiked. There was always a caveat, a 'but', a sting in every tail. 'There's more, isn't there? What aren't you telling me?'

Of all the things she'd read about Gage, there was one thing she should never have forgotten, that part of his skill in business was due to his freakish instinct. His ability to mine the secrets no one else could. He was right about there being more, but she could never let him have all of her secrets. She'd held them too close, for too long, until they'd become part of her. The burden she always carried.

'Why do you think there's more?'

'This document…' He motioned towards her tablet now lying on the table. 'It shows an excitement, a passion. Sure, the business is holding its own, but there's nothing here to be passionate about.'

Their eyes locked. A glorious heat settled in her belly then unthreaded and curled its way through her. The air seemed electric with possibilities, each one tempting but as unattainable as the other. Her passions had stopped being about a person long ago and had become about the little things accessible to her day to day. The smell of a rose, the cool breeze brushing sun-warmed skin, the sweet burst of a chunk of wild strawberry in this morning's jam. But now...

There was so much she could be passionate about here, if she allowed it. The hint of chest behind Gage's open-necked shirt, the strength of his tanned forearms sprinkled with golden hair, the pull of crisp cotton over muscular shoulders. All of that had inflamed her passions once, and it would be so easy for her to allow it to be so again. She eased her thoughts back to safer ground. Away from sliding her hands over those broad shoulders, pressing her lips to the pulse on his neck, letting him wrap his arms tightly around her...

Thoughts that would take her nowhere good. She ignored their allure.

'We've been trying to grow an enhanced rose. One with slightly different notes in the scent. Last year a bush showed promise so we cultivated a field of them and invited a few parfumiers here. Let their best noses smell it.' She paused, allowed the anticipation to build because there was joy in this, for her at least. Something she'd worked hard for and achieved on her own. And there was a tiny nugget of hope inside that people would be *proud* of her achievements. That Gage might be proud. A small thrill skittered through her at making him wait. Making him interested in what she had to say. Enticing him.

As the silence stretched, he raised an eyebrow and she relented. 'It started a bidding war for exclusive access. We're still in negotiations, but people are willing to pay a lot. It's—'

'Exciting' Gage finished the sentence, looking at her over steepled fingers. 'And an achievement.'

What she'd dreamed of when her dreams of having Gage had died.

Warmth coursed over her, heat rising to her cheeks. She must look as pink as the roses in her field right now. Here was a chance. It might be tiny, but it was a chance nonetheless.

'What are you saying?' Her words might have been a little too urgent, her voice a little too breathy, but she didn't care.

The corner of his mouth quirked up in something of a smile, which looked a bit triumphant for her liking, but if this was a lifeline, she was taking it.

'I'm not bloody-minded about the process. If a business stands up to scrutiny, it stays. The farm does. For now.'

The whole of her unwound, as his words sank in. Eve couldn't help the smile that broke out on her face. In business she'd learned to hide her emotions, but she didn't care about that now—this was something to celebrate. She walked over to where he sat, and he turned in his chair to face her. He could still take her breath away with those eyes of his, as perfect as a cloudless summer day. Her heart fluttered a few silly beats, as it always did when he was near. Around him she reacted like a girl barely out of her teens. He tilted his head back to look up at her.

'Thank you,' she said. All her tension seeped away, and something else entirely overtook it. A sensation so unfamiliar she'd almost forgotten what it meant. The surge in her pulse, the butterflies in her stomach. The bursting in her chest evidence of true happiness. She'd had so little of it in recent years. At that moment she didn't think too much about what she was doing as she leaned in and kissed him on the cheek, the merest brush. Something entirely platonic. Except the smell of him, all earth and spice, made her linger a bit longer than she should. Maybe she sighed.

Maybe her breath brushed his cheek in a way it shouldn't have before she pulled away. She should move back to her seat, but she didn't.

'My pleasure,' he said. His voice was low and soft, better suited to dimmed lights and late nights than this morning in a breakfast room. And the sensations coursing inside her morphed into something else, something liquid, hot and potent. 'But that's not the type of kiss you'd give your fiancé.'

Her heart picked up its rhythm to something harder and faster. She should be terrified by this, but she wasn't. The anticipation of a coming dare overtook her. 'What do you mean?'

'We're having dinner with Greta Bonitz tonight. Our engagement won't be convincing to her if that's how you act.'

'I thought you were convinced I could fake it?'

'Time to prove it.' He held out his hand, palm up. His voice was a murmur, like a breeze through rose petals. 'Touch me.'

She should back away but his hand was there, and she craved to feel his skin against hers once more. He was right, in public they'd have to hold hands, at least try to look adoring, if this were to work. Maybe, just maybe they could reach some sort of truce here and now. She placed her hand gently in his. He wrapped his fingers round hers, stroking the backs of her knuckles with his thumb. All she wanted to do was close her eyes and give in to the sensation, his warmth, the gentleness of his touch.

'You scared, Eve?'

It was the game they'd played when they'd been kids and had sneaked off to the bottom of their respective gardens to see each other through the vine-covered hole in the wall. She'd always risen to the challenge of that taunt.

Whether it had been climbing trees too high or catching garter snakes, a dare had always been her call to action.

She gazed into the everlasting and perfect blue of his eyes. She could drown in them they were so deep. 'You don't scare me, Gage Caron.'

His pupils were wide and dark, his nostrils flared. The knowledge that she still affected him jolted through her with the hot roar of power. He might be able to destroy her and her business, but she held something too. His desire. She wanted it, to wrest back some control of her own. Then he tugged at her hand. She followed with no resistance, allowing herself to be reeled in. Gage widened his legs so she stood between them, and drew her close with a smile that was all triumph. She swallowed, a pulse thrashing wildly in her throat.

'Who's afraid of the big, bad wolf now, *cher*?'

# CHAPTER FIVE

SHE SHOULD RUN yet all Eve craved was to sink into Gage and take everything that his wicked smile promised. He was all dry heat and the crack and fire of an electrical storm, dangerous and thrilling. She was rooted to the spot, watching him blaze in front of her with a hypnotising energy.

This was a test of her determination. But if he thought the look of him sitting there as sinful as Lucifer would chase her away, he was sorely mistaken. She didn't run anymore. She never would again.

'Sugar, you'll learn that I'm no Little Red Riding Hood,' she said, her voice low and raw in a way that sounded alien to her ears.

'Who are you then?'

She cupped his cheek, traced the smooth, freshly shaven skin as she leaned down, her lips a whisper away from his. Breathing the same breath as if in that moment they shared one life together.

'I'm the woodcutter.'

Eve dropped her lips to his. She'd always marvelled at how soft his mouth was, but something about it caught her off balance today. That the hard man he'd become could have any gentleness left in him. This should stop, but she cupped his face and he slid a hand to her waist and gripped tight as he parted his lips and she followed.

Their tongues touched and she melted into the delicious taste of him, coffee and sweetness, and she could hardly breathe for the memory of it all. Those recollections flooded over her. Of their love, the adoration when everything had been perfect and unassailable. She slid her hands into his hair and gripped hard as he thrust his hands into hers, tugging at the pins that tamed her curls, scattering the infernal metal objects with a clatter on the table-top.

Their mouths clashed and warred and the kiss became a frantic thing with teeth and tongues and desperation. Gage hauled her onto his lap, never breaking contact. She twisted and then straddled him as he dragged her close till there was no space between them.

Years of dreams and desires collided in that one moment. She didn't care what it meant, what he thought of her. Gage had been her one and only. She couldn't contemplate another man touching her after he'd planted his seed during their one night of abandon, after she'd carried and lost their baby. It was too raw and too much and she just wanted to forget. Gage and his body could make her.

She couldn't stop as her hands roved over his shoulders and chest and relearned him, like a road travelled long ago. She worked his buttons with trembling fingers so she could stroke the hot, perfect skin beneath. Rocked on his hardness because he was right there with her, thrusting up as she moved, each movement causing a bright burst of pleasure to explode through her.

One hand released her hair, trailed down her body to her breast. His questing fingers stroked over her nipple. She groaned into his mouth so he plucked at it harder in the way she'd loved as she rode him. He remembered everything that drove her wild and repeated it, their bodies still in perfect tune with each other. Their breaths panted into the room as he grappled with the button of her trousers. Slid the zip down too slowly then eased his hand inside and stroked gently over her underwear.

'More,' she gasped against his lips, and the word was met with a low chuckle and fleeting pressure but not enough. She burned, wanted to tear off her clothes as they itched and prickled her skin. He eased his thumb beneath the waistband of her panties, sliding it with steady pressure over her slick clitoris. It took only moments for the burn to build and twist then explode outwards, her screams of pleasure trapped by their fused mouths. He kept going and the orgasm went on and on, wreaking destruction.

When she'd shuddered for the last time and sagged into him, limp and wrung out, Gage tightened his arms tight around her waist and stood. She barely had the wherewithal to wrap her legs round his waist as he placed her on the table in front of him. Her hands tangled in his hair; his mouth never left hers. Frantic hands grappled with the buttons of her shirt, tugged down the cups of her bra and he dropped his head to her nipple and sucked, torturing her till she writhed against him. She wanted him again, the exquisite emptiness building deep inside.

Gage somehow manhandled her pants down and off her legs. He pulled her forward so that she perched right on the edge of the table. The clink of a belt buckle and the burr of a zip told her they were far from finished and she didn't care. She never wanted this moment to end.

She reached out, craving to feel the heavy, warm silk of him in her hands, and then she took and gripped hard, marvelling at his glorious size and stroking him in the way she remembered he loved. He pulled back, moaned, mouth at her neck, kissing and nipping as a flood of heat built between her legs, aching to her core. He ran his teeth over and along the shell of her ear and the sounds they made were barely human, guttural expressions of need.

He tugged down the straps of her bra, pulled her shirt off her shoulders, trapping her arms, and she arched back, gloriously exposed. Gage's one hand slipped between her legs, fingers probing deep. The other tortured her nipple.

'I don't damn well care anymore,' Gage growled in her ear. It was like the words weren't meant for her, as if he was giving himself permission to take what he wanted. Then he kissed her again, all heat and battle, and she shook as though she was overwhelmed by a fever, with the impending orgasm hanging just out of reach. He pulled her closer or did she guide him? Then his fingers withdrew, leaving her empty and bereft till he notched himself at her entrance. She wrapped her legs around him again, encouraging, drawing him forward with her heels. He entered her with a sharp thrust and a groan. She tensed at the sensation, swift and over-full. It had been years and, no matter how wet she was or how much she wanted this, she couldn't help the gasp that escaped at the size of him. Gage stilled.

'*Cher?*'

It had never been Eve when he'd been inside her.

'A moment,' she whispered. She wanted his hands and his lips and possession, so she didn't have to think about him between her legs, invading her very soul. The short, shallow thrusts that had her panting and wanting even more. She raised her mouth to his, softer this time, gave a languid kiss that he mirrored as he slid in and out in a way she would have said was gentle and loving if it had been seven years earlier. The kindness of him at this moment would be her undoing. She drove her heels into the back of his thighs and tried to spur him on to something harder, less tender.

'Just...*take* me,' she said as she nipped at his collar bone.

'No.'

He slowed right down then, rocked into her, and she thought she'd go mad. He threaded his hand into her loose hair, wrapped its unruly length around his fist and eased her head back, her neck bared to him. Her breasts thrust forward, pushed up by the ruined cups of her bra. He licked and kissed and sucked and she was sure he'd leave marks everywhere as she groaned in frustration, bright light sparking in her eyes and the cliff of oblivion looming just out of reach.

All the while he kept up the rhythm, gentle and slow, and she despised him for it because what she wanted was hard and hateful, not this…undoing. Unpicking every seam she'd so tightly stitched up over the years. Only when he slid his hand between them again, stroked and teased and she began saying who knew what—unintelligible mutterings that were probably begging but she didn't give a damn about her pride—did he begin the hard thrusting that she'd craved, his rhythm breaking and irregular because he was as lost as her with the pressure and changes of angle.

In a roar of pleasure she fell apart, screaming his name, and he followed with a shout on one final hard thrust, filling her with his heat.

They stayed there for a few seconds, heavy breaths ragged in the room, the smell of salt and musk and sex hanging in the air, fused with the spicy scent that was all Gage. She closed her eyes, her head against his chest. The thump, thump, thump of his heartbeat in her ear. What had she done? His hate she could deal with. But a gentle, kind and passionate Gage Caron had the power to destroy her utterly and she wouldn't let him. She'd barely recovered the last time she'd let him go. She needed to move, protect herself from her own critical mistake. Allowing herself to touch him. Thinking the fire of their passion wouldn't burn her.

Eve raked up her bra straps. Shrugged her shirt back over her shoulders and pushed at Gage.

'Move.'

He slid out of her, still half-erect, hair a mess and looking confused as he stepped back, hands up and off her body. She ignored him and wrestled with her underwear, trousers. Anything to get away as fast as possible, to begin the process of putting herself back together.

'Eve?'

She shook her head as he tried to reach for her, tears stinging her eyes. Clutching her crushed clothes to her body as she pushed past him and ran to her room. She slammed the door and turned the key before stumbling to the bed and sitting on the edge.

Her body wasn't listening to what her head was trying to tell her, that this should never have happened. The unprotected sex, whilst blindingly stupid, wasn't going to lead to pregnancy. She had an implant so there was no risk of that.

No, it was that her body wanted more. More of Gage, his lips and his hands driving her out of her mind. Driving out the thoughts that whispered that if her father never recovered, some secrets would remain safe and she and Gage might one day have a chance, when there was none to be had at all. Not now or ever, because secrets had the power to destroy, and there were some secrets she would always have to keep.

What if he wanted more, too? She shivered, like she'd plunged into icy water. She craved that more than anything else in the whole world but there could never be any truth between them because she wouldn't destroy the family he loved. So they had nothing, because that lack of trust between them would rot everything away from the inside. Eve took a deep breath. She'd shore up her defences and inject the coldness into her blood that she'd become re-nowned for.

A sharp rap sounded at the door.

Time to be cruel to be kind. And the crueller the better.

No answer.

Gage did up his belt, having chased Eve to her room with his trousers half-open. Head still reeling at how out of hand one kiss had become. How much more he had wanted until Eve had fled down the hallway, half-dressed herself. He'd never hurt a woman during sex before, but she'd gasped and now he wasn't sure, not after she'd pushed him away and run, leaving him quite literally with his trousers around his damned ankles.

He had to get his head together, but sanity was somewhere back with their bodies locked in ecstasy at the dining table, with nothing on his mind other than the feel of being inside her again. The warm silk of her skin, the wet heat surrounding him. Eve's kisses, which had been desperate and wanting. The smell of her still clung to his skin, so heady and sweet it might never wash away.

It was as if he'd been transported back to a time where life had been perfect, a kind of surety that everything would work out. He hadn't felt that way for so long, the sensation shocked him. And Eve had been right there in the maelstrom of it all. So why run away at the end? Instead they should have both taken to the bedroom where he could have spent the day buried inside her, working her out of his system.

Gage tested the door. *Locked?* Hell. His heart began beating a sickeningly fast rhythm and he swallowed. All those rumours of him forcing her to go with him came back to the fore as bile rose in his throat. It was a moment's worth of insecurity that took him right back to her rejection. How he'd misread the situation totally. Had he done the same here today? He raked his hands through his hair. No. She'd been right there with him, screaming as they'd exploded together...

*More... Just...take me.*

She'd come twice and there had been *no* doubts in his mind she'd wanted him inside her, the passion overwhelming them both. Still, something was wrong, and he wasn't standing outside this room until he found out what it was. He knocked again, harder this time.

'Eve...' Damn, what was she doing? He felt like an utter fool, impotent with the inability to do anything other than ask for her attention yet again. He listened. Heard muffled sounds that he couldn't identify... Was she crying?

'Open up... Eve... Eve!'

He pounded on the door like a lovesick fool and hated himself even more for it, but he couldn't stop. Finally, the lock clicked and the door opened.

She'd changed her top to something black and body hugging. Tidied herself, with her hair now tamed and neat rather than spilling over her shoulders, perfect to grip. Presenting as cold and aloof as the day he'd called her, and she told him in no uncertain terms there was no *them* anymore.

'Stop that, sugar,' Eve drawled.

He hated that damned name. She only ever used it when she was trying to needle him and it worked the same now as it always had. But past that icy shell he could see the cracks that blurred and softened her. Mascara had smudged under her eyes, making them smoky. Her cheeks bloomed with a healthy, beautiful blush. Maybe not so icy and unaffected, then.

'We need to talk,' he said.

Her eyes widened a tiny fraction as a look passed through them. Something like fear. She swallowed, but her mouth held a tight, brutal line. Then she sighed theatrically and waved him away like an annoying child. 'I don't suffer from anything inconveniently contagious, and I'm on contraception. Unless you have something to add, there's nothing to discuss.'

Maybe he should have walked away. He didn't chase women, not anymore. He'd had a taste of humiliation at her hand once, and it was never happening to him again. And he would have walked had he not been certain he'd hurt her somehow. Asking the question was self-protection. He wasn't having any more rumours spread about him, not from her quarter at least.

'I'm clean too. There's no need to worry.' It was laughable how long it had been since he'd last had sex. He'd been so absorbed with his pursuit of Knight Enterprises he hadn't had time. Or that's what he'd told himself. The sad reality was that when he'd become focussed on Eve again, any other woman had ceased to exist. She'd become his sole obsession. The thought of touching anyone else left him cold, which had only added to his frustration and fuelled his desire to exact the retribution he'd sought for seven long years.

'We still need to talk. And I'm not having this discussion in the hall.'

He wasn't sure why it all seemed so hollow at this moment, but he wasn't letting the conversation go.

Eve stood back, held out an arm as if welcoming him in, but the hand holding the door gripped tightly enough he could see her fingers blanch white. He walked inside, looked around the space, focussed on the huge bed with soft cushions and creamy plush covers that loomed large in the room. How he wanted to carry her there and strip her cool façade layer by layer till she ignited again.

'It was *sex*, Gage.'

The way she'd said that word, spitting it out at him like they'd done something wrong.

There had been nothing wrong with what they'd done. On the contrary, it was the rightness of it that had shocked him the most. How natural it had felt, as if they'd never been apart.

'And if you need your ego appeased,' she added, 'an itch pleasantly scratched.'

'I'd say you found it more than pleasant. Since it took around two seconds of our kissing for me to have you on the table and coming, *twice*. That's reason enough for my ego to be doing fine.'

'It's been a while. And I didn't realise we were keeping score. Are you going to claim I owe you one now?'

He had been accused of many things in his time, but he *never* held expectations of a woman where sex was concerned. For him, giving pleasure was as heady as receiving it. While she owed him many things, the roil of anger began tightening in his gut at the suggestion she owed him that.

'Don't be ridiculous.'

She shrugged. 'Remember, I kissed you. And while it might have been my ass bare on the table, that one kiss proved I could have you right where I wanted you... Again.'

Her words hit him like a punch in the gut. At the time it had felt *all* mutual, but had she simply been using him, like last time? The burn inside turned molten, a furnace of rage that transported him back in time, welling and threatening to spill over. His jaw tightened hard enough to crack teeth. He'd let it damn well happen again and he loathed himself for it. He glared at her, standing there triumphant. So damned aloof. How could he have been fooled? She'd not always been cold like this. She'd once been a young woman full to the brim with emotion, or so he'd thought. Except…

He took a breath through that surge of fury and as he did so realised that she wouldn't look him in the eyes right now. If she didn't care, she'd be looking at him straight on and not somewhere in the middle of his chest where she seemed to have developed a fixation with his shirt buttons. So instead of listening to what she said, he focussed on how she'd acted instead.

The flush over her skin, her pleas for more, *harder.* Leaning against his chest, accepting his arms around her as they'd taken a moment and come down from the cataclysm that had been the intimacy between them. Screaming out his name and then pushing him away hard and running like the devil himself was chasing her. Locking the door. He hesitated.

*She's scared.*

Of him…

No. It wasn't him. It was something else and he'd find out what it was if it killed him. He could taunt her like he'd always done as a child, when something had terrified her. She never backed off from a dare but now he began to suspect her lashing out with claws unsheathed was something else. Her trying to force his distance. Right now he enjoyed her claws a little too much because they were both spoiling for a fight. He could give it to her, because making up could be a thrill all of its own. Except he didn't want to fight with her, but *for* her, and he knew the ways he could play dirty and win.

What had always had her melting like butter on a summer's day had not been playing rough—though they'd done their fair share of that and it had been fun—it had been the gentle, tender moments. So she was angling for a fight right now. He wouldn't give it to her because it was easy to fight when he bit at the hook she cast for him, the one that fed the anger he carried. He'd just have to play smarter, not harder.

'I'm sorry I didn't think about contraception. It was irresponsible and wrong. If you don't trust me, I can get tested again, for your peace of mind.'

Her eyes widened a fraction.

'No, I trust you.' Her whole body softened, wilted like something had come loose. Like he might be winning this game, with the rules he didn't understand. Then it was as if she'd reminded herself she wasn't allowed to be vulnerable anymore, and everything in her hardened again. 'But you are a man after all. Led around by one thing. It's always the same.'

He took the barb, absorbed the sharp stab of it. Ignored the twist of possessiveness like razor wire wrapping round him, at the thought of any other man with her. He had no rights here, none at all. But being around her flung him into a kind of insanity that made him a fool.

'Cutting me down to size?'

She held her head high and proud. 'It was easy to do. You're soft wood.'

He laughed, because now he *knew* she was lying. She dangled that damn bait so enticingly, but he wouldn't take it.

'Yet only minutes ago you were ecstatic with how hard I was. I wasn't hearing your complaints, only your screams.'

Eve glanced at the bed, at him, then back at the bed. Took a small step away from it like if he was too close to her, she'd tumble him onto the mattress. He was enthusiastic about that idea. It was right where he wanted her, eventually. There he'd get more truth than any conversation they were having right now. Something was going on here and he'd find out what it was sooner or later.

'Eve. Enough of this. Let's agree you're an expert at hurting me. Thing is, I'm worried I might have hurt you.'

He'd lowered his voice, tried for something more conciliatory. 'I'm sorry about that too.'

She turned away towards the windows, reached to her face and swiped her fingers across her cheeks. Was she crying? He took a step forward, wanting nothing more than to reach for her. Her tears had always broken him, and that sensation of needing to comfort was an overwhelming thing that had his fingers itching to take her into his arms and soothe away whatever pained her.

She gave a sharp, shaky kind of laugh. Wrapped her arms round herself as if holding something in. 'I... It didn't hurt. As I said, it's been a while.'

It would have to have been a hell of a long while for it to surprise her, hurt her, or whatever she'd experienced. He had no rights to her. She was an adult woman who'd left him long ago, but masochist that he was, he needed to know or it would niggle like a splinter under his skin.

'How long?'

'Long enough.' She shook her head, looked at him with her pale and haunted eyes. 'Not that it's any of your business.'

Eve looked at her bed again, yet with so much yearning this time it almost cut him off at the knees. A pulse began beating, seductive and low, that primal drive he knew too well, one that he accepted now that he'd probably always have around her. He was half-hard again, and she'd be able to see that. Earlier he might not have wanted to give her that power over him, but he didn't care anymore.

'I could guess.'

'And in the unlikely event you were right, would you expect a prize?'

A slow smile slid across his face. 'I'm thinking a better idea is something where we both win.' Part of him was secretly pleased he still knew the ways to make her come apart at the seams.

'I refuse to play these childish games. It's a mistake to mix business with pleasure and, anyhow, I can get pleasure anywhere.'

'You can't get it while you wear my ring on your finger. Anyhow, you don't want it anywhere, you want it from me.'

She tugged the gleaming sapphire from her hand. He gritted his teeth as she walked to a feminine-looking dressing table and gently placed it on the pale wood.

'Every man thinks they're special. You're not. Please leave, I have things to do.'

He needed to go. She wasn't giving up her quest for an argument, and he still wasn't in control enough not to risk uttering hurtful things that couldn't be unsaid. In his darker moments when he'd thought back to that night she'd cast him aside, he'd imagined her gloating at the pain she'd caused. She didn't look like she was gloating now. Her face was pale, her eyes tight as she chewed on her lower lip. At this moment Eve did not look like a woman who enjoyed hurting him. She looked like the young woman he'd thought he'd known and had believed he'd spend his whole life with. One who'd been kind, protective of her mom and sister. Loving.

'Then I'll leave you to wrestle with your feelings for me,' he said, and walked from the room. What had happened to her between the time he'd left with only their kisses under the sound of the rain as memories, and the day she'd ended it all?

Hugo Chevalier had happened, and Gage was determined to find out what that man had done. There were any number of ways he could go about getting that information but she'd tell him in the end because he had a weapon she couldn't fight.

She still wanted him.

# CHAPTER SIX

EVE SNATCHED UP her evening bag and headed for the door of her room then stopped, looking around. There was a needling sensation, like her world was not quite right. Like she'd forgotten something. She turned and her gaze lingered on the dressing-table, where her engagement ring glittered in the low lights.

She looked down at her left hand and the sense that something was missing increased. Eve turned back, tossing her clutch onto the bed as she passed. Grabbing the ring, she slid the extravagant cluster of gemstones onto her finger. They lay cool against her skin, easing the burn of her overheated flesh.

Eve tried not to think about how comforting the weight of the engagement ring was whenever she wore it. She hadn't realised properly how any of this would be, having believed she could cope with her feelings. Sadly, she'd underestimated how crushing unrequited desire could really be. How the cruel words she'd forced herself to say would chip away at her soul and blacken it for ever.

It had been one thing as a desperate, besotted twenty-year-old. When her father had found her in that rundown hotel, she'd been fuelled by fear and exhaustion, and in the horrible weeks that had followed she'd agreed to anything to protect Gage, her choices horrible yet clear. She'd also had the advantage of not seeing him. That distance had made the terrible choices seem easier. No one had witnessed her weeping into her pillow every night.

Soon she'd been a continent away from him after their last, terrible call when she'd destroyed his love for her and succeeded in turning it into blind hatred. But nothing had prepared her for the wearying exhaustion of the act she continued to play.

Eve smoothed her hands over her blue dress, perfect for travel because it was soft and body-hugging and had once made her feel beautiful. It also now made her feel exposed, the fabric the same vibrant colour as Gage's eyes, matching her engagement ring to perfection. It clung to her body and reminded her with each movement she made of Gage's hands softly stroking her.

She tried to ignore that sensation as she walked from her room down the stairs to travel to dinner with Greta Bonitz, blinking back the threatening tears. Kissing Gage, touching him. Making love, because it had been far more than sex. They had all been a critical error. Once their lips had touched it had been like her body had come home. The soul-deep sigh of relief.

But now she was left with lonely nights in a bed in a house where he lay just down the hall, because as much as her body wanted him again and again, she couldn't let him have her. That realisation crippled her. If she let him touch her again, she might never let him go, and where would that leave them?

He wanted her, that was clear. They still burned brightly when they were together. While she had nothing to compare it with, their bodies didn't lie like their minds did. They knew how to work together in perfect synchronicity. She shivered. Closed her eyes and let herself indulge in the guilty pleasure of recalling the feel of him inside her again. A flood of warmth washed over her.

And now she was simply avoiding him. She took a deep breath to steel herself and walked down the hall to the lounge. Gage waited there, staring out the doors that show-cased the view of her fields of flowers. Night had fallen now and everything was in darkness, but the breeze still blew in perfumes of roses and lavender. He had his hands in his pockets, coat slung over the arms of a chair. His shoulders were broad and strong. Once they'd carried so many of her burdens. Now she only had herself. She let herself indulge in the look of him, surveying the darkness outside as though overseeing his domain.

'The car will be here soon.'

She didn't know how he knew she was there but, then, she'd always known when he'd walked into a room so perhaps he had the same sixth sense about her too. It comforted her and distressed her all the same, with the what-ifs. What if she'd ignored her father's threats? What if she'd still run back to Gage? Would they still be together? Would their baby…?

No. There was no use to these thoughts. She'd punished herself enough for the last one. She didn't need any more.

He was such a beautiful, masculine picture framed in the doorway, glowing in the low lights of the room. The golden boy indeed. Gage turned and raised a tumbler a quarter full of golden liquid.

'Drink?'

Not unless it was straight bourbon. That might be the only thing that would get her through this. But she needed her wits about her, especially tonight when everything felt so ragged and raw. 'No, I prefer not to drink before an important business deal. The celebration can come afterwards.'

'Looking forward to getting rid of me that quickly?'

The smirk on his face told her exactly what he thought she might say, and exactly what her answer really would be if she told the truth. And that was a worry in and of itself.

'You know we both want to move on, sugar.'

The corners of his beautiful mouth curled in a sensual smile.

'So certain of that, are you?'

His voice was as gentle as the warm breeze floating into the room, but it packed the power of a punch. Did he want her, still? The slide of his gaze over her body gave her the answer, but she wouldn't admit it.

'I'm certain of what I want.'

'Hmm.' He didn't press further, merely sipped his own drink, the ice clinking in the glass, and watched her. Blue eyes were supposed to be cold, icy, but his burned hot and ignited her. If she didn't know it was impossible, she might worry about self-combusting right here in the middle of the room.

'You look beautiful,' he said, and strolled towards her, moving in close. He placed his half-finished drink on a side table then reached out his hand and hesitated. She didn't move away, and he seemed to take that as a kind of permission. He gently grasped one of her blonde curls between his fingers. 'I love your hair like this.'

His voice had a kind of wistful, contemplative tone to it. She couldn't deal with that. His anger, his dislike— they were easy things to accept. Not this quiet man, the one who reminded her of the twenty-three-year-old she'd run away with.

'Thank you,' she murmured, and didn't think too hard about how she'd left it down on purpose. Gage looked magnificent himself, standing there in a blue striped shirt, open at the neck and showing a tantalising slice of chest. The narrow taper of his waist. The way the trousers framed his strong thighs. Thighs she'd wrapped her legs round only hours ago. Heat rose to her face. An ache bloomed deep inside her.

'I like the look of my ring on your finger.'

That doused her heat like falling into a pond in winter. The problem was she liked the *feel* of it on her finger. She loved the sensation that it was his claim of ownership over her. Something about that thought slid way too much warmth and pleasure through her blood, like a good shot of spirits. She'd never wanted to believe anyone owned her, but Gage had. He'd claimed her heart and she hadn't been able to entrust it to anyone else. Damn him. She looked down at the exquisite gems with as much disdain as she could muster, which was hard when the ring was the most beautiful thing she'd ever seen.

'Your ring might be on my finger, but you don't own me. You never did and you never will.'

'I owned you this afternoon for a little while.' He held up two fingers and his smile was all devil. 'Twice, if I recall.'

'You're not being a gentleman about this.'

'I learned my lesson well. You taught me there was little point.'

'I'd rather forget about this afternoon.' If she didn't, she'd just throw herself into his arms and beg him to tear the clothes from her body. They might never make dinner.

'Whereas I'd like to do it again. Many, many times.'

She stopped breathing. No air would come. The atmosphere was too syrupy and thick. She wanted it again too. Craved it. Would do almost anything to be in his arms again. All she had to do was to walk forward. Kiss him… But no. That would end in disaster.

'You're deluded.' Her voice sounded more like a breathy whisper of desire than a denial.

'I'm a realist. Sex was never the problem between us. We're adults. Why not enjoy ourselves?'

Because he'd move on and she'd be wrecked for ever. Except the temptation of it rang loudly. To forget everything but the feel of his lips and hands on her body. Him inside her. To be lost and found all rolled into one. She tugged at the tie around her waist, loosening it a fraction. Everything seemed too tight. Her skin was fit to burst with wanting.

'I promise we'd enjoy ourselves. It would only be better the next time. And the next.' Heat radiated from his body. The smell of him, all bespoke cologne and something else. The essence of the man himself. Earthy, raw. She wanted to lean in, rest her head on his hard chest. Give in to this thing between them. It was all she could do not to slide into his arms again and tuck herself in where she felt safe, one of the only places she did. But he wasn't safe. He was her greatest danger and she'd be a fool to ever forget it.

Still she looked up at him, into his fathomless blue eyes. She couldn't tell what was ticking away in that clever brain of his. They were so close now and in her heels she could tilt her head up and kiss him. Allow herself to forget for a little while…

But forgetting was dangerous. She'd tried over the past seven years and hadn't been able to. The contents of her small yellow suitcase were testament to her obsession and her grief. Then the sound of an alert interrupted the moment and Gage broke his gaze from hers. He checked his phone and she stepped away from him, taking a deep breath to regain her equilibrium.

'The car's here,' he said, and began walking to the door

as if their conversation about sex had never happened. And perhaps for him it didn't matter. She was a means to an end. A vehicle for his revenge against her father. To her, it was like her world had tilted on its axis. She was sure people could be grown up about this. That adults could sleep together and not care. Just have fun. Scratch an itch. She wasn't one of them. She'd never be casual about Gage Caron.

Letting him touch her in the first place had been a mistake.

The night air was warm as they slid into the back of the car, a driver holding the door open for them. She steeled herself for the journey to the restaurant. Tonight was important, playing her part even more so. Success here meant her freedom sooner. Once Gage's business with Greta Bonitz was confirmed, their engagement would end and she could melt into obscurity. Retire to her flower farm, grow roses and forget Gage Caron existed. But the thought of handing back the engagement ring and trying to pretend she and Gage had never touched, never kissed filled her with torment. Better to remind herself that this was a business arrangement.

'How close are you to finalising something with the Bonitz companies?'

'We've stalled.' His voice was tight with the sound of repressed anger as the car began the journey to Nice. 'Greta is an extremely family-minded woman. Her own marriage lasted forty-seven years before her husband passed away and left her at the helm of the Bonitz group. It's important for her to work with like-minded people. I caused her some…concern.'

She didn't ask why and he didn't seem keen to offer more, simply staring out the window and shutting her down. She did the same for the rest of the drive. Tried to forget that Gage was so close, that she could simply reach out, touch him if she wanted. Take his hand.

None of that was clever or wise, yet she didn't feel either of those things right now.

The car slid to a halt outside a restaurant. Her heart began to race with a sickening rhythm. Her mouth dried. She wasn't sure she could do this. There'd been no need to pretend when they'd been alone. Here it was another thing entirely. Her mother and sister's futures hinged on the success of tonight. In many ways, hers did too.

'Don't you think she'll wonder about the convenience of you suddenly producing me?'

'No.'

Gage didn't wait for the driver but opened the car door himself and hopped out. Eve followed. He held out his hand to her and she looked at it for a few seconds.

'Hold my hand, Eve.'

She slid hers into his. The warmth of him engulfed her, but she was rooted to the spot. Rather than drag her into the restaurant behind him, Gage drew her close. Took his free hand and cupped her cheek.

'Do you want to know why she's not going to question a thing?'

Eve couldn't speak. She shook her head, wanting to melt into the warmth of his touch. Absorb the strength he exuded.

'This,' he murmured.

Gage dropped his head to hers. Their lips brushed. And her mind blanked.

Kissing Eve was like heaven and hell. Something he craved. Something he'd give almost anything to do again and again. When his lips touched hers the shock of it jolted through him. He forgot that they were standing in a street in front of a restaurant. He forgot everything but the feel of her soft lips on his own. How she opened underneath him and gave to the kiss as much as he took. This might be one of the most important nights of his career, but he didn't care. He wanted to call the car back and take her home. Peel off the soft dress that clung to her curves. Take her to bed. Bury himself inside her for hours. Hell, they mightn't even make it home the way he felt. Even the back of the limo sounded good right now. Dark. Private. Anything to be alone.

A click. The burst of a flash. Gage came to his senses and broke the kiss. He turned and there stood a man with a camera.

'The cameras,' she said, her voice husky and low. Her cheeks flushed a glorious pink. Eyes glazed, pupils blown wide. A tendril of satisfaction curled through him that he could make her look like this. Drugged with desire. 'Are they—?'

'Here for us. Yes. The news of our "engagement" dropped today. Our romance will be all over the gossip sites in no time and that kiss is why Greta won't doubt a thing.'

Eve seemed to come back to herself, the blush on her cheeks intensifying.

'If that's all it takes, I could have been anyone.'

He gritted his teeth. She still wasn't taking responsibility for how she'd got here. For the rumours that he'd plucked her from the loving bosom of her family, and she'd been *afraid* of him. Morphing their past into something twisted and dirty.

'You know why it had to be you.'

A slight frown marred her brow. A look of confusion if he hadn't known better, but those rumours had to have come from somewhere and she'd never tried to scotch them.

'I don't—'

'We should go inside.' He refused to hear excuses, how she was not completely aware of what she'd done, how she'd not been party to the rumours that had surfaced time and again. Whenever he'd felt like he was getting some purchase, another ugly whisper had started. That he was a man not to be trusted. 'We don't want to keep Greta waiting.'

He led Eve into the restaurant, and was ushered to the table he'd booked in a softly lit and private corner. Greta was already there, waiting. An elegant older woman and a powerhouse of the European business landscape. She stood as they came to the table. No smile, which didn't bode well, but at least she'd agreed to meet him. It wasn't something she accorded many people. He smiled instead, held out his hand and they shook.

'Frau Bonitz.'

She waved him away. 'Please. You make me sound ancient. It's Greta.'

'Thank you,' he said. 'And this is—'

'Eve Chevalier.' Greta cocked her head, her brown eyes intelligent and intent. 'I know all about you. I've been watching your activities in France with interest. Your efforts at building the European side of Knight Enterprises are impressive.'

Gage glanced at Eve. She smiled, and this one was wide and genuine. 'That's an accolade, coming from you.'

'I'm always alert to young women on the rise in business, because their efforts are missed by most.' Greta turned to Gage. 'But not you, it seems.'

He shook his head. 'I've had my eyes on her for years.'

Eve's hand jumped in his. He squeezed it gently. She seemed to relax as they sat at the table and he ordered champagne. Discussed choices with the sommelier, all the while listening to Greta and Eve talk.

'Knight's portfolio is an interesting one.'

'Yet we're looking to reorganise and sell a few companies that don't quite fit into our current strategy. Gage and I are in France, trying to decide which ones. Our vineyard is likely to be the first to go.'

'Hmm.' Greta took a sip of water as the waiter poured their champagne. 'We may need to talk some more about that.'

Eve cleverly guided the discussion, but she clearly already had Greta on the hook for the vineyard. Her skills in drawing out the conversation about a possible sale were subtle and impressive. So subtly done that it didn't affect the mood of the evening at all. He might be wrong, but it seemed Greta had warmed to him by a few degrees, and that was all Eve's doing.

Greta picked up her glass of champagne. 'I understand congratulations are owed to you both.'

Eve smiled and looked down at her ring, which sparkled under the low lights. Something about her seemed wistful and a little sad. 'Thank you. They are.'

They toasted, glasses clinking round the table. 'And yet your families' rivalry is renowned. I hope for your sakes they took it well.'

'Mine were circumspect,' Gage said. The lie niggled uncomfortably. He'd travelled to see his parents to give them the news, not wanting to tell them in a phone call or, worse, for them to find out through the media. While he'd told Eve they just wanted him to be happy, his mom and dad had not reacted well.

'*Still, Gage? Didn't you learn last time? We told you a Chevalier can never be trusted. Ever.*'

His mom and dad wanted a wedding, grandchildren, but that would never happen with Eve. Right now he couldn't see it happening at all. Would his parents be happy when he ended things? Likely. Gage took another a swig of his champagne, a waste of a magnificent vintage because he was unable to savour it. None of this felt like triumph to him. It all seemed hollow and pointless.

Eve toyed with a napkin on the table-top. She huffed out a laugh. 'Mine will take a lot of convincing.'

The honesty and pain of the answer surprised him. Without thinking, he reached out his hand, placed it on hers and squeezed. Eve's skin lay soft and cool under his own. She gave him a watery smile and a moment passed between them, something he couldn't explain but which felt a lot like understanding.

'I'm sorry. Family is important and my life's greatest reward,' Greta said. 'To work with my children, I can think of nothing more fulfilling, and I hope that for you. Although usually the gossip magazines have tales of burgeoning romances like yours, there's been no hint of anything between you, which is a surprise given your reported history.'

Gage stiffened. Pictures of him in his twenties being hauled out of a police car with a bruised and bloodied face had been excellent fodder for the gutter press. Gage's greatest shame was the suspicion he'd brought on his family in those times. He had said nothing to reporters, maintaining a dignified silence. But those pictures were easy for anyone to find, if they looked. Even though he employed people to ensure his online reputation was clean, there were some things you couldn't hide, no matter how much money you paid.

Gage let Eve's hand go and was about to reach for his glass when a discreet waiter leaned in to refill it. If Greta had any suspicions about the truth of their engagement, a check of the internet tomorrow would have photographs of their kiss and that would quell any uneasiness.

'You don't look like a person who'd read gossip magazines.'

'Usually I don't, but I'm interested since I'm a romantic at heart. Given the past, what started your reconciliation?' She turned to Eve. 'Since you've spent the past seven years in France, it would have been difficult for you both to cross paths.'

Eve leaned forward like she was going to tell a secret.

'Few people know this but Knight's having some liquidity trouble in the States. Gage offered to invest,' she said smoothly, placing her hand on his arm. Gazing at him with her head to one side, her pupils big and dark. 'He rode in like a knight in shining armour to save the day.'

Gage laughed, that recollection absurd but sounding so real. 'I think, *cher*, that description owes more to fantasy than reality. I seem to remember I was more corporate raider than white knight.'

She laughed too, something in her eyes flaring as she did. 'Maybe you were a bit piratical. Somewhat of a marauder.' Her lips curved into a sultry smile. 'I obviously like that about you. That's the power of our love. It's never changed.'

The words tore through him like an electric current. A waiter handed them their menus, but for him the words blurred on the page. They'd said they'd loved each other so many times in the past. He'd believed they had but had come to learn love wasn't for him, it hadn't been for years. He'd lived first-hand through the pain of betrayal and couldn't do it again, although on some nights, late, the thoughts crept in. What if they'd stayed together all those year ago? Could they have had a relationship as long as Greta's?

He'd never know. Gage quashed the thoughts, ignored the ache inside. Of overwhelming loss, of missed opportunities. He was made of harder stuff than this. And he didn't care anymore. This was all a means to an end.

They ordered their meals. Ate the exquisite food, which he barely tasted as he watched Greta and Eve talk because any involvement by him proved unnecessary.

Eve was perfection—warm, engaging, genuine. There was no flighty socialite at this table, no precious society princess. She and Greta connected as if they were old friends. He was mere garnish on the side.

And even though it was all going to plan, his anger began to simmer and boil. He breathed through it. Sipped more wine. Sat back and laughed on cue, commented where necessary, but couldn't completely hold back the burn. This could have been them for real. Yet Eve had thrown it all away, and for what? Daddy, Mommy, a trust fund? A damned flower farm in the South of France? He would have bought her the world if she'd asked for it. They could have done it all together, not spent these years apart.

But Eve *couldn't* have loved him. Love wasn't cruel, like she'd been. Love was about protecting the person you adored. No matter how good the sex still was between them, no matter that there appeared more to their story than he'd assumed over the years, she'd still strung him along and dumped him when convenient. Once this was done he'd do the same and walk away without a backward glance. He *had* to.

The twisting in his guts only hinted at the lies he told himself.

'This has been a most engaging evening,' Greta said, bringing him back into the conversation.

Gage smiled. 'I hope there can be more.'

'I'm holding a soirée in Munich in a few months' time. I'll send an invitation to you and your lovely fiancée.'

Gage glanced at Eve but didn't wait for her affirmation. 'It would be our pleasure.'

Or a descent into hell if they couldn't burn through this consuming attraction between them. But none of that mattered right now. He'd do almost anything to get this deal across the line. Eve didn't look happy with Greta's suggestion. The too-wide smile that didn't reach her tight eyes was a giveaway, to him at least. Good, this wasn't about her entertainment but about paying him back for the *years* he'd spent trying to undo his youthful foolishness.

Though why did it feel all so petty?

'Your approach to me was interesting,' Greta went on. 'I don't work with just anybody and I am gratified to see the rumours aren't true.'

'What rumours?' Eve asked. Gage tensed, all of him on high alert. She might not have spread them herself, but she would sure as hell have known what her daddy was whispering about him.

'You know, *cher*.' He turned to her. He'd look her in the face when he confronted her. The whole charade they were playing was about this. Redeeming his image so he could take his rightful place at every table without snide whispers. 'The story that says you didn't want to elope with me. That you weren't a willing participant.'

'That's ridiculous.' The words were adamant but all colour drained from her face. She gripped her napkin tightly in her hands. So tightly her knuckles paled.

'Of course it is,' Greta said. 'People saw a romantic story and took joy in making something unpleasant of it. *Schadenfreude*. But I can see it isn't true. I only wish you as long and as happy a marriage as my husband and I had.'

Eve turned to Greta, gave her a tight smile.

'Thank you. We can only hope to be as lucky.' She

dropped her napkin on the table and stood. Grabbed her clutch bag. 'If you'll excuse me, I need the restroom.'

Then she left the table as if the hounds of hell were chasing her. Gage watched her go, watched the brisk walk, the way her hips swayed, moulded by the soft blue fabric of her dress as she was pointed in the right direction by the helpful waiter.

'Perhaps that conversation was indelicate of me. Eve's a charming woman and it must be distressing.'

'She sometimes forgets how cruel people can be. She's a sensitive soul, my fiancée.' He hesitated for a moment. It was the truth. How could he have forgotten that? She'd always seen the best in things and people, even when life had thrown up the worst.

But she'd looked shocked, truly shocked by the revelation, and his brain wouldn't let him process it. His life had been lived under the assumption she'd been complicit in all the attempts to ruin his reputation. He didn't know how to think any other way. It was his frame of reference for all his thoughts and beliefs about their relationship.

'I hope I haven't upset her.'

Eve's horrified tone, the blood draining from her face, all the colour gone. He couldn't stop thinking that this had been a complete surprise to her. What if it was? What if she'd had no idea at all, exiled as she'd been over here in France? He couldn't process any of it, it was as though his whole life had been upended. 'Perhaps I'll go and check…'

'You should. I'll sit here and continue to sample this delightful wine. We have much to discuss over the coming months, Gage,' Greta said enigmatically.

But somehow he couldn't see it as a triumph as he stood and left the table.

All he could think of was Eve, and how shattered she'd appeared.

# CHAPTER SEVEN

EVE STOOD AT the basin, staring into the mirror. She took a deep breath, trying to calm her pounding heart, to ease the twist of pain. She'd never heard the rumours. How could anyone claim such an awful thing, that she hadn't gone willingly with Gage? She'd so badly wanted to be Gage's wife that nothing else had mattered, not even her family. She'd have travelled to the ends of the earth for him. And people were saying that he'd effectively kidnapped her?

But that wasn't the worst of it. It had been the look on his face as they'd been discussing it. Anger and certainty, as if he was convinced she *had* known. She lifted a trembling hand and brushed at the smudges under her eyes that no amount of concealer could hide. It had been impossible to sleep over the past few months with worry about the business, her family and then being around Gage. Some days she barely functioned, and yet she needed to go back out there. Perform. Play a part when all she wanted to do was curl up into a tiny ball and weep.

She turned on the cold tap and ran her wrists under the bracing water. Closed her eyes and tried to steady her throbbing heart. Stop the tears falling. She'd done it once. Survived the worst. All alone, thousands of miles from home, in a small church with a tiny white coffin and only a priest to see her tears. She'd woven that pain into the tapestry of her life and moved forward. What was one more time?

'Let's do this,' she said to her reflection, gritting her teeth and straightening her spine. She wrenched open the bathroom door, head down, and smacked straight into a wall of hard muscle and chest. Hands clasped her arms to steady her. She didn't need to be afraid of who it was. She knew. That heat, the smell of the man that made her crave to nestle her head against all that strength and soak it into herself for a while.

*Gage.*

But if she did, she might never let him go and she would always have to leave. Still, she couldn't muster the will to fight him. Not right now. She leaned back and met his gaze. A slight crease in his forehead was the only sign of all the questions she could never answer written there. Something soft and unreadable in his eyes. It undid her. As if looking back at her was the twenty-three-year-old young man she'd loved and left. The billionaire businessman was gone.

'Are you okay?'

No one had ever asked that in all these years. The doctors had talked about scientific probabilities. Nurses had patted her arm and said she was young; she'd have another baby. The priest had talked about God's will. No one had asked about *her*. Of course she'd hidden it from her family, not wanting her father to rage at the knowledge that a Caron had touched his daughter. Not wanting any of them to express relief that her baby had been lost, because that would have broken her completely.

Not even her mom or sister had asked how she was coping with losing Gage. It was as if, for them, that part of her life had ceased to exist. When for her there had been no relief, only bottomless grief.

She had run a business and people had assumed she was okay. Her family had relied on her. No one had ever thought about what *she* wanted, *ever*. Except for Gage. Now he cupped her cheek because he could always see through her. Saw what others might miss. Part of her wished she could tell him what had happened, to share the pain, but what good would it do? It was better that he remain blissfully unaware. The burden was hers to carry. No one else's. And at that moment she let go. If he hadn't been steadying her, she would have fallen apart completely.

'The rumours. What were they exactly?'

His gaze hardened. 'You know.'

She shook her head almost hard enough to give herself vertigo. Tears pricked at her eyes. 'You have to believe me. I don't.'

'Wasn't what you heard enough? You didn't want to come with me. I forced you to. You were scared of me and had a lucky escape.'

She gripped at the fabric of his shirt, crushing it in her fingers. 'Who said those things?'

'I thought it was you.'

'Never!'

'Okay. Let's assume it wasn't you.' He didn't sound convinced and his frown remained. 'I can't believe you'd be so naïve as to not guess who else might have had a reason. There's only one possibility.'

*No.* Her father had promised Gage would be left alone. That had been their deal. He'd be left to live his life…and she'd try to pick up the pieces of hers. 'People make up stories all the time.'

'And still you defend him. Sure, people make up stories. But every time something great was happening with Caron, a quiet word and investors melted away. I had to fight harder than anyone to keep things going. These anonymous whispers only came out when it would do most damage. And who would want to hurt me if not you? Your father.'

She released the crushed cotton of Gage's shirt and buried her head in her hands. How could anyone sully the memory of that time? It had been terrifying, exciting, full of promise and hope for the future. That's what she remembered. And the sense of desperation that they had been each other's one and only, and no one could tear them apart. Once it had ended, clinging to the hope that what they'd both have left were beautiful memories, and for her that would be enough to survive on.

But to dirty their past this way was unforgivable, hitting deep at the heart of their young love. She'd always believed the deal she'd struck with her father. That she'd leave Gage, and nothing would be said about his family or what had happened. He'd *promised*.

'Who promised?'

She'd said that aloud? Part of her wanted to tell Gage, to shout that she'd never stopped loving him and had made a devil's bargain to protect him.

No wonder Gage hated her, wanted revenge, this charade of a relationship. Because someone had been dripping poison into people's ears about him for years, poisoning him in the process. Yet another thing she'd have to atone for and fix. Because she *would* fix this. She'd work day and night to repair the damage her father had done, even if it meant once again sacrificing herself.

'We should get back to Greta. She'll be wondering where we are.'

Gage cupped her cheeks and stared down at her in this dim corridor, trying to delve into her soul.

'You carry a world of pain in your eyes. I want to know why. What's hurting you?'

How could she answer?

*Your dad's not really your father. You're someone else's son. I lost our baby.*

She could say all those things. The secrets she'd held onto for years. But what good would it do to unburden them all now?

'Nothing, other than revisiting our past. I'm all for moving forward.'

He scanned her face, one corner of his mouth quirking up in a tiny smile.

'Why did I ever believe you were a good liar?' he murmured.

Because it was easy to lie when she wasn't standing in front of him. But this had been the flaw in agreeing to the deal to save Knight. Because the man in the flesh was her Kryptonite. She'd been a fool to think that she could carry through with this game. She always held the losing hand, craving his warmth and strength. Especially now. And maybe that was exactly something she could take, something to distract them both from the truths she could never tell. So she grabbed the lapels of his jacket as his eyes darkened. Went up further on her toes and pulled his head down to her lips.

Her kiss demanded hard and passionate, but their lips touched and all Gage gave was gentle. Arms sliding round her back, holding her with a kind of reverence she didn't deserve. His lips moved over hers, coaxing her to give more than she wanted to. And, still, she couldn't help falling into it. This kiss that whispered it was more about love than desire. Timeless and endless. Not like the stolen kisses of their youth but something older, wiser and infinitely more dangerous because it carried all the hurts of the past mingled with what felt a lot like forgiveness.

She was held safe, ensnared by all the slick and hypnotising rhythm of it. Never wanting the moment to end. And maybe even if she couldn't tell him how she felt, she was showing it here. But she was terrified that he was showing her something too. Gage's hand delved into her hair, holding her tight, giving and taking. His body was hot and hard against hers, his arousal obvious, making her want. The core of her ached, needing him to fill her. Then he slowed, pulled away, his breathing heavy.

'We need to go,' she said. She didn't look at him, because if she did it would likely end her.

'We're not done, Eve. This conversation isn't over.'

That didn't matter to her so long as it was over for now. Then she could pull herself together before she completely fell apart, because she held secrets Gage was never going to find out.

Eve and he had walked back to the table hand in hand. They'd finished up with Greta, and she'd promised to call Eve about the vineyard. It was everything he could have dreamed of, the deal not yet sealed but he was sure it would be. The whole thing had been so laughably easy it was almost an anti-climax to all that had gone before.

And yet the night felt as if something had irrevocably changed. All those years he'd believed that Eve had been a party to the insidious rumours about him and she was adamant she'd had no idea. Once he might not have believed her denials, had he not witnessed her reaction tonight. The shock, the horror was so genuine he doubted even the best actress could have played the part so well. It convinced him she'd had no idea at all.

If he'd been wrong about that, what else had he been wrong about? Gage couldn't fathom the possibilities. He'd suffered through that excruciating phone call when he'd promised to take Eve away from her family, when she'd viciously rejected his love, treating him like a foolish boy. The scorn in her voice. That had all been painfully real. The question now, all these years on, was why had she done it?

For seven years he'd been certain of where he stood in the world. Now he wasn't sure of anything. In the back of the car, on the way home to Grasse, Eve had pressed herself so far against the door on the other side of the car it had been as though she was in another country. Why had she been so far away? That kiss she'd given him had rocked his foundations. Something he wanted to explore because he was sure she'd used it to distract him from getting to the truth. As if it would have all spilled out if she'd allowed herself to get close.

The car travelled up the long farmhouse drive and halted at the front doors. As Gage thanked the driver Eve jumped out of the car, almost fleeing to the door, except tonight she didn't have the key. He strolled towards her, formulating his plan because this night wasn't ending here. Eve was still like a drug flowing through his veins and he craved more of her.

'Have a drink with me,' he said.

'I think I've had more than enough tonight.' Her voice was soft, a little breathy. He knew that tone, the one that told him how much she desired him. In all this time he hadn't forgotten the things that made her tick.

'I'd like to discuss the dinner, see if there's anything I've missed.'

Business. He gave her that to hide behind. She sighed, and the sound of it caressed him like a feather down his spine.

'Now?'

'While it's fresh.' Gage pushed the door open. 'Come into the kitchen.' She'd think that was neutral space, whereas he saw no part of this place as neutral. It was all a war zone, one way or another, and he'd never been known to lose a battle.

He followed Eve through the house, the scent of her trailing behind like that of the fields of flowers surrounding this place. As they entered the kitchen, with its stone walls and exposed wooden beams, he could see how this home suited the very core of her. Except right now she didn't seem comfortable here, edging around the counter area and away from him. She dragged out a barstool and sat, slipping off her stilettos.

Pink. Her toenails were a pretty pink.

'Would you like warm milk, bourbon and honey to help you sleep?' He went to the refrigerator.

'Sure, why not?'

She sounded like he'd just asked her to chew glass.

'I'd appreciate your opinion on how tonight went.'

He didn't give a damn about the drink or the dinner. Greta was on board. They'd have to play a few more rounds of getting to know each other but Greta had liked what she'd seen. All that he cared about now was the woman sitting in front of him. Because after what he'd learned tonight, everything was *not* as it seemed.

As he mechanically grabbed what he needed and began preparing the nightcap, Eve sat there, working through her observations. They were insightful and damned clever. Proving herself to be the businesswoman she'd claimed to have become. No longer a precious society princess or trust-fund child.

Once he'd believed she'd been given the job in France out of nepotism. He'd bet now that she'd been sent here to keep her away from him. Gage finished making the sweet, milky concoction with a solid slug of spirits and poured cups for them both. Eve took a generous sip and didn't even blink at the amount of bourbon in the cup. He wondered whether she often had trouble sleeping and how much she used this particular remedy.

'Of course, with Greta set to invest, you won't need me soon,' Eve said. That jolted him right back into what had been a one-sided conversation.

'She's invited us to her party in Munich in a few months. We're not done till that deal is signed.'

Eve fished her phone from her bag, flicked through a few screens. Hesitated.

'I see we've hit the press. What a sweet picture you've painted.' Her voice burned as caustic as lye. But he stopped listening to the words and went back to watching the woman. She wasn't looking at her phone anymore but at her engagement ring, which she twisted to catch the light. 'I assume you have a plan for when we end it. Something suitably nebulous, like work keeping us apart? A respectful uncoupling?'

No. He'd planned on dialling things up to thermonuclear. A story that told the world exactly what sort of woman she was. A liar. But that didn't suit him now because he wasn't sure what she was. Still, he smiled, humoured her.

'Something like that.'

She looked at him with her china-blue eyes soft and with a wash of something else that, if he had to guess, looked like regret. He didn't want to talk about endings at all. He wanted to talk about beginnings. Reconnections. The things that lit a fire inside her because he loved her glow. He looked around the rustic farmhouse kitchen, with Eve at its heart. Her corn-silk curls gleamed like an ethereal halo under the soft lights. She looked right, here in this place. Like she should be nowhere else.

'You must find the farm hard to leave.'

Eve raised her eyebrows and took another sip of her drink. He might have taken some of his too but he didn't want to go to sleep and he didn't need to be intoxicated. He was man enough to admit she did that to him already. She smiled, something soft and mysterious that lit her up from inside.

'It is. I try to stay here whenever it's not rented out, which isn't often enough.'

'Why rent it out at all?'

She shrugged. 'I have a loan I want to pay off faster and tourists are happy to pay a premium to stay here. I do what I have to do.'

'And when you don't need to anymore?'

'I'll come here and stand on the back terrace, over-looking *my* fields, smelling the roses and lavender on the breeze. And I'll never leave.' A blush rose on her face, as beautiful as the sun breaking over the horizon at dawn. 'It's silly, really. Following the seasons. Sitting back and watching things grow.'

He drank some of the bourbon mixture, grimaced. Turned out this was *not* one of the things he enjoyed.

'There's nothing silly about it. It's always been your dream.' Gage noticed there was no talk of relationships or family. He didn't know why that left him with a pang of something like sadness.

The simple things he'd once loved were all tied up with memories of Eve. Sneaking off and meeting through that hole in the wall. Threading flowers into her hair so she looked like some ethereal fairy princess, all golden and beautiful. When she'd rejected him, he'd stopped dreaming of simple, even frivolous things and had driven him-self in a never-ending quest to redeem his name. It had been exhausting. What a pleasure it would have been to merely sit somewhere and look at a landscape. To…stop.

'It wasn't my only dream once,' Eve said. Her gaze met his. There was so much unsaid, and he couldn't seem to find the words to pick a way through the maze of the past that stood between them. 'What's yours?'

He should have said the deal with Greta Bonitz. That's what he'd wanted more than anything only weeks before, but he couldn't say that because it would be a lie now. His dreams were shifting things, dredging up fantasies held so long ago they'd been forgotten. Of marriage, children. Old desires he'd tried to cast aside, along with the painful memories.

The sad truth was his dreams were still tied up in her.

'You,' he said with no plan or forethought, leaving himself open to attack. He didn't care if what came next left his blood on the floor. He needed to get to the bottom of what was going on here.

Eve grabbed her cup and clutched it on her lap in both hands. Not looking at him now but into her drink. Her lower lip trembled till she sank her teeth into it. For a few moments he worried she might draw blood.

'No. I can't be your dream. I'm your nightmare.'

'My dreams are my own. Sure, they've become nightmares because I shouldn't touch you. But in my fantasies... I can do anything.' He moved around the counter to where she sat, still resolutely avoiding his gaze. 'Do you fantasise too? Maybe about me untying that distracting bow at your hip? Teasing those tight nipples I can see right now through your dress. Undoing you. Is that what you're fantasising about?'

He ached for her, but this was a long game he played now. Gage reached out and brushed the tangle of her golden locks over Eve's shoulder. The drink in her cup quivered. She gave an imperceptible shake of her head. 'I'm tired.'

If he had his way, there'd be no sleep in this house tonight. A heavy pulse beat low and insistently in him. 'I can think of better ways of getting to sleep than milk and bourbon. Let me show you.'

Her lips parted, the death-like grip on her cup loosening a fraction. He grabbed the rim and eased it out of her hands.

'What are you doing?'

Her voice was low and husky. A flush ran up her throat. She knew exactly what he was doing. He cupped her cheek, stroked his thumb against her smooth, soft skin. Eve finally looked at him, her eyes bottomless pools, almost all pupil surrounded by a sliver of pale blue.

'I'm going to kiss you,' he said, the anticipatory pleasure surging through him making him hard, desperate, when he needed infinite patience tonight. He leaned down to whisper in her ear, 'Then I'm going to carry you to my room. Peel that tempting dress from your glorious body.' The panting of her breath teased at his neck. 'I'm going to caress, kiss, explore every part of you.' He skimmed his lips feather-light along her throat. 'And only when you're trembling, wet and mad with desire will I make love to you. For hours. I want to hear you scream my name. Over and over.'

He skimmed his lips over the side of her neck, past the base of her ear. His eyes drifted shut as his nose brushed her cheek. 'Say yes, *cher*, and I'm yours for tonight.'

He wanted more than a night, but Eve was afraid of something and if she thought their time was limited she might just let go of that tight control…enough. She twined her arm around his neck and pressed her lips to his. Her lips parting. Their tongues touching.

There was nothing bold about her, just uncertainty. Something about that, how tentative they were at this moment, made him feel young again. Like the world had possibility rather than being full of disappointment. He wanted her here. Now. On this cold marble counter. The drive to tear off the dress and lay her out rode him hard. But he'd told her his plans and wouldn't deviate from the promises he'd made her. He kissed her back, relishing in the softness of her mouth, the hesitant stroke of her tongue. Let himself believe they were back…before. Before any of the pain and hurt. He pulled away from her and looked down, her lips dark pink and moist, her breaths heavy, matching his.

'Bed.'

'Yes.'

He swung her into his arms, where she clung on, so light and breakable. Something precious to be cosseted and adored. She nuzzled into his neck as he carried her to his room, striding with purpose, in a hurry to get there because the night ahead loomed large and pleasure-filled. He'd have her again, and again and again. Hell, he needed to take a few breaths to make sure he'd last. Even the thought of being inside her once more unravelled him. He walked through the door of his room into darkness. Found the bed and gently laid her on the covers then moved away.

'Where are you going?' Eve asked, voice low as if whispering some naughty secrets.

'A light. I want to see you.'

'No!' Her voice was strident, a strange discord in the evening. 'I… I want you now. Like this. Don't leave me.'

The blood surged through him again. That wasn't something he could ignore and now his eyes had adjusted to the lower light he glimpsed the way the moon glowing through the expansive French doors cast her in its silver light.

'Whatever the lady desires, she shall have.' He moved to her dress. That bow at her side, which had been plaguing him all night. He plucked at the end of the tie, ever so slowly, pulling as the loop of the bow slipped through. He eased apart the remains of the knot and peeled the dress open. She lay splayed on the fabric, her body pale, her bra and panties a dark trace of lace on her moonlit body.

He craved to see those breasts again without a bra. To taste them, toy with her nipples till she writhed in ecstasy. Something wild and possessive grabbed him, wanting her to beg him to satisfy her. To prove she should never have left him. To prove that no one else could ever give her what he had.

As much as desire drove him to tear off her clothes and pound into her like a crazed man, he wouldn't. Her rapid breaths were like music in the air. He eased her panties down her legs and tossed the flimsy lace to the floor. Leaned over her, stroked his fingers whisper-light up her leg till she shivered and moaned, then dropped his head and kissed the soft, pale skin of her stomach, lower and lower. Breathing in the scent of her sweet arousal. He hovered for a moment, one hand stroking, his breath on the juncture of her thighs because he wasn't ashamed to admit he wanted her too. He was aching and hard, his clothes gripping him too tight.

Eve squirmed underneath him. 'Please.'

He smiled. Kissed his way up her body. Settled his lips over her left nipple, already a hard peak, and sucked it through the lace of her bra. Her groan was deep and carnal and sliced through him with shards of anticipatory pleasure.

Gage pulled down the other cup of her bra, twirled her free nipple between his fingers as Eve reached her hands and grappled with the buttons on his shirt. He loved her desperate, staccato movements, her frantic tugs at the fabric, pulling it from his trousers.

'Too many clothes,' she groaned. He shrugged the shirt

from his body and threw it to the side. Undid his belt and whipped it from his trousers.

'Get rid of this damned bra.' He kissed the side of her neck as she rolled to one side and he undid the clasp at the back, freeing her. He sat back on his haunches, looking down at her body in the cool light. Sprawled out on the bed with her hair feathered on the pillow. Her features were smudged and blurred like a charcoal portrait in the soft light. Gage dropped his head again, kissing her perfect breasts. Laying his body over Eve and relishing in the contrast of her softness to his hardness, her edges and angles underneath him.

He didn't care that he still had his trousers on. If he took them off, this would be over too soon. Eve wrapped her legs around him, ground her body against his hardness as he captured her lips in his own, their kisses wet and frantic with nipping teeth. He wanted to see that, see her lips, swollen and well kissed, and know that he had done that. Wrecked her, like she was wrecking him. Her legs gripped tighter as he lost himself in the grind of their bodies, plucking at her nipples with his fingers, tongues exploring, their movements in such synchronicity it was like they'd never been apart.

She pulled her mouth away. 'I need you.'

The bright burst of arousal tore through him, his body heavy with it. Aching. 'I know,' he murmured against her lips. He rolled to the side, his trousers now an impediment. He reached for the zip.

Eve rolled to the side too. 'Let me.' She slid the zipper down all too slowly, reached her hand into his trousers and gripped his length through his underwear. He dropped his head back. Relished her touch. She slipped below the waistband of his briefs. Stroked him with her cool, firm touch and he almost shot off the bed at the shock. It was his turn to groan, throw back his head. Take. Savour.

Her firm fingers rubbed over the tip, working him like he'd shown her he enjoyed so many years ago. But this wasn't about him as the prickle at the base of his spine sounded a warning, the heaviness that told him he'd lose control soon. It was about her, breaking her apart.

He moved off the bed and looked down at her, unable to judge her expression in the darkness. He stripped himself of his trousers, underwear and knelt on the bed, dropping his head to the juncture of her thighs. Breathed in her sweet musky scent.

She spread her legs wider, fell open for him as he traced her with his tongue, relishing the salty sweet taste unique to her. He delved between her legs. Concentrated on the tight little bud and made her squirm and moan, lavishing her with attention. He slipped his hand between her thighs, probing her wet depths as he slid one finger inside then another and curled them to hit the spot he knew drove her wild.

Her back arched. She gripped the sheets, her thighs trembling as he lapped at her body, taking her higher and higher, but he wouldn't let her fall yet. He eased off a touch, bringing her back down. He could make this pleasure last for hours if he wanted to. He knew all about delayed gratification and patience. He had warned her after all.

Her hands released the sheets and one thrust into his hair, gripping tight. He relished the bite of pain, the desperation it showed.

'All of you.' Her voice was like the slip of lace over beautiful curves. As soft as the moonlight caressing her body. 'Inside me. *Please.*'

He'd wanted to hear her beg but it didn't hold the pleasure he'd thought it would. He needed to be inside her, to slide into her hot, wet depths and lose himself right along with her.

'Yes.' He rolled over and opened the bedside drawer.

'*No*,' Eve said, and he halted immediately, a sinking feeling hitting his stomach. She'd changed her mind? She reached out her arms and tried to pull him back to her. 'Only you. Nothing between us. Just you inside me.'

The rush was like a drug. Like being hit, hard. In all the time since Eve he'd never had sex without a condom. The only time he ever had was with her that long-ago morning.

'I trust you. I need you.'

And that's all it took, the expression of trust so heady he almost came then and there without her hands even on his body. He didn't care anymore. He rolled over onto her, settled between her glorious thighs. Positioned himself and hesitated for a second before slowly pushing home. His mind blanked. The white-hot spike of pleasure almost undid him. Eve gripped his body hard. He hesitated for a moment.

'Good?' He ground out the word through gritted teeth because this was better than good. Just having her underneath him, being inside her, felt life-altering.

'Yes.' Her voice was barely a whisper and then he began to thrust, long and slow, a hypnotic rhythm of push and pull. Her lips on his, tongue exploring his mouth. All slick and wet and barely controlled. She moved with him; her legs wrapped around his. Meeting him with every thrust. Moments of exquisite sensation that had him thanking the heavens she'd allowed him back into her body again. He didn't care right now what had come before, only this moment, pure and perfect.

The grind of her against him, the movements not so controlled now, told him she was close. She chased her pleasure and he was happy to give it to her. He dropped his head and sucked on her nipple as she tensed then splintered around him. Crying out his name. He buried his head into the side of her throat, breathing in the sweet scent of her hair as she brought herself up to meet him and gripped hard. He knew she was going to come again and held out for as long as he could till she grabbed his backside hard and dug her nails in deep. She could draw blood and he didn't care. A bright burst of light exploded in his head as he tumbled over the edge. Her sobbing cries announced she'd gone over with him, again. And as the world righted itself, he heard the whisper he was sure she'd never meant him to hear. Three words that changed everything.

*'Only ever you.'*

# CHAPTER EIGHT

MORNINGS WERE FOR reckoning, and Eve wondered how swift that reckoning would be today. She'd woken to a body aching, sated and boneless. But her heart and soul weren't sated. They'd never get enough of this. The touches in the darkness, the furtive kisses. The screaming want that would never go away.

And this morning the fantasies in the darkness collided with the brutal reality of the daytime. What had she said last night? Hidden by the moonlight, it seemed as if any of her most furtive imaginings could be real. That time could be turned back, and she and Gage could pretend they were in their early twenties again, when anything had seemed possible.

So little was possible now, all their history wound up with secrets. She should get up, move. Leave this bed and this room and flee, and to hell with everything. Her family, the company. This, here, was risking her soul and she didn't think she had enough strength to keep the charade going any longer.

'Morning.' Gage's midnight voice didn't suit the sunshine filtering into the room through gauzy curtains. It spoke of the night, of twisted sheets and whispered caresses that could be hidden. In the daylight there was nowhere to hide.

'Morning back at you.'

In moments her world flipped, and she found herself rolled over and underneath a hot, hard body. Any thoughts of getting up and running away evaporated in a welling of need. She shifted under him and winced. It had been a long, passionate night with little sleep, but her aches eased, to be replaced by another—the hot slide of desire working low down. There was no ending to how much she craved this man.

'Are you hurting?' His voice sounded so gentle. The look on his face concerned. It was worrying, this time spent with him. He was less the hard businessman, more the generous lover. Someone dangerous in every sense to her health and happiness. He pushed himself further up on his elbows and looked down at her, as if checking.

'A few aches and pains.' She shrugged, trying for a nonchalance she didn't feel. 'As I said, it's been a while.'

His eyes darkened to the blue of a stormy sea. His pupils almost swallowed any colour.

'How long?'

Gage's voice was soft, the question sounding innocent enough, and yet a thread ran through it, something dark and dangerous. It felt important and screamed a kind of warning. She'd broken open, leaving herself vulnerable in a way she hadn't allowed for years. Words had spilled out of her like she'd been given a truth serum, and while most of them could have been excused as being whispered in the throes of passion, the heat of the moment, some couldn't. She'd hoped he hadn't noticed, but with Gage she'd never really had room to hide. This soft and caring man unravelled her every time. She looked away.

'Long enough.'

Why couldn't she say something sophisticated, urbane? Something a woman experienced in having great sex would say. Something to shut him down rather than crack the door open even wider.

'Last night you said—'

'Sugar, I say a lot of things when I'm chasing an orgasm.' She would not let him use her words against her. Not words spoken in the heat of the moment. 'Don't believe everything you hear.'

She covered the lie well enough and what she'd said was designed to be brutal. She could deal with him angry. It's what she wanted. Safer that way for her and for him. But the words left a sour taste in her mouth, felt tainted, because last night had been something special and beautiful.

She expected him to pull away in disgust, to leave the bed. Instead he settled down, over her. His gaze might have changed fleetingly, a tightness that she couldn't read, but he didn't shift. His forearms remained either side of her head, his thumbs stroking at her hairline. She wanted to close her eyes, to soak in the gentleness and the caring, but that would leave her exposed again.

'I'm coming to realise what I should believe and what I shouldn't,' he said, skimming his lips over her mouth. The whole of her flooded with a slick heat. She didn't care that she ached, she revelled in his hard body against hers. If they made love again, he'd forget this, they could lose themselves in pleasure and he wouldn't ask the hard questions anymore.

When Gage's lips descended on hers, she captured them, the kiss soft and coaxing. He groaned and the sound punched right through her. He was hard against her, aroused again with that one kiss and the tangle of their tongues, and she threaded her hands through his hair, widening her legs and rolling her hips against him. He was in the perfect position to slide easily inside her and carry them away to bliss again, but he didn't, just let her grind against him till they were both panting and desperate. Then he adjusted his position and she sighed at the feel of him easing inside her. He whispered words in her ear that had her melting. *'The feel of you against me. So perfect. Never wanted this so much.'*

And she wanted it too. She wanted it all.

The impossible. *Everything.*

Tears pricked her eyes. Maybe she could lie about why she'd ended what they'd had, but then this would be like a house of cards, bound to blow over in a rough breeze. With their families loathing each other, there would be plenty of those. Better they remain here in a physical relationship and that was all. The sensation built inside her, that glorious burn, a wave of pleasure that she'd soon ride to oblivion so she could forget everything but his touch.

Except Gage pulled back, threaded his fingers in hers and raised her hands above her head, trapped her. His thrusts were gentle and shallow and avoided the contact she craved. His eyes were intent on her, so blue it hurt to look at them.

'Look at you. So beautiful underneath me.'

She arched her back but he wouldn't let her finish, watching her writhe against him. 'Gage. Please.'

'I love seeing you want me so badly.'

A sheen of sweat misted his skin. The room was warm from the morning sunshine hitting the glass as he kept up the slow, relentless rhythm that wouldn't let her finish.

'Memories taunted me for years and now I have you.'

She arched back, groaned. 'I need.'

'I know.' And yet he didn't relieve the ache, it only intensified. She chased the pressure, him grinding against her. His hand. Anything other than this torture. But he didn't relent. 'I'll make you scream if you answer.'

Her body was wound so tight she thought she would

tear apart. She trembled underneath him. 'Anything,' she panted. Closed her eyes because if she concentrated hard enough she might get there, with or without him. But he eased off even more and that delicious fall over the edge remained just out of reach.

'How long?' he murmured. She tried to ignore the question but she couldn't as the sharp bite of pleasure went on and on. Gage leaned down and grazed his teeth on the shell of her ear. 'How long has it been since someone's touched you like this?'

*Only him.*

She shook now. Their bodies coming together but never enough for her. He knew what it took to get her over the edge, that hadn't changed. Her body hadn't learned anything different because he'd been her only lover. In her own guilty explorations after they'd parted, all she'd been able to think of had been him. She'd tried to imagine sex with anyone else, but no one other than Gage entered her fantasies. Now he was denying her and she didn't care about secrets. All she wanted was him.

'Don't be afraid, *cher*.'

Tears burned her eyes and ran down her cheeks. Tears of frustration and need, sure, but more at the loss of this. All the years they'd missed.

She opened her eyes and he looked down at her, his gaze searching her face. His golden hair had fallen over his forehead and his eyes were intent, as if he could see everything like he'd used to—her hopes, dreams, fears. So many fears. And for a few moments she wanted to give him a truth so it could set her free. She'd stitch herself up with lies later.

'Seven years.'

Seven long, lonely, devastating years. A look scudded across his face, a thousand thoughts hidden there, all of which were unreadable. Then he pulled away. She was left empty and aching.

'*No*. That's not—'

'You promised,' she sobbed.

He hesitated then kissed the middle of her chest, lingering over where her heart pounded. 'And I keep my promises.' He kissed her navel, trailed his tongue down lower, and lower. 'I'll look after you.' His breath was a warm caress between her legs. He lingered for a few moments then dropped his head. 'I always will.'

Gage stroked his tongue over the centre of her. That's all it took to make her scream and lose herself in the promise she could never allow him to keep.

# CHAPTER NINE

THE MORE THINGS appeared to have changed, the more Gage realised they'd stayed the same. Except life wasn't imbued with the innocence of seven years ago. It had been tainted by something unknown, lurking in the shadows. A brooding monster he'd try to get to the bottom of, if Eve would let him.

She lay sleeping in his arms, where she'd been for a few hours now after turning his world on its head with one truth. Now he was frozen at the information she'd disclosed. Like a sliver of glass in the sole of his foot, the thought stabbed at him. Seven years. As if time hadn't moved on for her at all. He'd thought she didn't want him, that her trust fund or marriage to a society prince was all she'd sought, with him a toy along the way to play with. He'd been convinced that he wasn't good enough, and yet in all that time there'd been no one else for her.

She could be lying, but he knew deep down that she wasn't. The question was, why? He would get to the bottom of it, but telling him seemed to cost her a great deal so he allowed her a break, letting her sleep while his thoughts whirred. He couldn't escape the realisation that the choice to reject him might not have been hers. What threats had been made against her? What had been done to turn their love into this twisted charade?

The burning heat of rage threatened to ignite in his gut. All this time. The wasted years. For what? And whoever was responsible, they'd pay. He'd get to the bottom of what happened, and then burn it all down.

Eve stirred. An elegant stretch of her body as she gently woke in his arms. Parts of him stirred with her. He could tell the moment she realised where she was. Her body, previously languid and soft, now stiffened and moved away from him. She looked at him, the barest of creases between her brows, her eyes watchful. He hated that, the uncertainty in them.

Once they'd been certain of each other. He craved that certainty again. He brushed a soft kiss over her lips and gloried in the pink flush that bloomed over her skin. He didn't want to break the moment, but he needed answers. And he needed to ask the questions carefully. But Eve continued to distance herself from him.

'When are we leaving for the US?' she asked, her voice husky from sleep.

'Keen to get home?' *Home.* That word held a tantalising hint of what might have been between them. Building a haven against the world. What still could be, if he allowed himself to be honest…

'America hasn't been home for a long time.' Eve's fingers tortured the sheets. 'No. I can't get any information about my father. Mom and Veronique aren't making any sense about what's going on.'

It was as if someone had thrown a bucket of iced water over him. Gage resented mention of Hugo Chevalier entering the hallowed space of this shared bed. He breathed through the ever-present burn of anger that the man still had some malevolent power over Eve.

'I'll check flight arrangements. I've got some things to tie up in Mississippi first, before we head back to Seattle.' Except every part of him railed against leaving here, a sickening knot in his gut only getting tighter. As if reality would intrude and nothing would be the same again.

She nodded, looking far away. 'I should get up and—'

'There's no hurry.' He didn't want her getting out of the bed and leaving, not yet, when so many questions needed answering. 'Why, Eve?'

Her mouth firmed to a tight line. 'I don't know what—'

'Yes, you do. Why has there been no one else? Seven years is a long time.'

Her closing down to him began right then, the shuttering behind her eyes clear, like she'd pulled down a blind and excluded him from the room.

'I was studying and then thrown into managing the business here.'

The lie was written all over her face. The way her eyes avoided his. The way her throat convulsed as she swallowed. Her words sounded genuine but the look of her screamed volumes. If he'd been able to see her face to face in their final conversation, would he have seen the truth? Because all he'd heard had been the words, and he suspected now that those words had been blatant lies too.

'You're a beautiful, passionate woman. Men would have flocked to you.' They would have wanted her. He'd taunted himself for enough years with thoughts of her and any man other than him, till he'd hardened his heart to granite. Nothing and no one had been let in since.

She shrugged. Wriggled away. She still wouldn't look at him and all he saw was embarrassment and a spark of something else, hot and angry, in the flare of her pale blue eyes.

'Men did, but I had *focus*. Something to achieve. I'd been given a job to do here, and I excelled at it. I didn't need the attentions of a random man to make me feel good about myself.'

She rolled over and almost threw herself from the bed in her haste to escape. Glorious. Naked. He wanted to drag her back like some caveman, spend hours buried in her till they had to leave for their flight. Although it was tempting to skip it altogether and stay, continue the fantasy that they could remain cocooned from the outside world.

'Come back to bed. I won't ask any more questions. Let me make love to you instead.'

Her eyes softened for a moment. He drew back the sheet and patted the mattress beside him. There'd be no mistaking how badly he wanted her, and if Eve didn't want questions asked for now, he could do that.

Eve's gaze raked his body like her nails had scored his skin. Flares of heat ignited where it lingered. His face, chest, lower and then her pupils flared wide and dark. He smiled because he had her, and she knew it. They could resist many things, but not each other. He held out his hand to her. 'C'mon. You're not scared, are you?'

'Nothing scares me anymore,' she said in a husky whisper.

He reached out and she placed her hand in his. He tugged and she tumbled onto the bed and into his arms. Their truth screamed loudly in every touch and caress when they were in bed, tangled together. Here there were no lies between them, only raw honesty. If this was all Eve had to give for now, that would be enough.

Eve slept through most of the flight. The long, passionate night when they'd made love over and over, taking its delectable toll. It was as though they were trying to exorcise the demons of the past, as though when buried in each other they could regain something they'd lost.

She allowed it, the fantasy that this could last, because she'd come to the blinding realisation that she'd never stopped loving Gage. She now knew it was why she rarely returned to the US, to the place where they'd begun. She'd stayed in France and video-called the family. Had attended obligatory holidays when her presence had been unavoidable—Christmas, Thanksgiving—and only when internet alerts had told her that Gage was somewhere else so there'd been no chance of ever bumping into one another.

Now, in a car on the soil of the place she'd once believed was home, her anxiety ratcheted higher. Eve took some slow, steady breaths. Checked her phone. Still no real word about her father, just some bland-sounding messages from her mom and sister about him improving and coming out of ICU.

'I thought you'd have an apartment here,' she said as they pulled up outside an anonymous boutique hotel where a doorman waited for them.

Gage shook his head, gazing out the window, his mouth narrowed to a tight, hard line. 'I'm not here often enough for somewhere permanent. On the rare occasions I stay, it's at the guesthouse at Mom and Dad's. I didn't think you'd want to go there.'

He was right, but for reasons Gage would never know. That place carried too many memories of the night they'd been foolish and had lacked caution just before they'd run. The night she'd fallen pregnant.

She shoved that thought down into the recesses of her memory where it silently taunted her, and exited into the cool, rarefied air. She held her breath as their bags were taken from the car. Even though the bellhop was careful with their luggage, her small, battered yellow suitcase wasn't treated with as much reverence as it deserved.

Usually she didn't allow anyone else to touch it. It didn't feel right. That one small case held all the wounds of her past. She flexed her fingers. Itched to go retrieve it. Ignored the sensation. Gage had looked at her oddly when she'd demanded she carry it onto the plane herself. There had been too many questions on his face. She didn't want them asked of her.

In the lift to their room Gage grabbed her. Pressed her up against the cool, mirrored wall. Dropped his lips to hers hard, in a kiss that took and conquered. Desperate, as if being here would tear them apart again if they didn't reconnect immediately. She gave in to it, wiping away the memories of being back here. The place that had seen the beginning and the end of them.

They entered the suite, all warm neutrals that said nothing. Their bags would be up soon. She walked through, put down her tote on the plump couch and stared out the window at a city that now seemed foreign to her.

'I should see my family.' She hadn't wanted to mention it because she knew the hatred that ran deep, but she couldn't avoid the inevitable. Her father would know by now, if he was well enough, about Gage. About Knight. But if the man was conscious, she needed to see him, to reset the boundaries of their agreement. Ensure that the secrets he'd promised would be kept dead for ever.

'I know. Has there been any more news on your father?'

She turned away from the view she had no real interest in to look at Gage. His face gave away little. Not anger, or hatred. Nothing but acceptance.

'Not as much as I'd like...' She'd asked to speak to Hugo and the only message she'd received back had been from her mom: *'Reap what you sow...'* 'I suppose you'll want to see your mom and dad too?'

'They're away right now.' He hesitated for a moment, enough for her to notice. 'We can visit when they get back.'

A cold prickle of dread ran down her spine. It was as if everything was slowly escaping her control. Already

Gage seemed to be incorporating her into his life. Even though this was fake, meeting his family as his fiancée *meant* something, she knew it. And how could she face them, knowing what she did? She thought about calling his parents. Demanding they speak with Gage, tell him the truth. But weren't some things their secrets to keep? Did Gus Caron even know himself? It was too much. What she needed wasn't a confrontation but time...

'I don't think that's a good idea.'

'Why?' That question. One word. So innocuous, when her answer could leave her exposed.

'I'm wondering how you're going to explain things when it all ends.'

'Thinking of me, *cher*?'

*Always.* 'I don't want to make things more difficult for you than they have to be.'

'I'm an adult, I can take responsibility for my own decisions.'

'What if I disappoint them?'

'You told me you weren't scared.'

'I'm not.'

Gage cocked his head as if he was about to say something but a knock at the door interrupted his response. He let the porter into the room with their bags. The man dealt with the larger cases and left the small ones for them. Gage thanked him. Gave him a generous tip. She moved to grab her yellow suitcase, to place it somewhere safe. Maybe the back of a wardrobe where it could be hidden from Gage's questioning gaze. Gage snagged it at the same time as she did. She jumped at the shock of his warm hand touching hers as they held the little case between them.

'I can take it,' he said.

She shook her head. He was so close to the truth about everything with his fingers on the handle. He let go as she pulled a little too hard and the latch gave. Her heart jolted to her throat as her life for the past seven years spilled onto the carpet in sheaves of paper and scrapbooks. She let go of the handle and the case tumbled with a thud to the floor.

'*No.*' She bent down, scrambling to snatch everything up, her frantic fingers ineffective at sweeping the scattered papers into a pile and away. Gage bent down to help and her mind blanked as he picked up a scrapbook that had fallen open. The articles she'd collected over the years. Most were on her computer but those she'd found in hard copy she'd carefully cut out and glued onto now yellowed pages. She'd followed Gage's every success and failure with an obsession, to make sure her sacrifice had been worth it. And it had, or so she'd thought.

He flicked through, hesitating on some pages. Picked up another. Seven years of news about him, all collected and curated. His gaze met hers. A frown on his face. His mouth opened, closed. Confusion. She snatched the book from his fingers.

'That's not yours to look at.'

'If not me, then who? Because it's all *about* me. You collected…' His voice choked as he waved his hand over the remaining pages, lying about the carpeted floor like autumn leaves. She spied the corner of an official document, stowed in a plastic sleeve. One that had the power to tear the lies of the past seven years apart.

'So what if I did?'

'So *what*? You told me… You said… And yet you've been collecting articles about me. You didn't forget. You didn't put us behind you. Why?'

She gritted her teeth. Steeled herself for untruths to hide even greater secrets. This had to end now. 'We were too young. It would never have worked long term. Better the recriminations then than divorce lawyers now.'

'No.' He wouldn't stop looking at the papers on the floor, now running his hands through them, sorting, shifting. 'I do *not* believe you had so little faith in us.'

Eve didn't know what to do. She trembled, fighting back the tears threatening to fall.

*'Stop.'*

Gage didn't look up. He didn't acknowledge her at all and then there it was. Safely pressed into a journal. The midwife working at the hospital had done it for her. Tiny footprints and handprints in blue, from a soul who had come too early and left too soon. Gage held them for a few seconds before they slipped from his fingers, the precious papers falling back to the carpet to join the rest. He scrabbled through what remained until he came to the printed official French document.

Eve froze to the spot. She couldn't do anything but kneel there and watch the past years of their lives unravel like a skein of wool.

Because their son had breathed, he had a birth certificate. Louis Gage Chevalier. A name they'd always loved. Louis for a boy, Catherine for a girl. They'd dreamed every dream when they'd spun those fantasies with one another, when they'd been barely out of childhood themselves.

'A… a baby?' He scanned the page, looked at her, scanned it again. The paper shaking in his hands, *'Our* baby?'

'Yes.' Tears she'd promised she wouldn't cry anymore began sliding down her cheeks.

The heat of banked anger flared in Gage's eyes. 'How could you keep our son…*my* son…?'

She bit her lip hard to try and quell the pain with something physical but the sharp bite did nothing to ease the hurt that had never quite healed, like a constant bruise. A lifetime was still too soon. But their child deserved to be finally known and acknowledged by someone other than her. And if Gage knew, maybe he'd stop asking questions that would lead to the most important secret of all she kept from him. A secret that was becoming harder to keep as time slid by.

'I didn't realise I was pregnant, not at first.' The stress, the heartbreak. Not eating, not sleeping. They'd all taken a toll and she hadn't put together what it meant when she'd missed her period. 'And when I did… You can't imagine.'

Being in France made it easier but she'd been terrified that someone would find out. Her father would have lost his mind if he'd known, and she'd already hurt Gage too much. In the beginning it had been what had driven her to succeed, to study and put everything behind her because she'd needed to keep secret the child she carried. At least for a while till she could plan, because after what she'd said to Gage it would have killed her if he'd questioned who the father was or, even worse, denied their baby.

'Where the hell *is* he?'

She couldn't say the words. Instead Eve gently sifted through the detritus of her life lying scattered on the floor. She found the document she was looking for and gave it to him. Whilst he might not be able to understand all that was written on the page, he'd recognize what it meant. Another official paper that had marked the end of all her dreams.

'I finally saw a doctor and it was going okay. Then at twenty-three weeks, it didn't.' She couldn't express the hope that had died then. It had felt like she had too, and a new Eve Chevalier had been carved from the winter of all that grief. Colder. Harder. The softness pared out of her. 'He was born so small. They tried to save him and he fought so hard, but…' She shook her head. In the days after that she'd become a zombie. The emotions too big to suffer alone and yet there was no alternative. Trying to hide what had happened because she'd been determined no one would ever find out.

'You should have said. I would have…' The look of anguish in his eyes as their worlds crumbled before them, all the things she'd hidden stitched tightly inside. Gage had that way of unpicking them one by one. 'Why didn't you tell me? Were you ever going to?'

'I was terrified.' At least that was a small part of why she'd done what she'd done. 'Scared of what my father would do.' If he'd known, he would have told Gage the truth about his parentage. She remembered that time of fear. Carrying Gage's child. Wanting to protect him, wanting to sort out the risks for them all in her heart before she announced to the world she was pregnant and the father was Gage.

'That man.' Gage surged from his knees towards her, a fire igniting in his eyes. 'Did Hugo ever hurt you because of me?'

His rage burned like molten metal, thick and scorching. Not at her, but *for* her. She shook her head.

'No. But I thought if I told him about the baby, he might have done something.'

'There is nothing he could have done to you because I *would* have come for you.'

'You were another country away. He had all the power. And by the time I thought I could say something it was all over, so I kept it to myself because you didn't need to suffer this pain.'

Yet as much as the ache now always lived inside her, it felt good to share. To finally acknowledge with another person that their little boy had lived, if only for a short time.

'I'm suffering it now,' Gage said, his voice as cracked and broken as her heart. He flicked through more of the material till he found an old, faded photograph of her, holding their little boy all swaddled and hidden. The pain, raw on her face. Her midwife had said it would help, one day, to have this photo. That at some time in the future she'd want these memories.

'You've carried this case around since then,' he said.

'I carry it everywhere. It's always with me.'

Gage hunched over the papers as if curling into himself. The photograph dropped from his fingers and fell to the floor. He buried his head in his hands as his shoulders shuddered. He uttered no sound, but she knew his pain. She'd carried it around with her for too long. Six birthdays, six Mother's Days. Every milestone she should have been celebrating with their child, lost to her.

She draped herself over Gage's trembling body. Wrapped her arms around his shoulders and let the years of unshed tears fall. *Finally,* there was someone who knew. Another person who could mark the date as it passed. And as they clung on to each other a selfish, wicked thought grabbed hard at her like a kudzu vine and wouldn't let go. What if she could have Gage after all these years? But wanting was a dangerous thing. She still had secrets to keep, though holding them back now felt like trying to stop sand running through an hourglass.

It just ran through her fingers instead.

# CHAPTER TEN

THIS PLACE HELD too many memories of his failures and regrets, and those regrets almost crushed Gage now. The pain in his chest wouldn't go away, a tearing, cutting kind of agony. He wondered if it ever would. All the things he and Eve had missed together threatened to slice him to pieces. The child lost to them both. He didn't know how Eve had dealt with it on her own, away from any support. How it didn't crush her now.

What if he'd ignored her cruel words seven years ago, had followed her across the world and fought for the woman he loved rather than giving up and wallowing in self-indulgence over her rejection? They could have been a family or, even if things had still turned out badly with their baby, they would have had each other to cling to. Instead, Eve had suffered in a foreign country. Alone.

Her weight lifted from his back, where she'd held onto him and poured out her grief along with his. He couldn't understand how she could forgive what he never would—the end of everything they'd hoped for. He took a deep breath against the sadness that threatened to overwhelm him. He'd never forget what had been done by Eve's family. If he had to maintain the rage for both of them, then so be it. It was bright and hot enough to consume the grief of a thousand people and still have room to devour more.

He straightened up to look at Eve, her beautiful face marred by tears, blotchy and red. He gritted his teeth. 'Hugo *will* pay. For it all. If it's the last thing I do with my last breath, he'll know the meaning of suffering. A lifetime of it isn't enough for what he's done. Where is he now? Because, God help him, a reckoning is coming.'

Her eyes widened and she paled to the colour of parchment. The ruins of her mascara stood out as dark, wet tracks under her swollen eyes. She shook her head. 'No.'

*'No?'* Gage stood and began to pace. She was still defending him, after all that man had done?

'If you go to see him, what will you do?' Her voice trembled and choked as she stayed on her knees, as if begging him to stop what he never would. *Ever.* 'What will it achieve?'

He wheeled round. How could she not see? Her family, her *father* had destroyed their lives. Tainted the last seven years with his special brand of poison.

'I want to show him that he's lost, and I have it *all*. His company, and especially what he tried to keep from me. *You.*'

Eve scrambled to her feet. 'So I'm still being used as a weapon?'

She was talking in riddles.

'What the hell do you mean?'

'There's a future that holds love, not this hatred.' She clasped her hands in front of her. 'My father will reap his reward. There's nothing you can do to him that will make him unhappier than he is now, than he has been for most of his adult life.'

He shook his head, unbelieving. How she could even acknowledge Hugo after all that had gone before was unfathomable. 'You're protecting him?'

She shook her head, eyes wide. 'I'm protecting *you*. That's why I won't let you go.'

'You can't stop me.' He snatched his phone from his pocket, called for a car. 'Tell me where he is, or I'll find him on my own. He'll know what he did!'

His ride would be here in under ten minutes. So little time and too much, when he wanted to rush out and tear her father's world apart, like he'd done to theirs. Gage paced the carpet, unable to stop because if he did, he feared he might fall and never get up. Eve didn't move. How could she be so still? With her arms now wrapped tightly around her waist, biting into her lower lip. Then she reached out, grabbed his arm and he had no choice but to stand there, forcing himself to stay upright.

'Gage, *please*.' Eve's grip was tight and strong for such slender fingers, her voice a bare tremor in the otherwise brutal silence of the room. 'You can't go… There are things you need to know… The truth of why I ended…us.'

The answer to the questions he'd asked for seven years hung just out of reach. Now nothing would get him to move from the spot in which he stood. Yet Eve seemed frozen, her eyes wide and pupils mere pinpricks. A pulse thrashed wildly at the base of her throat, as if they were on the edge of something too big to be knowable.

If anyone were to break the inertia, it would have to be him.

'What?'

The word jolted like a shock through Eve. She pulled her hand back as if he'd burned her. Now she was the one to pace, hands fluttering restlessly as she spoke.

'You've got to understand. At the time he said things were bad with Caron and that if he told everyone what he knew, it might fold. You love your parents. I didn't want you hurt like that.'

And still she didn't make sense. None of this did, her defence of Hugo. *Nothing.* 'What the hell are you talking about?'

'I can't… I have to…' She stopped. Her chest heaved as if every breath was an effort. Her eyes spilled over with tears. He almost moved to hold her up, because now it was as if she was the one who might fall. 'You need to know. Your father… Gus…is not your father.'

Everything froze, like the room had been hit by an ice storm.

*'Chevaliers are charlatans and cheats, never to be trusted.'*

His dad's words screamed in his ears. Gage shook his head, pointed at her, punctuating the air with his finger.

'No. You're lying.' Eve reared back like she'd been struck. 'It's not true. It's—'

'You need to talk to your mom and dad. Why would I lie?' Her hands were stretched out, as if imploring him to believe her when what she said was unbelievable. 'I've seen the evidence. My father said if I didn't end things, he'd tell everyone you weren't Gus's son. Better you hated me than you lost everything. I had to do it. To protect you.'

Gage shook his head. It couldn't be true. He was a Caron. Gus was his dad.

'Doesn't wash, *cher.* How were you going to explain us to your daddy now? That promise you demanded he keep was worthless with us together.'

Though only hours ago if Eve had told him she'd had a baby, he might not have believed that either…

'I thought we'd be done by the time my father recovered, if he did… Then things changed…' She tortured the sapphire ring on her finger, twisting it back and forth. Staring at the gleaming gems. It hit him so hard it felt like the breath had been almost knocked from his lungs.

Those questions he'd asked of his parents when he'd been a child. How he didn't really look like his dad. The dread of realisation frosted over him because in the end, here was the perfect explanation for Eve's cruelty, the only one that made sense.

He'd been going to confront her father, and Eve knew Hugo would tell him what she'd kept hidden all these years.

Gus Caron was *not* his father.

That knowledge now fired the burn inside, a blinding realisation of all the lies told and toxic secrets kept.

'If your daddy had died you'd have kept this secret, wouldn't you?' he hissed. 'When I *deserved* to know.'

She walked up to him, a tentativeness about her as if she was approaching a wild animal. Maybe that's exactly what he was. The feral desire to lash out and hurt those he loved bit down hard. He barely held it in check because he knew only too well that words, once spoken, couldn't be unsaid.

'You did need to know but it wasn't my story to tell and it should never have been told to you in hatred. The story needed to be told to you in love, by your parents. I—I was going to talk to them. Ask them to speak to you, and then…'

She looked at all the papers and scrapbooks lying in a scattered mess across the floor, like their dreams. Nothing could ever be the same after today. His world had ended and he wasn't sure how to start living again.

'So I'm not a Caron.' Gage turned his back on her. Walked away towards the window with fists clenched. Looked out at the view of a city he now loathed. 'It's too late now. This. Everything.'

He'd been a father, and hadn't known it. He was a bastard, and hadn't known that either. Nothing seemed stable anymore, like the ground had cracked beneath his feet. He dropped his head and looked at the floor to make sure it was solid because it felt like it would open up and swallow him whole. The hair on the back of his neck pricked, warning of someone close. Then there was a gentle press of a palm, which he supposed was meant to comfort, but instead it felt like a stab in the back. Just one more knife in the multitude that had struck there and stuck, leaving him permanently wounded.

'So much that's happened has been so wrong, but we can make it right. There's a future and we can—'

Gage wheeled round, and Eve took a step back. What could she see on his face that made her want to give him space? Not even he could read the emotions now churning inside him bar one. An endless hatred, focussed laser bright on one man.

'Your father deserves to be punished, and I will *relish* meting it out to him.'

Eve looked up at him, those blue eyes of hers so pale and sad. He wondered when he'd become inured to all the grief.

'And what happens when you're done with that? What then?'

He frowned. What did she mean? He'd triumph, that's what would happen.

'Then it'll be over.'

'Do you have any idea how to live a life where revenge isn't part of it?' She held out her hand and placed it on the centre of his chest, where his heart should be beating. He wasn't sure it was anymore. 'When will it ever be enough?'

The answer rang clear: it would *never* be enough, not for him. 'How can you let this go? He stole everything from us.'

'I don't care about that man. I can't control what he does, only what I feel. All I care about is you. Trust me, this will eat away at you like it's done to him.'

The heat of her palm burned into him, a reminder of how cold he'd become.

'I'm *not* your father.'

'No. Not now. But one day, if you keep going, you will be. What if my father's gone? I'm his daughter. Will you end up hating me too? This needs to stop.'

He moved away from Eve with her imploring eyes and gentle hands. Softer emotions had no place here, not in this room where all his hope had been smashed and broken. 'It'll stop when I say it does, or your father's in the grave.'

Eve clenched her fists by her sides. 'He could live another twenty years, and you want to carry on hating him for that long?'

He'd never stop. 'I'll loathe him till I'm in the grave myself.'

Her tears fell again, slipping down her cheeks, tracking down her pale skin. There'd been so many tears today they could have filled rivers with them. Eve wiped at her face, took a deep breath. Stood firm and proud.

'I have loved you for almost my whole life. I will continue to love you all the days I have left,' she said, taking the engagement ring from her finger and holding it out to him. For a moment he had trouble understanding what it all meant. 'But I can't do this anymore. I won't allow hatred to rule my life or infect another day.'

He stared at the ring for a few moments, then looked back at her. There was no way she would walk away from him, not now, not after everything. Not with so much left unfinished.

'We have a deal, and you're breaking it? If you don't carry this through to the end—'

'Then you'll what? Destroy me too?' She didn't look angry, she didn't look sad, just worn down and tired. Like someone had carved out all the vibrant parts of her and left a pale husk behind. 'I beg you, try your hardest because *nothing* could hurt me much more than I'm hurting now. I'll keep to our deal. You want to wheel me out as your fake fiancée for Greta Bonitz or anyone else? Fine. But us? We're done. Because your hatred for my father is stronger than your love for me, and I deserve more than that. I deserve *everything*.'

Her voice cracked and broke. She turned around, placed the ring on the side table and walked out the door, leaving all his dreams a tattered ruin in her wake.

# CHAPTER ELEVEN

GAGE DROVE HIS rental car through the iron gates of his parents' home, roaring up the long drive past flowering hedges. He'd learned to ride a bicycle on this drive when he was five. His dad had taught him. Wobbling on training wheels with Gus always at his side, murmuring encouragement. The day those wheels had come off, he'd pedalled recklessly down to the end, the breeze whistling in his ears and his dad whooping and cheering after him.

His hands gripped the steering wheel hard. He parked the car, wrenched the door open and hurled himself out, slamming the door behind him. No, not his dad. Had both of his parents kept the secret, or was Gus ignorant? It was as if the people he'd loved his whole life, were now strangers to him.

He stood outside the front doors of his family home and looked up at the expansive portico above. When he'd been younger he'd seen this place as his heritage. All lies. His world was steeped in them so deeply he couldn't see the truth for the darkness anymore. Couldn't see any way out as everything he'd believed and known crumbled around him.

For so many years, he'd thought he'd known the enemy. Eve. Visions of her demanding better. Handing back the ring. Walking with her head held high out the door, that was a gaping wound he was sure would never heal. Yet again she'd left him. But she'd only been a bit player in this game, and he couldn't process that pain right now. His enemies had turned out to be closer to home. The one place he'd believed he was safe from lies and it turned out even here truth was lacking.

What was left for him now? He'd been conducting this quest for revenge on behalf of a family that wasn't even his. Every foundation he'd built his life on was an illusion. He didn't even know *who* he was.

He grabbed his keys to the house and opened the front door. Maybe he should give them back, since it didn't feel he had any rights here. This place had once been the happiest of homes. That had changed when Eve had left, the estate containing too many memories of her presence, so he rarely visited. Now he wondered whether there was reason to visit ever again.

His father would likely be in the den, so Gage made his way there, everything passing by in an amorphous blur. He was an imposter, with no place here. As he walked, he tamped down the sensation that grabbed his throat and squeezed till he reached the doorway. There the choking feeling increased till there was hardly enough air to fill his lungs. The man he'd once believed to be his father, a man he'd looked up to and admired as honest and good in a world full of fakes, glanced up, saw him. A smile broke out on his face as he stood.

'Gage! What are you doing here? We weren't expecting you.' His father looked happy after his break away. A prelude to retirement and handing over the reins of a company Gage wasn't sure he wanted any longer. Then the smile stuttered, died. Replaced by the tight mask of disapproval unvoiced. 'Is Eve with you?'

The wound in his heart opened and bled a little more.

While this place held too many memories, his parents had been the bedrock of his life. He'd always pitied Eve's family and the conditional love she'd been shown. Now all he could do was stare.

He wasn't this man's child. If that dirty secret hadn't been kept, he and Eve could have been together. All that had gone before came down to this. His family's secrets and lies were the cause. His father, because he didn't know what else to call him, frowned.

'Son. What's wrong? Are the Chevaliers causing trouble? Has Eve...?'

He could hear the unfinished sentence. *Has Eve left you again*? How could he say what was wrong when everything was now over? It was too much to articulate. Eve had gone. He didn't know who the people who he'd once called his parents were anymore. His whole world had shifted and tilted, as if he'd woken up in an alternate dimension.

'I'm not your son, am I?'

He didn't know how he got the words out. They cut at his throat like ground glass. His father paled.

'What do you mean?' For a few moments Gage almost hoped that his father didn't know. That at least one of his parents hadn't been part of the duplicity. But the man who had always looked him straight in the eye now wouldn't meet his gaze.

'I'm. Not. Your. Son.'

Gus's legs gave way and he fell back into the leather chair. He buried his face in his hands. After a few moments he looked up at Gage, eyes moist with tears.

'How did you find out?'

Gage shut his own eyes for a moment as the words struck him with the force of a blow. Gus could not have hurt him more if he'd hit him. A punch would have been preferable.

'Does it matter?'

The final conversation with Eve screamed loudly in his ears. Then her rejection. Nothing mattered, with his world collapsing around him.

'No. It doesn't. Because you have always been my son.' The lines on Gus's face were etched deeper now, like his father had aged twenty years in a matter of moments. Gone was the strong man, the head of their small family. This man was a ghost. 'You were my son the day you were born.'

Gage shook his head, stabbed his finger at the air in front of him. 'But you're not my father.'

Gus flinched. Stood again. Walked out from behind the old oak desk that Gage had once been destined to inherit. 'I took you fishing for bass. I taught you how to cast. We went to Little League together. I was with you every step as you pieced back together the heart a damned Chevalier shredded. I loved you then. I still love you, and you will *always* be my son.'

They sounded like fine words, but now it was all just a charade. His father glanced over his shoulder, a crease forming between his brows, pain written all over his face. Pain he'd last seen when Gus had bailed him out of a jail cell with a broken nose and terror in his heart. Pain Gage didn't give a damn about right now.

Let them all suffer. Let it all burn.

'Darling, it's lovely to see you…' His shoulders sagged. His mom. At least he knew one parent here was his. Gage didn't turn to look at her. She'd hidden as much from him as the man in front of him had.

'Betty, he knows.'

His mom stepped forward into his peripheral vision and grabbed the back of the chair in front of her.

'Darling.' Her voice was the barest of whispers. 'Please understand…'

He didn't want to hear. In this room the lies were the cause of all his hurts.

'There's nothing to understand, *Mom*. You lied to me. That man…' He pointed to the man who'd raised him. Whom he'd once loved. 'That man is not my father.'

Gus Caron looked at him. Stricken. His colour was grey. Gage didn't care. The pain on his parents' faces could never match the pain that was tearing him in two.

'Betty. This is a conversation I need to have with my boy.'

'I… I'll get some iced tea.'

'No. I think we need something stronger.'

'Then I'll leave you to talk.' His mother looked at him, tears dripping down her cheeks, before she left the room. He'd made a woman he loved cry, yet again. His father walked to a sideboard, grabbed a bottle and held it up.

'Want some?'

Gage shook his head. Gus poured himself a three-finger slug and his father was not a drinker.

'Hiding this from you was never planned. It just…never seemed a good time to say anything.'

Gage gritted his teeth so hard he thought they might crack. 'I asked you when I was nine why I didn't look like you. You both said I took after Mom's family.'

'You need to understand—'

'You all keep saying that and I've tried, but I'm out of ideas. Why don't you explain it to me? Because you've had *thirty* years!'

Gus gulped down half his drink. Winced. 'We were overjoyed to have you. And it didn't seem to matter. You were all your mother and I wanted. We tried to have children when we first got married. We couldn't. There was a problem with me.'

Gage had a small, sharp moment of bright hope, a shard that inserted itself and stuck. 'So you used a sperm donor?'

His father shook his head and that hope was dashed.

'You know your mom and I married young. It was one of the *many* reasons we were so against you and Eve, but especially given what happened to us… Marriage. It isn't easy. Which is something you'll learn with Eve if… But you're both older. Better able to deal with what will come your way.'

Gage looked down at his hands, gripping the leather seat back of the chair he stood behind. His nails cut into it. There was no relationship anymore. He and Eve were done. He held on even harder, because it felt right now like he was bleeding out all over the floor.

'We tried for so long to have a baby. Everything failed. Doctors said there was no explanation. Just one of those things. *Idiopathic infertility.*'

His father twirled the crystal tumbler in his hands. Took another mouthful of liquor.

'We weren't happy, son. Things were going wrong. And your mother and I, we both sought to ease our pain elsewhere.'

Gage rubbed his hands over his face. For as long as he'd been alive his parents had loved each other. He'd thought their marriage had been perfect. They had been an immutable force and now this? He shook his head. 'I don't want to know.'

'You're an adult and you need to hear this. It's where it starts. Your mom fell pregnant. It wasn't planned. It just happened. She didn't want to be with the father. He didn't want her either.'

'Who is he? Do I know him? Did he know about me?'

'Yes, he knew about you. No, you don't know him. I can give you his name. He's a businessman in California with a wife and two grown kids of his own. A whole lot of folks made a whole bunch of mistakes back then and in the end he didn't want to be in your life. Your mom and I had a choice to make. We wanted children. And here was our chance.'

Gage couldn't stand any longer. He pulled out the chair he'd been holding onto and sat, trembling. He regretted refusing his father's offer, wanting a drink of whiskey now himself to numb the feelings that rioted inside him. 'I wasn't a commodity.'

'No. You were our greatest success and greatest love. And yet you were a product of our greatest failings. Neither your mom nor I were innocent in this thing. In the end we had to fight hard for our marriage, and we succeeded. You're a blessing. I didn't care who your biological father was. I'd been no prince myself and it would have been hypocritical of me to criticise your mom for failing when I had first, and more than once. It wasn't easy fixing our marriage. Both of us had a great deal to forgive the other for. The easy thing was always you. From the moment you were born you were my son. You were no one else's.'

'How did you do it? How did you forgive her?'

His father downed the last of his glass, sat back in his chair. Looked at him with soft warmth in his clear brown eyes. A look that had once been familiar and was now strange and confusing.

'While saving the marriage was one of the hardest things I've done, in the end forgiving was easy. I forgave your mom because I love her.'

Gage left the house, wandered through the sprawling gardens, down to the edge of the property, to where the large magnolia grew. He leaned against the trunk, sliding down to sit on the ground underneath. Not caring if he ruined his trousers in the tree's detritus, not caring about anything at all. He felt numb, broken by the revelations of the past few days.

About Eve leaving him.

He shook his head, refused to think about it, about her final words. Gage stared at the huge wall separating his parents' land from the Chevaliers'. From a vantage point in the branches above he used to watch Eve in the garden. He'd been lonely, an only child with not many friends to play with, and a bright little girl picking flowers hadn't seemed like the enemy but a possible friend.

To this day he still didn't know why the Carons and the Chevaliers held such enmity towards each other. It had been ingrained in his psyche for so long he hadn't questioned it. From imploring him never to go over the fence if he lost a ball or a paper plane there to the open hostility when they saw each other in public, he'd grown to accept something he should have fought, for Eve's sake and for his own. As children they hadn't embraced the hatred that had poisoned every interaction between their families. As young adults they'd naïvely thought they could end it. Until seven years ago when he'd believed he'd finally understood that a Chevalier could never be trusted. Turned out the people he shouldn't trust had been far closer to home.

More fool him for believing *anyone*.

Footsteps scuffed through the fallen leaves surrounding him. He looked to his left, up at the pale, drawn face of his mom.

'Darling, I'm so sorry.'

He shrugged. What did it matter now? Apologies changed nothing. He was here. Eve was gone. His father wasn't his father. Nothing was right with the world as he knew it.

'At least you're my mother.'

'Do *not* say that to me. I understand you're angry. You have every right to be. But think.' She pointed up to the house, her voice trembling. 'That man has been *nothing* but your father since the day you were born.'

If he tried to intellectualise it, his mom was right. He couldn't fault Gus. Apart from how they looked and that one question when he'd been nine, he'd never guessed his dad was not his blood. The man had given him unflinching love and support, had bailed him out of jail when he'd been arrested after he and Eve had run. Paying lawyers to clear his name. Never, ever questioning what had led Gage to flee in the dead of night with the daughter of a sworn enemy. Nursing him through the hangovers and poor behaviour after Eve had told him never to speak to her again.

Other kids had always been envious of how much his dad loved him, including Eve. He'd always thought how lucky he'd been. He knew it, but that didn't stop the pain scouring through his veins like acid.

'Were you ever going to tell me?'

His mom sighed, sat down next to him in her pretty dress on the leaves and raw earth. She'd get dirty too and he wasn't sure why that worried him. His mom cupped his cheek. Her fingers were warm, but a tremor ran through them.

'I wish I could say we were bigger people. But no. Time passed and the harder it became till we wondered what the point would be. Then you told us you were engaged to Eve—'

Pain struck him straight to the heart. He rubbed his chest. 'You don't have to worry about that. We're not engaged now.'

The silence his words met flayed him some more. His parents' disapproval had been clear. It had needled in the beginning, even if the arrangement with Eve was a fake. But right now he couldn't bear to hear it. His mom took a deep breath.

'Oh, sweetheart. Why?'

The words caught in his throat. A tight lump that he swallowed down before it choked him. 'She knew all along about me not being dad's son. Her father threatened to tell me if she didn't break it off all those years ago. She was pregnant. She lost the...'

He couldn't go on. The pain of it was too much. His mom wrapped him in her arms, like she'd done so many times when he'd been a child.

'I'm sorry,' she murmured into his hair. 'I know platitudes will never be enough. As adults, we have so *much* to beg Eve's and your forgiveness for. We've all failed you because we acted like children and couldn't let things go.'

He took a deep breath. 'She says I'm like her father.'

'You must have made her furious to use that insult.'

'I said and did things I'm not proud of.'

His mom patted him on the arm. 'That one statement tells me you're not like him, because you have the capacity to learn. Hugo Chevalier doesn't. He never did, which is one of the reasons I fell in love with your father. We may have had our problems. Serious problems. But your father could think and reason and he cared. He's the best of men, even with his human frailties. You take after him, not that man next door who only ever wanted to tear things apart.'

Gage looked up at his mom, the belief in what she saw written in the gentle smile on her face. 'You have so much faith in me.'

'Your father and I both do, darling. It's time you had faith in yourself.'

He didn't know what to do, how to fix this. All he knew

was that he loved Eve, had never, ever stopped, and he wasn't sure how to tell her, how to forgive…either of them.

'There's one question I've never asked. Why do our families hate each other so much? How did it come to this?'

His mom looked at the fence separating the two properties then back to their home.

'That's a long story,' she said.

'Then tell me.' Gage leaned back against the trunk of the old tree. 'Seems I've got all the time in the world.'

# CHAPTER TWELVE

EVE PUFFED OUT a breath, blowing at a strand of unruly curls that had fallen across her face. She wiped her hands on her dusty jeans and looked around at the packing boxes now filling her Paris apartment. She'd made a few hard choices after leaving Gage and America behind.

The agony of that decision still sliced right through her, stinging as fresh as a papercut, but she'd finally concluded that she deserved *more*. All her life she'd danced to the tune of others. She was tired of living the way everyone else expected, and now she'd had enough. This time was her own.

So she'd flown back to France, given notice that Knight needed to find another CEO for the French operation, and had walked away from it all. Putting hatred and anyone determined to hang onto it behind her. She'd seen the way that emotion destroyed. It had no place in her life anymore.

As soon as she packed up her possessions here, she'd move and start growing the plants she loved. A simple life worrying about the soil, sun and scent and nothing much else. At the same time she'd try to heal her broken heart, though she knew that there were some things from which she might never fully recover. Putting her heart back together was one, because some of the pieces were missing. They probably always had been.

But thoughts of heartbreak weren't going to get this apartment packed, and the drive to move and move forward was the only thing keeping her upright. Kitchen, she'd do that next. As Eve grabbed a box and began taping it, her intercom sounded. It was the apartment's concierge. She answered.

'Mademoiselle Chevalier, a delivery.'

She breathed out a sigh of relief. 'Thank you. Send them up.' The extra packing boxes she ordered. At a knock, she opened the door. Only it wasn't packing boxes, but two men, each holding a vase of flowers.

These weren't just any flowers either, but blowsy English roses in a riot of pinks and apricots. Perfect, rambunctious blooms spilling from their containers, filling the hall with a glorious scent.

Her heart throbbed as she gripped the hard wood of the door, frozen. Staring like a fool at the men, who were only trying to do their jobs. She shook herself out of her inertia, stood back and let them in, asking them to place the roses on the dining table and sideboard.

'Is there any card?' She didn't really need one. There was only one person who they could be from. A surge of emotion welled inside, threatening to break her. She bit her lip to tamp it down.

One of the men shrugged. '*Non*. Only flowers.'

They left and she moved to close the door but one of the men stopped her with a wry smile.

'There are more.'

She stood back as the flowers kept coming, filling her apartment. Magnificent vases were placed on every flat surface with roses bursting from them as she directed where they should go.

She looked around at all the colour overwhelming the space and realised it had never really been a home to her because it hadn't held all of her heart. Those missing pieces she'd left years ago with Gage. He'd always kept a part of her, always would. She wiped away a tear that threatened to fall. He wasn't her future. That was now a quiet, peaceful life. Let Gage and her father wage a war of revenge and attrition. Too much had been lost, and for what? She was sick of the game and the hand she kept being dealt, so she'd folded. Tossed her cards on the table and walked away.

The final vase was placed on a small side table, which looked like it would topple under the weight of the outrageous arrangement.

'Is that all?' she asked, looking around the room that seemed more like a florist's shop than an apartment now.

'Not quite.'

She stilled. That voice, the deep burr of it igniting a fire in her that would probably never go out. She whipped around.

Gage stood there in the doorway to her apartment, cradling in the crook of his arm a large bunch of purple and lavender roses wrapped in petal pink paper and Cellophane. He wore soft, faded jeans and a crumpled shirt. Stubble shadowed his angular jaw, his golden hair all messy, as if he'd raked through it with restless fingers. It looked like he'd rolled out of bed, thrown on clothes left over from a long night before and run over here. But he couldn't have done that. Instead, he'd travelled halfway around the world. To see her.

Her traitorous heart skipped a few beats.

He was so beautiful it hurt. The way his worn clothes hugged the muscles of his strong body. The planes of his face more angular than she remembered. Honed. *Determined*. His blue eyes like the summer skies in Grasse that would always haunt her. She'd loved him her whole life, no matter how many times she'd lied to herself, trying to convince her wounded heart they'd never had a chance. Every part of her was attuned to him, even when they'd been apart.

It was something she had to come to terms with because he couldn't be the man she wanted. She needed to put the warring behind her. She deserved more than being a pawn on a chessboard built of loathing. The terrible thing was that Gage deserved more too but he wouldn't see it. She couldn't bear to witness the man she'd loved for most of her days becoming a slave to hatred, being eaten away by degrees.

'May I come in?' he asked, still standing outside the door, not even a toe over the threshold.

She somehow convinced her trembling legs to move and stood back, whilst he edged past. She shut the door with a soft snick behind her and he followed her into the lounge area.

'These are for you.' He held out the bouquet. She took it from him and buried her nose in the velvety petals, inhaling their scent. Lemon and raspberries.

'I think I probably have enough.'

'You can never have too many flowers.' He looked around the room, down at the floor, then his gaze rested on the packing boxes. 'You're moving. To Grasse.'

It wasn't a question. A jolt of surprise spiked through her. 'Is that an educated guess?'

Gage ran his hand through his hair. 'A large parcel of Caron shares has been sold. Your loan's been repaid. The farm is off the rental market and you've resigned as CEO. It's no guess.'

She put the flowers on a chair. They could go into water later, once she'd dealt with this and moved on, but tell that to her body, which vibrated at the impossible thrill of having him near, in her space. She cocked her head. 'You been keeping an eye on me?'

'Always.' Gage's voice ground out, wounded and raw. His throat convulsed in a swallow. 'I don't know how to look away.'

And there was the anguish of them, described in one sentence. Neither of them knew how to stop this. For days after she'd come here she'd barely been able to haul her sorry self out of bed each morning. It had been a struggle to simply put one foot in front of the other and not to scour the internet for any news about him. She'd wondered if she'd ever fully get over him and had resigned herself to that answer being 'No'. He would always be part of her. Even now, she craved to reach out, to touch him. To comfort and be comforted. To trace her hands over his strong arms. Arms where she'd once felt protected. Loved... And yet going back felt like an end, not a beginning.

Finally, someone had to say *enough*.

'Gage, what are you doing here?'

'I've come to talk. I've been so focussed on...what's gone wrong in my life.'

She planted her hands on her hips. 'You can say the word. It's *revenge*.' She'd been in denial for so long she refused to accept the same of him.

Gage nodded. 'You're right. I've been so focussed on *revenge* I lost sight of everything that might have been good.' He shoved his hands in the pockets of his jeans and for a moment looked like a chastened schoolboy. 'I've spoken to my parents.'

That conversation must have been awful. Her heart, which she was struggling to harden, softened a little further. 'I'm sorry to have been the one to tell you, but you needed to know. If only—'

'No.' Gage shook his head. 'There's no need to be sorry.

In the end you were the only one with the courage to say anything. I'm glad it was you, and not Hugo.'

Something inside her unknotted a fraction because that final and terrible decision to say anything at all had tortured her, even though she'd known she'd had no choice. 'How did the conversation with your parents go?'

He shrugged. 'As well as can be expected when finding out the man you've loved as a father all your life, isn't your father. But I learned some things.'

He took a deep breath, looked at her with his summer-blue eyes. Her heart broke all over again every time she was close to him. No more. While it was a difficult habit to overcome, *she* was the priority now. She just had to stay strong.

'Did anyone ever tell you why our families hate each other?' he asked.

'"Carons are liars and thieves."' She repeated the words her family had tried to etch in her consciousness from birth.

Gage cocked his head. '"Chevaliers are charlatans and cheats."'

'Now we've established that, does any other reason matter?'

It didn't really. People had choices. You could move forward and get on with your life or you could wallow. Forward was the only direction for her now.

Yet with Gage here again in her home, surrounded by flowers, the idea of moving forward on her own didn't seem like a triumph. It seemed like a recipe for loneliness, because even when they weren't together, he'd always been her destination. She swallowed back the burn in her throat, the stinging in her nose.

'It matters. Because it's what led us here. It matters because we can't move on unless we know how it began in the first place.' Gage took a step forward, flexing his fingers as if he wanted to touch her. She took a step back and steeled herself, when all she craved to do was tumble into his arms and forget warring families. His shoulders slumped for the briefest of moments then he straightened, like a warrior readying himself for battle, and began pacing.

'It started with a business deal between friends, and bringing the telegraph to Mississippi. Your family claimed mine had a side investment in the company supplying utility poles that wasn't disclosed to Chevalier. Mine say yours inflated quotes to skim the extra and make an outrageous profit at Caron's expense. The hatred grew from there. It waxed and waned over the years depending on which family was doing better. Those things aren't really a surprise.' He stopped tracking across the parquet floor, turned to her. 'Your dad being engaged to my mom is.'

'What?' Her legs almost folded under her. Luckily there was a couch close. She sat down hard, her hand to her chest as if that would somehow settle her pounding heart. 'That's…that's *impossible.*'

Gage remained standing. 'My mom said their parents knew each other, were old friends. An engagement between Mom and Hugo was expected. Then she met my dad. He'd come home from college for the holidays and it was love at first sight. They married young and your dad never forgave her. It caused a scandal at the time, given the rivalry between our families. Though I wouldn't be surprised if Gus secretly liked stealing Mom away from a Chevalier. But things only went nuclear again after Mom had me.'

Eve wrapped her arms around her waist. Gage's voice was distant and remote through the buzzing in her ears. She could put a few things together and the truth of them plunged like a knife and twisted. 'He always wanted a boy.

He was jealous of what your mom and dad had. Two girls were never enough for him.'

'He was a fool. You are enough, *cher*.' His voice was soft and gentle. 'You're more than enough.'

Whatever the truth in Gage's words, the realisation still hurt. 'It's why he was so happy when he found out about you. It meant the dream he assumed was your parents' lives wasn't the fairy-tale he'd imagined.'

Gage walked forward, sat on the couch but as far away from her as he could, like he was giving her space to glue herself back together. It didn't matter. Another country was too close where he was concerned.

'Mom and Dad went through a really bad patch in their marriage. They almost broke up. Of the many reasons they objected to us, our being so young was one of the biggest. They wanted me to have lived my life, be older. Be sure.'

She picked at a loose thread on the knee of her old jeans, anything to resist the urge to close the space, crawl into his arms and never leave. 'I was sure then. The arrogance and innocence of my young self. I thought love would conquer everything. But we would have burned out.'

He shook his head. 'No. We wouldn't. I was sure back then too, and I'm even surer now.'

Her heart pounded a wild and desperate rhythm, crushing the breath right out of her. Hope was something she could not allow to spark, not now. Because that tiny pilot light of hope in the face of all the futility surrounding them had the power to burn her to ashes.

She was terrified of who might rise out of them.

'Gage, stop.'

He ran his hands through his hair again, some golden strands falling over his brow. It almost undid her, seeing this self-contained man so messy and rumpled, all because of her.

'Tell me you don't want me, and I'll walk out the door right now. But I never want you to live under the assumption I didn't love you. I did. I do. I have for years.' Gage turned his body to face her, his gaze steady and sure. 'I'll never stop.'

And it didn't matter what seemed sensible and rational and right. That hope burst to life in a bright, hot conflagration and all she could do was let herself burn.

Gage sat on the edge of the couch, that precarious position a metaphor for his life right now. All that he desired was in this room. There was no plan B for him. It was a case of either living his best life or merely existing. Eve looked away from him, at all the vases that decorated every surface. This gesture, grand as it appeared, wasn't enough. In all reality, probably nothing would be enough to earn her forgiveness for how he'd behaved.

She looked so beautiful and fragile sitting here, like the blooms that filled the room. One wrong breath, a careless touch and the petals would bruise and fall. It was all he could do not to reach out. To brush away the smudge of dust on her cheek. To kiss away the look of sorrow in her eyes, for which he was entirely responsible.

She shook her head. The crack in his heart widened a little more.

'But…you've got no room in your life for me. You want to destroy my family. Life's about living. Building things, not tearing them down.'

The look on her face almost broke him; the corners of her mouth trembling in a futile fight not to turn down. Her eyes were a little red, gleaming with tears he knew she refused to shed. He didn't deserve them anyhow. Didn't deserve her, but he couldn't leave without trying. In the end, all he wanted her to know was that she was loved.

'I was wrong. So wrong in so many ways. Pursuing Knight Enterprises like I did. Forcing you into this situation. They were the actions of a cruel man. You were right to accuse me of becoming like your father. Loving someone means letting them go and I should have done that. Instead, I treated love like a possession. But it's not. It's something bestowed not something you take and hoard. I love you, Eve, but I *will* walk away if that's what you need to be happy.'

Gage inched closer, close enough so their knees brushed. Even that hint of a touch sent shockwaves right through him. Eve didn't turn away, she didn't move at all. This close he could see the tired, dark circles under her eyes that she'd tried to conceal. They reflected his own. Both of them looked wretched.

She stared at where their knees barely touched, before looking at him. Her brows rose a fraction, eyes wide and blue, the question in them clear.

'Can you promise me no revenge?'

In the end that was the easy part. Getting her to trust him would be harder and he'd work at it for ever if he had to. Gage nodded.

'All I want is you. It's all I've ever wanted, I just didn't realise it.' He took her hands in his own. They were cool and the barest of tremors shivered through them. He hoped he could warm her, now and for ever. 'I'm so damned tired of looking for the worst in everything. I want to see the best, and you were always the best thing that had happened in my life. I should have trusted you and our love. If I'd come after you back then, rather than believing the lies, maybe things would have been different.'

She dropped her head, looked at their joined hands. 'You believed me when I was unspeakably cruel. I can hardly forgive myself for what I said to you because my father demanded it.'

'Your words were cruel, but I should have known they were a lie. I should have trusted you more.'

Eve squeezed his fingers, and Gage squeezed back, holding on tight.

'I should have fought for us instead of giving up,' she said.

'I wasn't worthy of you then. And I'm sure as hell not worthy of you now.'

'You were always worthy.' The threatened tears in Eve's eyes now brimmed and overflowed, tracking down her cheeks. 'If you weren't, I wouldn't have tried to protect you.'

He couldn't stand the distance anymore. He reached out to her and hauled her onto his lap. She didn't resist, nestling into him as he wrapped her tightly in his embrace. Closing his eyes and relishing the feel of her again, all soft and pliant. At that moment something about his upside-down world righted itself again.

'It was my job to protect *you*,' he said, murmuring into her unruly hair as it escaped from its tie. He stroked his hand over it, a marvel of twisted silk under his fingers. 'And I failed, in every way.'

'We were both young, neither of us knew what we were doing then.' Eve's fingers traced over his chest, stroking him like some overgrown cat. He could almost have purred at the pleasure of her tentative touches, as if learning him all over again. 'All I know is that I can't live with hate. I want to surround myself with love.'

'You'll have it every day, *cher*. That's one thing I can promise.'

Her hands left his chest, moved to his face and drifted to stroke the bridge of his nose, under his right eye, the places where he carried the scars of that terrible night seven years earlier.

'I'm sorry for these. For my father.'

'I earned them, loving you. You have nothing to apologise for.' It was all he could do not to take her face in his hands, to kiss her. But he held back. There was more that needed to be said. Building a solid foundation for the future he craved, one with Eve as his wife. 'Do you want some company growing your roses?'

She pulled back, looked up at him. 'Don't you have an international conglomerate to run?'

He shrugged. 'I can do that from wherever there's an internet connection. What I want more is you. And I'll be wherever you are. I'll do whatever you need. We'd always planned on making a home like the house in Grasse.'

'So dreams can come true?' Eve's eyes were wide and questioning. He didn't want to make her question, he wanted to be her every answer.

'I think we've spent our lives apart preparing to come back to each other, even if we didn't realise it. So now I want to make our engagement real. To marry you, like we planned once. Does that fit in with your dreams?'

The flicker of her pulse beat strong and solid at the base of her throat. He'd kiss there first, if she let him. When she said yes. For now, holding her, being allowed to love her was enough.

Eve plucked at something on his shirt, gave a light, tremulous laugh. 'Working out place settings for guests at the reception would be a nightmare. Maybe we should elope.'

He placed his fingers under her chin and tilted her face so she'd look at him again. Her eyes were tight, wary. He hated that uncertainty there, the things family enmity had forced upon them. 'You will be the most beautiful bride and I want to see it. It's what I always wanted for you. In whatever dress you've dreamed of, at the wedding you deserve. Nothing less.'

'I never cared about that.' She slid her arms around his neck, threading her fingers into his hair. He relished each touch, caress as a gift of trust. He hoped he could prove himself to her so she'd never doubt anything again. 'All I wanted was you.'

That was the last bit of encouragement he needed. Gage made sure his hold on Eve was secure and stood, cradling her in his arms. She squeaked in surprise but her body didn't tense, as if she was confident of him at last, and that was his promise to this amazing woman. He'd never let her down or let her fall. Ever again.

'You've got me, you always have. But I need to grab something out of my pocket.'

She pouted, tightened her arms around his neck a fraction. He almost gave up on what he'd planned to do. They could find the bedroom instead, stay there all day. Then they could finish packing and move. Together. He wouldn't leave her alone again. But this time he was determined to do it right. To make up in a small way for generations of wrongs. He loosened his grip and she sighed, untangling herself from him and sliding down his body as he bit back a moan.

Gage reached into his pocket, pulled out the glittering engagement ring and held it up. At the time he'd bought it, all he'd been looking for had been something large and valuable. A message to the world and nothing to the woman who would wear it. Until he'd seen this ring, and then all he'd been able to think of was her.

'Our dreams start today. Simple, wild, whatever you want we'll make them true together.'

Eve placed her right hand over his heart, which pounded under her palm. 'My knight in shining armour.'

She smiled, wide and bright. There were tears in her eyes but he knew those were tears of joy. He'd do all he could to never see her cry tears of sadness again.

'Or piratical marauder. I can be either. I can be everything you want and anyone you need.'

Eve's smile turned sultry, her pupils huge, dark caverns in the pale blue. Soon he'd explore everything that wicked mind of hers was conjuring up. Now they had all the time in the world.

'You already are,' she said, her voice low and soft.

He closed his eyes for a moment. Thanking the heavens for this, for her. For second chances. 'Marry me, Eve. We both deserve a happy ending and I'll fight every day to ensure you get it.'

'Yes,' she said, and the power of their love filled him with its warmth as he slipped the ring on her finger. 'There's nothing in the whole world that would make me happier than that.'

# EPILOGUE

*Later*

EVE LAY BACK in Gage's arms on the couch, his fingers tracing along a fine chain round her neck where her wedding and engagement rings lay. It had been a few months now since they'd fitted her fingers. Warmth flooded over her at his gentle caress. He plucked the chain, lifting it so the rings dangled in front of her, swaying back and forth.

'Happy anniversary, Mrs Caron,' he murmured. She loved the sound of those words on his lips. Her dreams spun into a perfect reality with that sentence.

'Two blissful years, Mr Caron.'

She hadn't realised how wrong everything had been until they'd married. Now all seemed right with the world. As if she'd found the last piece of a puzzle, finally fitting it into place. Their wedding had been everything she'd dreamed of, and more. Her dress a confection of antique lace and tulle. Blooms crowning her head as they'd been married surrounded by the flowers of her farm. Roses, lavender, jasmine. Such magic had infused those moments after they'd said their vows, she'd felt like a fairy princess marrying her prince. A day so full of joy she hadn't stopped smiling since.

Even the absence of her family hadn't dented her happiness. They'd made their choices, she'd made hers. She'd promised herself two years ago that the only direction she'd look was forward. With Gage as her husband, it was an easy promise to keep because he was right there with her, supporting her at every step.

Eve reached her arm behind her, running her fingers through Gage's hair as he allowed the rings to nestle back against her chest. She turned her head and he lowered his, capturing her lips in a gentle, lingering kiss.

'You were the most beautiful bride.' His hands slid over her large and still-increasing belly. 'Even more beautiful now. How's our little bean doing in there?'

Eve laughed.

'She's not little anymore, and *definitely* not a *bean*.' Eve shifted to get comfortable then settled again into Gage's embrace. They enjoyed lazing here in the Paris apartment they'd moved back to as her pregnancy had progressed, to be close to the hospital where she'd deliver their baby any day now. As she relaxed, a tell-tale jab struck her near the ribs. 'There! She did it again. Did you feel?'

'Yeah.' She adored the sound of wonder in Gage's voice at their baby's kick. His excitement over every moment of her pregnancy was infectious. Marvelling at the changes in her body, even her swollen fingers and ankles. He rubbed where their baby's foot pressed against his hand. 'Things getting a bit tight in there?'

She smiled. 'Are you trying to say that I'm ripe?'

Gage slid his hand over her stomach, up her arms. The tip of a finger drifted across her collarbone. She closed her eyes, relishing the pleasure of his caress.

'Like a peach. I just want to take a bite.' He dropped his lips to her ear and grazed his teeth over the shell of it, his breath feathering her skin. Goose-bumps shivered down her arms. 'I adore your curves.'

'I adore you,' she said. Their love had grown, expanded. Filling all the holes left behind by grief and loss. There was simply no room for sadness anymore. 'When are your mom and dad planning to come?'

It hadn't taken long for Gage to reframe his family's past, present and future. In a more contemplative moment he'd admitted Gus Caron was exactly the man he would have wanted as a father, if given the choice. And from then on Gus became 'Dad' again.

'A couple of weeks after our little girl arrives, so they say. I'm betting on earlier. How about your sister—have you convinced her to visit?'

Veronique had reached out after the wedding photos had hit the press with a simple text.

You've never looked happier.

The steps to communicating had been tentative, but that was okay. They had all the time in the world.

'She's trying not to show it but she's crazy excited to be an aunty. I'm betting about a day after you send her the first picture, she'll be right on a plane, claiming her status.'

Gage groaned. 'Remind me to delay the photos a bit or the house is going to get crowded.'

'Even if you do, they'll be beating down our door anyhow. There are a lot of people excited about this baby.'

Gage placed a hand over hers, threaded his fingers through her own.

'Call me selfish, but I want a little time to introduce myself to our daughter. To get to know her. Have her get to know us…' His voice caught. Sometimes emotion overcame them both. The excitement, the joy. And for Gage the fierce need to protect.

That was fine, because she protected him right back.

She squeezed his fingers. 'Your daughter will love you just as much as I do. Even more than you love her. I promise.'

'I know. You showed me the way, reminding me *how* to love. I'm so full of it there's no room for anything else.' He lifted their joined hands and pressed hers to his mouth. 'I've loved you my whole life, *cher.*'

The words she'd said to him, the words they'd written into their wedding vows. Their promise to one another. Words of love that filled every day of their lives, now and for ever.

She turned to him and smiled. 'And I'll continue to love you all the days I have left.'

\* \* \* \* \*

# MILLS & BOON

## Coming next month

### THE COST OF CLAIMING HIS HEIR
Michelle Smart

'How was the party?'

Becky had to untie her tongue to speak. 'Okay. Everyone looked like they were having fun.'

'But not you?'

'No.' She sank down onto the wooden step to take the weight off her weary legs and rested her back against a pillar.

'Why not?'

'Because I'm a day late.'

She heard him suck an intake of breath. 'Is that normal for you?'

'No.' Panic and excitement swelled sharply in equal measure as they did every time she allowed herself to read the signs that were all there. Tender breasts. Fatigue. The ripple of nausea she'd experienced that morning when she'd passed Paula's husband outside and caught a whiff of his cigarette smoke. Excitement that she could have a child growing inside her. Panic at what this meant.

Scared she was going to cry, she scrambled back to her feet. 'Let's give it another couple of days. If I haven't come on by then, I'll take a test.'

She would have gone inside if Emiliano hadn't leaned forward and gently taken hold of her wrist. 'Sit with me.'

Opening her mouth to tell him she needed sleep, she stared into his eyes and found herself temporarily mute.

For the first time since they'd conceived—and in her heart she was now certain they *had* conceived—there was no antipathy in his stare, just a steadfastness that lightened the weight on her shoulders.

Gingerly, she sat beside him but there was no hope of keeping a distance for Emiliano put his beer bottle down and hooked an arm around her waist to draw her to him.

Much as she wanted to resist, she leaned into him and rested her cheek on his chest.

'Don't be afraid, *bomboncita*,' he murmured into the top of her head. 'We will get through this together.'

Nothing more was said for the longest time and for that she was grateful. Closing her eyes, she was able to take comfort from the strength of his heartbeat against her ear and his hands stroking her back and hair so tenderly. There was something so very solid and real about him, an energy always zipping beneath his skin even in moments of stillness.

He dragged a thumb over her cheek and then rested it under her chin to tilt her face to his. Then, slowly, his face lowered and his lips caught her in a kiss so tender the little of her not already melting to be held in his arms turned to fondue.

Feeling as if she'd slipped into a dream, Becky's mouth moved in time with his, a deepening caress that sang to her senses as she inhaled the scent of his breath and the muskiness of his skin. Her fingers tiptoed up his chest, then flattened against his neck. The pulse at the base thumped against the palm of her hand.

But, even as every crevice in her body thrilled, a part of her brain refused to switch off and it was with huge reluctance that she broke the kiss and gently pulled away from him.

'Not a good idea,' she said shakily as her body howled in protest.

Emiliano gave a look of such sensuality her pelvis pulsed. 'Why?'

Fearing he would reach for her again, she shifted to the other side of the swing chair and patted the space beside her for the dogs to jump up and act as a barrier between them. They failed to oblige. 'Aren't we in a big enough mess?'

Eyes not leaving her face, he picked up his beer and took a long drink. 'That depends on how you look at it. To me, the likelihood that you're pregnant makes things simple. I want you. You want me. Why fight it any more when we're going to be bound together?'

*Continue reading*
THE COST OF CLAIMING HIS HEIR
Michelle Smart

*Available next month*
www.millsandboon.co.uk

# COMING SOON!

We really hope you enjoyed reading this book.
If you're looking for more romance, be sure to
head to the shops when new books are
available on

# Thursday 10<sup>th</sup> December

# MILLS & BOON

## THE HEART OF ROMANCE

---

## A ROMANCE FOR EVERY KIND OF READER

---

**MODERN**

Prepare to be swept off your feet by sophisticated, sexy and seductive heroes, in some of the world's most glamourous and romantic locations, where power and passion collide.
**8 stories per month.**

**HISTORICAL**

Escape with historical heroes from time gone by. Whether your passion is for wicked Regency Rakes, muscled Vikings or rugged Highlanders, awaken the romance of the past.
**6 stories per month.**

**MEDICAL**

Set your pulse racing with dedicated, delectable doctors in the high-pressure world of medicine, where emotions run high and passion, comfort and love are the best medicine.
**6 stories per month.**

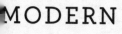

Celebrate true love with tender stories of heartfelt romance, from the rush of falling in love to the joy a new baby can bring, and a focus on the emotional heart of a relationship.
**8 stories per month.**

Indulge in secrets and scandal, intense drama and plenty of sizzling hot action with powerful and passionate heroes who have it all: wealth, status, good looks…everything but the right woman.
**6 stories per month.**

**HEROES**

Experience all the excitement of a gripping thriller, with an intense romance at its heart. Resourceful, true-to-life women and strong, fearless men face danger and desire - a killer combination!
**8 stories per month.**

**DARE**

Sensual love stories featuring smart, sassy heroines you'd want as a best friend, and compelling intense heroes who are worthy of them.
**4 stories per month.**

---

To see which titles are coming soon, please visit

**millsandboon.co.uk/nextmonth**

# DARE

## *Sexy. Passionate. Bold.*

Sensual love stories featuring smart, sassy heroines you'd want as a best friend, and compelling intense heroes who are worthy of them.

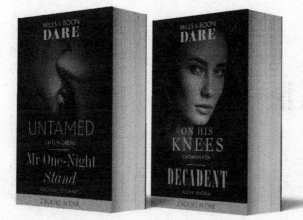